THE ICE

THE ICE

A Novel of Antarctica

LOUIS CHARBONNEAU

DONALD I. FINE, INC.
NEW YORK

Library of Congress Cataloging-in-Publication Data

Charbonneau, Louis, 1924–
The ice: a novel / Louis Charbonneau
p.   cm.
ISBN 1-55611-177-0
I. Title.
PS3575.O7I27   1991
813'.54—dc20   90-55024
CIP

Manufactured in the United States of America

10   9   8   7   6   5   4   3   2   1

Designed by Irving Perkin's Associates

This one is for
Caprice and Tracey
with love

THE ICE

Part One

DAMAGE
ASSESSMENT

ONE

———————

KATHY MCNEELY WAS AWAKE EARLY, listening, in the dim shadows of her polar tent, to the stillness of the Antarctic night. It was a vast, impersonal, mind-assaulting silence, the pure quiet of the earth's last true wilderness. Outside, she knew, the white continent lay brilliant under the sun—it was January, the middle of Antarctic summer, unending days without darkness. In that immense, cold and silent whiteness only a few fragments of human presence could be found—life clinging to the borders of death, she had read somewhere. Jacques Cousteau, she remembered.

But those who came were quickly linked. Her mind flashed, unwillingly, to Dr. Carl Jeffer's casual revelation the night before—the reason for her early wakefulness. "Have you heard the latest, Dr. M?"

"I'm sure you're going to tell me." Expecting some amusing bit about the Russian scientists, or the ongoing feud between two American colleagues over the eating habits of *homo sapiens*.

"Your friend Hurley is nearby. He's set up camp near the foot of the Hartsook Glacier. They say he's going to make a run at it."

Kathy was momentarily speechless. She felt a warmth in her cheeks.

"I imagine we'll be seeing some of him. Does that bother you, my dear?"

"No . . . why should it? He's doing his thing, I'm doing mine."

"Mmm. If you ever feel the need to talk about it . . ."

Carl meant well, of course. He had been there at McMurdo Station when, in the biologist's phrase, she and Hurley paired. He had watched the sudden conflagration, worried about her, and offered quiet support after the breakup.

"If I ever feel the need, Dr. Jeffers, you'll be the first."

Hurley. Why couldn't he have made his attempt at a sledging record from the Ross Ice Shelf on the far side of the continent, following in Robert Falcon Scott's legendary footsteps?

Why did he have to come *here?*

They had met the first time back in early December when the television crew that was to film Brian Hurley's adventure had set their chopper down near the scientist's camp. The remote location director, Hal Berkowski, wanted to get some penguin footage as background. The visitors had shared the instant hospitality typically found at Antarctic camps, where isolated researchers were starved for any change in their daily routine. The two Russian scientists had produced vodka, the television crew some of their picnic rations (including, to Alex Volkov's astonishment, some Russian caviar), and Kathy had spent an evening being stared at by a dozen men instead of only six. Hurley had been one of them.

He was an attractive man in a rugged, outdoors way—strong hands, muscular build, sun-browned features, bright blue eyes. Quieter, more thoughtful than she had expected. Publicity-hungry adventurers, she thought, should be noisier, more assertive. Instead, it was the TV director who clamored for all the attention.

4

After the chopper flew off she found herself thinking of Hurley more than once. What drove a man like that, she wondered, to come to so forbidding a place, to challenge nature so recklessly in the way he planned?

They met again at Christmas in MacTown, the familiar nickname for America's McMurdo Station on the edge of the Ross Sea. If it hadn't been Christmas, Kathy thought later, and if this hadn't been Antarctica, where normal barriers so quickly fell away, nothing would have happened. In her academic milieu he might never have approached her; she might never have noticed him.

But approach he did. She had just entered the noisy mess hall and was looking around for Jeffers and some of her other colleagues when Hurley stepped in front of her. She felt her heart give a surprising skip.

"Dr. McNeely! We met—"

"I remember, Mr. Hurley."

He grinned, seeming pleased. In the background recorded Christmas carols filled the hall, a few men joining in ragged chorus. "Some grog, Doctor? A beer? Chipped beef on toast? A hamburger?"

She laughed. "I haven't eaten."

"That sounds like hamburger to me."

Whatever distance there was between them melted away over hamburgers and Cokes. After eating they met some of Kathy's team, sang a few carols badly, and got a little merrier than expected. Kathy and Hurley ended up alone together walking down an ash-blackened McMurdo street under the midnight sun, Hurley carrying a bottle of champagne he had cadged from the television crew's supplies. They ended up in her room, spilling champagne and their life stories in equal amounts. They ended up fumbling at each other's layers of clothing, laughing at the absurd clumsiness of the process, the joyful unexpectedness of the moment. Pulling off her sweater, lifting her thermal undershirt to reveal small, firm breasts, Hurley stared as if he had never seen a woman before. She watched him anxiously, wanting him to be pleased. He hurried her naked under a pile of blankets and held her until their body heat warmed the space in which they lay. She felt out of control, a little frightened, all of her protective layers of caution and independence shed as easily as the clothes that kept out the Antarctic cold. In his eyes she thought she saw a mirror of her own panic. How could this be happening? And was he feeling the same astonished wonder?

Kathy and her group had reached McMurdo on Christmas Eve to pick up a shipment of supplies and equipment, intending to stay only through the holiday. They were delayed a full week when the transport plane failed to arrive. Hurley said it was destiny, but after that first night Kathy drew back a little, wary of their headlong rush into something neither was prepared for. She told herself that Hurley wasn't the kind of man to stay long in one place; he had mountains to climb. And she had long promised herself that casual, temporary involvement came at too high a price.

After three days he came late to her room again. She opened her door to his shamefaced grin, smelled his breath, and allowed him inside to give him coffee. When he touched her, her skin seemed to merge with his, burning. He stayed the night.

By the end of the week she felt emotionally drained—whipsawed between sensuous nights with Hurley and anxious days of frustration over her prolonged absence from the field camp. She kept wondering when Hurley might say something to suggest that this meant more to him than a brief holiday fling. Then one morning she saw the television crew Hurley was involved with staring at her from a table across the mess hall, grinning and nudging each other. One of the men made a comment she couldn't hear. The others burst into laughter. Kathy's cheeks burned. It seemed to her that Hurley's friends had answered her question.

She and Hurley spent New Year's Eve together. The boisterous clamor that ushered in the new year left her melancholy, fighting tears, sensing not a beginning but an ending. At noon on New Year's Day the Hercules transport rumbled in from

6

Auckland with the badly needed supplies. That night she and Hurley quarreled.

She told herself that the breakup was predictable, that they had nothing really in common, that she had simply been carried away by the spirit of the season and the place, parceling out her gifts more freely than usual.

But it had hurt. No amount of wry or bitter wit could cover the hurt.

The argument had started innocently, as most lovers' quarrels did. Or not so innocently. Had her question been meant to set him off? Was she so frightened by the possibility of losing her cherished sense of controlling her own life, making her own way, that she had to provoke his anger?

"Is this what you do?" she asked him that evening at dinner. She had glimpsed Hal Berkowski and the television crew at another table, laughing raucously once again.

"What do you mean?"

"I mean, running off to the far corners of the earth with a TV crew in tow?"

For a moment he was silent. "The cameras aren't always there."

"They are this time."

"They're a necessary evil."

"Ah!"

"I gather you don't approve."

"It's not for me to approve or disapprove."

"I thought maybe . . . it might matter to you."

"Why should it? It's what you do, right?"

"I guess it is."

He was staring at her, his expression small-boy quizzical.

"Antarctica will still be here when you leave," she said. She wanted to stop herself but couldn't. "Did you ever think it might be better off without all the glamorous TV exposure?"

"That's kind of smug. What I want to do is important to me. Maybe just as important as the way you scientists spend your time counting penguins, writing a paper, getting another grant."

7

"There's more to it than that!" she answered hotly. "We're actively involved in protecting the environment here, about preventing it from being trampled over by every Tom, Dick and Harry . . . "

"There's more to what I do than—"

But he had stopped then, his retort unfinished. For a long time they were both silent, alone with their own thoughts.

"If I did anything wrong, said anything . . . "

"No, Hurley, it's nothing you said."

They had tried to repair the damage, spending the rest of that evening together, but it didn't work. She had pleaded being tired, reminding him that she was leaving in the morning for her field camp. He looked as if he wanted to say something more, but remained silent. She convinced herself that they were both relieved. What had happened between them had been too intense, too extreme, too improbable to last.

She had left McMurdo Station the next day and hadn't returned. She'd buried herself in her work, her true passion, the real reason she had come to Antarctica. She was grateful for it—even more than usual.

Why did Hurley have to come back into her life now?

When Kathy McNeely burrowed through the tunnel-like exit from her tent, the rush of bright cold air seized her throat like a fist. Even when you thought you were ready for it, Antarctica took your breath away.

She hesitated at the opening before easing from the warm cocoon of her shelter onto the ice, long enough to snug her dark sunglasses into place over her face mask and to pull on the fur-backed mittens Alex Volkov had given her. The sunglasses concealed inquisitive hazel eyes; the knitted balaclava mask covered naturally curly hair the color of bar cocoa, clear skin dusted with freckles, and rather thin features. Only her mouth, both generous and determined, showed through a hole in the mask.

The eight-by-eight-foot, pyramid-shaped polar tent, a design little changed for a century, other than the use of nylon sheeting instead of cotton burlap, had been home since late November. It was snug and warm. The single tunnel-like opening with its dual flaps provided a rudimentary airlock between the cold outside and the warmth within. Though every inch of the interior was crowded with her cot, trunk, clothing, books, research materials, primus stove and other gear, it was a luxury hotel as far as the other members of the scientific research team were concerned; she was the only one who had a tent all her own. Being the only woman had some advantages.

While her eyes squinted against the snow glare, all of her other senses reacted. Her skin felt tight with cold. The icy air was crisp in her throat. Her ears seemed thick with the incredible stillness, pierced now by the ululating conversation from the adjacent emperor penguin colony. The stunning sweep of snow all around her dwarfed the cluster of small tents. She had heard a visiting scientist describe Antarctica's immensity of snow and ice as appalling. She could understand the feeling even as she rejected it. Nowhere else had she felt such an awesome sense of space and grandeur—or felt herself so small and insignificant.

Behind her a finger of the Transantarctic Mountains punctured the snowscape in a series of spiny projections like the vertebrae of a dinosaur. Some of the peaks were completely shrouded in snow, only their shapes defined; others thrust brown shoulders and granite wedges out of the whiteness. This great mountain chain, separating Greater and Lesser Antarctica, ran more than three thousand miles across the continent, its highest peaks thrusting twelve thousand feet above sea level. The mountains never appeared so high because much of their mass was snow-covered. Where the chain reached its zenith at the center of the continent, the ice plateau itself was over two miles thick, masking the bedrock beneath it.

To the west, a portion of the Hartsook Glacier—Hurley's challenge—poured out of the mountains toward the sea in a massive frozen river. From Kathy's perspective it was a blinding sheet of white, its dangerous fissures and crevasses hidden by distance and glare. Glittering off this endless expanse of snow and ice, the sunlight was caught by millions of scattered ice crystals that, like a medieval alchemist's dream, turned instantly to gold. Closer, the light struck a cubist formation of twenty-foot blocks of blue ice, which glowed in their depths like uncut jewels.

Near the foot of the glacier, smaller tongues of ice forked off it, one of them running like a corridor into the sea. Elsewhere the flowing mass collided with shelf and coastal ice, which heaved upward in huge chunks, creating infinitely varied formations that resembled a frozen city rising steeply from the edge of the sea, buildings and towers, arches and parapets of ice, their colors ranging from the purest white to aquamarine to a blue as intense as the sky overhead.

Much of this northern Antarctic coastline presented steep ice cliffs and broken faces impossible to penetrate from the sea. But at this location the ease of access offered by a sloping sheet of ice had attracted the penguin colony Kathy and her team had come to study. The ice shelf on which the cluster of tents made such a tiny impression ran gradually downward to the water's edge and a thin apron of sea ice. Beyond this fringe was the Southern Ocean, blue and gentle on this still summer day. It was dotted with the pancake shapes of pack ice and ice floes. Farther out to sea were larger icebergs, some of them as large as ships or islands, drifting slowly away from the continent toward the north.

Vast and forbidding, as cold and dangerous as it was beautiful, Antarctica was a land almost beyond imagining, Kathy thought. But no longer safe from man's corruption, as last year's disastrous oil spill had so harshly demonstrated.

When the penguins within view of the tents saw Kathy emerge, they fell silent all at once, like a crowd in a banquet hall suddenly silenced by the unexpected entrance of a stranger. Then the activity of the colony resumed undisturbed. Some of the birds, cradling youngsters on their feet, gazed off toward the sea as if contemplating a trip. Many parents were busy feeding their young, while other chicks in their fuzzy coats clustered together for mutual protection like teenagers. And a stately procession of the penguins waddled or hopped or tobogganed on their stomachs across the ice to and from the water, gathering food for themselves and their fast-growing chicks, many of whom were now old enough to join the parade.

As Kathy plodded across the snow, it was just past five o'clock in the morning. Without a watch or a change from darkness to light, her chief clue to the time of day was the silence and lack of human activity around the other tents. Walter Corbin and Emil Zagorsky, two other members of the American team of scientists, had been up late the night before, drinking with the Russians. Corbin, a marine scientist from the University of California's Scripps Institution of Oceanography, was a thin-featured, ascerbic man with a mind as sharp as his tongue. His focus this summer was on evidence of damage to phytoplankton in the ocean from the *Kowloon* oil spill. Zagorsky, balding, round-faced and amiable, was a sea bird specialist from Ohio State, his interests dovetailing with Kathy McNeely's. Zagorsky in particular, whom the Americans referred to amiably as "our Russian," seemed to feel duty bound to try to keep up with the real Russians, who drank vodka daily, quite literally, like water.

A small group of emperor penguins had been gossiping near the Jamesway, an insulated canvas hut, more than twice the size of the tents, that served as mess, meeting and recreation hall. As Kathy approached them, the giant birds waddled toward her, holding their stubby wings out as if for balance. But they veered off before reaching her, leaving Kathy to wonder with wry amusement if they had been coming to greet her or simply going on about their own business.

The Jamesway bore a hand-lettered sign over the entrance: PRIVATE CLUBHOUSE—MEMBERS ONLY. Carl Jeffers, a marine biologist from UCLA, already had coffee ready. The oldest man on the team, he was their *de facto* leader, whose studies were directed toward the presence of oil on the ocean floor and in the sea ice a year after the triggering event, with an analysis of its lingering impact on marine life.

Pulling off her face mask, Kathy gratefully accepted a steaming mug along with a bar of chocolate. "Smitty has a cold and has taken to his bed," Jeffers said, referring to Harold Smithson, an environmental scientist from New Zealand, the only member of the team who was neither American nor Russian. "Our other two colleagues won't be out jogging either this morning," Jeffers added cheerfully. "At any rate, not for a few hours."

"At least they shouldn't freeze."

"God no, not with that alcohol level in their blood."

"I suppose the Russians will be sleeping late, too."

"Think again, my girl. Alex was in here a half hour ago, cheerful as a porpoise. He and Comrade Simanovich are already off to work. They're taking some algae samples from the bottom of that floe that drifted by yesterday."

"Niki is diving?"

"But of course. Being the junior member gives him the honor." Jeffers grinned at the prospect of Simanovich descending into the icy waters in an insulated wet suit. His expression, visible as a kind of smirk through his gray beard, suggested that the perks of rank were no different in the Soviet Union than in the halls of American academe. "Alex seems to think the slimy green is quite clean. No evidence of oil."

Oil remaining from last season's spill tended to seep down through the pack ice, turning it the color of coffee, and inevitably contaminating any algae on the bottom ice. Algae grew in abundance, like a shaggy greenish-brown coating, on and in the bottom layers of sea ice. During the warmer summer months enough of the ice would melt to release the algae into the sea, where it became part of the southern ocean's vast food chain. Great swarms of krill, a tiny shrimplike crustacean, fed on the algae, and the krill were food for everything from fish to baleen whales to penguins, who were in turn the delicacy favored by leopard seals.

"We're making progress, my dear, and we'll make more if the

weather continues to cooperate. I can't promise that, though. The news from MacTown this morning isn't promising. They're predicting what they call an unstable pattern for the next few days."

"That could mean a howler."

"Precisely. Smitty may never emerge from his tent until it's time to go home."

Though crowding fifty, Carl Jeffers seemed undaunted by the hardships of their present circumstances. He remained tirelessly energetic, cheerful, restlessly curious. Kathy had studied under him and admired him; she doubted she would ever be able to keep up with him.

The first time they were at McMurdo Station, before leaving to set up their camp, Jeffers had looked around the crowded mess hall and mused thoughtfully, "Look at them. It's like I never left the UCLA campus. They look as if their biggest worry is, will Dad let them have the car Saturday night. This is a young man's party, Kathy."

"You do all right."

"I'm losing it."

"Sure you are."

"No, I'm serious. I think this is my last time."

And Kathy had wondered if he meant it this time, or if he would be back again, as if the ice exerted some irresistible pull. Sirens beckoning from a floating iceberg, or dancing just beyond the edge of sight, obscured by blowing snow . . .

"And what are you up to today, Bird Woman?" Jeffers said. "Or need I ask?"

"I'm tending my flock," Kathy said.

Jeffers chuckled. "Ah, the things that pass for wit when you've been down here long enough at the bottom of the world."

"I'm trying to remember, Carl, some of your funnier lines from Westwood."

"They're elusive, I admit, but that's the essence of wit."

She finished off the hot coffee and the chocolate bar, reflecting that her indulgence in the latter had added a layer of fat that was both curse and blessing. Curse because she would have to go on the most painful of diets when summer was over and she went back to the real world (Antarctica was fantasy, a place of magic); blessing because it was, like her long johns and her red parka and the wool mask over her face, a sheath of insulation against the dangerous cold of the ice. She hung her mug on its designated hook, grinned at Carl behind her face mask, braced herself once more for the impact, and stepped out of the warm clubhouse into the shining cold.

For two hours Kathy McNeely sat under an improvised canopy near the edge of the ice, shifting position occasionally to keep her back to the sun rotating above the horizon, in a vain attempt to reduce the snow glare. She was positioned in the middle of the penguin colony, which was the size of several football fields, every square foot occupied. Unafraid, the birds tottered around her or stood in groups nearby. Their hooting and trumpeting, even the high-pitched whistling of the chicks, like the pervasive smell of their guano, became simply background noise, an accepted part of the scene. Her kind of Muzak, she thought.

Penguins were her special field of interest, emperors claiming top priority. The largest of the penguins, adult emperors stood more than three feet tall. True to their regal name, they were not noisy and squabbling, like the smaller penguins. Though they established breeding grounds, they did not make nests or mark a specific territory, so there was none of the quarreling common in other penguin rookeries. Some penguins seemed born comedians, like the Adelies that had entertained sailors for nearly two centuries. The emperors were more solemn and sedate. They were fascinating due to their impressive size, stately strut and striking coloring, highlighted by white and yellow patches on either side of their heads, and long bills marked by mandibular plates of vivid orange, coral pink or lilac.

Twice this morning Kathy had spotted penguins bearing the "K" signature she had stenciled under the wings of injured birds nearly a year ago after the SS *Kowloon* oil spill. Out of a colony that currently numbered about thirty thousand—Zagorsky had taken the census—she had now counted 108 penguins carrying her mark. Her records showed that she had put her initial on 273 other birds last February and March; these were still unaccounted for. Were there still a few in this colony she had not yet spotted? Were the missing birds part of another rookery, located somewhere else along the vast frozen apron of the continent? Or was the answer a grimmer one?

These were some of the questions that had brought Kathy and her international team of scientists—dubbed Operation Second Chance—to Antarctica this summer. With environmental and marine specialists included in the group, their work ranged well beyond Kathy's primary concern for sea birds, seeking to document and assess the extent of the damage from last year's oil spill to the entire ecology of this coastline. How serious, prevailing and long-lasting were the oil-based hydrocarbons released into the ocean? How much damage had there been to marine life in general? To the ocean floor and the fundamental food chain? How had the residual oil been affected by the harshness of the Antarctic winter? What would be the effects of an even larger spill?

The disaster had been almost predictable. As activity in and around earth's last unspoiled continent increased, as Antarctica became a giant laboratory and even a novel tourist attraction, the probability of an accident increased many times. The wreck of the Argentine tourist ship *Bahia Paraiso*, which foundered on the ice early in 1989 near the U.S. Palmer Station in the Antarctic peninsula, had been the first clear warning. Then came the SS *Kowloon* disaster.

She was a Chinese supply ship, an icebreaker trying to smash through heavy pack ice to reach Zhongshan, the Chinese station in East Antarctica. The ship had arrived late, near the end of the austral summer, and was in a hurry to leave its cargo and escape to the open sea to avoid being trapped by the thickening sea ice. But a submerged iceberg ripped a gaping hole in the ship's hull. Diesel fuel erupted from the ship into the water, seeped into the surrounding ice, lapped onto the rocks and shelf ice of the coastline, and drifted down into the depths of the crowded ocean.

When news of the *Kowloon* disaster reached the nearest pockets of civilization, a rescue effort was hastily organized. Volunteers from the Antarctic bases manned by New Zealand, Australia and Britain joined those from McMurdo, along with a handful of marine scientists who were able to reach the ice. There were none from the Chinese station, as old hands of the Ice had caustically noted.

Kathy McNeely, a marine biologist-ornitholigist with a special interest in penguins, was in the Falkland Islands at the time, on a penguin sighting. Upon hearing of the disaster and its threat to a penguin colony, she rushed to Antarctica on the first available flight. After a briefing at the U.S. station at McMurdo, she was flown with other volunteers in a ski-equipped transport plane to an ice shelf overlooking the spill.

By then the SS *Kowloon* had broken free of the ice and was limping home, leaving fifty thousand gallons of oil in its wake, and thousands of dead or injured birds—Antarctic and snow petrels, tiny birds that flew in clouds of snow-white, smoky blue or flashing brown; large, dull brown, gull-like skuas, a scavenger coastal bird that preyed on penguin eggs; and penguins.

The accident had occurred directly opposite a large emperor penguin rookery. Unlike most penguins, emperors often set up their breeding site directly on sea ice near the coastline rather than on the mainland. Such was the case here, making the rookery especially vulnerable to the slick of oil.

By chance the spill had come between breeding seasons. Most of the colony had gone to sea. But those who remained, including many chicks hatched in the dead of the austral winter and now six or seven months old, were immediate victims. The birds had nowhere to go for food but the ocean. Innocent of danger, they dived and hopped into the water. The oil engulfed them. It coated their bodies, clogged eyes and beaks, finally worked down through the dense layers of small feathers, destroying the insulation they provided against the cold of the environment. Depriving the birds of that protection was like sending a human being naked into the freezing cold of the Ice. It was possible for a man to survive for a minute or two in such circumstances— bravado "streaks" were an initiation rite even at the South Pole —but after a few moments the cold seized, the sweat froze on the skin, the skin turned blue, the chills began . . .

The young penguins were most vulnerable. They died faster, and in greater numbers.

When Kathy McNeely and the other volunteers arrived, the penguin colony was in disarray. Hundreds of oil-soaked emperors lay on the ice, along with thousands of smaller birds and a number of helpless seals. Many were dead or too badly injured to survive.

There were only a few weeks remaining before winter. The weather turned foul, lashing the coastline with repeated storms. The would-be rescuers found themselves poorly equipped for what they faced. Supplies were scarce. The oil, after the more toxic chemicals evaporated in the first week after the spill, became a thick black goo that seemed impossible to remove from densely layered feathers. The rescuers turned to dishwater detergent for cleaning, used hairbrushes and combs, even their toothbrushes, to scrub the birds' feathers. They tore up bedsheets, towels and thermal underwear for cleaning and drying.

The days became a blur of frantic activity. Then the mercury plunged, the storms became more violent. Sea channels choked with ice, and high winds threatened to make air travel impossible. The exhausted rescuers were forced to leave, turning their backs on countless birds they had been unable to help.

An estimated two thousand penguins had died, hundreds of the scavenger skuas, additional thousands of the smaller, fish-eating petrels, scores of young crabeater seals. Older seals and whales in the immediate coastal waters seemed to have survived without serious injury, perhaps because their thick skin would not absorb the oil, though some marine scientists remained un-convinced. Toxic damage, they argued, might not yet be visible. And deaths in the depths of the ocean were not recorded.

Among the last of the volunteers to leave, Kathy McNeely flew to New Zealand barely in time to escape the arrival of the austral winter. She was exhausted, despairing and angry. Soon she found it hard to remember clear details of those mind-numbing days battling the oily slime. The ugly images were mercifully blocked out.

She began planning her return to Antarctica before she left Auckland for her home in the coastal hills near the University of California at Santa Barbara, driven not only by her continuing concern for the survivors of the *Kowloon* spill but by the lure of the Ice itself. She pulled every string she could find, bullied Carl Jeffers into using his influence with the NSF—he ended up joining the team—and put her first sabbatical on hold. Two Russian scientists and one from New Zealand joined to give the study an international authority. Nothing could have kept Kathy away.

When Kathy and the rest of her team came to the Ice in late November, they found the immediate site of the *Kowloon* trag-edy made inaccessible by dramatic changes in the coastal ice. Moreover, there were few penguins or other marine animals in the vicinity; obviously the damaged emperor colony had relo-cated. Flying along the coast by helicopter, the scientists found a large new emperor rookery about a hundred miles west of the old one. Close enough, they decided, given the prevailing ocean current in the direction of the new site, for their assessment of the oil spill's impact. And a broad, sloping ice shelf made setting up a camp and carrying out their studies both possible and practical.

At that time the new penguin colony was busy with family affairs. The youngsters, three to four months old, were fuzzy chicks with an appealing white mask and black cap. Unlike other penguins, emperors stayed in Antarctica through the cold, dark winter to breed. The eggs arrived in the depth of the coldest season on earth, and while the female went off to feed in the ocean—often a journey of two months or more—the male kept vigil, holding the egg on its feet, clear of the ice, with a loose fold of skin draped over it to keep it warm. On her return, the mother took over as the egg was ready to hatch. She carried her new chick on her feet, insulated from the ice, in the same way the male had protected the egg, until it was old enough to survive on the ice.

For Kathy the next six weeks had been both anxious and joyful. Like the penguins shuttling back and forth between the rookery and the ocean, her emotions had rocked from one extreme to another. Each surviving penguin found with her "K" marking under its wing brought a surge of elation. Each day without finding one of her birds meant disappointment or, after successive days, dejection. That kind of emotional involvement was unscientific, she knew; it could cloud her thinking. But she couldn't control her strong reaction, and after a while she didn't try.

The number of identified survivors seemed pitifully small. But each one, as Dr. Jeffers had patiently reminded her, was important. Each was a tribute to the work of volunteer rescuers nearly a year ago—and a grim reminder of the fragility of the Antarctic environment. . . .

A noisy squabbling jarred her out of her reverie. She crawled out of her canopy and stood up for a better view. The screeching came from her left where, at the edge of the ice tongue, a tumble of rocks and gravel stood in sharp contrast to the surrounding ice and snow. Here a small Adelie penguin colony had settled for their breeding season. There was no rivalry between these smaller penguins and the emperors. Unlike the larger birds, Adelies used pebbles for nest-building. Their rookery was occupied by about two hundred adult Adelies. Their eggs had hatched around mid-December, not long after the humans had taken up residence nearby. The chicks, only a few weeks old, were covered with a soft, gray, fuzzy down. In the past week the small colony, which made up in raucous activity what it lacked in numbers, had been joined by a few dozen two- or three-year-old Adelies, too young for breeding but not for posturing and playing.

As Kathy watched, a group of the Adelies hopped onto the ice and, after strutting back and forth a few moments, dove one by one into the water in what seemed like a choreographed procession, like swimmers in an old Esther Williams movie.

Smiling, Kathy turned toward the camp. Beyond it, at the far end of the ice shelf where the sloping sheet met an ice cliff on the right and the sea on the left, a flutter of movement caught her eye.

Volkov, she thought instantly.

It was a flash of color, bright red against the vast expanse of white, that had attracted her attention. Alex Volkov had traded with Zagorsky, giving the American a Russian fur anorak for the standard NSF red parka issued to Americans on the Ice.

Puzzled, she wondered what Volkov wanted. The glare from the dazzling expanse of snow and ice between them made the tiny red image dance in her vision, but the Russian seemed to be waving in her direction. There was urgency in the gesture.

Kathy had met Aleksei Aleksandrovich Volkov during that frantic rescue operation nearly a year ago. Volkov had been doing research at Russkaya, the Russian station on the Marie Byrd Land coast, and had been among the first volunteers. Like her other colleagues at the time, he had receded into the general blur that defined those terrible weeks. Not so this new season. The Russian scientist wasn't a man to be easily dismissed.

Aleksei Volkov worked for the Institute of Evolutionary Morphology and Animal Ecology, a division of the Soviet Academy of Science in Moscow. Kathy guessed his age at between thirty-five and forty. His younger colleague, Nikolai Simanovich, was visibly in awe of him. The Americans addressed them familiarly as Alex and Niki.

Like everyone else who came to the Ice for any length of time, the two Soviet scientists had grown beards since their arrival. Volkov's was black and luxuriant, already scissored into

a handsome shape; Niki's was a straggly reddish-blond sugges-
tive of a teenager's attempt at a mustache. The difference was
characteristic. Alex Volkov was an ebulliant, opinionated, char-
ismatic personality who tended to dominate any gathering,
while Simanovich was quiet and reserved to the point of diffi-
dence. Carl Jeffers had once suggested that Volkov seemed more
American than any of the Americans.

Though not intimidated, Kathy McNeely was nevertheless a
little uncomfortable around Volkov. He was too attractive a
man for comfort. And he had a way of watching her with an
amused and speculative glint in his blue eyes, matched by the
slight curve of a smile, that flustered her. It had been a long
time, she thought, since any man had caused her that schoolgirl
insecurity.

Such thoughts were far from her mind as she started across
the broad ice shelf, the width of several football fields, toward
the gesturing Russian. As she did so another figure climbed into
view close to Volkov. Over the distance the tiny, white-faced
figure, clad all in black, might have been a friendly emperor
penguin.

Niki in his wet suit, she realized. What had he found in his
dive? Was that why Volkov was signaling her?

A dip in the ice shelf—though it appeared as level as a playing field it was actually riffled by spiny ridges and folds made
invisible by drifting snow—caused her to lose sight of the two
Soviets. When she saw them again, she was fifty years closer.

Volkov was waving at her again. Something in his body
lauguage triggered alarm. She began to hurry, her movements
clumsy in the layers of padded clothing and thermal bunny
boots she wore. Before long she was breathing hard in sharp
puffs of vapor. Like a tired old locomotive chugging uphill, she
told herself, trying to lighten the feeling of unease that was
beginning to oppress her.

It didn't work.

From a hundred yards off there was no longer any question.
Something was wrong. Volkov and Simanovich were both star-

ing toward her. What could Niki have discovered? She could see the dark blue water beyond the two men, pocked by a field of pack ice that resembled white poker chips scattered across blue felt.

She was laboring now. Running in Antarctic cold was never a wise idea. You began to sweat under the layered clothing. The undergarments soaked up the moisture and lost much of their insulating effect. Then the skin cooled and chills set in . . .

She could feel the clammy perspiration on her body, the pull on her thighs as if she carried weights attached to them. Though the ice was covered only with dry powder snow, the drifts dragged at her boots. Puffs of snow kicked up around her feet with each step. Hurrying through it was like trying to trot through shallow water.

Clouds drifted over the sun and the morning swiftly darkened. She felt the sudden drop in temperature. Where had those clouds come from? They were like an omen, reinforcing the mood of foreboding awakened by Volkov's manner.

Closer to the two men now, forcing herself to walk quickly rather than trying to run, Kathy was able to see the white frost in Niki's beard and eyebrows where moisture had frozen after he came out of the water. White beard, white eyebrows, icicles dripping from his nostrils. He made no attempt to brush them away. There was shock in his rigid posture.

A small black bundle appeared in the snow at Volkov's feet. For an instant Kathy thought it was a young penguin exhausted from a swim—chicks would sometimes collapse and lie prone on the ice for a short time when fatigued.

Her emotions raced ahead of her understanding, and she felt a clutch of panic in her breast.

Two of the prone birds were now visible on the ice near the two Soviet scientists. One of them gave an odd, uncharacteristic lurch. Kathy had a sudden flash of memory to the previous year, a horror show of images of penguins flopping helplessly in the snow, of the pure white surface turning black with ugly stains where the birds lay dying.

"Oh my God!" she cried out as the truth exploded in her brain.

Heedless of the darkening sky and deepening chill, she began to run, her anguished gaze fixed on the two penguins lying in the snow, their feathers saturated with fresh oil.

TWO

———

CARL JEFFERS HAD SPENT two hours on the radio trying to raise someone at McMurdo who could speak with authority about the possibility of a new oil spill anywhere in Antarctic waters. The answer, which came late in the afternoon, was about as disturbing as a positive report would have been.

"There's nothing," said Lieutenant Commander Larry Hayes, the deputy chief of station at McMurdo, which was administered by the U.S. Navy under contract to the National Science Foundation. He sounded disgruntled, as if the urgent field message had ruined his day. "I mean *nada*. Zero."

"There has to be," Jeffers insisted.

A burst of static blotted out Hayes's reply. It made Jeffers think of cartoon cursing. "—didn't make myself clear. We've had no report of any accident. For Christ's sake, don't you think we'd know?"

"Maybe you haven't heard yet."

"What, someone's going to keep it a secret?" The navy officer was clearly in a testy mood. He was a career navy man who, insiders said, didn't regard his Antarctic posting as a high point.

"The fact is, Doctor, there isn't even a ship along that entire coastline that could have got into trouble."

"Something's happened," Jeffers said. "That oil didn't just materialize. You're sure there's no tourist boat that might have changed course? They can be unpredictable."

For several seconds Hayes was off-line. Jeffers could hear someone else talking in the background. When the officer spoke again, his voice was suddenly very loud, as if the radio signal had cleared. "There's a tourist ship heading your way, but it reports no trouble. I spoke to the captain myself an hour ago. Same goes for the Russian icebreaker near you. Your man there can verify. You have a Soviet in your camp, haven't you?"

"Yes, we do."

"Maybe they'll tell him something they're not telling us, but I don't think so."

"What about an air search?"

"We don't have any planes to spare, Dr. Jeffers. This is a very busy time for us, and yours isn't the only expedition with special needs. Anyway, where would they start looking?"

"The site of the *Kowloon* spill—"

"Is clean, Doctor. There may be residual oil in the ice, but even that's no longer in the same area. Not only does oil move, but the sea ice moves, too. And breaks up, and melts."

"We know all that, Commander, but—"

"What you have, Operation Second Chance, is an isolated incident. Your penguins must have found an old pocket of oil."

Jeffers did not bother to say that the possibility had been discussed and rejected. The oil from the *Kowloon* had spilled in an area of sea and pack ice. The ice itself had helped to contain it; very little oil had lapped onto the landmass. Two-thirds of any such spill evaporated in any case. And even though oil degraded more slowly than normal in conditions of extreme cold, the rest of the *Kowloon* oil had either seeped into the ice or been dispersed by the pounding waves during the past winter's storms. Some of it had found its way to the ocean bottom—that was the focus of Carl Jeffers's research—but none of it, as Hayes asserted, remained on the ice or in the water as surface oil.

Which left, Jeffers thought, a worthy conundrum. The penguins Niki had found had encountered fresh oil in an icy wilderness where there was none.

"A ghost ship," Walter Corbin said sardonically in the silence following the message from MacTown.

"So it would seem," said Jeffers shortly. He was still disgruntled over Lieutenant Commander Hayes's dismissive attitude. Also, like the others in the team that made up Operation Second Chance, he didn't care much for the navy's tendency to slap a code name on any activity, as if it were a military operation. Operation Second Chance indeed!

The joint American-Soviet team, with one Kiwi thrown in, tried to gather once a day in the Clubhouse for the evening meal, even though they often worked on different schedules and the bright days did not break down into normal segments. For some, if not all of them, it was the only formal meal of the day.

Even in an isolated field camp, food was no longer a problem for Antarctic workers, shortages no longer the life threat they had been as recently as Admiral Richard Byrd's time. In addition to easily carried, lightweight freeze-dried rations, it was easy now to store frozen meats, vegetables and fruits, even pastas, bacon and eggs, most of which could be quickly prepared on a Primus stove—a duty that was rotated evenly among the members of Operation Second Chance, as was the more onerous chore of seeing that enough snow was melted to fill their daily needs for precious water for drinking, cooking and personal ablutions. When food shortages did threaten, an air drop or helicopter visit on request was seldom more than a week away.

The Jamesway was an extendable, double-layered unit, this one about twenty-four feet long, large enough to accommodate a cooking corner, folding chairs and cots for sitting, a long mess table, some shelves holding books, and a rack for hanging outer clothing that was always removed indoors, even a makeshift shower (permitted once a week). Short-wave radio equipment occupied another corner, the camp's only link with the outside world. The Clubhouse had a tough, waterproof vinyl floor that extended beyond the walls and was covered with insulating mats. Though crowded when everyone was inside, there was elbow room, and the interior was both warm and bright—power provided by a generator housed in an adjacent small tent.

The one communal meal of the day in the Clubhouse was a social occasion that provided welcome relief. It was also a good time to review and discuss individual projects or needs. The discussions were not always productive; most scientists were individualists, jealously guarding their own research; in spite of their common purpose, these were no exception. But the evening sessions had proved useful as a break in the routine of work that frequently went on around the clock and a way of easing tensions.

The latter was no small matter. The isolation of Antarctica tended to draw people close together, creating instant friendships. Paradoxically, in the confined circumstances of the camp, two men sleeping to a tent, no change of routine for weeks, small differences escalated out of proportion. Minor irritations —clicking teeth, a snore, a whistle, a tone of voice or speech pattern—became intolerable. Emil Zagorsky, for instance, was the most amiable of colleagues; but he habitually chewed with his mouth open, and Kathy had reached the point where she couldn't bear to look at him during meals. Similarly, Walter Corbin had started out sharing a tent with Smithson, the Kiwi, but Corbin—a man of cool, aloof arrogance that some said was justified by his brilliance as a scientist—couldn't stand Smithson's habit of whistling through his teeth when he was absorbed in thought, which happened often when he lay on his cot unable to sleep. The two men had had to be separated. Corbin now bunked with Zagorsky, whose table manners were lacking but who didn't snore or whistle; Smithson shared a tent with Jeffers. And recently, as all the men tended to hover more eagerly around Kathy McNeely during the nightly gatherings—they hadn't seen another woman of any kind for six weeks—even the good-natured Zagorsky had got into a shouting match with Carl Jeffers over who was entitled to sit next to Kathy one evening.

Tonight there was none of the customary joking and arguing among the scientists. They picked at their food, saying little. Even a rare treat, some canned peaches, was consumed with indifference until Corbin remarked with asperity that Zagorsky had got four peach slices while he, Corbin, had received only three. Finally Carl Jeffers brought out his favorite libation, a bottle of hundred-proof Southern Comfort, and poured a shot into each cup. "Enough already," he said, settling back on his bench seat against the wall, "let's see what we know. Anyone have any suggestions?"

"Is a new spill," Alex Volkov said. "Is no other explanation."

"From Walter's phantom ship?"

Volkov started to reply and stopped. He gave an eloquent shrug and sipped his Southern Comfort, which brought an appreciative nod. No one else said anything for a while.

Smithson suddenly sneezed, and everyone in the hut glared at him accusingly. The New Zealander, a tall, thin man with a tall man's habitually stooped shoulders, had dragged himself from his tent in an effort to help when he heard about the two injured penguins; but his cold was still at its peak, and no one wanted to share his germs. As Carl Jeffers said, a cold in the Antarctic was nothing to sniff at. "Sorry," Smithson mumbled, dabbing apathetically at his red nose with a tissue.

"I don't care what McMurdo says," Kathy McNeely said. "We're looking at a new problem here, not the one we already knew about. We can't just let it go."

"But as our good Commander Hayes pointed out," Walter Corbin said, "where do we begin to look? This is a very large continent, Dr. McNeely, most of it relatively inaccessible except by air. A sea search would take much too long, even if it were possible to explore very much of the coastline, even if we had an icebreaking ship at our disposal, which we don't."

"I will talk to captain of Soviet ship," Volkov said. "But ship is three, four days from our position, perhaps more. I do not know."

"We'd appreciate that, Alex," said Jeffers. "Maybe your captain does know more than he's told them at McMurdo. It's worth asking, anyway."

Volkov nodded. Simanovich, as usual, watched Volkov and said nothing. He did, however, seem to be enjoying his Southern Comfort and made a point of studying the label on the bottle. Both of the Soviet scientists read and spoke English; that was more than any of the Americans could claim about Russian.

"I think we have to go back to the area of the *Kowloon* spill," Kathy said.

"What for?" Corbin demanded. "That emperor rookery was on sea ice that's drifted, melted, broken up, changed. The damage may still be pervasive; it's certainly not specific to that original location. Anyway, we flew over that coastline on our way here. There was nothing to see. The penguins have migrated, showing more intelligence than humans when it comes to sharing space with oil. The place where we are now has the largest rookery along this coastal area. The *Kowloon* site offers nothing other than bad memories."

"This oil came from somewhere!"

"Maybe the authorities aren't telling all," Corbin said.

"What's that supposed to mean?" Zagorsky demanded.

"Yes, Walter," said Volkov. "Tell us, please, what you mean."

Corbin stroked his new beard, which had been carefully scissored so that it made Kathy think of portraits of Sir Walter Raleigh, and said, "Perhaps there are things going on that the NSF isn't telling us, that's all. That could, of course, mean ship movements we don't know about. Or air shipments. An expedition that hasn't been publicized, for instance. A large expedition transporting fuel for its own needs. A fuel dump that may have been set up on unstable ice. An accident . . ." He shrugged.

"That's pure speculation," Zagorsky said.

"The NSF isn't the enemy," Kathy said. "They're why we're here."

"They're not *why* we're here," Corbin sniffed. "They just made it possible."

"The trouble with the NSF is, the State Department is running the show," Carl Jeffers said, his words surprising Kathy. "They're telling the NSF what to do. State's idea of ecological responsibility is to ask the developers to make an environmental assessment for us. Did you know the Antarctic Advisory Committee of the U.S. State Department has representatives from ARCO, Gulf and Exxon on the committee? What the hell does that tell you? Asking them to assess the environment is like the chickens asking the wolves to set up a security system for the coop."

"It's not that bad," Kathy said, smiling in spite of herself. "The NSF is in the middle."

"It shouldn't be in the middle! It should come down hard on the side of preserving this place. I don't have to tell any of you how important it is. I tell them that the Southern Ocean accounts for twenty percent of the total marine photosynthesis on this planet, and they nod indulgently. Remind them that Antarctic deep-sea currents feed all the oceans, and they're nodding right off. Oh, they'll perk up a little bit if you mention the ozone layer or the greenhouse effect because those are now fashionable questions. But if you begin talking about ultraviolet radiation destroying phytoplankton and actually jeopardizing the entire food chain, you've lost them. Half the scientists you talk to, if it comes to that, don't take the danger seriously." Jeffers paused a moment as a memory surfaced. More quietly he said, "Right here on the Ice, I ran into a guy, does research for some energy outfit, who insisted to me that Jacques Cousteau is a fascist. He actually said he thinks all this talk about polluting the last true wilderness on earth is crapola for the masses."

"What's he doing in Antarctica then?" Kathy asked curiously. "Who is he with?"

"Very good question, my dear," Jeffers admitted, a little shamefaced. "And the answer is, I don't know. We'd both been drinking, hit a couple of the bars in MacTown, and I think he was running off at the mouth a bit. I know we had some heated discussion, but frankly the last part of that evening isn't very clear. After that I never saw him."

"Well, he shouldn't be here."

"But he is. That's my point. He's here, which means he has the blessing of the National Science Foundation. That's just what I'm trying to say. If you go to them these days with a project, you want to find out a little more about how the earth got to be the way it is, and this continent is the most beautiful laboratory for geological research on earth, you'll get some chin stroking and some hems and haws, and they'll get back to you soon. But if you go to them and say, 'Hey, I think maybe if I do some digging around, I might come up with some ideas on the available mineral resources underneath all this ice or find out how much manganese we can scrape up off the ocean floor,' and they'll tell you, 'Here's your authority, let us know what you need!' "

"If you're going to start in again on the minerals regime," Corbin said, "I'm going to bed."

The minerals issue was a point of sharp and continuing discord between Jeffers and Corbin, who were on opposite sides of the argument. A minerals agreement was signed in Wellington, New Zealand, in 1988, by representatives of thirty-three countries, including the signatories of the 1959 Antarctic Treaty, that potentially opened up the Antarctic continent to controlled exploitation of its mineral resources, from gold and platinum to oil and even uranium. The United States had pushed strongly for the agreement—feeling the pressure from major energy companies, Carl Jeffers claimed. Australia and France, after initially signing the accord, had later withdrawn their approval. Their dissident action now threatened not only the Wellington agreement but the 1959 Antarctic Treaty itself. That remarkable accord rested entirely on the continuing willingness of all the original twelve nations that had signed it, and the twenty-six other nations that honored it, to suspend national claims and differences while preserving the entire continent of Antarctica for peaceful scientific inquiry.

"Is different in my country," Volkov said. Everyone looked at him. A small smile hid behind his black beard. "With us it is so simple to know what scientist should think."

"All right," Jeffers said, "I'll bite. How do you know?"

"They tell us."

He laughed abruptly, and everyone soon joined in.

"Even with *perestroika,* Alex?"

"*Perestroika* is come to Communist party, is come to new parliament. Is not yet come to Soviet Academy of Science."

Volkov's joke had its effect. The atmosphere in the Clubhouse relaxed visibly. Then Smithson, who had had an extra dose of Southern Comfort "for medicinal purposes," dabbed at his reddening nose with a tissue, blinked bloodshot eyes and said, "We could use a little more *perestroika* right here on the Ice."

"What's that supposed to mean?" Corbin snapped.

Smithson lifted bony shoulders in a shrug and held his cup out toward Jeffers, who, after a brief hesitation, poured another hearty shot into it. Smitty was already feeling the effects of the hundred-proof liquor, Kathy thought.

"Well, there are the Chinese, for starters. They're still on everyone's hate list after last year. And it's still being whispered that they're eating seals and penguins, living off the land. You've all heard some of the stories. And there are other disturbing stories, or rumors, I suppose you might call them. About things going wrong this year on the Ice. There was one about a shipment of supplies being airdropped at an abandoned campsite in one of the dry valleys, while another expedition's base camp went hungry."

"You always hear tales like that," Zagorsky growled.

"That's true, Smitty," Jeffers said. "Except for work there's not much to do at McMurdo or any of the base camps except drink and gossip. Rumors are a way of life down here."

"Yes, quite. But not so many bad ones, I think. There was

quite a bit of talk about it at MacTown. You know, suggestions of bad karma or a year of bad luck." He paused. "The bad luck always seemed to be linked somehow to the treaty problems."

"You're drunk," Corbin said.

"Not just yet," Smitty said with a leer. "But it does seem like an excellent idea."

"Next thing you'll be saying those oil-soaked penguins are part of the bad luck streak. Luck has nothing to do with it. There's a logical explanation. We just haven't found it yet."

"There is misconception, I think," Volkov said after a moment of silence brought on by Corbin's blunt reminder. "Because oil is no longer visible where SS *Kowloon* was struck, it is convenient to think problem is gone away. Even your Commander Hayes speaks like this." He glanced around the hut. "We know this is big mistake. Today Nikita find oil residue in the ice. Is very long way from spill."

Kathy's reaction was quick. "Could that account for the penguins you found? Is that possible?"

"Is not possible. Oil on two birds is chemically active, still very toxic. Is maybe twenty-four, forty-eight hours in water, exposed to erosion and atmosphere. You saw this?"

"Do you have any theories?"

"Not yet." Volkov shook his head. "Is very big mystery."

"I have to go back to the old emperor rookery, at least to the original location of the spill. It's too much of a coincidence that more injured penguins would show up along this coastline."

"Coincidence is not easy to accept," the Soviet said gently. "But sometimes is only explanation."

"I still have to see for myself."

Volkov, seeing the stubborn line of her mouth, looked even more interested than usual.

"That won't be easy, Kathy," Carl Jeffers said. "Our motor toboggan won't take you safely over those mountains to the south of us, and they're between us and the bay where the *Kowloon* leaked. And you heard what McMurdo has to offer. No planes available."

"Those helos are in and out of McMurdo all summer. One of them should have time for us."

"I think we have to be a little more convincing. I'll give it another try tomorrow."

Alex Volkov said nothing, but the expression in his probing blue eyes was thoughtful.

Fatigue set in early after the long, trying day. Smithson tottered off to his tent. Carl Jeffers said that in the interest of avoiding germ warfare, he was bringing his sleeping bag into the Jamesway rather than bunk alongside the Kiwi. He reminded the others of McMurdo's weather warning, and they all went out to make sure the tents were battened down, the ice screws and storm guys secured, the safety rope in place connecting each of the tents with the Jamesway and the separate tents used as an outhouse and a storage shed. If a blizzard blew in during the night, that rope was an essential lifeline even for the short walk from one tent to another. Without it, in a typically blinding Antarctic storm, your sense of direction could be turned upside down with a single misdirected step. Even trying to bridge a span of ten yards or less, you could become lost. . . .

Kathy went to check on her two patients. The larger penguin, a male three and a half feet tall, was standing, his neck bent in a curve as graceful as a swan's as he stared down at the ice. His coat appeared matted and ragged, but Kathy was encouraged to find him standing, however disconsolate the pose. The smaller female, however, probably the bird with which the male had paired, was another story. She lay on a towel where Kathy had left her in a corner of the storage shed. She was alive but weak. When Kathy touched her, she squirmed feebly, whether from fright or not Kathy didn't know.

She had reason to be frightened, Kathy thought.

So did they all.

She stood for a moment outside the entrance of her tent, feeling tired and depressed. In the distance the ice moved and cracked, and a mammoth chunk slid into the water with a sound like thunder. Listening, she could hear the brushing of the brash ice, the murmuring from the emperor penguin rookery, the shriller chatter of the small Adélie colony. A veil of snow lifted on a noiseless gust of wind and drifted past her like a ghost. The beauty and wonder of the sunlit night seeped into her mind, and the momentary feeling of despair blew away like the powder snow.

The deeper anger stayed. She needed that.

THREE

————————

WHEN BRIAN HURLEY STARTED OUT across the ice sheet that morning, the weather was cold but clear with little wind. It was only a practice sledge run, but he had taken the precaution, in spite of the fine day, of carrying flags on slender poles, which he stuck periodically into the ice to mark his route. He might be new to Antarctica, but he was no stranger to Arctic cold or the danger of sudden, unexpected storms. And his first two months on the southernmost continent had taught him respect for its capricious moods. He knew that a storm could come howling down the slope of the glacier without warning, blinding him with blowing snow, covering his tracks completely in the first minute.

He took a watchful pleasure in the brilliant day, the squeak of harness, the huffing and occasional excited barks of his dog team, the banging and lurching of his sledge over the uneven ice, which was serrated by sastrugi, sharp-edged furrows formed when the ice alternately melted and froze again.

Hurley was, in his own description, an unemployed archaeologist. He was not in Antarctica to dig into the exposed rock of the dry valleys, however fascinating that would have been to him. His restless streak had, at least temporarily, lured him away from his chosen field.

He had first become interested in archaeology as a child growing up in New Mexico, where even in high school he had been able to secure summer work at nearby archaeological digs. After graduating from the University of New Mexico, he had found the patient, dogged donkey work of field research more frustrating than rewarding. But the work had opened up corners of the world he would never otherwise have seen, and it had awakened a hunger for exploration as well as for testing himself out on the edge of human experience. He would get back to digging, he knew; the restlessness had to work itself out.

It had taken him to Alaska, after various other sojourns; there he had labored on tuna fishing boats and on the construction of the giant oil pipeline. He spent one whole summer in remote mountains armed only with a camera, and holed up for the winter with a crazy trapper who thought he just might be the Son of God.

It was in Alaska that Hurley became acquainted with husky dog teams. He admired both the dogs and the competition they inspired, and before long he was working with a team of his own, begging and borrowing to purchase the valuable huskies.

He had placed third in his last Iditarod race, a grueling test of survival lasting eleven days across more than eleven hundred miles of the frozen Alaskan wilderness between Nome and Anchorage. He had a natural way with animals. His love of the dogs, and his search for new challenges, had caused him to join an Arctic expedition. Now it had brought him to the wildest, emptiest, most elusive horizon on earth: Antarctica.

The only thing Hurley disliked about his current venture was the financial part. For a proposed one-man dogsled run challenging the record to climb the Hartsook Glacier and race from there across the high ice plateau to the South Pole, he needed financial backing. The tab had been picked up by a cable television network, HTV, which proposed to film different stages of the journey to highlight its drama, its dangers and its harrowing difficulties. The run itself would not be made until next year—it was already too late in the Antarctic summer for a try this season—but Hurley was conditioning both himself and his dogs to Antarctic terrain and weather and the formidable obstacles they would face.

The TV crews were already filming his training and trial runs. "We can splice these into the film of the actual race," the young producer had explained to Hurley.

"But it won't be the same thing," Hurley had protested.

"You're gonna make the run in one piece, man, you're not cheating anyone. But we need film, man. We need all the film we can get."

"If you try to fake anything, the deal's off."

"Hey, what did I tell you? You're calling the shots."

So with some misgivings Hurley had reluctantly made his bargain with the TV devil. He had agreed to let the HTV cameras record his work this season, on the condition that events or segments of the final film would be properly identified.

To his relief the film crews had little liking for the Antarctic cold. They had spent most of their time this summer in the bars at McMurdo, venturing out occasionally in good weather by helicopter or transport plane to shoot some film. They wasted a lot of time and money, Hurley thought. It meant nothing to them.

For Hurley their money meant a shot at something new, an adventure he might otherwise only have dreamed of. He hated the commercial part of it, he told himself. But no one had bludgeoned him into it.

The truth was that he savored some of those moments when the cameras were trained on him. Liked the respectful attention of the camera crews when he was working with the dogs. Didn't even mind the sound of his own voice speaking into the microphones.

Okay, he also wanted the damned record. Wanted to do something better and faster than anyone else had ever done it. Wanted it to be seen by millions.

It might not go down in history. It might not make up for being soundly beaten in the Iditarod by a woman musher. It might last as an enduring achievement only until the next ego-driven adventurer came along, a new fast gun eager to cut down the aging gunslinger. But it was still worth doing.

And it wasn't going to be a cakewalk. Even these practice runs were grueling trials. He would need luck with the weather, luck with his gear, healthy dogs, and—

Dutch, the lead dog, was barely across the camouflaged snowbridge when it collapsed and the hidden crevasse beneath it opened up like jaws.

There were nine dogs in the team, Dutch alone in the lead, the others pulling in tandem. A husky like the others, Dutch was big, mean-tempered, quick to anger, like the Dutchman he was named for, boss of a pipeline construction crew for whom Hurley had once worked. He was a superb team leader, loyal, powerful, absolutely courageous, aggressive enough to keep the other dogs in line. The others had names that were signposts in Hurley's life. Sam for his father. Vixen, the only bitch, running in the second row as a lure for the young males pulling behind her, as a wry tribute to his ex-wife, who couldn't take his wanderings. Muley, for his stubborn kid brother, still trying to make it as a pitcher in the Cubs' minor-league system at age twenty-seven. Kipling, in honor of the writer. Crazy for the trapper he had wintered with. Oscar, an older dog named after Dr. Oscar Whitson, the archaeologist who had taught him as a teenager how to sift the dust of history reverently. Bones, the big, good-natured, lazy dog in the last pair, for his best friend, who had a weakness for rolling dice. And Bones's partner in the last row, Niner, the latest addition to the team, who had been named for his position rather than for Alaskan gold seekers of another century.

Dutch lunged when he felt the snowpack giving way. He made it across the crevasse safely, pulling most of the team after him. The third pair, Crazy and Oscar, were nearly caught when the bridge buckled. A scrambling thrust pulled them to solid ice beyond the chasm.

With startled yelps and a muffled howl of pain, the last pair dropped out of sight.

Hurley, riding the back end of the sledge, jumped off and braked with all his strength. The lightweight, loose-coupled and highly flexible sledge looked as if it would fall apart any minute, but it was ideally designed for the pounding of Antarctica's uneven, spiny, treacherous ice. It was also lightly laden. The bulk of Hurley's provisions and gear was back at his staging camp. The lack of weight kept the sledge from plummeting of its own momentum into the crevasse, dragging the entire dog team—and Hurley as well—into an icy grave.

The rig slowed, skewed on the ice and shuddered to a stop. The nose tilted downward at the edge of the drop.

The crevasse was at least a hundred feet deep, but narrow. Many that Hurley had carefully detoured around were yards wide. At the point where the snowbridge had caved in, this fissure was about five feet across. The ice was as clear and blue as water.

Bones was visible a few feet from the edge of the deep cut in the ice, struggling in his harness, his paws scrabbling wildly at the snow and ice. Hurley saw the panic in his eyes. Just beneath him, hanging out of his broken harness and secured only by the nylon trace that linked all the dogs, was Niner, the dog that had howled in pain.

Hurley's actions were reflexive and swift. He slapped at the quick-release catches, freeing the dogs from the sledge. The rest of the team would have to bear the weight of the two dogs in trouble. He dragged the sledge back from the edge of the crevasse. For a few reckless seconds he considered trying to jump across the gap. Reason cut through the foggy notion. In his bulky gear, on the slippery surface, he would never make it.

Across the narrow chasm the dogs were milling around, barking and whining. Dutch snapped at the complaining Vixen, who gave a yelp inordinate to her distress. All the dogs were excited and worried. Old instincts of danger crowded them. If the whimpering victim dangling from the trace had been within reach, the pack might well have turned on him. The husky was wolf-bred; his instincts were not far removed from the wild.

"Stay!" Hurley called out in a firm but calm tone. "Easy, Dutch. Let's keep calm. We'll get out of this." He felt no incongruity carrying on a conversation with his dogs. In the wilderness they were his only companions; conversation was normal. "Just stay."

A dozen paces to his right, where winds had blown most of the snow from the surface of the ice, he found a narrowing of the crevasse. He tested the ice on his side of the gap and eyed the other rim with suspicion. Then he jumped.

When he landed, his boots skidded and shot out from under him. He sprawled on his back. The ice was firm—and hard. Hundreds of feet of it, he thought gratefully, solid beneath him.

The dogs became more excited at his approach. Hurley knelt cautiously at the rim of the crevasse and leaned over the edge. Bones was within arm's reach. His harness, made of sturdy cotton lampwick, was intact. "Careful, Bonesy, don't snap," he said soothingly. "I'm here to help."

He pulled off his right mitten to get a better grip on the harness. When he took hold of it, he felt the searing bite of a metal clasp against the back of his hand. A patch of skin, bonded to the cold metal, tore loose as he hauled the struggling dog over the edge to safety.

Like a fallen mountain climber at the end of his safety rope, Niner still dangled from the trace that linked all the dogs.

Hurley shoved his hand back into its mitten. He used both hands to grab the trace. Niner yelped once in agony. Then he was silent.

Hurley stared down at him. "You goddamned beautiful son of a bitch," he said aloud. "Your leg's broken, isn't it?"

Broken up near the shoulder, Hurley guessed. The angle of his left front leg was wrong.

And the nylon rope had wrapped around the broken leg. To pull the dog up meant intolerable pain.

"Sorry, boy," Hurley muttered.

Behind him Dutch snapped at one of the other dogs, provoking a brief, snarling melee. "Goddamn it!" Hurley yelled in his own best imitation of a snarl. "Cut it out!"

The dogs immediately quieted. Hurley looped the trace around his right hand and forearm, ignoring the burning sensation where the flesh had peeled off. He let the dog team on the surface feel his weight while he eased over the rim of the crevasse. Then he let himself down into the fissure.

Within the icy canyon the light changed, as if he had entered a room glowing with soft blue light. The young, injured dog watched him with wild, rolling eyes. Above them the team, as if sensing a change in their situation, danced about restlessly, pulling against Hurley's weight. He was now completely dependent on them and the trace they supported.

Hurley spoke to the dog trapped in the crevasse with him. His tone was light, conversational. "You know what my father used to say to me when he took off his belt? He'd say, 'This is going to hurt me more than it does you.' " Hurley paused. He was close enough to Niner to reach out and touch him. The dog's lips curled back in a reflexive snarl. "He knew different, we both did, but I appreciated him saying that, even though it was bullshit."

He touched Niner's muzzle gently, let his fingers rest there.

"What I'm trying to say is, I've got to get hold of what's left of that harness and drag you upstairs if I can, and it's gonna hurt like hell."

Without warning he fell about a foot deeper into the pit. One of the dogs up above had lost his footing on the ice. Hurley felt the shock all through his arm, which threatened to pop from its shoulder socket. He banged against the wall of blue ice and hung free, his feet scrabbling at air.

After a few seconds he felt the rush of fear begin to drain away. His thoughts unscrambled. "Steady up there!" he called.

Though startled by the sudden drop, Niner had not whimpered or tried to bite. Hurley decided to wait no longer. Reaching out with his free hand, he hooked it under the broken harness that still crisscrossed the husky's chest. "It's you and me, kid. And them." He called out sharply, "Dutch! Pull!"

There was a short delay, during which Hurley could hear some scrambling movement beyond the rim of the ice canyon. "Pull!" he shouted again.

Out of sight, the dogs fell into line, responding to Dutch's lead. Snow sifted over Hurley and Niner, and he thought the ice shifted. A chunk of it tumbled past his ear. The chill went straight to his heart. He waited, the survival instinct screaming in his brain, telling him to lunge, claw, scream.

He waited another piece of eternity.

The trace moved. It scraped over the edge, cutting into the ice. Hurley felt the heavy pull on his right arm, which, wrapped around the nylon rope, bore his 180 pounds and another 140 pounds of muscular young husky.

Though he was new to the team and Hurley had had him for only six months, Niner proved his trust. He did not slash at Hurley's vulnerable arm with those long, sharp canine teeth. He let himself be held, Hurley trying to keep as much weight as possible off the length of rope tangled around the broken leg.

Foot by foot, they scraped slowly up the wall of the crevasse. Now Hurley could hear the dogs above them clearly. They were barking with excitement, pulling more cohesively.

As he was hauled over the edge onto solid ice, Hurley rolled onto his side, putting his body between Niner and the sharp rim.

He had been unconsciously holding his breath. It exploded from him as he tumbled onto the ice. He scrambled away from the crevasse, dragging Niner after him.

At the other end of the chain Dutch stopped pulling. His mission was accomplished.

* * *

For a long minute Brian Hurley lay flat on the ice, his heart slamming against his ribs. Sweat chilled under his layered garments. He brushed snow and frost away from his eyes and his nostrils, felt the stiffness of his frozen beard.

Niner was biting at the rope around his leg, drawing blood. "No, boy!" Hurley said. "Easy . . . easy."

Gingerly he began to unravel the tangled trace. When the husky growled, Hurley ignored him. "We got us a problem here, son, but let's get the damned rope off you first."

He unwrapped the length of rope as carefully as he could from the broken leg, releasing the pressure. The big dog accepted his touch. The last loop fell away from the shoulder. Hurley eased it from under the dog's body. As soon as he felt the tension of the trace drop away, Niner struggled to get to his feet. Hurley put a hand on his side, applying steady pressure, holding him down. "Stay, boy . . . stay."

After another moment the husky relaxed. His eyes rolled toward Hurley, but the wildness had left his stare. His steady panting told Hurley that the dog was in pain. His left leg was pulled up, toes curling in.

"That leg needs to be set. I'll do my best, but . . ."

He thought of Dr. Katherine McNeely. The Bird Woman. Every day since she left McMurdo, and every long night, he had replayed their brief quarrel in his mind, trying to understand what lay behind it. He refused to admit that their fierce attraction had been nothing more than a fleeting fancy, born of loneliness, isolation, the easy emotions of a sentimental season. But if he was right, what had made their words turn so quickly bitter? Why had they been so seemingly eager to seize on the first sign of difference between them, as if they had been waiting for an excuse? Or had those days in MacTown meant less to her than to him?

Hurley remembered everything about her—her dark eyes, intelligent and lively, the way her mouth opened when she laughed, small, perfectly shaped breasts, the vulnerability he sensed beneath her confident manner. Now he remembered

44

something else as well, something she had said during one of their long, murmured conversations in the early morning when they probed their mutual histories, eager to learn everything about each other. (He had not imagined that, he told himself.) She had taken some undergraduate courses in veterinary medicine at UCLA before her later specialization as an ornithologist.

Okay, so she wasn't a veterinarian, Hurley thought. But she knew *something* about caring for sick or injured animals.

And, maybe, setting broken bones.

What Hurley did not articulate, even to himself, was the blunt fact that the young husky needed immediate help. Without it he would not survive long in Antarctic conditions.

He told the dog to stay. The others were watching him calmly now, sitting or lying down on the snow-covered ice. The cold, he knew, didn't bother them. In fact, they probably thought it was a little too warm today.

Hurley retraced his steps to the narrowing of the crevasse, crossed over and returned to his sledge. It took him fifteen minutes to unload. Then he pulled the sledge by hand over to the crossing point and easily ran it across. Repacking his gear on the sledge, he formed a flat bed in the center. His backpack with its braces made a rough stretcher on which he was able to lift Niner onto the sledge. Hitching up the dog team, Hurley put the easygoing Bones up front to run in tandem with Dutch. The lead dog didn't care for the arrangement, snapping once at Bones to show his displeasure; but the latter acted as if this were the normal course of friendship, and Dutch grudgingly settled down.

Though the sun rested just above the horizon, it was shortly past noon. Hurley plotted a course to the eastern flank of the Hartsook Glacier. An ice tongue, like a side road branching off from a superhighway, led to the east of the glacier, passing near the scientists' base camp and a large emperor penguin rookery.

About a six-hour run, Hurley judged. Niner seemed relaxed enough for the moment; Hurley guessed that shock had set in, dulling the dog's pain. But he would take a beating riding in the sledge for six hours. Hurley never gave a thought to whether the dog team could or would do what he asked of them. They would. What he didn't know was whether that effort would be good enough to save the injured dog. No matter. He had to try.

Setting off, Hurley noticed for the first time a dark bank of clouds sitting over the coastline to the west, beyond the intervening mountains. The clouds brought a little nudge of warning. Antarctic storms often moved very fast.

Sledging, the snow glare almost blinding him, Hurley kept a sharp watch for any other unexpected opening in the ice. But he put most of his trust not in his eyes but in Dutch's instinct. The lead dog had been fooled by the deceptive snow cover once today; it would be unusual if it happened again.

The dogs adapted to their four-pair hitch and fell into a steady, ground-covering rhythm. They followed the glacier where it bludgeoned its way through a wide mountain pass, descending toward the sea. Glaciers moved at varying paces, but Hurley had been told the Hartsook mass was traveling about sixty yards a year.

In the pass the wind sharpened and seemed colder. The line of dark clouds stood higher on the horizon, reaching up into that piercing blue sky like a spreading stain.

Sometimes Hurley rode the sledge. As often he trotted along behind it, giving the dogs less weight to pull and quickening their pace. As he inched across the seemingly endless sheet of ice, Hurley recognized the reason for the excitement that steadily grew. Each mile brought him closer to Kathy McNeely.

FOUR

THE TRUCK BRAKED AT THE EDGE of the hard-packed ice runway of Williams Field, the airstrip serving McMurdo Station. Michael Davis bounced against the torn vinyl seat; he felt the shock of the jolting stop travel up his spine.

As he clambered out of the heated cab, the cold air slammed into him like a door shut in his face. His breath caught; the skin tightened over his face in spite of his woolen mask; his body prickled with a chill under the layers of clothing. *What the hell?* he thought.

The temperature had been a relatively mild twenty degrees above zero during the three days he had spent at the U.S. Palmer Station in the Antarctic Peninsula, and not much colder when he arrived at McMurdo Station. There had been little wind, and with the air so dry the cold had actually seemed tame in comparison with a January day when the wind was blowing off the lake through the canyons of downtown Chicago, where he had served his journalistic apprenticeship with the *Tribune* before moving to Los Angeles and the *Times*.

Today was different. The temperature had plunged to about twelve below zero and was heading down. Cloud cover threat-

47

ened the sun. Gusts of wind sent powder snow whirling across the runway toward him.

What the hell are you doing here? Davis thought.

He spotted the stocky figure of Hank Forbes, the veteran navy helicopter pilot he had met the night before, standing next to the Huey helicopter, its bright red body vivid against the white mass of Mount Erebus behind it. An active volcano, Mount Erebus had contributed the lava bed on which McMurdo had been built as well as the ash that blackened its streets. Forbes, retired from the service but reluctant to abandon the joy of flying, was now a contract pilot for the National Science Foundation, jockeying choppers around the coldest, windiest, most dangerous place on earth for such aircraft. Forbes gave Davis a genial wave before going back to his conversation with a mechanic who had been fueling the helicopter.

There was no sign of the two men Davis would be flying with. Still warm and snug in their room at the euphemistically named Ross Hilton, Davis thought. He should have known they'd be late, but he hadn't wanted to miss them. Rupert Merrill, the man in charge, had said they wouldn't be able to wait if Davis couldn't be ready on time. In the conviviality of the noisy MacTown barroom it had seemed important to heed his warning.

Davis had stumbled on Merrill by accident while making a tour of McMurdo's four bars—although, with a reporter's arrogance, Davis didn't believe that such fortuitous encounters were ever entirely by chance. Merrill, a geologist, had proved to be a cheerful drinking companion. Though his partner, Len Sears, had had little to say, he'd done his share of drinking, and even he had loosened up as the evening wore on.

The trio had moved on to a second bar when Merrill expressed interest in the journalist's assignment to write a series of articles about Antarctica for the *Los Angeles Times*. In the noisy, crowded room it was possible to talk with a surprising degree of privacy. No one could listen to anyone more than two feet from his elbow.

"Any special focus, Mike? You must have something in mind."

"No, no . . . but with the Antarctic Treaty up for review, my editor thought it would be a timely subject."

"The Antarctic Treaty!" Sears made a garbled sound into his glass. He set it down and mumbled something unintelligible before stalking off in search of a urinal.

"What did he say?"

Merrill laughed. "Don't mind Len, he's not a fan of the Antarctic Treaty."

"How could he not be? Look what it's done for Antarctica."

"What would that be, Mike?"

"Well . . . since 1959 it's insulated this continent from most of the world's quarrels and self-destructive pursuits, made it a peaceful preserve set aside for scientific research . . . your kind of work. How can you be against that?"

"You'd be surprised. The way the treaty is administered, SCAR—that's the international Scientific Committee on Antarctic Research—and the separate national committees hold very tight reins on research. It's not exactly freedom of inquiry. Not everyone is happy with the treaty."

"But there *is* freedom of sharing information, right? From what I understand, that's been the greatest benefit over the past thirty-something years. The whole concept of international co-operation in Antarctica is a model for what nations can do if they just set aside national prejudices and selfish interests."

"Mmm. Tell that to Greenpeace," said Merrill.

The terse comment stopped Davis. "Okay," he said. "So the Japanese are still killing whales in Antarctic waters. What else, Mr. Merrill?"

The geologist's smile turned wry. "Don't get me wrong, Mike, the treaty has been a great thing overall for the Ice. Just don't overestimate its successes. It caused most of the represented nations to set aside territorial claims to this continent, and that's been all to the good. But you have to remember, back in 1959, when the treaty was signed, Antarctica was just a big ice cube. It was too cold, too inhospitable, too barren to be important. In the 1990s that view is outdated. Antarctic waters are a potentially rich resource, quite aside from killing whales, which everyone but Japan has agreed to stop. Krill fishing, for example, has enormous potential. And the continent itself isn't as barren as we once thought."

"Which brings us to the minerals regime."

Merrill looked at him approvingly. "Exactly. That's why the signatories to the treaty established a minerals regime in 1988. We know there's oil here, minerals, precious metals. It's important to have general agreement on minerals research, so we can control development for minimum impact on the ecology of the continent. What's done in Antarctica is no longer insignificant to everyone but a few explorers."

"That agreement has already caused dissension."

For the first time Merrill's equanimity seemed ruffled. "France and Australia withdrew their agreement to the minerals regime. But they'll come around. Resources development has to come. Controlling it, sharing its benefits, is a goal we can all accept. The only disagreement is on how to get there."

Davis sipped his drink before saying casually, "I've heard talk about other problems on the Ice."

"Oh? What kind of problems?"

"I don't know . . . disagreements between different missions. Unusual accidents, stuff like that. You heard anything?"

"Nothing at all," Merrill said after a moment's hesitation. "If you're after scandals down here, Mike, I'm afraid you won't find any."

It was the hesitation that Davis remembered.

Sometime later, in yet another bar, Merrill talked about his own work in Antarctica, which involved drilling into the ice to remove core samples for study. "Antarctic ice is essentially a time capsule," he explained, "built up layer upon layer over thousands of years. Our own core samples record such events as a volcanic eruption over three thousand years ago, changing climatological patterns over the centuries, even such specifics as radioactive fallout from nuclear tests in the 1950s."

"Is that where your work is directed?"

Merrill shook his head patiently. "We're using our core samples to measure concentrations of methane and carbon dioxide at different periods in recent history. And nitrous oxide, the chlorofluorocarbons, which are suspected of creating a hole in the ozone layer over Antarctica during the summer, as well as trapping more heat."

"You find all that shit in the ice?"

"Of course. And we're able to compare measurements in the atmosphere today with those deposited in the ice in the past and recorded in our core samples." Merrill paused. "What we know is, current levels of atmospheric pollution are higher than ever."

"TERCO is interested in these studies?"

"We're an energy company, Mike. It's in our interest as well as everyone else's. TERCO is very interested in how burning fossil fuels affects the global environment."

It was too pat a speech, Davis thought, glib words Merrill had used before. He said, "So what are you learning? Are the carbon dioxide levels high enough so the Antarctic ice sheet is going to melt? The so-called greenhouse effect?"

Merrill smiled. "Done some research?"

"So far all I've learned are the buzzwords. What about it? Is Cape Cod going to be underwater?"

"It's not that simple, Mike. The scientific community is like any other. There are alarmists, doomsayers walking around proclaiming, 'The end is near!' And let's face it, there are some who just like to see their names in the paper or their faces on television."

With a reporter's skepticism Davis wondered what Merrill was trying to sell him. He wished he hadn't had quite so much to drink. The conversation was one he wanted to remember and use.

"Does that mean you're not one of the believers?" he asked.

"As a matter of fact, our studies are inconclusive. There's just as much evidence the earth might be in for a cold trend as a warm one. The same conditions that are said to threaten a greenhouse warming, by trapping infrared radiation from the sun that would otherwise be reflected into space, may conversely bring about more cloud cover and more rain. Instead of melting the Antarctic ice sheet, we could have a cooling effect."

"Isn't that a minority theory?"

"If you look at the history of science, Mike, minority theories are quite often the correct ones."

Merrill sounded so damned reasonable, Davis thought. Why didn't he fully trust him?

After Len Sears rejoined them, the trio moved on to another bar, where, with Willie Nelson singing his melancholy version of "It's a Wonderful World" in the background, Sears joining him in a tone-deaf baritone, Rupert Merrill cupped his hand over Davis's ear so he could be heard and said, "Why don't you come and see for yourself?"

"What?"

Merrill said that he and Sears were flying out to their research camp in the morning. Davis was welcome to come along, see what TERCO'S Antarctic field research was all about. Davis's NSF transport plane could pick him up there, Merrill suggested, and he could then go on about his tour.

Ordinarily Mike Davis would have said thanks, but no, thanks, and stuck to his own agenda. The National Science Foundation, eager to cooperate with an award-winning science reporter from the *Los Angeles Times,* had set up his itinerary, supplied him with an earnest young yeoman first class as a tour guide, lined up a large, reassuringly sturdy ski-equipped Hercules LC-130 transport plane to ferry him and a couple other DVs —local NSF code for distinguished visitors—about the continent. One thing changed his mind: Merrill's reminder of his employer.

TERCO was an energy conglomerate that, like many other U.S. and multinational oil and energy development companies, had a legitimate interest in sending a research team to Antarctica. What particularly interested Davis wasn't the Houston-based company itself but its CEO, Ron Kusic. During the free-wheeling 1980s Kusic had won a reputation as a corporate raider. Brash, brilliant, ruthless—suitable qualities for any pirate —in 1981 he had acquired a controlling interest in Travis Oil, a small Texas company, before its owners knew what was happening. Then, in a series of progressively bolder maneuvers, he had targeted ever-larger companies, building on his previous acquisitions along with junk bond financing for hostile takeovers. The climax of a decade of maneuvering had stunned Wall Street and the energy industry. In less than ten years the upstart Kusic, a man with relatively little oil industry experience, had leaped from the springboard of little-known Travis Oil to a successful manipulation of stockholder unrest and greed that brought him control of one of the industry's giants, TERCO. It had been a risky move, coming at a time when the financial community was beginning to pull back from the wave of speculation that characterized the eighties, and junk bonds had become a dirty phrase. But Kusic, a salesman of legendary prowess, had somehow won over both the stockholders and the bankers.

Davis hadn't heard Kusic's name as often lately or seen it on the business pages of the *Times*. He wondered what the man was up to now and whether or not his plans had anything directly to do with a team of geologists in Antarctica. The question was pertinent enough to cause Davis to accept Merrill's invitation.

In the cold clarity of the morning, he wasn't as happy with his decision as he had been last night.

Davis shivered and moved about, stamping his feet. He gazed back toward the sprawl of McMurdo Station, squinting against the snow glare as he searched for another vehicle heading his way. McMurdo reminded him of one of those service bases made up of temporary buildings still in place from World War II. There was a haphazard, improvised look to the place, gray burlap-and-board or sheet metal buildings slapped up with little sense of planning, streets of gray volcanic ash from Mount Erebus that had turned to black mud on the relatively warm day of

Davis's arrival, stacks of huge shipping crates and drums waiting to be moved by the trucks and tractors grumbling along the streets.

The dump on the hillside in back of the station wasn't as horrific as he had been led to expect. "Hey, we dropped a bundle cleaning the place up," his guileless navy guide, Steve Drexler, had told him. "I mean, I think it was like ten million bucks last year. You should've seen it before the cleanup. It was just a huge pile of old truck tires, rusty machinery, empty shipping crates and drums, trash, you name it. Trouble is, nothing disintegrates here, it's too cold for that. You come back ten years from now, or fifty years, and whatever you left behind most likely will still be there."

"Like Scott's last hut, the one you showed me." Robert Falcon Scott's last fateful expedition in 1911, his heroic struggle to reach the South Pole, the irony of reaching his goal at last only to find that the Norwegian explorer Roald Amundsen had planted his flag a month earlier, and the tragic fate of the five men in Scott's party—Evans, Oates, Bowers, Wilson and, finally, Scott himself—on their terrible return journey that ended only a few miles from safety, was as much a part of Antarctic legend as the Pole itself. The neat wooden hut Scott had built on Ross Island, facing McMurdo Strait, remained as he had left it, with cans of food and broken bottles and other articles scattered about. Drexler's voice had taken on the hushed tones of reverence when he led Davis to the site.

"Yeah, like that. I mean, yes, sir."

"So what happens to all the stuff now?"

"Well, we got the fenced landfill now. And what's too big or too toxic or dangerous to bury, we ship it back home."

Davis had an image of ships low in the water, heavy with trash and waste, struggling across the stormy straits. How many thousands of tons of it each year? McMurdo would have been a small town back in the States, but there were more than a thousand people there during the summer season, enough to generate prodigious amounts of trash. During the winter the population dropped to about a hundred personnel, who holed up for the season. "There's not a whole hell of a lot going on in winter," Drexler had informed him, sounding morose at the reminder of approaching winter. "You watch the same video movies and thumb through the same old magazines or books and then start over. You wonder what the hell you're doing here, you know?"

I know, Davis thought, shifting his weight and rocking back and forth as he stared down the hill toward the station. He slapped his mittened hands together and decided that when he was old enough to retire, he would settle in some place, like Key West, where it was never cold enough to see your breath.

The arrival of the van carrying Merrill and Sears precipitated a flurry of activity. Mike Davis didn't even have time to complain about the two geologists keeping him waiting in the cold. Within minutes they were on board the Huey helicopter, the overhead blade making an infernal racket until the doors were closed. Then, before Davis was really prepared for it, the chopper lurched into the air, climbed briefly and heeled over like a bird tilting on its wing. Davis felt the seat belt bite into his middle while his stomach was left behind. "Jesus Christ!" he muttered.

It was his first time up in a helicopter, a fact he had not wanted to admit to Merrill and his partner. He had tried to think of the junket as a lark, an adventure, as well as an interesting sidebar to his articles about troubles in the paradise of Antarctica. The bright red helos, as most of the regulars at McMurdo called them, clattered into and out of Williams Field all day long. They were part of the story of life on the Ice, and Hank Forbes, the grizzled pilot, his face weathered and burnished by sun, wind and cold, a younger version of Chuck Yeager, made a good background character. Now, however, looking down at an immense sheet of snow and ice that seemed to go on forever, feeling the aircraft shake like a vintage wooden crate from the steady chopping of the overhead blades, Mike Davis experienced a sudden longing for the comfort and security of an ordinary aircraft, complete with solicitous flight attendants.

What am I doing here?

The question catapulted him from the noisy interior of the chopper, a tiny moth fluttering over the vast white wilderness of the Ross Ice Shelf, to what seemed a safer, saner world—adjectives not usually reserved for Southern California. *That bastard Shafter,* he thought. *I wish him a week at McMurdo in winter without his jockstrap.*

Lee Shaefer, commonly known to the staff as Shafter, was Davis's managing editor at the *Times.* Davis remembered the moment, three months ago, when Shaefer had first spoken the mysterious, unexpected word. Davis had repeated it after him in disbelief.

"Antarctica?"

"That's right, Mike. Antarctica."

Davis felt a tickle along the back of his neck, a chill of anticipation or dread. He remembered a recent story, page four or five of the first section, not enough of a grabber to make the front page, quoting Jacques Cousteau's warning of the worldwide disaster that would follow disruption of the food chain in the Southern Ocean. "It's been done," he said.

His managing editor shook his head. "Uh-uh. This one's getting bigger. It's got everything. Holes in the ozone. Penguins. Seals. Whales."

"And krill," Davis said dryly. "Don't forget krill."

"It's made for you." Shaefer hadn't risen high in the echelons of *Los Angeles Times* editors without being able to turn on what passed for charm when he desired. "It's the perfect follow-up on that Alaskan retrospective. Did I ever tell you, I damn near cried over those otters. And the eagles, they really did it for me."

"You're a cynical, manipulative bastard."

Davis didn't have to be reminded that his by-lined stories in the *Times* documenting the misery left behind in Prince William

Sound a year after Exxon pulled out had done more for his journalistic status than anything else he had written. He had been nominated for a Pulitzer, losing out to a *Detroit Free Press* science writer who had written a hard-hitting series about toxic pollution in Lake Huron fisheries.

The reporter sighed dramatically. "Okay, Antarctica. What have you got for me? What's the angle?"

Shaefer grinned his wolf's grin that showed the gaps between several of his front teeth—the grin that had helped win him his nickname of Shafter. "What I have for you, Michael, is approval from the National Science Foundation, without which nobody goes there, for a summer vacation on the Ice." He tapped a thick manila envelope on his desk. "They've even sent you some helpful hints on how to stay alive while you're there."

Davis stared bleakly at his editor. He made no move to take the information packet. "Why me, for God's sake?"

"Who else? You've got the credentials. You're a scientist—well, you can write about science, anyway." Shaefer didn't want to give more credit than was due. Davis was the newspaper's number one science reporter, which either gave him a leg up in two fields or made him neither scientist nor journalist, depending on your point of view. "You spent time in Alaska, so you know all about ice and snow."

"Antarctica isn't Alaska."

"Yeah, no polar bears, they tell me."

Staring at Shaefer's complacent smile, Davis heard the whistle of an icy wind blowing off a glacier and shivered. "My God, Shafter, do you have any idea how *cold* it is down there?" But even as his protest found voice, Davis again felt that quiver of anticipation. It was more than excitement. Fear, curiosity, wonder, anxiety, that whole bundle of conflicting emotions that came with the apprehension of something new and different, a horizon never seen before.

"Take your woollies," the editor said equably. "They say it really is spectacular, Michael. I envy you."

"Be serious."

"I've never been more serious in my life. There's a story there, Michael. It's as simple as that."

"What story? The New Zealand conference disputes? That's been hashed over. And Cousteau's been on television all over the place. I respect his message, but—"

"Just be quiet a minute and listen." Shaefer glanced out of his interior office window. Not much to see anymore. Not like the old days, when you could stare out of his office over the entire length of a busy, crowded, disorderly newsroom. Now it was all cubicles, each one with its own computer terminal. A lot more information was available instantly at your fingertips, but there was also a lot less bullshitting about the Dodgers or the Raiders or the winter meeting at Santa Anita. "I've got this source," he said. "his name is Sam Namura. I went to Stanford with him."

"Name-dropper," Davis muttered.

Ignoring the comment, Shaefer said, "He's a marine biologist at Berkeley now, just got back from Antarctica a couple months ago. He'd been down there doing research for a year, and this thing has been bugging him ever since he got back." When the editor paused, Davis knew he was being careful in his choice of words, making his appeal. "The way Namura tells it, it's like one of the Nixon crowd was accidentally shipped to Antarctica and has been busy executing dirty tricks."

Appealing to the liberal in me, Davis thought.

"What kind of dirty tricks?"

"What Sam heard was mostly secondhand, stories over drinks, rumors, the usual, except that the stories often had a nasty edge. After a while they began to paint a disturbing picture. This wasn't someone going around getting his jollies. This was malicious stuff, even dangerous."

"Give me a for instance."

"Like feeding rivalries and jealousies among the different scientific missions. Spreading stories about affairs hetero and homosexual. Or getting into the navy's computer system at McMurdo and fixing it so supplies were misdirected. A research team in the field not getting food supplies or heating oil could be disastrous, Namura says."

"You haven't sold me."

"You're a newspaperman of sorts, you're supposed to be skeptical. But you're also supposed to be able to sniff out a story. I'm telling you, Michael, Namura is no alarmist. This thing has a smell."

Davis tried to think of a put-down, some way to squash the whole Antarctic notion with a single tart phrase. It wouldn't come. Instead the tickle of anticipation became more pronounced.

Shafter was right, as usual. Namura's unease rang true. And if there was anything behind it at all, someone had to go down there and find the story.

Why me? he thought. But he knew the answer to that question. *Because you want it.*

FIVE

_____

An hour out of McMurdo Station Davis was snapped back to his immediate surroundings by a change in the pitch of the helicopter's rotors. By then he had become comfortable enough with the ride to enjoy the remarkable views on all sides. The chopper climbed steeply past a wall of ice. When it rose over the top of the cliff, Davis saw that the ice formed the front of an enormous glacier extending as far as he could see toward the peaks of the Transantarctic Mountains. The expanse of snow and ice also stretched for miles to the left and right, a blanket of pure, dazzling white, unmarked, untouched.

There's no feeling like it. You step out onto that snow and you know that no man, no living creature, has ever set foot there before. There is a purity to that moment which simply must be experienced to be understood.

Dr. Sam Namura's words. When Davis first met the marine biologist at his editor's urging, he was startled by Namura's passion for Antarctica. Namura was a short, stocky man with thick eyeglasses; he reminded Davis of Mickey Rooney's comic caricature of a Japanese in *Breakfast at Tiffany's*. But Namura couldn't have been more serious when he spoke of his year on the Ice. "It was an unbelievable experience, Mr. Davis. It's like no other place on earth. It possessed me. Perhaps that is why my year there seems like a small lifetime. In spite of the cold, the constant problems with equipment and my experiments, not being able to get parts or supplies I needed for weeks or months, I hated to see the year end. I cried when we left."

Namura's strong attachment to Antarctica was part of his concern for what he perceived to be happening there. Recalling the scientist's words, Davis stared down at the muscular folds of the glacier beneath the helicopter. "You must understand, Mr. Davis, there is more than a little possibility of paranoia when people live and work for prolonged periods in such isolation and physical stress. Still, there were too many incidents to be put down entirely to the conditions of life." Namura paused, sipped a salt-rimmed margarita and gazed out of a restaurant window at the sun-drenched beauty of Marina del Rey, where he and Davis had arranged to meet for dinner, as if he were contrasting the hedonistic scene with the harsh beauty of Antarctica and had found it wanting. "I'm not speaking of familiar complaints, such as Greenpeace enthusiasts placing their boats in the path of Japanese whalers. Such conflicts are well known. They are troublesome but not surprising. I'm speaking of something else . . . something like dirty tricks, to use the political analogy."

"Dirty tricks?" It was Lee Shaefer's phrase.

"Switching shipping labels, for example, so supplies were misdirected. In Antarctica such a mistake is no small thing, Mr. Davis. It can be disastrous. And it also creates suspicion, animosity, distrust, which is all the more damaging because the culprit is unknown and everyone becomes suspect."

"A prankster . . ."

"A prankster did not put snow in the gasoline tanks of three New Zealand snow toboggans shortly after an American group visited their station. Or leave the remains of dead seals on the ice below the Chinese station, as apparent evidence that they had been killed for food—an accusation that the Chinese vociferously denied. A prankster did not cause an oil leak in one of the fuel storage bladders at our base camp. Not only did we lose most of our heating oil, but it seeped into and contaminated the ice. These were not pranks, Mr. Davis. These were acts of malice . . . or worse."

Namura fell silent. The reporter waited, his journalistic curiosity now racing at full throttle, sifting the few facts Namura had revealed, weighing the emotional debris, searching for glints of truth.

"I'm probably not conveying this very well—it's difficult to describe without sounding melodramatic—but . . . have you ever worked someplace, a university or even a newspaper office, where the atmosphere became poisoned? By rumors, theft or vandalism, deliberate acts of subversion, rivalries, jealousies, character assassination?"

"Hey, you're talking about my workplace," Davis joked.

Namura forced a smile. "It is the concentration of events that caught my attention while I was in Antarctica. You must understand, Mr. Davis, that in the beginning I found the people on the Ice extraordinarily hospitable. Friendlier, more open than one usually finds. There were no hostilities of any kind. But between the time I arrived and my departure, the atmosphere changed. People were becoming less open, more suspicious of strangers or of those who were not in their own group or of their own nationality. A certain . . . freedom had been lost. I'm not simply talking about cabin fever, Mr. Davis, as it used to be called, a common phenomenon at the end of an Antarctic winter. No, this was something much more disturbing. I sensed a deliberate hand behind the change. As if someone had a grievance against the Antarctic community."

Mike Davis shook his head. Now that he was in Antarctica, fluttering over the mass of a glacier a thousand feet thick, Namura's dramatic words sounded less convincing.

The helicopter lifted unexpectedly, like a bird catching an updraft, and climbed so rapidly that Davis's reflections flew out of his head. He saw that they were close to the mountains. In the distance the snow-covered peaks had seemed small. Now they had assumed the shape of a formidable mountain range. As the chopper raced toward them, Davis tried to suppress his alarm. There was nothing to worry about. Hank Forbes knew what he was doing, didn't he?

Helicopter crashes, if not exactly commonplace, were a fact of life in Antarctica, he had been told. At the time, hiding his inexperience, he had brushed off the statistics even while he jotted them down in his notes. Like most statistics, they had little to do with him personally.

He became aware of being watched.

Rupert Merrill smiled. "Getting the hang of it, Mike? This is your first helo ride, right?"

"Does it show that much?" Merrill was quick with first names, Davis thought. A facade of geniality without genuine warmth. "It's a trip."

"We'll be there in another hour or so."

The helicopter passed easily between the nearest peaks and began a descent parallel to the slopes of the mountains on the far side. Here another glacier appeared, creeping like white lava toward the distant sea. In the incredible clarity of the air, Davis saw patches of deep blue far to the west, more than fifty miles away, and a series of huge tabular icebergs rising out of the water like the skyline of a great city.

The chopper drifted lower, turning toward the coastline.

"Why are we changing direction?" Davis asked.

Hank Forbes threw a reckless grin over his shoulder. "Look behind you, Mr. Davis."

Davis glanced back, expecting to see the massive thrust of the mountain peaks, the source of the glacier flowing downward. There was nothing but a universal whiteness, as if a curtain had descended over a stage.

He sensed, for the first time, tension in the cabin.

"Make sure you're strapped in tight," the pilot called out. "We might have a little turbulence."

Forbes spoke in the reassuring tone of a commercial airline pilot, Davis thought. It did not leave him reassured.

Inside the chopper there was no sound other than the steady hammering of the overhead blades and an occasional banging, as if someone were outside trying to get in. The aircraft appeared to be moving faster than before, in a hurry. It flew low over the long sweep of the glacier, low enough for Davis to see pressure ridges where the ice had folded over upon itself, sculptured snowdrifts, the deep blue of crevasses splitting the ice. In all that vast white expanse there was no living thing, no monument to human presence or passage, no spire or tent or track. The helicopter was alone in the cold, dazzling wilderness.

Behind it the world had disappeared.

Davis remembered Satchel Paige's admonition: *Don't look back. Something may be gaining on you.*

The helo dropped suddenly. Cargo shifted in the back of the cabin; a box broke loose. As the aircraft righted itself, Rupert Merrill said, "He's got to get away from the mountains."

"Why?" Davis asked nervously. "You mean we might not get high enough?"

Merrill shook his head. "If the storm catches us, he won't be able to see them."

Ignoring the old star pitcher's advice, Davis stared back over his shoulder. He hadn't thought of the silent whiteness as a storm. There were no black clouds, no streaks of lightning, no crashing thunder.

In that moment the familiar reality of earth and sky, mountains and valleys, light and shadow, disappeared. There was only an all-enveloping whiteness into which the helicopter sank as if into a white ocean.

Even the sound of the rotors was muffled.

"My God, what—what's happened?"

"A whiteout!" Merrill snapped.

The geologist's imperturbable manner had vanished with the horizon. Beyond him Len Sears gripped the arms of his seat, his hands white-knuckled. Ahead of them, leaning forward over the pale glow of his instrument panel, Hank Forbes peered intently through the windshield at the featureless brightness through which he flew.

Mike Davis remembered seeing a photograph, in one of the books he had consulted in preparation for his Antarctic sojourn, of the imprint of a large bird, identified as either a skua or albatross, that had flown into the snow-covered surface of the ice, unable to see it. The bird had lost its depth perception in a whiteout. The condition occurred under conditions peculiar to Antarctica, the result of uniform refraction of light from thick clouds overhead and the snow on the ground. There was no point of reference. On the surface a man might seem to be floating in midair. But in the air, Davis thought, sweating under his cold-weather clothing, he was like that helpless bird in its suicidal plunge into the snow. They were completely disoriented, flying blind. Hank Forbes's radar altimeter told him how far he was above the surface immediately below, but it gave him no horizon line or flight path. Experienced as he was, the pilot could fly into a mountain or into the ground before he knew it was happening.

"Goddamn it, Forbes," Len Sears snarled, "get us out of this shit!"

The pilot did not answer or acknowledge the demand. His concentration was so complete Davis wondered if he had even heard. His bearded, weathered face was reflected in the glass before him, dominated by the dark goggles that concealed and protected his eyes. Merrill also glared at Forbes's back, as if he, too, were blaming the pilot for endangering them all by flying into a whiteout condition no one could predict.

Staring through the windows into blankness as the minutes crawled by, the reporter was eerily disassociated from reality. Were they flying sideways? Skimming over the glacier's surface or hurtling skyward? His stomach was queasy. Did that mean they were falling, plummeting like a runaway elevator? How far were they above those empty wastes of snow?

Ten minutes seemed an eternity. Davis wanted to pray, an impulse he had not felt in twenty years.

Veteran pilots of the Ice recognized two different kinds of whiteout. A true whiteout was an optical illusion, akin to a mirage. The fact that such conditions were unpredictable made them especially dangerous to aircraft. But an Antarctic blizzard created snow blindness as complete and as demoralizing as a pure whiteout. Demarcation between earth and sky vanished. Landmarks disappeared. Navigational instruments became unreliable. Moreover, a blizzard brought an additional element of danger: fierce winds.

Mike Davis's first helo ride had plunged him into the cone of a true whiteout. There was no awareness of winds outside the aircraft's cabin. There was no sound but the turbine whine and the muted whack-whack-whack of the rotors, no visual sensation but the blank whiteness, as if they floated like a fly trapped inside a giant milk can.

Fifteen minutes into the whiteout, the bizarre experience ended as abruptly as it began. The whiteness poured the Huey and its occupants back into their familiar, dimensional universe.

"Yes! Yes!" Len Sears shouted.

Mike Davis whooped with elation. Thrown into the crucible on his maiden helicopter flight, he had survived to write the tale! He grinned from ear to ear, slapped Merrill on the back, didn't even mind Merrill's enthusiastic pummeling in return.

Only Hank Forbes was silent, grimly intent at the controls. He knew they were not out of trouble.

Antarctic storms came up suddenly. They might whirl about the continent in a single day and blow themselves out, or they might linger, pounding the Ice and its few vulnerable inhabitants with violent winds and snow blowing hard enough to etch a windshield. Unlike a whiteout, a blizzard could generally be tracked, and there were some thirty weather stations scattered over the vast white continent. The network was effective, but given the sudden weather changes and the area covered, a mass the size of the United States and Mexico, it was not perfect.

This morning there had been no hint of a severe storm developing. Nothing to deter Forbes or his passengers from taking off as planned. The storm rose out of McMurdo Sound an hour after the helicopter took off. On the radar screens at MacTown it did not even appear to be a major storm in the beginning. An hour later, however, the winds had doubled to gusts of forty knots. Aircraft at Williams Field were tied down. Even heavy trucks and bulldozers grumbled to a stop, their drivers seeking shelter. All helicopters were grounded. Radio warnings went out over the thinly spaced network of weather stations and from them to field research camps and aircraft scheduled to be in flight.

Hank Forbes received the alert in the midst of the whiteout, which commanded all his attention as he tried to guide the helo through the mist. As soon as he emerged from the dreamlike whiteness, he turned to the next potential hazard. A storm was chasing him. He sifted his options, thoughts racing. Those options were few. MacTown was too far away, the storm between them. To sit down immediately on the Hartsook Glacier, over which they were flying, would enable them to escape the buffeting that was sure to come in the air, but that choice created other risks. Glacier surfaces were treacherous at best. And even if they succeeded in landing safely, they faced the necessity of mooring the chopper and digging in. On that great river of ice, five or six miles wide and two hundred miles long, they would endure the battering of the blizzard.

Forbes chose to run. Turned the helo down the long sweep of the glacier toward the coastline and the nearest camp he spotted on his map. Behind him the storm rose over the mountains until it filled the sky. The day, once dazzlingly bright, became as dark and gray and cold as a winter sea.

Forbes saw the wind in action before he felt it, in the form of snow devils dancing and pirouetting across the glacier. Inside the chopper's cabin the shouts of relief and euphoria subsided. Forbes's passengers sensed that like a puny child in a playground of bullies, they had escaped one menace only to confront another, even worse.

Then the blizzard enveloped them. They were drowning in snow.

"Jesus Christ!" Len Sears swore.

Mike Davis, seeing the fear in the others' faces, felt his own settle in his belly like undigested pasta. He didn't see how anything could be more frightening than the whiteout they had escaped, but his companions' reactions told him he was wrong.

Merrill confirmed the worst. "He's got to take us down fast. Helos can't fly in this!"

"What do you mean?"

Merrill's glare was angry, directing his emotion at Davis. "You can't fly these things in winds over twenty knots. If he doesn't find a place to sit down quickly . . ."

Merrill left the words of doom unspoken, but there was no doubt of his meaning.

The first wind gusts lifted the chopper and hurled it down the long face of the glacier. Mike Davis felt the unnatural speed but little else. Miraculously the pilot seemed to have the helo under control. Everyone else in the cabin was staring at the back of Forbes's neck, the hunched shoulders, the weather-scarred hands at the controls. Everyone held his breath.

Without more warning they flew into the heart of the maelstrom. Mike Davis slammed into the plane's fuselage, hurting his shoulder. Then he was lifted out of his seat as the helo plunged downward with sickening speed. Only the seat belts kept him and the others from bouncing around the cabin like Ping-Pong balls. Merrill was shouting something unintelligible at Forbes. The banging and crashing as the helicopter was thrown about by the raging winds obliterated any reply. The fury seemed to go on interminably, the helo tossed about in the raging winds like a canoe in white water.

A lull came suddenly. For the first time in minutes Davis heard the beating of the chopper's blades. Through the dense curtain of blowing snow, which rattled against the windows like shrapnel, he glimpsed a flat sheet of ice off to his left, some broken ice cliffs, the dark blue of the Southern Ocean.

And, half buried in the snowdrifts that whirled across the ice, a tiny cluster of tents or shelters.

"Hang on!" Hank Forbes shouted, breaking his silence at last. "We're sitting down!"

The helo fell out of the sky.

SIX

THE BLIZZARD CAUGHT BRIAN HURLEY in the open, completely exposed to the driving winds on a tongue of ice that forked like a side road off the superhighway of the Hartsook Glacier. At the coastal field camp he was trying to reach, still twenty-five miles away, the temperature was recorded that evening at twenty degrees below zero Fahrenheit. For Hurley, katabatic winds of twenty to forty knots—gravity winds created by cold air flowing down the face of the glacier from the high plateau—created a chill factor of approximately eighty below.

Pinned down, unable to see more than a few feet in front of him, Hurley knew he couldn't go on blindly over unfamiliar snow and ice or risk exposure to the killing cold.

Before being cleared by the NSF for his dog sledge run, Hurley had been given the same survival training other long-term visitors received, which had included instruction in digging an emergency snow trench, improvising a snow cave or building an igloo from blocks of the hard, lightweight snow called firn that was the best building material Antarctica offered.

There was no time to cut, shape and lay firn blocks, even if he could have found the right kind of snow. Instead he threw a tarp over the sledge and hastily heaped snow over it, packing it down with a shovel from his gear. Then he began furiously to scoop snow out from under the center of the sledge, creating a hollow opening beneath while leaving both ends of the sledge supported by the ice.

The hollow cave was cramped. There was not enough room for him to sit up or change position easily. He would have to lie on his side, legs drawn up toward his chest. On the other hand, the confined space would more quickly be warmed by his body heat.

The huskies of his team were better adapted to the severe conditions than Hurley. Before he had finished digging his shelter underneath the sledge, the dogs had already scratched out shallow holes of their own and disappeared into them. The openings were quickly covered by blowing snow.

Only Niner was unable to fend for himself. Hurley lifted the injured husky from his bed on the sledge and made room for him at one end of his snow cave.

The dog growled when Hurley set him down. "Hey, don't knock it," Hurley said. "Two bodies are better than one. We'll keep each other warm."

The snow blew over the opening above them, sifted down, gradually blotted out the sky. A feeble trickle of light seeped through the curtain of snow. Then even that faded out.

It became very dark and quiet.

Except for the moan of the wind itself and the scurrying of fine-grained snow over the frozen surface, the storm had no voice. No sound penetrated Hurley's shelter. Within his cocoon, Hurley sensed only the weight of the deepening snow.

A month earlier, during a similar snowstorm, Hurley had had his first experience of digging into the snow during an Antarctic blizzard. Within minutes a smothering claustrophobia had nearly had him clawing and screaming to escape the tomblike trench in which he lay. He had had to fight through the feeling of panic. This time he felt more confident, more secure about being able to draw sufficient oxygen through the powdery blanket that covered him and more certain about himself.

Besides, this time he had company. Instead of turning into clumps of ice inside his thermal boots, his feet were warmed by the husky's body.

Deliberately Hurley refrained from checking the luminescent dial of his watch. When the storm blew itself out, it would still be daylight, whatever the hour. Meanwhile, the blizzard might last three hours or three days. Counting the minutes wouldn't help.

Neither would thinking about those hardy souls who had challenged the Ice before him and disappeared without a trace.

Should have got all this on film, he thought.

Where were those television cameras when you needed them?

The Soviets thought it was a good excuse for a party.

Of course, Alex and Niki thought just about anything was a good excuse for a party. The arrival of the helicopter out of the blue, chased by the blizzard, simply offered a better pretext than usual.

With everything from tents to piles of supplies to the snow toboggan securely tied down before the storm's arrival, the entire group at the Operation Second Chance camp turned out to help moor the helo and prevent it from flying away on its own. A safety line strung from the Jamesway enabled the new arrivals to pull themselves safely through the blizzard to the hut.

There the newcomers—two geologists, a journalist and the helicopter pilot—were greeted with enthusiasm and pumped with eager questions. What were the odds on the San Francisco 49ers repeating in the Super Bowl? My God, was the game already over? What happened to January? There was news about a crisis in the Baltics; Volkov pressed the reporter for details. California had had another earthquake, centered in the mountains near Riverside, 5.1 on the Richter scale, not the Big One. The Dow Jones index, in a bullish stampede, had smashed through the three thousand barrier. At the remote and isolated research base, where the routine of the camp focused entirely on the work at hand, to the exclusion of everything but erratic sleep, day after day, week after week, with little or no contact with the outside world, the stuff of everyday events back home was exciting news.

The blizzard was a less welcome presence. It drove everyone, scientists and visitors alike, into the Jamesway. That first night of the storm no one was eager to retire to his own small tent. The hut offered food, company, a radio link with McMurdo, an illusion of relief from the tearing and pulling winds that threatened either to rip the tents apart or to snatch their ice screws and weights from the ice and hurl the tents off into the white fury.

Kathy McNeely was late joining the others in the hut. After the helicopter's occupants had been escorted to safety, she had gone to the supply tent to check on her two wounded charges. The male penguin was standing inside, nearly fully recovered. He strutted around the tiny enclosure when she entered, making a peculiar squawking sound. He seemed content to remain inside, however. The female was still too weak to try to escape.

When Kathy crawled out of the tent and tried to stand, the wind almost blew her off her feet. She grabbed the lifeline with both hands and hung on until she gained her balance. She couldn't see the Jamesway through the blowing snow—she barely made out her hands gripping the rope—but she hauled herself hand over hand along the rope until she sensed the presence of the hut. Her groping hand found the flap covering the entry.

Entering the low access passage—Carl Jeffers called it the foyer—she heard the rising tumult of conversation from inside. With a fierce kind of joy she slipped out of dark chaos into brightness, warmth, noise. It was like being born again, she thought in a momentary daze.

A Primus cooking stove roared at the far end of the hut. With relief Kathy shrugged out of her parka, adding it to the huge pile near the entrance. Still too warm, she slipped out of her cardigan, unmindful of the instant sensation she created. The men all tried not to stare too obviously at her breasts, clearly shaped by the soft fall of an old plaid wool shirt.

Someone grabbed her by the arm and thrust a cup of vodka into her hand. Alex Volkov beamed down at her. "Drink up, Katya! Now party can begin!" For him she was Katya or Katyusha, familiar Russian forms for Katherine.

In the midst of the hubbub in the crowded hut, Michael Davis found himself pushed into a corner with Rupert Merrill, both men gripping china mugs half filled with icy vodka, so cold it made Davis's teeth ache.

Neither man tried to move; for the moment the hut was as jammed as a subway car at rush hour. After a few moments Merrill said, "You remember what you were asking me back at MacTown that night . . . about problems on the Ice?"

"Yes, sure." Davis tried to focus on what the geologist was saying, blocking out the babble around them.

"Would that be for publication, Mike?"

Davis became more alert, curiosity sparked. "That's the idea."

Merrill shook his head. "Off the record."

Davis hesitated. He was reluctant to commit himself. You never liked to concede that much without knowing what you were going to hear. Merrill had something, he thought, but he wasn't the kind of man to give it away. He was too cool for that. Davis decided he didn't really have a choice.

"Okay, off the record, then."

"Good. I wasn't entirely candid with you, I'm afraid."

Niki Simanovich lurched in front of them, grinning broadly. He lifted his mug so enthusiastically he slopped vodka down the front of his sweater and said something in Russian. A wave toward the entrance tunnel spilled more vodka. Niki grinned expectantly at the bewildered Americans.

Alex Volkov, on his way out of the hut, paused near them to

explain. "Niki say, this storm, she is like Moscow summer." Volkov grinned. "Is a joke."

Davis laughed belatedly. Pleased, Simanovich stumbled toward the narrow bench set up as a bar. The Russians seemed to have an unlimited supply of vodka on hand.

Turning back to Merrill, Davis said, "Go on. You were saying?"

"Hm? Oh, yes . . . about discord on the Ice. I've heard of a few things—more than the usual glitches, that is. You understand, Mike, you get a bunch of specialists like this group anywhere and you're going to have some bickering, quarrels, bruised egos. That's not what I'm talking about."

The level of conversation in the Jamesway was high enough to cover their low-voiced exchange. Davis was regretting his quick agreement to keep this talk off the record. Hell, this was the story he had been sent to Antarctica to find.

"I was at Palmer, on Anvers Island, for a few days. That's just across the way from Faraday, the British station, so I paid them a visit. The Brits are doing some parallel studies to mine this summer, taking carbon dioxide readings, and I know one of the men on their team."

So far, so dull, Davis thought. It was going to be hard enough making a hole in the ozone layer readable, without getting into details of chemical readings of ice core samples. At least with the ozone you had something that sounded scary: a hole.

"The Brits were very hospitable and invited me to stay overnight. I guess it was about three in the morning, there was this loud explosion. By the time I threw some clothes on and got out of my room, there was a lot of confusion in the hotel where I was staying as well as outside. People running about, shouting. Soldiers with automatic rifles spilling out of their huts on the run, as if we were under a terrorist attack, yelling at me to go back inside. A siren began to wail, and then I saw the smoke."

Merrill paused to sip some vodka. Following suit, Mike Davis realized that he couldn't even feel the vodka going down. It had to be a hundred proof; his throat was numb. Another shot or two, and he'd be numb from head to foot.

"The smoke got everyone's attention; fire's a real terror down here. We all started running toward it. It came from the north edge of the station, and a couple of fire trucks were already there, along with British station personnel and soldiers, all of them just tumbled out of their beds and looking the worse for it. When I came close enough, I saw that the smoke came from a separate building with an antenna tower—or what had been an antenna."

His interest thoroughly aroused, Davis longed for a tape recorder; he had been discouraged from bringing one into Antarctic cold. He consoled himself that the raucous din in the crowded hut would have made the recorder useless . . . and Merrill might not have talked freely if he'd known he was being put on tape.

"What was it?"

"The radio-TV antenna. An explosion knocked out the whole communications system. The fire was already under control, and the British authorities cordoned off the building. No one knew exactly what had happened, and the Brits weren't saying . . . but it didn't take long for some of those soldiers to make an educated guess. Sabotage."

"By whom, for Christ's sake?"

"The Argentines, who else? There's bad blood between them, going back to the Falklands War. The Argentine base isn't very far from Faraday, an easy run in a motor toboggan or any snow vehicle. And the thing was, there'd been some Argentine skiers in the vicinity the day before. The soldiers put two and two together. They were really pissed off. Having your radio and television signals knocked off the air is about as bad as anything could happen on the Ice."

"What happened then? Did they find out what caused the explosion?"

"No one would say. But those soldiers didn't need proof. The Argentines had been nearby; the tower blew up; ipso facto, they

76

did it. Some of the Brits were all-fired up for organizing a commando raid on the Argentine base. If one of their officers hadn't kept his head and stepped in and put a stop to it, we'd have had our own little war on the Ice. Once a thing like that gets started, Mike, it can be like a runaway truck."

"Yeah . . ."

At that moment Alex Volkov popped through the entrance into the hut, exuding cold. Snow and frost crusted his black beard and eyebrows. Smiling, the Russian shrugged out of his snow-covered parka and stamped more snow off his boots. *All that for a short walk to the john,* Davis thought with dismay.

He had been shown the way to the Outhouse, a utility tent used as a toilet, equipped with buckets as well as holes cut into the snow and lined with plastic trash bags. At the time he had been cautioned about holding on to the safety rope that linked the Outhouse with other tents and the Jamesway. "If it's really bad outside, or you aren't sure you can handle it," one of the American scientists had told him, "there's a pail in your tent."

"Is not such a bad joke, what Niki say," Volkov declared. "Like Russian summer out there!"

Volkov stayed with them for a few minutes, warming up from his brief outing. After asking Mike Davis how he was enjoying his Antarctic summer, Volkov insisted that in spite of the jokes, Moscow was really very beautiful in summer. Just not for long.

When the Soviet scientist moved off in response to a shout from his younger colleague, Davis said, "So what happened at Faraday?"

"Nothing," Merrill answered. "The officer cooled the men down, and it turned out there was no fire, just a lot of smoke."

"That's it? What about the explosion?"

"The British authorities clamped a lid on the whole thing. Two days later the station was back on the air, and officially that was the end of it. Not that any of the people at Faraday forgot. The Argentines won't be welcome there this summer."

Davis puzzled over the incident. Why would the administration at Faraday hush it up? What really happened?

"Quite frankly," said Merrill, leaning close to Davis so he could be heard without raising his voice, "if I weren't so reluctant to believe it, my hunch is that someone blew up that antenna tower. It wasn't a gas explosion or electrical failure. Those soldiers had it right. It was deliberate sabotage."

"Kind of hard to swallow."

"Not so hard. National priorities don't disappear, even on the Ice. The Antarctic Treaty has lasted this long because it was convenient all around. But the Argentines haven't given up their territorial claims. Neither have the British, the Aussies or the Kiwis. We've held our own claims in abeyance, like the Russians, but—"

"What's this about the Kiwis?" A tall, reed-thin man stood swaying before them. He had a red nose, as if he had a cold. "I'm Smithson. Smitty, for short."

Davis brightened. "The New Zealander on this team, right?"

"Quite so." Smithson tilted at an angle that seemed to defy the laws of physics. "The one and only."

"Just the one I want to talk to."

"Oh, you mean you've heard about the Yanks stuffing snow in our petrol tanks? Our lads will have an answer for that, never fear."

Davis nodded at Merrill, took the New Zealander by the elbow and steered him away. "Tell me about it," he said. "I'd be interested in anything you've heard . . ."

Crammed into another corner, Carl Jeffers found one of the men from the helicopter looking at him.

"I didn't have this gray beard then," Jeffers said.

"What?"

"That night in McMurdo. I'd just arrived from Christchurch, and I hadn't started on the beard."

The other man frowned, seemed puzzled. He had the hard-muscled, weathered look of someone who had worked out of doors for a long time. A geologist, Jeffers remembered, worked for one of the energy companies. What was the name? It would come to him.

"It's Sears, right? Ah . . . Ken?"

"Len," the geologist said reluctantly.

"Carl Jeffers. Don't tell me you've forgotten?"

"You look different with the beard."

"More distinguished, I trust. I'm thinking of keeping it when I go home. At least until my wife sees it." Jeffers smiled, wondering how he could have spent a presumably convivial evening in the company of so sour a drinker. The wondrous ways of what Thomas Jefferson called ardent spirits, he thought. Jefferson, of course, had been a wine man, favoring that milder libation. "We had quite a night of it."

"I guess we did."

"You really don't remember?"

"Not much."

"Too bad," said Jeffers with a laugh. "I think we solved most of the world's problems. Not to mention life on the Ice."

"I talked a lot?"

"As I recall . . ." The UCLA scientist chuckled; details of that night in MacTown were hazy in his own memory. "I believe very little went unsaid."

Len Sears didn't smile.

After Jeffers moved off, Sears glanced around uneasily. He gave a guilty start when he found Merrill beside him.

"What was that all about?" asked Merrill.

Sears wondered if he should try to lie his way out of it. Trouble was, if he had talked too much to the UCLA guy that night, Merrill would find out sooner or later.

"He's the guy I was drinking with that night I got smashed at McMurdo. You remember, I told you about it."

"That's him? Dr. Jeffers?"

"Yeah, he's the one."

Masking his reaction, Rupert Merrill studied Jeffers, who was talking to the thin-featured but pretty young ornithologist from UC Santa Barbara. Unlike Sears, Jeffers did not appear to be agitated over their meeting. How much had Sears told him that night? And how much did the scientist, who had also been drinking heavily, remember?

Damn Sears anyway! Normally closemouthed and reliable, he became a surly, boastful talker when he drank too much. There was a core of anger in him that Merrill had sometimes found useful, but in unguarded moments it had got Sears into trouble.

"Did you run off at the mouth that night?"

"Hell, no . . . shit, I don't know. Why would I talk to a professor?"

"You were drunk, Lenny. Shit-faced drunk."

Sears flushed, though the reaction was hard to detect, covered by Sears's suntanned features and the quantity of vodka he had consumed tonight. "I don't think he remembers any more than I do."

"But what if he does? He remembered *you*, Lenny. You didn't know him from Adam."

"That doesn't mean anything."

"Let's find out, shall we?" Merrill put his face inches from Sears's, smiling for the benefit of anyone who might be watching them. Looking into Merrill's eyes was like peering into the blue ice of a crevasse. "Have another talk with the professor, Lenny, okay? Find out what he knows about our project—how much you told him."

"I didn't tell him anything he shouldn't know."

"You don't know that. You're not certain; it's all over your face. We blow this now, Lenny, Kusic will have my ass for breakfast. And I'll have yours."

Still flushed, Sears mumbled a reply.

"What's that? If you've got something to say, say it!"

"No, I got nothing . . . I'll talk to him, okay?"

"Just don't mess up."

SEVEN

FOR ONE OF THE VERY FEW times that summer Kathy McNeely
felt like an outsider. Not that she was slighted or ignored; the
opposite was true. The men took turns clustering around her,
anticipating her slightest wish. But even as they talked and joked
with her, she sensed that she was the odd woman out, not part of
the club. The party was boisterous enough even with her present. Without her, she knew, it would have been different.
Louder, probably. More raucous and vulgar, certainly. More
relaxed, too.

And, she thought in her own defense, more adolescent.

But there was another problem. Besides feeling tonight like
the one woman who had crashed an exclusively male enclave,
she couldn't get into a party mood.

"What's wrong, my love?"

She glanced with relief at Carl Jeffers's familiar face, half
hidden behind the unfamiliar beard. She wondered how it was
that no matter what he wore, whether in a classroom, laboratory
or office at UCLA or in a crowded hut in Antarctica, Jeffers
managed to look shaggy and rumpled and wise.

"I'm fine."

"I know you too well. It's that business with the penguins the Soviets found, isn't it?"

"I know I shouldn't keep imagining the worst, but I can't help it."

"Which is?"

"That there are others, who knows how many. Why would there be only two?"

"An isolated incident? It's possible."

"I think, Dr. Jeffers, if I offered that explanation to you in a seminar, based on the evidence, you'd call it wishful thinking."

"Hmm. I suppose I would. What do you propose to do about it? Your work here—"

"Is almost done, at least for this season. I keep thinking, how am I going to feel if I walk away without making a real effort to find out what happened to those birds?"

"Aren't you being a little overzealous? You can't be the shepherd —or shepherdess—for the entire flock, if you'll forgive the mixed-up metaphor. There's only so much you can do . . . so much any one person can do."

"I know you're trying to help, Dr. Jeffers, but that's a cop-out."

"I hoped you wouldn't notice. Let me refill that cup from our Russian friends' inexhaustible supply."

It took Jeffers a few minutes to fight his way across the hut to the bar. While she watched him, Kathy noticed that one of the geologists, the one Jeffers had been talking to earlier, was also staring at the scientist over the rim of his mug. Something about the stranger's stare made her uneasy. She shivered, gooseflesh rising on her arms. The man's expression was baleful. What could Carl possibly have said to him?

"Here you are, my girl. You need to relax tonight. We'll attack your problem again tomorrow or as soon as this storm clears. I've an idea or two of my own."

"You do? What?"

"Oh, no, you don't. Not tonight. Anyway, we'll get nowhere shouting in this din."

She had a sip of Posolskaya, a brand of Russian vodka she had never heard of before this Antarctic summer but a name now as familiar to her and the other members of Operation Second Chance as Coca-Cola. Starting out as ice in her throat, the vodka became a fire down below. *There's a problem in physics for you,* she thought; *how could anything so deliciously cold feel so warm by the time it reached your stomach?*

"Who is that man you were talking to?" she asked. "The one with long hair?"

"Who—oh, that's Sears. Len. My drinking buddy from McMurdo. Looks like an actor or an undercover cop, doesn't he? He's actually a geologist."

"You're buddies?"

"In a manner of speaking. Why?"

"The way he was watching you. Very unbuddylike. How did you meet him?"

"How many bars have you seen in your sheltered life, Bird Lady? You bump into someone, start talking, the drinks flow. . . ."

"And pretty soon everyone's an old buddy."

"Exactly so. For as long as it lasts."

"Well, it looked to me like the pals had a falling-out. If looks could kill . . . what were you talking about anyway?"

Jeffers laughed. "As a matter of fact, Sears wanted to know how much I remembered about that night. I think he's worried he might have been . . . ah, indiscreet."

"Was he?"

"If he was, I'm afraid I don't remember. It does seem to me, though, that we clashed horns at one point." The scientist shook his head ruefully and picked at his beard in the manner of all men with a new and itchy growth. "Don't ask me what about. Every man deserves one lost weekend."

"I'm not so sure about that," she said dryly.

"There is one thing . . ."

She waited, eyebrows raised, sipping her vodka, and at that

moment Aleksei Volkov started to sing. Jeffers turned toward him, as did every eye in the hut.

All but one, Kathy saw.

Len Sears was staring at her and Jeffers, and the hostility she had sensed a few moments earlier seemed seasoned by another emotion.

Fear, she thought. *He's afraid of Jeffers's remembering.*

Only later did Kathy recall that Jeffers had never finished what he started to say.

Volkov had a rich, deep baritone and a good ear. Niki Sima-novich had brought out his balalaika, a triangular-shaped guitar-like instrument with metal strings. Kathy thought of poor Niki playing it outside anywhere on the Ice, and the picture evoked an image of fingers shredded by frozen strings—the sort of violent image that rarely occurred to her, in spite of her famil-iarity with the casual violence in nature. It was a product of the storm, she thought. And possibly of the unease that had stayed with her since the discovery of the injured penguins, the feeling that something was unaccountably wrong.

Perhaps that was what had her imagination running wild, feeding alarm over a hint of anger in a stranger's stare. Maybe that was also why she seemed so acutely tuned to whispers of discord or animosity, her attention zeroing in on fragments of phrases spoken by the Los Angeles reporter, by Jeffers, by the visiting geologists.

Davis had the wrong end of the stick, she thought, vowing to talk to the journalist before he left. There was no pattern of dissension on the Ice. There had been only a few isolated inci-dents.

Two oil-saturated penguins.

> *"Raztsvetali yabloni i groushi*
> *poplyli tumani nad rekoy . . ."*

She glanced up as she heard the Russian words, sung in a

84

husky voice throbbing with emotion. She sensed that others were watching her, grinning openly.

> *". . . vykhodila na bereg Katyusha*
> *na vysokiy bereg na krutoy . . ."*

Oh, my God, Volkov was singing to her! Katyusha!

"The apple and pear trees were blooming . . .
mists were winding over the river
Katyusha went along the steep shoreline . . ."

"Well, you seem to have survived that ordeal," Mike Davis said.

"What makes you think it was an ordeal, Mr. Davis?"

"I was going by the look of dismay on your face when you turned around and saw Alex was serenading you."

"That wasn't dismay; that was plain ordinary shock."

As it happened, Kathy McNeely had remembered the science reporter's by-line from the series in the *Los Angeles Times* on the effects of the *Exxon Valdez* spill a year later. The articles had gripped her. They were well researched, detailed and, from her own experience, accurate. She said as much.

"Hey, thanks . . . coming from an expert, that means something." To cover his reaction, Davis glanced around the Jamesway, where the party to end all parties, as Emil Zagorsky had dubbed it, was simultaneously winding down and picking up speed, like the last mile of a marathon. "You're not the kind of woman I'd expect to find at an isolated camp like this," he added.

"Where would you expect to find my kind of woman?"

"Uh-oh." Davis winced. "Did it again."

"I hope you don't make it a habit." Her amusement took the bite out of her words. "Are there women where you work?"

"At the paper? Sure."

"Do they go wherever they have to go for a story?"

"Yeah . . ."

"Then you have your answer as to what I'm doing in Antarctica."

Chagrined, Davis accepted the mild rebuke and gratefully seized upon her comment to change direction. "I heard someone call you the Bird Woman. I take it you work with penguins?"

"Yes."

"And you're here because of that spill last year. A Chinese icebreaker, wasn't it?"

Someone jostled him in passing, grinned sloppily at McNeely, apologized to Davis and stumbled off. "You'll never catch them, Emil," she called out after him. "They've got too much of a head start! Dr. Zagorsky is our own Russian," she said to Davis, without trying to explain the inside joke. "He thinks he can keep up with Alex and Niki in the vodka wars."

"He's dreaming."

"To answer your question, our project this summer is to measure the lasting damage from that *Kowloon* spill, not only to the penguins and seals but to the ecology in general. It's a scientist's version of what you were trying to discover in Prince William Sound. Each of us has particular interests and projects, but our overall focus is the same."

"Was that spill very far from here?"

"About a hundred miles up the coast. This was the nearest large penguin colony we could find this summer. Much of this coastline is steep ice cliffs, completely inaccessible from the sea. We were lucky to find this rookery."

"Do you find much evidence of that spill now?"

She hesitated. He was a reporter, after all, capable of quoting —or misquoting—her words. "This environment is very severe, Mr. Davis, as you're finding out. Much more severe even than Alaska's. It's tough on oil, too. Our studies indicate that most of last year's oil was broken up by the winter storms and dispersed. What we don't know yet is what percentage of injured marine life survived, what corruption of the marine environment might have occurred, how much toxic damage persists, how much of the oil is still in the ice where we can't find it, working its way back up to the surface. We're still at the asking questions stage. Too early for very many answers. We know that spill was a disaster. What we don't know yet is the full extent of the damage . . . just how bad it was for Antarctica and for this planet."

Her passion cut through all the noisy confusion surrounding them. Listening to her, liking her, Mike Davis wished they had got off to a better start. He also wanted to keep her talking. "I heard one of your people"—he nodded toward Smitty, who had proved amenable to being pumped for information—"say something tonight about finding a couple of penguins suffering from recent oil damage. Does that mean a new spill?"

Her green eyes were cool, wondering how much he knew. That gaze could be intimidating, he thought. "Are you really a journalist, Mr. Davis? Or some kind of inspector?"

"Like, for the NSF?"

"Perhaps."

"Scout's honor, I work for the *Times*. I'm just your basic dirty-fingernails reporter. They want a series on Antarctica. More specifically, since that's what I asked you, they want news about any new problems that might be surfacing on the Ice, what with the Antarctic Treaty up for review and all. Like the stories I've heard about friction between groups . . ."

He left the sentence hanging, hoping she might fill in the blanks.

"I'm sorry, I'm afraid I can't help you, Mr. Davis. And I seriously doubt you were ever a Boy Scout."

"I dropped out because I was no good at selling things. I'd like to see you at work with your penguins," he added with all the sincerity he could muster. "That is, if this damned snow ever stops blowing."

His dirty-fingernails self-description wasn't as idiotic as he made it sound, Kathy thought. She had a sudden, very strong feeling that she didn't want him prying into her work, asking pointed questions about the injured penguins that she could not answer, trying to make something sensational out of a tragedy.

"When the storm is over, we'll all be very busy here, Mr. Davis. It's a very short summer, and there's not much of it left;

this storm is a harbinger of what's coming. I don't think I can help you."

"I wouldn't get in the way," he persisted.

"You would even if you tried not to."

"What if I asked the NSF to intercede? They have a highly developed PR sense. . . ."

"Ask away," she answered tartly.

"No offense, Dr. McNeely—"

"No, you're just doing your job, and I'm doing mine. Let's leave it at that."

"I hope you don't mean that." Sensing that the interview was nearly lost, he tried another tack, nodding toward Volkov who, with a different accent, reminded him of Charles Boyer in the movie version of *Arch of Triumph*. "I see you're getting along fine with the Russians, Doctor. How about your colleagues? No problems with *glasnost* on the Ice?"

"Good heavens, no!"

Davis grinned. "Good heavens, no? Hey, can I quote you on that?"

Kathy felt herself reddening. "Do whatever you like, Mr. Davis. Excuse me . . ."

She escaped across the hut before Davis could think of a way to stop her. *You botched it,* he told himself. But he had struck a nerve somewhere. All he had to do was keep probing until he found the sensitive spot.

"Good heavens, no? Hey, can I quote you on that?" The words played mockingly in Kathy McNeely's ear. Davis would have preferred four-letter words, she thought angrily, the more familiar coin of a coarsening human discourse.

After a few moments her anger began to cool. She smiled ruefully at her touchy pride and Irish temper. Davis hadn't been deliberately offensive, she admitted to herself. Reporters pushed, that's all. Scientists pushed boundaries in their search for truth;

good journalists pushed people to the edge, trying to get other answers.

As for herself and the Russians, *glasnost* was real, and thank God for it. Her smile broadened as she thought of Volkov. *Maybe I'll sic the reporter on him,* she thought.

But what was Davis really after? What had prompted his questions about antagonisms in Antarctica?

Carl Jeffers was the last of the scientists to leave the Jamesway, having elected to rejoin Smithson in their polar tent, making room for the four visitors from the helicopter to roll out their sleeping bags in the Jamesway. Glancing at Len Sears, the marine scientist seemed about to say something. He thought better of it, wished them all good night and crawled out of the hut into the merciless battering of the blizzard.

Behind him, the men crawled into their bags and lay in darkness pierced only by light from the stove, which continued to heat the hut. Mulling over what he had learned since arriving at the camp, Mike Davis glanced toward Rupert Merrill, lying near him, his face indistinct in the dimness. "That story of yours about Faraday . . ." Davis said.

"Yes?"

"If I develop more information on my own, get the story from other sources, I'll use it."

Merrill did not immediately reply. Davis wished that he could see the man's face, read his eyes. He considered himself a good reader of faces.

"I suppose I can't object," TERCO's geologist said. "As long as you keep me out of it."

Davis promised himself to follow up on the story. When his head wasn't whirling so much, he thought. It needed a sober touch. If he had been a little more in control, he might have been able to dig more information out of McNeely without getting her back up.

"Did you hear about those penguins?" he muttered.

"What's that?" Merrill sounded wide-awake.

"Dr. McNeely," Davis said. "She's found some emperor penguins saturated with oil."

"Last year, you mean."

"No, I mean now. A couple days ago, from what I heard. She's treating them right here."

Davis thought he heard someone suddenly stir across the hut, but no one spoke. After a moment he shrugged and turned away, a vague queasiness from too much strong vodka causing him to dismiss the impression of tension in the hut that hadn't been there before.

Only later, drifting on the shore of sleep, did it occur to him vaguely that, in following up the Faraday story, he might be doing just what Rupert Merrill wanted.

EIGHT

KATHY MCNEELY ROSE EARLY as usual. Most of the others were still in their tents when she made her way through drifting curtains of snow to the Clubhouse. The winds had diminished to a twenty-knot gale. Though the sky remained leaden gray with clouds, and whitecaps stood up in stiff peaks like meringue out on the water, she hoped that the worst of the storm was over. Visibility, about fifty yards when the snow curtains parted, revealed masses of emperor penguins huddling together for warmth and a cluster of fuzzy chicks clumped like a congregation of dandelion puffs.

Hank Forbes had apologized for setting his helicopter down so close to the camp and the adjacent rookery. She realized that he had had no choice. In any event, the storm had muffled the sound of the helo and screened its approach from the birds' view, eliminating any consternation it might have caused. Penguins were quite interested in vehicles, including the bright red helos, but only when they were on the ground and approachable. Such a giant, noisy bird dropping out of the sky too close to the colony was more terrifying than an armada of skuas.

She appreciated Forbes's sensitivity. Most of the helo pilots loved the Ice and shared a concern for its inhabitants. An easy man, she thought. After five minutes in Forbes's company he was like an old friend, someone from the neighborhood.

Somewhat to her surprise, the four men who had slept in the Jamesway were all up, drinking coffee, all of them red-eyed and party-haggard with the exception of Rupert Merrill. Either he wasn't a heavy drinker—she couldn't remember anyone abstaining—or he was a very disciplined one. Equally surprising was the discovery that the two Soviet scientists were *not* up and about. *Maybe the competition with Zagorsky is getting to them,* she thought.

Carl Jeffers and Walter Corbin piled in behind Kathy, brushing snow from their parkas. Corbin drank little; like Merrill, he was not the kind of man who would allow himself to lose control. He had made a discreet pass at her once, as most of the men had; he had accepted her deflection of the attempt with a cool smile and had never made reference to it. This morning he showed no ill effects from the party, nor any emotion other than mild irritation over the inconvenient persistence of the blizzard. Jeffers, by contrast, was more subdued than usual, as if he had something on his mind. She made a mental note to ask him.

The hut quickly filled with the smells of hash and onions browning in a skillet. Hank Forbes was the volunteer guest cook. He folded a heap of onions, grilled in what seemed to be a half pound of butter, into the contents of several cans of corned beef hash, commenting, as he watched the skillet, on the pros and cons of good and bad cholesterol. "You take all that high-fiber stuff," he drawled, "that'll kick hell out of your cholesterol. But who can eat that shit? Beggin' your pardon, Doc."

Kathy, whose stomach was growling from the tempting aroma, said, *"No problema."*

Forbes grinned. "What they don't tell you is, the things that make your cholesterol go right off the chart, like maybe a stick of this here butter, are the only damned things that make eating a pleasure."

"The kind of pleasure that kills," Walt Corbin observed.

"Yessir," Forbes agreed, unruffled. "But you'll go out laughing, as they say, not with your lips all pursed up and your bowels in an uproar." He paused long enough to dump generous helpings of the savory hash onto a series of plates, which were eagerly passed along. "You ever notice, you eat too much of that healthy stuff, your whole system gets out of whack? Now why do you suppose that is? Do you suppose maybe your body's tryin' to tell you something? Like, maybe it craves a thick steak medium rare, a potato with a gob of sour cream and some hot bread slathered with butter?"

Mike Davis, who had had his head buried in a book he had picked off the slim shelf of volumes in the Clubhouse, glanced up. Kathy read Sir Douglas Mawson's name on the spine of the book. "Listen to this," Davis said, ignoring Hank Forbes's question. " 'The world is a void, grisly, fierce and appalling . . . the merciless blast, an incubus of vengeance, stabs, buffets and freezes . . . the stinging drifts blind and choke.' "

"Leave it to a reporter to stomp on a good conversation," Forbes said.

"Doesn't sound like the *L.A. Times*'s style to me," Kathy said.

Davis waved the book at her. "Douglas Mawson's words. He could have been here last night, writing this during the storm." The journals of Mawson, Scott, Shackleton, Amundsen and the other great early explorers could be found on shelves in the remotest huts throughout Antarctica. They held an endless, sometimes morbid fascination for later visitors to the Ice, who, working in far friendlier conditions, remained in awe of those who had first challenged the fierce environment and seemingly endless reaches of snow and ice on the mysterious continent.

"It's not over," Carl Jeffers said gloomily.

Everyone looked at him.

"I checked with MacTown by radio first thing this morning. The forecast is for more of the same. Anything you want to do outside, you'd better take care of it in the next couple hours, while you have the chance."

"Does that mean we're not going to get out of here today?" Merrill asked Forbes.

"No way," the pilot answered. "I'm gonna try to break the chopper loose where she's stuck in the ice and see if the engines will fire. But we can't go up. Not till we know this blow is over."

Merrill appeared to accept the inevitable with a shrug. The reporter, on the other hand, looked unhappy at the news. Kathy had heard him say something earlier about having to rejoin his NSF-approved tour group as soon as possible, aborting a planned visit to Merrill's research base.

When Forbes bundled up and trudged outside to see if he could free the helicopter from the grip of surface ice around its runners, most of the others accompanied him. Kathy lingered over a last cup of coffee. She was a little surprised when Merrill poured himself a cup, added generous scoops of sugar and sat companionably on the bench near her.

She was prepared to dislike Merrill; she distrusted most of the men she had met from major oil and energy conglomerates (they were always men). They shared a view of the world and its resources that was alien to her. She had once compared it, caustically, with the rapist's view of sex.

Merrill confounded her expectations. Pleasant and good-humored in spite of the storm's persistence, he didn't come on to her or condescend. He spoke feelingly of the need to monitor pollution of the atmosphere and of the advantages of Antarctica for his work. "Let's face it, this continent has the purest air left on earth. We can isolate traces—carbon monoxide and methane, for instance—better than anywhere else."

When he asked about her work with penguins, he *listened* when she answered; the attention was flattering.

"Isn't the attrition rather high in the normal course of events?" he wondered after she commented on the diminished size of the emperor colony her group was studying. "It was a bad winter here."

"Yes, of course. But this reduction seems abnormal."

"Do you attribute that to the *Kowloon* spill?"

"It's not a scientifically supportable conclusion . . . at least not yet," she admitted. "The colony from last year's site may have fragmented, though that would be uncharacteristic. It's also possible that some of the penguins have returned to the area of the spill."

"That seems unlikely, surely. Didn't you say that area had been abandoned?"

"We've reason to think some of the penguins may have gone back," she said soberly. She told him about the discovery made by the two Soviet scientists. "Given the prevailing coastal currents, those two oil-saturated penguins could have been carried here from the vicinity of the disaster site. It's not the only possible explanation, but I want to go back there."

Merrill frowned. "It's late in the season, isn't it? I'm thinking of the weather mostly. But aren't many of the birds already going to sea?"

"If you'd seen these penguins, you'd know why it's so important to me."

"I'd like to," Merrill said with evident sincerity.

"Finish your coffee."

Outside the Clubhouse the day was raw. Low clouds and blowing snow obscured the mountains. The sea was visible only in shards of cold gray that reflected the gloomy, overcast sky. As Kathy and Merrill plodded through the drifts to the small pyramid tent where her penguin patients were being kept, she could make out the figures of the other men around the helo, bent over in various attitudes of frustration.

The male penguin came to greet her as she entered the tent, holding out his flipperlike wings and squawking. "He seems good as new," Merrill observed after following her inside.

"He's doing fine. It's the female I'm worried about."

Merrill watched her as she tried to feed the sick female. Kathy held her thumb and forefinger wide apart, like someone making a shadow figure on the wall for a child. The inverted V shape, positioned over the penguin's head, triggered a reflex reaction.

The penguin threw her head back and opened her beak, allowing Kathy to pop cut-up portions of fish far down into the bird's throat.

"That's fascinating," Merrill murmured. "You obviously have a way with penguins."

"That won't help if there are hundreds of them in trouble out there."

"Listen, Kathy—Dr. McNeely. My field camp isn't all that far from the area of the *Kowloon* spill. I'm sure if there was an established rookery there this summer, we would have seen it during one of our flights."

"If it's a small colony, you'd have to be looking for it. It would be easy to miss."

"Then why don't I check the area out for you? It wouldn't be that much trouble. If there's anything there, I can let you know by radio. It might save you a fruitless trip."

Kathy looked at him appreciatively. *You mustn't make snap judgments about people,* she thought. "Thanks for the offer, but . . . I need to see for myself. I know where to look and what to look for."

"Think it over, Doctor." Merrill smiled. "This late in the season, it might be your best offer."

Her reply was interrupted by a muffled shout. They both glanced toward the tunnel entrance. There were scrabbling sounds, like a brief scuffle. Then an apparition burst through the opening and stumbled erect, swaying slightly as it faced them.

"My God, who—"

Kathy only half heard Merrill's exclamation. Her heart raced. The unexpected figure, tall and bulky and sheathed in snow and ice, conjured an image of the monster in an old science-fiction movie, *The Thing*.

The monster tried to speak. The face mask he wore had been impregnated with a coat of ice, the frozen moisture from his own breath. A chunk of ice fell from his cheek, revealing a deep crack in the skin from frostbite.

"McNeely . . . need you," he gasped. "Got a dog with a—a broken leg."

Reaching out toward her, as if in a gesture of appeal, he toppled forward and collapsed on the floor of the tent.

Kathy McNeely was awesome in anger, Brian Hurley thought.

"I'm not a veterinarian," she said, more frustrated than angry. "I'm not trained to set broken bones. I'm not equipped for it here. It's just—just . . . impossible!"

"I'm sorry," he said lamely. "You were the only one I could think of."

"You had no right . . . do you always use people like this?" She made it sound more a statement than a question. "I suppose you do."

"Only when I have to. I had no other choice."

She wanted to tell him that yes, he damned well did have other choices. But the reality of his predicament up on the glacier stopped her.

She stared down at the husky, which Hurley had carried into her own tent, the only place she could think of to put him. The storage tents were full, the Jamesway overcrowded, and she couldn't have him in the utility tent with the penguins. Even if the dog were too incapacitated to attack them, the birds would have been terrified.

Without asking her, Hurley had placed the dog on her cot. The husky eyed her warily, panting. He had very large canines, she thought wryly.

"He's doing okay," said Hurley. "He's in pain when you move him."

"You just moved him twenty-five miles."

"Yeah."

She had been exasperated with Hurley for dumping the problem into her lap. For the smug presumption that she wouldn't be able to turn him down.

"Perhaps one of the others . . ."

"They all say you're the only one." Hurley paused. The effect, she thought a moment later, seemed calculated. "If you can't help him, he's finished. We can't fly out of here until the storm passes. By then . . ."

She wondered suddenly what it must have been like up on the glacier, fighting his way down the river of ice toward the coast through blinding snow, winds that threatened to hurl him off his feet, a wind chill hard to imagine.

"You could have stayed where you were, holed up until the storm passed. You took an awful chance coming down the glacier in a blizzard."

"Niner wouldn't have made it up there. I grabbed the first hole in the storm that opened up. It closed about a mile or so from your camp. That last mile . . ."

Must have been hell, she thought; *a hell not of fire and heat but of burning cold.*

"You're lucky you found us at all."

Hurley grinned. "I know."

"You're still a user, Hurley," she said. "And what kind of name is Niner?"

"He's the ninth dog on the team."

"It's not really a proper name."

Hurley stared at her. His blue eyes were unwavering. There was a nest of squint wrinkles around each eye. Below them, his cheeks were pale and cracked in several places, as were his lips.

He really was quite an astounding man, she thought, as well as infuriating. Just a few hours ago, when he stumbled out of the blizzard into the utility tent, he had been in a state of exhaustion. He was frostbitten, cold and hungry. Even more than his offhand description, his condition had told an incredible story of a harrowing journey down the glacier. Now, after a hot meal and a brief sleep, he seemed refreshed. His eyes were clear and alert. The dangerous whiteness had begun to recede from his cheeks and nose and fingertips. Though the cracks in his face remained, she guessed there would be minimal permanent damage.

"You help him pull through this," Hurley said, "you can name him whatever you want."

"I will," she said.

Hurley sighed contentedly. "That means you're going to do it."

"I don't know . . . damn it, Hurley, I have no anesthetic, I'll have to give him sleeping pills. There's a risk. . . ."

"There's more risk if you don't."

She glared at him. "All right, I'll try . . . and you can help. I'll need someone to assist me."

"Not me," Hurley protested. His sun- and wind-ravaged face paled visibly. "I faint at the sight of blood."

"Too bad," she answered without pity. "You'll get used to it. Just keep taking deep breaths."

She set the leg, which proved to have a fracture of the humerus just below the shoulder blade, that afternoon, while the blizzard raged outside the tiny polar tent with renewed fury. The young dog moaned and struggled feebly in his sleep, but Hurley was able to hold him relatively still.

Her fingers trembled as she sewed up the wound, using nylon fishing line as thread. Once the sutures were finished, Kathy began to breathe a little more easily.

She became aware of Hurley swaying on his feet. Recognizing the drawn look about his eyes, the raggedness of his breathing, she said, "You can step outside now and get some fresh air."

"Thanks a lot. In this goddamned blizzard?"

"I don't want you getting sick in my tent."

Before operating, while she waited for the sleeping pills to take effect, she had given some thought to what she might do to help the injured dog hobble around, presuming that she was able to set the broken bone properly. When the storm cleared, he might be flown to McMurdo on the first available flight, but she had no idea when another plane or helo might be along. Transportation on the continent was unpredictable at best; it might be a day or a week. She could hardly count on Merrill and his group's postponing their plans while Hank Forbes flew the dog back to MacTown on an errand of mercy; Merrill, too, had his priorities. So did the National Science Foundation, whose transport plane was supposed to pick up Michael Davis as soon as possible after the storm cleared.

Hurley crawled back into the tent. "You look a little less green around the gills," Kathy told him.

"I appreciate the sympathy."

She ignored him as she worked at improvising a sling crutch to harness the husky's leg and shoulder. She made a frame of rigid tubing borrowed from a backpack, forming it into an elongated shape that extended from above the dog's shoulder to below the paw. She strapped the injured leg inside the structure to prevent it from moving or bearing any weight directly. The frame allowed the stiffened leg to pivot freely at the shoulder.

"What are you doing?" Hurley asked after watching her for several minutes.

She stiffened at the skepticism in his tone. There was quite a lot about Hurley that caused her to bristle now. She couldn't deny the strong feelings that had resurfaced. Even during those tense moments while she worked to set the injured dog's leg, she had been acutely aware at every moment of Hurley's physical presence so close to her. Those emotions, and the struggle to hide them, lay behind her snappish responses. But during the past month she had almost succeeded in justifying to herself that sharp exchange in the MacTown mess hall before they parted. She'd acted wisely. Not because she was afraid of such a passionate collision, but because, she concluded, Hurley was self-centered and irresponsible and no lasting relationship was possible. His purpose for being on the Ice, making a dog-sled run for a television special, seemed self-indulgent, wasteful. There was so much constructive work that needed to be done on the Ice. She couldn't see any justification for allowing a publicity-hungry adventurer to come here, other than the National Science Foundation's desire to make the public more aware of the little-known continent at the bottom of the world . . .

"It's a kind of crutch," she explained. "I've seen it used. It'll protect his leg and help him get around. He probably won't put much of his weight on it, but it'll help him keep his balance and walk."

"He'll chew the damned thing off as soon as he wakes up."

"No, he won't," she retorted. "And if you know so much about it, why did you come to me for help?"

Brian Hurley grinned. "Because you know more than I do."

For some reason even that concession annoyed her.

NINE

THE MOOD IN THE JAMESWAY was gloomy that evening, in contrast with the party spirit the night before. The storm had lasted too long. It was getting on everyone's nerves.

The news from MacTown at six o'clock was not encouraging. Another twenty-four hours, the meteorologist thought. No promises, though. Antarctic blizzards were capricious.

Brian Hurley observed the gathering with bemused interest. He was an outsider here. None of the assembled scientists was impolite, but they managed to cut him out of the herd all the same. They saw his activities as pointless adventuring at the expense of their precious, fragile continent. What did they think James Clark Ross and Robert Falcon Scott and Ernest Shackleton were, he wondered, if not adventurers?

The Russians poured a mean vodka, though. In fact, Alex Volkov was friendlier to Hurley than the American scientists, showing a keen curiosity about Hurley's project. "You will do this alone?" he asked. "Travel by sled to South Pole?"

"Not this year; there isn't time. But that's the plan for next year. The television people want to call it the Treaty Run." He paused a moment. "They're always looking for a gimmick."

"What is this . . . gimmick?"

"A—a stratagem," Hurley said, fumbling for the right word. "A peg to hang something on. Or a trick . . . like some device a magician would use."

"Device, like peg, is gimmick?"

"Yeah, sort of."

"But Antarctic Treaty may not be such a good . . . peg," Volkov said. "What if all nations do not approve review and new accords? This is possible. There is much controversy."

"They'll come up with a new slant," Hurley said with a laugh. "A new gimmick."

"So what is it you do this year?"

"All this talk is making me thirsty." Hurley gazed pointedly into his empty mug.

"But of course!" Volkov sloshed vodka from the bottomless bottle into Hurley's mug, beaming at the American. "Drink first, then tell me what you do."

After sipping—he couldn't toss the vodka into the back of his throat like Volkov—Hurley said, "The sponsors want me to take my sled and dog team up the Hartsook Glacier. They'll film the run and use it to sell the expedition to the Pole next year."

"You can do this? So late in season?"

"I can try." *I can also freeze my ass,* Hurley thought, *or tumble into a crevasse. Or get killed in the ratings.* "I'm supposed to go next week, if weather permits." His nod toward the outside fury was respectful. "If this keeps up . . ."

"But it not last much longer. How many days is it to make this climb to top of Hartsook Glacier?"

"It should take about two weeks. That's the way I figured it with nine dogs. Now . . . it'll be a little tougher."

"But you try." Volkov smiled at him.

"Yeah." Hurley smiled back. "The old college try."

The Soviet scientist looked a little puzzled. Hurley did not enlighten him. A little mystery, he thought, was good for the Russian soul.

103

* * *

Hurley decided he should work the room. McNeely seemed to be making it a point to avoid him, he thought. Or was it that the other men wouldn't leave her alone? Hurley had noticed the phenomenon before on the Ice, even in a place like McMurdo, where one might see a number of women. They remained a distinct minority anywhere in Antarctica, attracting men as honey drew flies.

Once, the first time Hurley visited the camp, McNeely had commented on the reaction herself, laughing when Hurley suggested that she was very popular with all the men at the camp. "Back home I guess I'd be what you call a six, you know, on a scale of one to ten. In Antarctica I'm such a rare commodity that all of a sudden I'm at least a nine . . . and for the Soviets, a ten plus."

"That mean Volkov and Simanovich?"

"I was thinking more of the men at the Russian station when I visited there."

"I think you underestimate yourself," Hurley had said, surprising her enough to provoke a long, curious glance.

He noticed that Volkov had joined the group surrounding Kathy McNeely, and in a few minutes they were separated from the others, talking animatedly. The Russian made her laugh. *She likes him,* Hurley thought. Why not? He was a nice guy. *Why should you care?* Hurley asked himself. Whatever had started between Kathy and himself at McMurdo had ended, seemingly by mutual consent, when the last Christmas carols died away. Or so he had told himself . . . while asking, every night since Christmas, how he could have let it end without making a more urgent attempt to understand why.

Watching, he liked the way she laughed, without restraint or self-consciousness.

Too bad it was good old Alex making her laugh.

* * *

"How can you do it?" Mike Davis asked.

"Because it's there," Hurley said.

"No, come on, be serious. How can you go into that wilderness alone, just you and your dogs, facing all that ice and snow and cold?"

Hurley shrugged. "Same reason people climb mountains, I guess. Maybe I just have to find out if I can do it. Maybe I've never grown up."

The reporter shook his head. "You've got to be a little crazy."

"Reporters do it, too. Livingstone was an explorer, but wasn't Stanley a reporter?"

"I'm not that crazy," Davis said. He drew closer to Hurley, inviting a confidence. "You run into any flak over your polar expedition? They tell me Antarctica isn't as all-around friendly this year as it used to be. The treaty, and new accords like the minerals regime, have stirred up the pot."

"You couldn't prove it by me." Hurley grinned at the reporter. "They love me here."

Hurley listened to the geologist Merrill, who was discoursing on the hazards of the Antarctic environment to the creatures that clustered along its icy shores and in the neighboring waters. "There was one winter I read about, back around '68 it was, when something like a thousand penguins perished from winter storms. Isn't that right, Dr. McNeely?"

"Well, I don't know about the year, but . . . those things happen."

"What's your point?" Carl Jeffers asked, sounding unexpectedly belligerent.

"Nature can be very indifferent to her creatures."

"That doesn't mean *we* have to be."

"No, of course not, Dr. Jeffers. But we have been, haven't we? A century ago traders slaughtered penguins for their oil . . . as many as four hundred thousand in a single year."

"A century ago we slaughtered about two million buffalo,"

Jeffers said. "Now they're nearly extinct. Are you recommending that for Antarctica's penguin population?"

"Not at all. You misunderstand me. All I'm saying is, we need to keep these things in perspective. Sometimes we lose sight of our priorities. The work you people are doing here is important; I'm not denigrating it at all. We need to understand the effects of environmental disasters, so we know how to deal with them. But we also need to remember that given the complexities of servicing our activities on the Ice, accidents will happen."

"I'm not sure I think much of your priorities," Jeffers snapped.

Hurley saw the consternation on Kathy McNeely's face as Jeffers stalked off. *What's bugging him?* Hurley wondered. *She would like to know, too.*

Like the older American scientist, Hurley wondered what point Merrill was really trying to make, especially in this company. There was a slickness about him that Hurley didn't trust. Okay, so a geologist employed by a major energy conglomerate might be expected to defend exploitation of the planet's resources, but there seemed to be more to his argument than that.

"What is it, Carl? Something's been bothering you all day."

Jeffers smiled. "If it finally made you start calling me Carl instead of Dr. Jeffers, it's worth it."

"That's no answer," Kathy said.

"It's true, though."

"I'll always think of you as Dr. Jeffers. It's . . . a mark of respect."

"You can respect me and still call me Carl."

"Damn it, Carl, stop it! Now what was that all about with Merrill? That wasn't like you."

"No? I've never pussyfooted around the plunderers and predators of this planet, have I?"

"Merrill isn't like that. I had a talk with him this afternoon. He seems genuinely concerned about what happens here on the

Ice . . . and that means to the rest of world as well. His work sounds very important."

"He's waltzing you, my dear. Don't trust him."

"Why would you say something like that?"

"I've remembered something about Merrill's boy Sears. No, don't look at him, Kathy; he's watching. The son of a bitch is worried."

"What have you remembered?" Kathy was both puzzled and concerned. It wasn't like Carl Jeffers to be melodramatic or to make unfounded accusations. She thought of Mike Davis's questions concerning animosities in Antarctica, but such concerns hardly seemed to apply to this situation.

"Not now, but I do want to talk to you later, my dear. In private. Okay?"

"If that's what you want, Carl, sure . . ."

"That's what I want. Now how about a smile, so our watcher won't know what we're plotting?"

The suggestion startled her. It was all she could do to manage a smile.

"Stop staring at them," Rupert Merrill said to Sears.

"He's talking to her about me, I know he is."

"You don't know that. Anyway, what's to tell? Let's get back to those penguins of hers, Lenny. I thought you told me you'd take care of that little problem."

"I did!"

"Then how did they end up here?"

"I don't know. Christ, how am I supposed to know? They're not the same birds . . . there must have been another spill somewhere."

"Forget it, Lenny, there hasn't been another spill. What did you do with those birds?"

"I told you . . . I buried them."

"Where?"

"In a crevasse. Hell, it must be a couple hundred feet deep. No way these can be the same birds."

A stray thought caused Sears's expression to freeze. Merrill saw the reaction and snapped, "What is it?"

"Nothing, unless . . . you don't supposed that whole cliff . . ."

Merrill stared at him. "You're doing fine, Lenny, go on."

"If it broke off . . . shit, it'd be an iceberg the size of Long Island! That'd be the only way . . ."

Sears appeared more and more nervous as he talked. He thought of himself as an unlucky man. Whenever he got *this* close to something he wanted desperately, his luck always went bad. Something always happened. The discovery he shared with Merrill promised to be his big break. Now . . .

"I buried them," he muttered.

The fuel bladder bursting was a sample of his bad luck. Not his fault, although Merrill acted as if it were. Hell, they bought the damned containers from the navy at McMurdo, the same bladders used all over Antarctica, at fuel stops and field bases large enough or remote enough to justify fuel storage. They were used because they didn't expand or rust or become brittle like metal containers. This bladder had a flaw, that was all. It burst and dumped its load of oil. Not even that much oil, as Sears saw it, maybe a couple thousand gallons, no more.

Two things made the rupture particularly unlucky.

One was the location of the accident. It had occurred on a narrow, steeply sloping shelf of ice wedged between an ice cliff on the left and exposed rock on the right, the two walls forming a kind of canyon that was invisible from the nearby seacoast and difficult to spot from the air. This seclusion had made the site ideal for TERCO's purpose—secret exploratory drilling.

During the previous Antarctic summer TERCO's geologists had followed a vein of cobalt and copper found higher up on the flank of the mountain. Although the mineral deposit had disappeared under a sheet of ice, traces had been found far down the mountain, closer to the edge of the ice sheet and the sea, on a line consistent with the original find. Where there was copper there were often other, more valuable deposits. While continuing its highly visible core drilling higher at its main camp, TERCO had, early in this new summer season, set up this second drilling site.

It was here they had made an exceptional find.

Unfortunately the secluded shelf was in a specially protected area (SPA), a designation that Merrill had chosen to ignore when the geological evidence he was following pointed in this direction. In the mid-1960s the Scientific Committee on Antarctic Research (SCAR) had included SPAs as one of the agreed measures designed to preserve and protect the Antarctic environment from harmful disruption. One reason for an SPA designation was the presence of mammals and birds native to the Antarctic coast and its waters, whose normal living conditions might be interfered with.

The drilling site's proximity to the infamous *Kowloon* oil spill on nearby sea ice was pure coincidence. Not so was the presence of a colony of emperor penguins, some of which, in spite of the previous year's disaster, had returned to their traditional breeding grounds near the bottom of the canyon. Attracted by the human activity, many of them soon wandered up to the TERCO camp. When Sears and his men tried to drive the birds off, some of them didn't get the message. They kept coming back and hanging around. They were fascinated by the drilling equipment and the beating of the generator pump.

When the fuel storage bladder burst, the oil enveloped scores of penguins, both adults and chicks.

If the accident had occurred farther from the coastline, there wouldn't have been any penguins in the vicinity to be harmed. The ooze would simply have seeped down into the ice. No harm done, as Sears saw it. But the penguins were there, waddling around in their tuxedos, dipping their spats in oil. . . .

The other thing, the other truly unlucky factor, was that the rupture occurred so close to the rig where the TERCO crew was drilling. Any other place, they could have covered up the evidence, picked up their gear and moved away.

They couldn't leave *this* site.

For the past two months they had been drilling and removing core samples, probing deeper and deeper into the rock strata. Lured initially by the presence of copper, they had since found significant deposits of cobalt, silver and nickel. Most important, just a few weeks ago, they had found a much more spectacular deposit, not only in float ore, chunks of it lying at or near the surface, but in a wide, deep reef.

Merrill had been so excited by the find that he took off for McMurdo as soon as a helo could reach the main TERCO field base, which was on an ice plateau safely distant from the secret drilling site. He left Sears behind to oversee the mopping up of the fuel bladder spill. His instructions were terse: "Clean it up, Lenny. Hide it, bury it deep."

In all Antarctica there was only one direct telephone link to the United States. It was located at New Zealand's Scott base, not far from McMurdo. From there Merrill had made his guarded report to Houston. From McMurdo's Williams Field he had sent a high-priority shipment of ore samples to TERCO's headquarters for analysis that would confirm the richness of his discovery.

After burying the evidence as instructed, Sears had joined Merrill in MacTown to celebrate their discovery and wait for word from TERCO's headquarters.

Some things wouldn't stay buried, Sears thought bitterly.

He thought of that deep blue fissure in the ice into which he had dumped the oil-soaked penguins. He was certain that he and his crew had caught almost all the injured birds. A few might have escaped. Swept out to sea, they might have been carried on the current to the vicinity of the scientists' camp. That would account for the two that had been found.

But if the ice had weakened in that last warm spell . . . if, after centuries unchanged, deep down inside the ice mass the walls had parted along the seam of the crevasse . . . if that great mountain of ice had broken off from the mother cliff, slid into the water and drifted silently away from the main-land . . .

It would have been like opening up a communal grave, Sears thought with a shudder.

"I give you one thing to do, maybe the most important fucking thing you've ever done in your life. You tell me you'll take care of it, I expect you to take care of it." Merrill spoke softly. Watching them, no one else in the hut could have heard the menace in his tone. Only Len Sears.

"I—I did . . ."

"Did you now? The same way you took care of any problem with your drinking pal from UCLA?"

"He doesn't remember anything."

"Maybe, maybe not," Merrill said. "But something's bugging him tonight."

Another piece of bad luck, thought Sears. Why did it have to be one of these bleeding-heart rescue mission people he sat next to in a MacTown bar and had a couple of drinks with?

And why did he have to run into that same man again . . . and be holed up with him for days because of a blizzard, forcing the man to start remembering?

"I'll talk to him again, okay?"

"No," Merrill said. Then he added, "I don't want any more problems, Lenny, especially from these Operation Second Chance scientists. This thing is too damned big. If Dr. Jeffers knows something or even suspects . . ." Sears didn't have to be reminded of the implications for their plans. "Maybe it would be a good idea if you just make yourself scarce the rest of the time we're here."

"But—"

"Do it."

But Len Sears's run of bad luck wasn't over. As he left the hut, Carl Jeffers glanced up from the bench where he was sit-ting. The expression in the scientist's eyes told Sears everything he needed to know.

He had talked too much that night, and Jeffers was remembering.

Tired after the long day and weary of the storm's battering, Kathy McNeely said good night to her colleagues after checking on her recovering patients. The female penguin, to her great relief, seemed improved. The male was hale enough to be released soon. The husky she had operated on was awake but still dopey from the sleeping pills. But he *was* awake.

As she pulled her face mask on, preparatory to going out once more into the storm and feeling her way along the lifeline back to her tent, Brian Hurley caught her by the shoulder.

"How's our patient doing?"

"As well as can be expected." My God, that's the sort of thing doctors were always saying!

Hurley smiled. "I suppose that's good."

"Yes . . . yes, I think so. He got through the operation. Just how good a job I did with that leg . . . well, we'll have to wait and see."

"You did fine."

"So did you, Hurley. You didn't throw up."

His smile broadened. He was just about the most thick-skinned man she had ever met, she thought.

"Have you thought of a name?"

In her fatigued state she was a moment understanding the question. "Oh . . . you mean, for the dog."

"Yeah. An agreement is an agreement."

"Yes, I've thought of a name for him. A good one."

"What is it?"

"Survivor," she said.

TEN

_____

SMITHSON'S COLD WAS BETTER, but his nasal passages were still stuffed up. Asleep, he breathed heavily and noisily through his mouth. In the sardine can dimensions of the two-man polar tent, Carl Jeffers decided he might as well have a freight train passing through.

Jeffers lay far from sleep, listening to the muted buffeting of the storm as background music to Smitty's solo performance.

His bladder was full. Too much vodka before bedtime, though it was getting so he could hardly go through a night without a trip to the john. Sign of age, he mused.

It wasn't like getting up and trotting off to the bathroom at his home in Westwood. He dreaded leaving his comfortable shell to go out into the blizzard. With a small Primus stove burning, the little tent, so fragile in appearance before the might of an Antarctic storm, was actually warm and snug. Safe, Jeffers thought.

But he didn't feel relaxed. The real reason he couldn't sleep was not Smitty's snoring or the pressure from his bladder. It was Len Sears.

Meeting Sears again had jarred some buried memories loose,

leftovers from that night at MacTown when he had fallen in with the geologist by chance. Most of the memories were piecemeal. Like one of the icebergs drifting by offshore, they were 95 percent beneath the surface—but their emotional weight could be felt.

Jeffers was convinced that most of that night was highly forgettable. If Sears hadn't pressed him about it, he would have been content to let it go at that. But something about their conversations made Sears nervous.

Jeffers was fairly certain they had had at least one serious argument. He could remember them shouting at each other . . . but later they had toddled off to another bar, arm in arm, so how bad could it have been?

In the heat of their discussions, Jeffers reflected, Sears must have let something out of the bag, something he wanted to stuff back out of sight. What was it?

They had talked about TERCO at some point. Jeffers had heard about Ron Kusic, the Ted Turner of the oil business. Not as flamboyant as Turner, featured more in *Fortune* than in *People,* but the same kind of aggressive ego. Sears had been evasive about him. He had never met Kusic, he admitted, but his boss was a go-getter, you had to admire him. That Sears had never encountered Kusic personally wasn't unusual. Sears was a fieldman, rough around the edges; he would have no place in the executive suite.

The Antarctic minerals regime—was that it? A hot issue, one that caused people to take a strong stand on one side or the other. Jeffers and Walter Corbin went at it sometimes over the issue, and it stood to reason Sears would share Corbin's point of view, pushing for exploration and exploitation of the continent's resources. Maybe Jeffers and Sears had quarreled over it.

That might explain lingering animosity. Not Sears's apprehensiveness.

The layered fabric of the tent, with its sandwich of air, shuddered as the wind tore at it. Antarctic veterans said a polar tent, with its ice screws firmly driven in and weights in place around the edges, could withstand winds up to eighty knots. Jeffers hoped this little tent wasn't being put to the ultimate test.

Drill bits, Jeffers thought. The ice screws had reminded him. Sears had picked up some drilling equipment that had arrived by air at McMurdo the day they met. Jeffers had been curious about the kind of drilling Sears was doing.

Jeffers knew only some rudimentary facts about oil and gas exploration. He knew that the first stage involved scientific surveys, searching for the right kind of rock strata and whatever else it was that tipped off a knowledgeable oil geologist. Then there was more intensive localized surveying of a promising location. Then exploratory drilling.

A coherent conversational string popped into Jeffers's memory, like a thread pulled out of a dark hole. It had started with Jeffers's blunt question. "Are your people drilling for oil or gas?"

"Hell, no," Sears replied instantly. "We're drilling ice cores." It was part of an ongoing program of monitoring the atmosphere, he explained.

The answer was quick and plausible, and Jeffers had a sense that Sears had been primed for the question. "You think there's enough oil and gas on this continent to make harvesting it a realistic, cost-effective proposition?" he asked.

"Has to be. Maybe not in this decade, but in the long term. All it needs is for the existing oil resources to begin to dry up. When that happens, people will be willing to pay . . . and pay."

"That seems to make you happy."

"Why shouldn't it? You think most of the developed nations don't know it? Why do you think they signed that minerals resolution?"

"Not all of the nations did."

"Most of them—including the U.S. of A. We know what butters *our* bread."

"There are commercial quantities of minerals here?"

"Parts of the Transantarctic Mountains have a geologic

makeup similar to the Andes. Some experts think they were part of the same mountain chain millions of years ago. And you'll find some of the same deposits. There's coal, of course, copper, iron, some chromium and platinum. We know there have to be petroleum basins, too, we just don't know how big. Yeah, Dr. Jeffers . . . there's oil here, and gas, and minerals. And someday . . ."

"Someday you'd like to see big offshore oil decks sticking up out of the sea ice, I suppose, and rigs scattered all over these ice shelves."

"You got it, Doc. What, you want to turn it into a world park, like those Greenpeace nuts?"

"It's not such a nutty idea."

"It's nuttier than fruitcake. All it will take will be one nation stumbling on something . . ."

An odd look crossed Sears's face, and he fell silent. A moment later he stumbled off to relieve himself of some of the beer he had imbibed. When he returned, the conversation took another turn, down a road Jeffers could no longer remember.

They had disagreed, Jeffers thought. Some of his comments had been caustic. He and Sears might very well have reached the stage of raised voices.

But it wasn't a smoking gun.

Something else was worrying Sears. Something more specific, important enough to be a secret. That afternoon Jeffers had thought he had it, the elusive memory slipping around a corner just as he spotted it, leaving nothing behind but an imprint on the air. But it was there. He was sure of it.

They said you should stop straining to remember when something teased you like that. Let your mind relax; play out the original sequence of events; see where they took you. Let the memory come; don't try to force it.

Memory took him to another bar with Len Sears. Late at night now, both men besotted, sharing a condition that prevailed widely at that hour of the morning in McMurdo. Jeffers had been told that drinking was a problem in Antarctica, where bored men deprived of customary emotional and physical outlets too often turned to alcohol. Jeffers hadn't planned on being one of the boys, but that night, prepping for what he expected to be two months of austerity at the field camp, he surely was.

In his college days he had done it often enough, and later at faculty parties. But then at least there had been Significant Conversations, high-flown debates both social and scientific, to give a facade of respectability to the occasion, intellectual zingers to remember fuzzily in the morning with chagrin. But that night with Sears . . .

"They've found uranium in East Antarctica, you know, in the form of encenite, near Syowa Station—"

"That's the Japanese base?"

Sears nodded. His head kept bobbing like one of those wooden dolls you sometimes saw on dashboards. "Platinum, too, even gold. What you want to find," he said, lowering his voice to achieve an air of confidentiality, "is something precious, something very rare the whole world wants, something countries have to have to keep up. . . ."

"What are you talking about?"

Sears looked unaccountably smug. "No, no, Professor . . . what you don't know can't hurt you."

"Who says . . . ?" Jeffers burped loudly, surprising himself. He stared accusingly at his empty glass. "Stuff snuck up on me. That's from the Latin, you know . . . *snucko, snuckare, snuckavi, snuckatus.*"

"Huh?"

"Nev' mind. You can't do it anyway."

"Can't do what?"

"Dig precious metals or whatever out of Antarctica. Not enough to make it pay. Too many problems. Logistical problems, all that stuff . . ." Jeffers groped for some of them. "Supply, transportation, shipping, equipment freezing up on you or breaking. Hell, you know."

Sears's expression was both smug and sly. "What if you

found enough of it to dominate the whole world market, in a place where it was easy enough to get at it?"

Jeffers laughed. "Like your own diamond mine?"

"Yeah, yeah, like that. Only not diamonds. Third world doesn't need diamonds. But everyone wants—"

Sears stopped dead. At first Jeffers thought he might be having a heart attack. His mouth fell open. He was having trouble breathing. He pushed off his stool, staggering as he came to his feet. He stared wildly at the scientist.

"What is it? Are you all right, man? Are you feeling okay?"

"Too much . . . I said . . . too much to drink."

"Are you going to be sick?"

"Gotta go," Sears mumbled. He looked anxiously about the room, his manner frightened. Then back at Jeffers. He essayed a sickly smile. "Talkin' crazy. Hey, man, I'm smashed, what the hell am I saying? Forget it. Drank too much. I'm gone, Professor, okay?"

"Do this again sometime," said Jeffers without enthusiasm.

"Yeah, sure . . . see you."

Transported back to his tent, Jeffers sat up. Smithson gave a loud snort in his sleep, then settled back into sawing wood. Jeffers felt a chill in spite of the heat inside the tent.

Sears had betrayed himself. No doubt about it. Sears—or Sears and the TERCO group—had discovered something. They weren't simply taking ice cores for atmospheric monitoring; that was just for show.

What was it the whole world, including third world nations, wanted so badly? Platinum was becoming more precious than gold, but that somehow didn't seem to justify both Sears's sly excitement when he hinted at discovery and his later panic. On the verge of drunken boasting he had retained enough clarity of mind to veer away at the last moment. And to be frightened of what he had almost revealed.

There wouldn't be any other nights of camaraderie with Sears, Jeffers thought. How keenly the man must be regretting that one night! If his memory was as blurred as Jeffers's was, he would be tormented by doubts about what he had said, fears that he had blurted out more than he should have, questions about how much Jeffers remembered.

It had to be a major find, Jeffers reasoned. And TERCO had to be sitting on it. Why? According to the minerals agreement, any development would be controlled by the Antarctic community of nations. Activity would have to be approved by a regulatory commission . . . and all would share in any royalties. There was no way TERCO could keep any such discovery for itself or progress to the stage of production mining in secret.

It would stir up some excitement, though. A major coup for the discoverers, regardless of what happened next.

Now I've gotta go, Jeffers thought. Much as he hated to, he was going to have to haul his ashes off to the Outhouse.

Regretfully he slid out of his nest of blankets and began to pull layers of clothing over his thermal underwear. There was a disposal pail in the tent, but he didn't want to pollute the atmosphere while he had to sleep in it. The Outhouse it would have to be.

Not as if he were a virgin at this. For the first time in years Jeffers thought of those times as a boy he had visited his grandfather's farm in northern Michigan. There had been no indoor plumbing, a fact he had simply taken for granted in the way children do. At the farm you used the outhouse, a small frame building closer to the barn than to the farmhouse. It was a three-holer, Jeffers recalled, and came equipped with a thick Sears catalog, which had pages of black-and-white photographs of young women modeling negligees. Getting up in the night in summertime to hurry to the outhouse was no problem. In winter it was another story. Leaving the cold house, trotting across the frozen ground to the little wooden shack, shutting the door quickly against the cold, shivering as you hurried to take care of your needs, skin all gooseflesh as your bare ass hung over the chosen hole . . .

Here we go again, he thought, worming along the exit tunnel, bracing against the cold. That five-year-old inside this fifty-five-year-old, bundled up and wearing his mittens, slipping out in the middle of the night . . .

The wind nearly blew him off his feet.

He grabbed the lifeline and hung on. The first shock of cold air knifed into his lungs and froze the moisture in his nose. The wind was like a living, malevolent force, pulling at him, pushing him around as if he were a doll. Hurriedly he began to haul himself along the rope.

It took him safely to the Jamesway, from which lines ran out to each of the tents like spokes from the hub of a wheel. A separate lifeline extended to the utility tent that served as the outhouse. It was identifiable by a string of three knots near the end where it was secured to the hut.

Relieved to have identified the correct line so quickly, Jeffers set off. The driven snow obscured everything. It clogged the openings in his face mask, blinding and smothering him. He couldn't even see the surface where he stumbled along. He moved in a white blindness as total as any other.

He found the Outhouse by feel rather than sight. Went to his knees, fumbling frantically for the entry flap, his fingers numb with cold inside the gloves that were inside his mittens. He dived into the tunnel, scrambling on hands and knees until he erupted into the interior.

For several minutes he crouched in the dimness. A small stove was kept lit in the utility tent to provide warmth. It also shed a little flickering light. Jeffers stared at it with something like reverence.

He relieved himself quickly and tugged all his clothes back into place, topped by the red NSF parka. But at the opening of the tunnel he paused.

He didn't want to go out into that fury again. The combination of awesome winds and cold and blowing snow was worse than anything he had yet experienced. *A taste of winter,* he thought. *We've been enjoying the balmy summer down here.*

He sighed. There was nothing for it but to suck up and take the plunge.

His whole attention was on the savage attack of the storm as it tried to tear his clothes from him and hurl him off his feet. He had the lifeline in his hands and took two steps away from the Outhouse before he realized something was wrong. The winds and the fearsome cold demoralized him. He was like that boy fifty years ago, he thought, facing an unimaginable world.

He turned around, reeling.

The rope was slack in his hands.

With the first intuition of fear he turned back toward the safe shelter of the Outhouse. Took two steps back the way he had come. Then a third. Went down on his hands and knees, groping.

It wasn't there.

He staggered back to his feet, bent over to diminish the profile he presented to the wind. The lifeline had been torn from his hands—but it was no longer a lifeline. It must have broken or been ripped free somewhere between the utility tent and the Jamesway.

He thought he heard something—a shout. He yelled back, but the cry was plucked from his throat and obliterated by the storm.

He tried to orient himself. The Outhouse was behind him—had to be. Ahead were not only the Jamesway but the other tents that encircled it at short distances. Ropes from each of them to the hut. All he had to do was keep moving forward. He would find one of the tents, the lifelines or the Clubhouse. He would have another mug of Russian vodka to start a fire in his belly, and to hell with the consequences.

He plodded forward through the drifts of snow. He could feel the cold beginning to settle in his fingers, his cheeks, his nose and ears. No combination of clothing and gloves and helmet could completely shut it out. He would have to find shelter soon, he knew. Could he burrow into the snow, like one of those huskies young Hurley used to pull his sledge? Jeffers was terrified by the prospect.

A young man's game, he had told Kathy McNeely. And so it was. Like Willie Mays, maybe he had tried to stay too long.

He shook off the morbid fear that threatened to overwhelm him. *Keep going, you'll find something.*

But the seconds became minutes, the first few steps became a dozen, then another dozen. He should have reached the hut by now, or at least one of the tents. He should be close enough to see one of them, even in the blizzard. He felt bewildered.

The wind blew him off his feet, rolled him in the snow. When he was able to right himself, he stayed down on his hands and knees. He looked around him into the whiteness. There was nothing else to be seen.

He had missed the tents, missed the Clubhouse. Must have become turned around in the beginning, he thought numbly. Must have set off in the wrong direction.

He was lost.

For what seemed a long time he remained on all fours, unable to move, paralyzed by the fear that each movement might take him farther away from safety. That same fear finally goaded him into action. Tempting though it was to let himself sink into the soft snow, he knew that would be fatal. Stubbornly he refused to crawl on hands and knees. Pride drove him to his feet. He began to shuffle forward, leaning over and keeping his head averted from the icy blasts.

He had no idea how long he kept going. His legs began to tremble from the strain; a cramp seized his left calf. Ice formed over his nostrils and on his eyelashes. The sweat on his body penetrated his clothing and froze, stiffening his undergarments until he felt as if he were dragging a suit of armor. He was also struggling to breathe. Each breath was a painful wheeze in his chest.

He thought of Titus Oates, one of the men on Scott's fateful last expedition. Weak and unable to keep up with the party, Oates knew he was holding the others back, diminishing what little chance they had to survive. And he chose his own gallant, heroic gesture. He walked away alone into the white wilderness, never to be seen again. *God, what men they were!* Jeffers thought. *What a sense of duty and honor they had. We use adjectives to describe them that no longer seem applicable, words of another time, like heroic, gallant, intrepid.*

But Jeffers had not chosen death. He struggled on. The blizzard beat him down, battered away his strength and slowly, punishingly, blew away the last shreds of hope. Jeffers didn't know how far he had come in the storm, but he knew it was too far.

Too weak at last to stay on his feet, he crawled through deep drifts of the powder snow that was like the softest sand. One mittened hand pawed through the snow and bumped into a solid object. With a leap of hope he tried to trace it, searching for a stake or rope or flap of fabric that would identify a tent.

There was only a slender column, like a pole, inside the deep snowdrift. Jeffers's hand moved slowly up the pole, and stopped. Explored a new and larger shape.

Jeffers came to his feet, both hands fumbling now. Tears welled up and almost instantly froze on his eyelids.

He had found the helicopter.

ELEVEN

THE MORNING BEGAN IN STILLNESS. Drifts of the purest white lay over everything—over the broad shelf of ice on which the tiny shapes of the tents and the hut were mantled in snow, over the helo, whose rotors were the lone alien thing sticking up out of the drifts, the fuselage being almost completely covered, over the ice cliffs that defined the shelf like bleachers overlooking an amphitheater, over the river of ice that flowed down from the mountains toward the sea, over the brash ice at the edge of the water. Even the ice floes, drifting slowly past the shelf, wore thick, soft caps of white. On one of these a large, fat elephant seal lifted his head and shook himself, scattering snow like a cloud of light in the morning sun. His grunt in the incredible silence shook the air like a cannon's roar.

The sky was a clear, flawless blue. The sun, with only a few weeks of summer remaining, stood very low to the horizon. The storm had passed.

Kathy McNeely was awakened by the stillness. She stared at the sloping roof of her tent. There was no ripple or flutter of motion from the wind.

She sat up quickly. Sensing that she was not alone before

remembering, she glanced at the neighboring cot, an arm's reach away. Survivor, fully awake, watched her. His blue eyes were clear and alert. Their color was startling. Some wolves, she remembered, were said to have blue eyes.

She dressed quickly, anxious now to step outside and see what the weather was like and what damage the storm might have left behind. When she was ready, she turned again to the husky.

"Okay, then, Survivor—that's your name from now on—I think we have to get you on your feet. I don't mind sharing the tent with you, but not as a toilet."

Getting him off the low cot wasn't as difficult as she expected. He stood uncertainly for a moment, tried to walk and discovered the limitations of his brace. Tentatively he bit at the straps.

"Uh-uh," Kathy said. "That's a no-no." The dog glanced up at her. "Let's go outside. You'll get used to the crutch, you really will."

What she hadn't reckoned on was the difficulty Survivor would have maneuvering through the exit. He was quick to learn, however, and when she used pressure on the back of his head to get him to lie down, he obeyed readily, and she was able to push him ahead of her over the slippery surface. They emerged from the tent into a world so dazzlingly clear and bright her eyes ached even behind her dark glasses.

Almost simultaneously with her appearance, the blanket of snow that lay over the penguin rookery stirred into activity, as if a thick white comforter were disintegrating. Adult birds walked about in the powder snow, assessing the morning, and were soon busy looking for missing chicks or partners, calling out in their distinctive bugling chorus like a gaggle of brass musicians tuning up, or hurrying off toward the water to feed. Near the far side of the shelf a string of Adélies hopped, one after another, onto a passing ice floe. They stood in a row at the edge of their floating barge, heads bent as they peered into the blue water, wary of the presence of a hungry leopard seal. Another group of active young Adélies climbed onto the rocks at the edge of the field, as if for a better view of the morning's brilliance. A squadron of skuas skimmed overhead, causing both the smaller Adélie penguins and the emperors to squawk in alarm and cluster closer together for mutual protection, and out over the water a flock of much smaller snow petrels blew past the shelf like a cloud of snowflakes, flying so low to the water they frequently dropped below the edge line of the ice, disappearing and reappearing in undulating waves.

The blizzard was over. Antarctica lay bright and beautiful and alive before her stunned gaze.

Kathy sensed movement beside her, a quickening of the husky's attention as he stared at the nearest penguins. She grabbed the strip of harness she had looped around his neck. "That's another negative," she said. "No penguins for breakfast. Something you'll have to get used to as long as we're together. This way, Survivor . . . I think we both need to take care of matters. Then we'll see if Hurley has any food for you."

She was surprised to find the lifeline to the Outhouse half buried under the snow. Torn loose by the winds, she thought. Lucky no one had to use it during the night. She took advantage of the loose line to secure it to Survivor's improvised collar before she crawled into the utility tent, presuming that the dog would take care of his own needs while she was gone. True to his new name, he seemed to adapt quickly. He was able to hobble along on three legs well enough, his stiff, braced leg sticking out a little and banging against the snow. Even in the short time he followed her his awkward gait had improved rapidly.

When she emerged once more, she saw a figure in front of the Jamesway. Not Carl, like herself an early riser. Rupert Merrill, his gaze sharply taking in the scene she had already witnessed. Not with the same exhilarating wonder and awe, she thought; he had the eye of a surveyor, not a poet.

Seeing her, Merrill called out, "Morning, Dr. McNeely. It seems we didn't all blow away after all." In the brittle silence his voice seemed too cheerfully loud.

"I was worried about us last night."

She didn't really want to have breakfast with him, she thought, not alone anyway. She hoped others were up and about. She couldn't count on the Soviets; there were no footprints in the snow that piled deep against the flap of their tent.

She left Survivor temporarily secured to the broken lifeline. He seemed to prefer being outside to the warmth of her tent. The Clubhouse was bright and warm, and the men from the helo were all awake. Hank Forbes gave her a grin as warm as a lighted window.

"Friend Davis is doing the honors for breakfast," he said. "I can't promise much."

Mike Davis waved a spatula in greeting and went back to his chores. He had a platter of frozen scrambled eggs already prepared and was turning over some strips of bacon on the grill. The bacon, he said, had been borrowed from TERCO's stores, compliments of Merrill. Savoring the smell of frying bacon, Kathy told herself to be grateful for blessings from any source. And why was she being hostile toward Merrill anyway? He had been convincingly pleasant with her. Carl Jeffers was the one who had some kind of quarrel with the TERCO people, not she.

It's because you trust Carl's instincts, she thought. She wondered what it was that he had intended to tell her later and never got around to.

Over bacon and eggs and a bagel fried in the bacon drippings —one of Mike Davis's specialties, he proclaimed—there were animated expressions of relief over the end of the storm along with awed assessments of its violence. Kathy cleared her plate as someone else stamped into the hut. She glanced up, expecting to see Jeffers. Brian Hurley grinned at her. "I see Survivor is on his feet. Good job, Doctor. I came to the right place."

For some reason the comment both pleased and irritated her. Maybe it was the complacent satisfaction in his tone. He had got what he wanted, and that was all that mattered. "He's doing fine," she said, more coolly than she had intended. "But he won't be pulling a sled for a while."

"Not this year," Hurley agreed. "But next summer, yes." He took his place at the narrow table and attacked a plate of bacon and eggs with a nod of approval at the reporter. "Just remember, Doctor, he's part of a feisty team. He's not a house pet."

"I'll keep it in mind." She began to pull on her outer layer of clothing. "You might feed him when you have time. I'm going to see how Dr. Jeffers is. He's usually the first one up."

Jeffers was not in his tent. Smitty, who was awakened by Kathy's arrival, didn't know exactly when Carl had left. "But he's always gone before I wake up, love," Smitty said. "He's probably out scouting."

"I didn't see any footprints in the snow," Kathy said doubtfully.

She was standing outside the tent, puzzling out Jeffers's absence, when Walter Corbin strode briskly up to her. Behind him Emil Zagorsky was staring toward the sea.

"I think you'd better come see this, Dr. McNeely," Corbin said without preamble.

"What is it?" She was still thinking of Jeffers, beginning to worry. It wasn't like him to wander off so early, without taking time to savor the first cup of coffee of the day. The men in the helo hadn't seen him.

"Down by the water," Corbin said. "I think you should see for yourself."

The emperor penguin stood erect on the ice floe, which moved sluggishly with the current. He was a large bird, nearly four feet in height. Almost had to be a male, Kathy judged, going by his size. He had vivid orange head patches and a narrow lilac stripe along the curve of his beak. With his black wings and pure white chest, he was a handsome creature.

The thick black coating of oil began about halfway down his chest and enveloped his lower body, legs and feet. He stood motionless on the cake of ice, the blackness pooling about his feet, and there was such a disconsolate misery in his pose that Kathy McNeely could not fight back her tears.

"There are others," Corbin said, his tone as cool and contained as always. "Not all of them in as good condition as this one. It would appear that you were correct in your assessment, Dr. McNeely. We definitely have a problem. Somewhere, somehow, there's been a new spill."

It was Hank Forbes who found Carl Jeffers in the cabin of the Huey helicopter. The scientist's cheeks and earlobes and fingers were white and cold, the tissue frozen. There were circles of blood around his eyes where the metal rims of his glasses had touched and burned the skin. His pulse was feeble, but he was alive.

They carried him into the Jamesway. Kathy put water on the stove to heat; rapid thawing in warm water was the prescribed treatment for severe frostbite. While they were holding his hands in the water and bathing his cheeks and ears, Jeffers sat in a stupor, helpless as a child. Gradually he began to emerge from his torpor, but he remained dazed, unable to explain clearly what had happened to him.

Kathy mentioned the lifeline. A flicker of comprehension appeared in Jeffers's eyes. "It pulled loose," he said. "I couldn't . . . I became lost."

"You were lucky to find the helo."

"I know. Kathy . . ."

"Yes? What is it, Carl?"

He shook his head, befuddled.

He remembered nothing else.

The blizzard had temporarily disrupted air transportation out of McMurdo. Hank Forbes made a quick decision not to wait for an NSF transport plane to reach them. He would fly Jeffers back to MacTown for treatment as soon as he could warm up his turbojets. Davis and the TERCO people were welcome to squeeze in and ride back, or they could wait for another flight.

All three men chose to go along. No one knew when another aircraft would be available or how long it would take for it to reach the Operation Second Chance base.

Jeffers was carried aboard the helo. Merrill and Sears, hooded and goggled against the cold and snow glare, piled in after him. Mike Davis sat up front in the cockpit with Forbes.

Kathy McNeely watched the Bell UH-1N rise slowly through its own snow curtain. She watched it flap away until the helo became a speck that vanished in the blue brightness. Then, her heart heavy with anxiety over Jeffers, she turned a somber gaze toward the sea.

The sense of foreboding that had seemed to hang over this Antarctic summer had not been an illusion. Had she been too quick to dismiss that reporter's queries about a season of discord and disaster? There was no longer any doubt that the Ice was at risk, threatened by a new, pervasive evil that imperiled the fragile environment and the creatures she loved.

Down by the edge of the ice the Soviets and her other companion scientists clustered. All around them black patches stained the snow, defiling the pure white surface.

TWELVE

———————

THOUGH IT WAS SUMMER IN ANTARCTICA, it was winter in Houston when, late that January, Ron Kusic, the chairman of the board, president, chief executive officer and major stockholder of TERCO, Inc., stepped from a gilded, thickly carpeted elevator into the crystalline elegance of La Ronde, a revolving rooftop restaurant. He was followed out of the elevator by Pete Rodriguez, his chief financial officer and a close friend. Across the room from them, floor-to-ceiling windows provided a breathtaking panorama of city lights and a forest of high rises. Among the building's prestigious tenants was Brady, Ellis, Tomkins & Weintraub, one of the city's most successful corporate law firms, located on the thirty-second floor. Kusic and Rodriguez were meeting one of the partners for dinner.

Recognizing Kusic instantly, the maître d' snapped his fingers, calling a waiter to attention, and personally escorted Kusic and Rodriguez across the circular room to a window table, where Emmett Brady waited. The maître d', who wore a tuxedo, seemed not to notice that Kusic was wearing a white turtleneck, wash pants and boat moccasins, attire more suited to the yacht where he could often be found than to La Ronde. Many of the diners wore formal dress. Their eyes and a muted buzz of conversation followed Kusic across the room.

He was a sandy-haired man of forty-two, deeply tanned, with an athletic spring in his step. The full mustache that covered his upper lip was neatly trimmed in a perfectly horizontal line. It gave his mouth an expression of firmness that complemented the arrogance of his features and the air of self-assured power that radiated from him. Rodriguez, two steps behind and hurrying to keep up, was a stocky, muscular man with thick, bushy hair that came down over his brow like a cap. He wore black wool slacks, a tailored white jacket and expensive Italian loafers, informal but more appropriate to the setting than his boss's casual wear.

Emmett Brady, who rose to greet them, looked the part: a successful sixty-year-old attorney with silver hair, a solid belly that was a tribute to good food and drink, a thorough insider's knowledge of the acquisitions game and excellent political connections. He wore a blue silk suit with a western cut. His cold blue eyes had followed Kusic across the room from the elevator, not with warmth but with appreciation for the man's style. For the past six years he had been Ron Kusic's principal legal adviser.

A magnum of Dom Pérignon rested in a deep bucket of ice beside the table, and the waiter quickly filled slender flutes for the two new arrivals. Brady had ordered the champagne for Kusic and Rodriguez. He was on his second bourbon and branch water. Like most Texans, he regarded champagne as a sissy drink. Kusic, he noted, was his usual half hour late.

The pleasantries were brief, and the men ordered dinner immediately. Kusic didn't like to waste time on courtesies. When Brady spoke of disturbing news about Kusic's cash-flow problems, Kusic nodded toward Terrell. "Tell Pete," he said. Kusic didn't want to know the details; he was a big-picture guy.

While the other two talked, Kusic ignored the stares of several sleek young women in the room and gazed out the panoramic windows. The view changed very slowly as the restaurant revolved, and Kusic waited. There was an almost sensual pleasure in the anticipation.

He had been sitting there for about ten minutes when the silhouette of another high rise inched into view, about a half mile distant.

Kusic had had the TERCO logo created in blue neon and mounted atop the building, where it could be seen for miles. He watched for the entire time it was visible, about twelve minutes, before it passed out of sight. He thought of his father, who had beaten him routinely in drunken rages before abandoning the boy and his mother. "You'll never amount to nothin'," Joseph Kuscynski had said. "You got a big mouth; but you're trash, just like your mama, and you'll always be trash." *The logo's for you, Pop, wherever you are,* Kusic thought. Whenever he came here, watching the sign edge into the window frame was his favorite moment, and it was always accompanied by the same thought.

"You're going to have to address the problem," Brady was saying to him, the last words catching Kusic's attention. "It's not going to go away. Wishing it away won't work."

"If wishes were horses, beggars would ride," Kusic murmured.

"I didn't get that." Brady probably didn't look puzzled very often.

"Something my mother used to say." Kusic turned to Rodriguez. "Capsulize it for me."

"Essentially what it comes down to is, TERCO has assets that add up to about two-point-five billion dollars and total debts of three billion dollars, with cumulative interest charges close to one million dollars a day. More to the point, we've got bank debt in the form of short-term merger debentures of one-point-three billion dollars with big lump sum payments due over the next couple years, the first payment in June." Rodriguez smiled. "Emmett sees that as a problem."

Kusic's gaze swung lazily back to Brady. "That's news?"

"Unfortunately, yes. TERCO's potential financial shortfall was the subject of a feature article in the *Los Angeles Times* this morning. Most of the local TV stations picked up on it for a two-minute bite on the evening news. It'll be in other papers all across the country tomorrow for sure, with some Sunday editorializing to come. Disaster, real or potential, always makes the news."

"Two days, it'll be forgotten."

"Bankers don't forget," Brady said.

The subject rested while they finished dinner and ordered coffee and brandy. When the waiter finally left them alone once more, Kusic said, "You have your ear to the ground, what are you hearing?"

Brady sighed. He sipped his brandy before answering. "The first rumors, the first hints that you might have trouble coming up with the lump sum debt payment due on June thirtieth this summer."

"We'll pay it," Rodriguez said.

"It always starts with rumors," the lawyer persisted.

"We've heard the skeptics before," Rodriguez said. "They've always said Ron couldn't pull this off or that. He always has."

"This is a bigger game," Brady said. "And the rules have changed, thanks to Boesky and Milken."

For the first time a frown creased Kusic's tanned forehead. "You mean there's a problem with our stock offering? Is that what this is all about?"

Reluctantly Brady nodded. "The timing isn't good. Buyers are being overly cautious."

"There are always buyers. Greed isn't cyclical. It's a human condition."

"It's a different atmosphere now. Not enough confidence in the market. You're going to need a large infusion of cash, and these rumors . . . stories like this thing in the *Times* . . . don't help. The confidence isn't there."

Kusic was silent for a full minute. He nodded pleasantly at a long-haired blonde at a nearby table, whose escort scowled. The blonde looked as if she would melt under the table.

"It's all perception, isn't it?" Kusic said finally. "If people begin to think you're in trouble, you're in trouble."

"Unfortunately that's true. It happened to Trump—"

"So it could happen to me," Kusic snapped, dismissing the comparison. "What if TERCO came up with some good news, maybe just before we announce the stock offering?"

Brady appeared skeptical. "It would have to be something dramatic . . . and genuine. I mean, not some whizbang PR gimmick. The real thing."

"Even if it were long term? I mean, even if profit taking were a long way off?"

"That's not a problem in this business. Long term is the name of the game."

"Maybe I'll have something."

Brady's expression froze. "You've made a find? Something important?"

"Maybe."

"Maybe doesn't cut it."

"You'll have the details when I'm ready."

Brady was first startled, then intrigued, then encouraged. Excitement flickered behind the cold blue eyes. "You come up with something big," he said slowly, "something that will really grab the attention of the small buyer, you'll have your cash."

"Start working on that stock offering prospectus, Emmett. I want it ready to go."

They were finishing their coffees when a heavyset red-haired man approached the table, smiling too broadly and, in spite of the room's air conditioning, flushed and sweating. He rubbed one hand over his hair and said, "Mr. . . . Mr. Kusic? I'm Jack Aaron. I know you probably don't remember me, we met at the last sales meeting, but . . . I just wanted to say what a pleasure it is to see you here, sir, and . . . and to work for TERCO."

Kusic smiled. "Good to see you again, Jack." He did not offer to make introductions. "We're having a little meeting here."

"Oh . . . yes, sure, Mr. Kusic." Aaron nodded eagerly, still sweating. His hair, a candy apple red, seemed too young for the fleshy face. "I just wanted to say . . . we're all with you. I mean, things like that *Times* hatchet job, they don't mean a thing."

"I appreciate your saying that, Jack. It's nice to know my people are behind me."

"We're a team, sir . . . a team."

Kusic nodded pleasantly, and after a moment's hesitation the salesman hurried across the room toward a distant table. For a long moment Kusic said nothing. Then he turned to Rodriguez. "Who is that clown?"

"Your western regional sales manager."

Kusic's gaze was bland, but the cold-eyed Brady, watching him, felt a chill.

"Do we have to keep people like that around?"

"He's been a producer," Rodriguez said.

"Fine."

Emmett Brady got off on the thirty-second floor. Kusic and Rodriguez rode down alone in silence. The elevator was swift and soundless. It carried them to a subterranean garage. While they were waiting for Kusic's silver BMW 850i coupe to be brought to them, Kusic asked, "What's the latest from Antarctica?"

"It looks good. Merrill's sent ore samples by air for our lab to analyze, but there's not much doubt it's a rich find. We'll know more about the size of it soon."

"No leaks?"

Rodriguez hesitated. "Nothing significant."

"Don't hold out on me."

"Apparently one of Merrill's team got drunk at McMurdo Station and popped off to some environmental scientist. But it looks as if any potential damage has been contained."

"I don't like the sound of 'it looks as if . . .'"

"The scientist didn't appear to remember anything our man

might have said. Anyway, he got lost in a blizzard and nearly froze to death. He's being flown to New Zealand for treatment, and I imagine he's going to be too busy with his own miseries to worry about what some bigmouth said in a bar."

"Jesus Christ!" Kusic exploded. "You imagine! I want a goddamn lid on this thing until we're ready. We're talking image here. The way it is now, we don't even get to keep whatever we mine, we'll have to share it with every other Tom, Dick and Harry. We're on the verge of killing off this Antarctic Treaty, if the politicians don't kowtow to the crackpot environmentalists. And maybe the minerals agreement will die with it, may it rest in peace. But either way this discovery will put TERCO on the map. You make goddamn sure Merrill knows how important it is to keep this under wraps. What this is about is prestige and publicity. And, like Brady says, cash flow."

The parking attendant swooped down a ramp with the silver BMW, and the two men drove off, Kusic at the wheel. He drove very fast and with casual skill; celebrity Grand Prix racing was one of his hobbies. He cracked a window to let the cold night air rush in. After a while Kusic said, "What is it, Pete? Is there something else I should know? Down there on the Ice?"

Rodriguez squirmed uncomfortably on the leather bucket seat. "There was an accident with a fuel bladder near the drilling site. It ruptured, spilled a few thousand gallons of fuel oil. There were some penguins in the area that got caught in the spill. You know how the environmentalists will exploit that if the story gets out."

"So?"

"So they buried the birds in the ice. Apparently a couple of them got away and were found by some marine scientists."

"That's it? A couple of *birds*?"

"Shit, Ron, the public gets all upset if some minnow is endangered. Penguins are different. They're cute. Everybody loves penguins. Nobody wants them hurt. Including TERCO," he added.

Kusic shot him a sharp glance. Rodriguez was the only man alive from whom he would have accepted the implied rebuke.

After a moment's silence he said, "You get the word to Merrill. Tell him I don't want to hear any more bad news about the site. This is good news time, Pete."

"Merrill can handle it."

"He damned well better handle it." Kusic concentrated on his driving for several minutes. Then he said, "Whatever it takes, Pete. Tell Merrill that's from me to him, personal. Whatever it takes."

He lifted his face toward the stream of cold air blowing in through the open window, causing Rodriguez to turn up the collar of his jacket, and thought about Antarctica, a continent of ice.

And TERCO was sitting on a potential fortune.

Part Two

DAMAGE CONTROL

THIRTEEN

FOR A WEEK BRIAN HURLEY experimented with a fan harness system. Instead of a single long central trace from Dutch, the lead dog, to the sledge, with pairs of dogs clipped to either side of the trace behind him at spaced intervals, the fan system put each dog on its own trace. After some trial and error, Hurley adapted the system to satisfy Dutch's ego, letting the big dog trot out front on a longer trace than the others, in effect letting him lead, as he always had. Behind him the other dogs fanned out in groups of four and three.

The team had lost something with the injury to Niner—Survivor now; Hurley corrected himself with a grin—but not as much as he had feared. When they ran in pairs, it was possible for a lazy dog like Bones to cheat a little, keeping his line tight to the trace without really putting his weight into it. In the fan arrangement it was easier to detect any slackness or lack of effort. Dutch was even quicker to see it than Hurley was, and once, during a pause on a practice run, he turned the moment the sledge pulled up and attacked Bones with frightening ferocity.

It happened too fast for the other dogs to get excited and start their own melee. Hurley reacted instantly. He had been bitten on the arm once breaking up such a fight, and he had learned better than to get in the way of slashing teeth. Springing close behind the two fighters, he grabbed Bones by the hind legs and swung him clear. Dutch tried to dart past him in his rage, but Hurley was able to grab the big husky's trace and haul him up short.

During the half hour rest stop the good-natured Bones acted aggrieved, licking at a few cuts, but Hurley noticed that when they set off again, Bones was pulling hard against his trace.

Hurley had set up his own camp on the tongue of the Hartsook Glacier at a distance of about a mile and an elevation of three hundred feet above the Operation Second Chance camp and the penguin rookery, far enough for the dogs to present no threat to the penguins. The site offered Hurley a fine view of the field base below him, the sprawling rookery, and the curve of a shallow bay, a definition invisible at a lower level. It was also close enough for him to walk down to the scientists' camp almost daily—to check on Survivor's progress, he told himself.

Kathy McNeely had been in a somber mood during the week since Carl Jeffers's accident. Too depressed for Hurley to tell her about the rope, without being surer than he was.

Paranoia was an all too common condition when people lived under stress in extreme isolation. Maybe *he* was becoming paranoid. In any event, Hurley had saved the broken nylon rope that had provided a lifeline from the Clubhouse to the toilet tent the night of Jeffers's accident. He had substituted another line, and if anyone noticed the change, there was no comment. The break in the line had occurred where the rope was secured to the Jamesway. The severed ends of the line were not frayed. The break was clean and sharp, as if the rope had been cut.

Hurley told himself the winds had been wild that night, and their force could do astonishing things—including snapping a rope cleanly. Though not completely convinced, he was left with nothing but uncorroborated suspicion. Not enough to make wild charges, even if he could have thought of a reason for someone trying to kill Jeffers.

Still, the nagging suspicion persisted. What if someone had tried to murder the UCLA scientist? Or anyone else who tried to use the line that night, he thought. Had Jeffers been the specific target? Or was anyone in the Operation Second Chance camp at risk?

One morning, when he emerged from his tent into the brilliance of another cloudless summer day, he was presented with a remarkable scene of activity below him. A cruise ship, equipped as an icebreaker, had anchored in the bay opposite the emperor penguin rookery. Small orange-and-black Zodiacs chugged past a huge blue-green iceberg and threaded among drifting ice floes toward the edge of the shelf below the scientists' camp. Long before they were safely deposited ashore, some of the passengers foolishly stood up for a better view of the teeming activity around them. *Just what we all need,* thought Hurley, who had come to remove himself in his own mind from the category: *tourists.*

Hurley was debating whether to go down to the camp that day—he had thought of checking on Survivor again, even though the dog was hopping around the camp on three legs, his clumsy brace thumping on the surface, with remarkable agility —when an alien sound shattered the stillness on the glacier. Hurley glanced up, shielding his eyes with the palm of his hand. Out of the glare a small dark silhouette appeared, featureless in that frost blue sky, looming larger as it sped toward him.

Hurley groaned aloud. The HTV crew had had huge identification letters painted on the side of the navy helicopter that had been assigned to ferry them around the continent. It was visitors' day all around.

The helo made two passes over Hurley's tiny camp before the pilot selected a safe landing strip on the snow-covered surface about a hundred yards away. He set the skids down gently on hardpack so firm it was hardly dented by the weight of the aircraft. The side door popped open, and the red-jacketed passengers tumbled out onto the snow.

Smile, Hurley growled to himself. *You might be on camera . . . and isn't this what you wanted?*

The director of the remote-location HTV crew, Hal Berkowski, was a tall, straw-thin young man with a prominent nose and an unruly fall of shoulder-length blond hair. To Hurley he seemed too young to be directing anything more demanding than a home video of the family picnic, but Hurley acknowledged that this was prejudice. For all he knew, Berkowski was a genius; genius did not discriminate on the basis of age.

Berkowski, his long, thin neck poking out of the collar of his NSF-issue red parka, stomped around beside the plane as if determined to pack the snow down. His eyes were hidden behind huge dark goggles, but there was a delighted grin visible through the hole in his face mask. "It's perfect, Hurley! Look around you, man! We can even use the snow glare, you know, get some surreal effects."

"I wasn't planning on—"

"Fuck plans, man! You gotta grab the brass ring when it goes by. Look at this weather—gorgeous! And the shadow contrast is awesome. Isn't that right, Mark?" he called out to the cameraman, who was fiddling with a lens filter.

"Fantastic," Mark said.

"See, Hurley? Hey, man, it isn't like I'm asking you to fly to the Pole. Just go to the top of this glacier, that's all. What's it called?"

"Hartsook Glacier. And what do you mean, that's all? Hal, that's the toughest part of the run. It's a stiff climb all the way. And there are God knows how many crevasses."

"You can do it, I know you can."

"I'm short one dog—"

"You've been practicing, right? You told me so, everything is going great, you said, am I right?"

"Well, I said something like that."

"Fan-tastic! Now you're talking. When can you start?"

"Hal, you're not listening! I can't just decide to make a two-week run like that. It takes planning. I'm short of supplies as it is."

"You name it, we'll get it for you. I want this, Hurley. The geniuses back in L.A. who dreamed up this caper are all over my back."

"The deal was for a run next summer to the South Pole. It's in writing."

"You want next summer, you do something for me now. The bosses want some bites for their bucks. It's as simple as that."

"What's that supposed to mean?"

"They want some minutes to put on the tube. Didn't you tell me nobody's ever climbed the Hartsook Glacier in a single run to the big plateau?"

"Yes, but—"

"Then we've got a hook. It can be a summer special, maybe a fill-in for some dog of a show that's just taking up airtime. I mean the real summer in television land, June, July, August, like in there somewhere. It's going to be a bitch to climb, right?"

"Right."

"We'll play that up, use low angles on those mountains. We'll scout out some good locations on the way up the glacier, we can do most of that from the air, and we'll drop a film crew in to meet you where something looks good. We can set up a couple of base camps along the way, too. Hey, the weather stays like this, who's to complain?"

Me, Hurley thought, more and more dismayed as he listened.

Berkowski was on a roll. "And it's gonna look cold, all that snow and ice, it'll pull an audience when it's in the nineties this summer, better than any beer commercial. And it'll set up next year's polar run, kind of whet the Nielsen family's appetite."

"I don't like it," Hurley said, running out of objections. "You can't go at Antarctica like it's a spur-of-the-moment fling. Too dangerous."

145

Berkowski stopped packing the snow down long enough to stare at Hurley for a long minute. He looked from the busy scene below them at the edge of the sea, to the snow-covered mountains rising high above them, to the great river of ice that flowed downward through a long valley between massive peaks. "It's fuckin' beautiful, man. I want it. I want it now, while the bitch is all dressed up in her best. You hear what I'm saying, Hurley? You wanted in, you're in. But that means all the way."

It wasn't exactly a threat, Hurley thought. It was a description. In his own brash terms, Berkowski was even putting it to him gently. You want to do this, you want the glory and the gold, you take the garbage along the way.

"There's a bonus in it for you, Hurley."

"Stuff the bonus."

But Hurley knew he couldn't get out of it. Not unless another blizzard blew in. Or he gave up on the entire polar project, packed it in and went home. He supposed that he was no different from a screenwriter or director who was compelled to tailor his product to the demands of faceless men somewhere who signed the checks. This is show business, Hurley. Hooray for Hollywood.

"I'll need supplies in a hurry," he said. "There's not much summer left; this weather won't last. I'll have to start within a week. I'll make a list; I think you can get everything at McMurdo. Mainly I'll need food for the dogs. On the trail they need at least one and a half pounds of pemmican per dog each day. If I figure on two weeks—"

"What the hell is pemmican?"

"It's a mixture of oatmeal, meat, vitamins and lots of fat."

"Shit," Berkowski said. "They should put that on the menu at Spago."

"You just get me the ingredients. For a two-week run, say, fifteen days to be on the safe side, I'll need a minimum of a hundred and eighty pounds of the mix." Plus food for himself, he thought. Not much room for any extras, he thought, if he was to keep the overall weight of the sledge down close to 400 pounds. His full nine-dog team had been able to pull 450 comfortably. Eight dogs, uphill all the way, would be tested by a lighter load. Of course, if Berkowski set up advance field camps along the way as he suggested, Hurley could stash supplies at each stage and pick them up as he reached the camps. If it was—

Hurley caught himself. *You're going to do it,* he thought. *If that's the case, you're going to do it right.* Advance bases or supply depots were legitimate. The great Antarctic explorers all had used them, cutting down on both the risks of isolation and the weight of supplies they had to carry. Sometimes those depots had made the difference between life and death —survival and triumph for Roald Amundsen, who had managed his meticulously plotted expedition so well, but glorious failure for Scott, who, along with the last survivors of his fateful polar expedition, had died, too weak to go on, only eleven miles short of an emergency depot that would have saved them. Hurley could accept the HTV crew's leapfrogging ahead and waiting for him at advance bases, then, but that was as far as it went. If his effort was to have any meaning at all, it had to be a real test for both musher and dog team. That meant pulling a full load, and nobody to hold his hand.

Berkowski was grinning at him behind his woolen mask. "You figure fifteen days max, that what you're saying?"

"If we're lucky, and everything goes right . . . which is a very big if."

"But you've got it calculated, right?"

"As close as I can."

"There, you see, Hurley?" Berkowski's grin was triumphant. "The old girl has no reason to turn on you. You're not going to be treating her with disrespect. It's not spur of the moment, after all, is it? You've been planning to have a go at her all along!"

FOURTEEN

——————————

As if to make up for the unseasonal storm, Antarctica turned benign in the last weeks of summer. Its sky was a faultless blue. Temperatures rose toward the freezing point in the peninsula and along the northernmost coastline. So often shrouded in clouds and gray sea fog even in summer, the coast now bathed in brilliant sunshine.

Tourists on the *Southern Gypsy,* warned to wear their dark glasses against the glare off snow and ice, marveled as a massive portion of an ice shelf calved from the mother cliff with a crunching roar like an amplified train wreck and shifted slowly away out to sea, creating an instant coastal passageway and an iceberg half the size of Manhattan Island. The ship rolled as it rode the powerful swell from this act of creation.

A giant albatross wheeled slowly back and forth in the wake of the ship. Clouds of petrels rode just above the waves. Penguins performed on either side of the ship for the delighted passengers, diving and leaping, as if escorting the *Southern Gypsy* along a channel through the drifting sea ice. Cries of excitement followed glimpses of seals, black and gray and spotted, in the water and on the passing ice.

Ashore, Kathy McNeely watched the ship anchor opposite the emperor rookery, her initial tolerance tipping over into dismay as she followed the progress of several orange-and-black Zodiacs toward the shore.

Her mood this past week had been the opposite of the bright, sunny days. She almost wished for clouds and fog to match her depression. She threw herself into the round-the-clock rescue effort, helping clean and feed the dozen or so surviving oil-soaked penguins that had been pulled from the sea, along with a pair of fur seal pups young enough to be handled safely. All the while Carl Jeffers's near tragedy played endlessly in her thoughts. During one long, sleepless night she even entertained the possibility of hitching the first available ride to New Zealand, where Jeffers had been flown to a hospital in Christchurch, abandoning her Antarctic mission and accompanying Jeffers back to California.

By morning the grief-driven impulse had passed. She was needed here more than Jeffers needed her.

"He would not wish you to give up your work," Aleksei Volkov said to her when she voiced her feelings.

It was a simple answer, but true. Jeffers would hate that, hate being the excuse for it. The last word relayed from MacTown was that Jeffers was recovering nicely.

Nicely. One of those expressions used to comfort worried friends and relatives. What did it mean? Amputated fingers and toes? A shattered mind? "The operation was a success" meant only that the patient was still alive. Would Carl ever completely recover from his ordeal?

How could it have happened? They all had tried so hard to follow all the safety rules. Jeffers had made several previous trips to Antarctica; he had witnessed other mishaps; he knew better than to take chances. The lifeline must have been in place when he paused at the Clubhouse to shelter briefly from the winds, before making his way along the rope to the Outhouse. Otherwise he wouldn't have gone on.

A commotion out on the sea ice caught her eye. One of the

Zodiacs had pulled up next to an ice floe. An eager passenger, ignoring or not waiting for instructions, jumped instantly onto the ice from the landing craft. His pushing action shoved the Zodiac away from the ice. Though at first showing signs of alarm, the tourist quickly realized that the island wedge of ice, fifteen feet thick, was, if anything, safer than the Zodiac. He began to do a booted shuffle, an elated dance on the ice.

The guide in the boat yelled at him. The man answered with a clumsy pirouette, his binoculars flopping from a strap around his neck as he spun. Some of the other passengers laughed and shouted encouragement, drawing an angry glare from the guide.

A sleek, small-headed seal appeared at the edge of the ice floe. He peered over the edge at the dancing man. With a jolt of alarm Kathy McNeely recognized the mottled coat of an adult leopard seal, an aggressive and dangerous seal that grew up to nine feet long.

The tourist spotted the seal. "Look!" he cried, the sound of his voice carrying clearly over two hundred yards of water and ice. "A seal! Isn't he a beauty?"

He began to dance toward the edge of the floe, drawing closer to the seal.

"Stay away from him!" the guide shouted, frantically directing the Zodiac toward the cake of ice. "He thinks you're a penguin!"

"So?" the reckless visitor answered, laughing. "I just left my tux at home."

"You damned fool! He thinks you're dinner!"

At that moment the seal jumped out of the water onto the ice. The tourist gave it one startled look and scuttled toward the Zodiac. As the boat touched the ice, the seal flopped across the ice toward the man, propelled by its flippers with amazing speed. The intended meal threw himself headlong off the ice floe into the Zodiac, which immediately pushed off. From her vantage point Kathy could see the foolhardy man still upended in the boat, while the frustrated leopard seal barked after him.

The lucky man would have a story to take home, Kathy

thought, especially after he learned that leopard seals had been known to attack humans on the ice and drag them into the water.

Resigned to the inevitable interruptions and confusion, she started toward the penguin colony, hoping to forestall any incidents there. Some of the other landing craft had already reached the edge of the ice shelf. The passengers were clambering out, armed with cameras, gingerly testing their footing in the snow while they stared about in wonder and delight. One group, landing a few moments before the others, had collected near the ice edge to gape at a huge Weddell seal sunning on a stationary floe a few yards from the shoreline. The giant seal raised its head languidly and emitted a bellow somewhere between a cough and an elephant's trumpet. The tourists scattered backward in fright. They didn't know that the Weddell was the most amiable and sedentary of the big seals, harmless to humans in spite of its size.

These incidents quickly passed, and the tourists began to move about the ice shelf, converging on the penguin rookery. Most of them, it seemed, had listened to the briefings from their guides or the seminars given by the naturalists on board the ship. They approached the penguins slowly to avoid giving alarm, their expressions rapt, their cameras clicking.

A tall man with thinning gray hair, hatless on this mild Antarctic summer day, separated from the group, leading a woman carefully across the ice. He had a dignified, almost courtly manner that could not be disguised by his bulky clothing. He was the kind of man who would always find his own path, Kathy thought intuitively, watching the couple as they approached, the man holding the woman's arm as he escorted her.

The man was in his sixties. The woman appeared considerably younger, an appearance aided by cosmetic surgery about the eyes and chin and by hair still defiantly blond. Watching them, Kathy was reminded of her own parents, together for nearly forty years, devoted and trusting, at peace with each other. She felt a stirring of envy.

As the couple came close to a cluster of penguins, the birds scuttled away nervously. "You're too tall," Kathy called out on impulse. "You should get down to their eye level."

The patrician visitor glanced across the snow toward her. He had very piercing blue eyes that scrutinized her closely, making a quick appraisal.

"They're frightened by us?"

"Exactly. You're intimidating. If you want them to relax and stay close, you have to approach them very slowly, unaggressively and preferably at their own level."

The man seemed amused by the suggestion. He introduced himself and his wife as Joe and Miriam Carter, confirming that they were visiting Antarctica for the first time. "You're one of the scientists at this camp?" he asked, nodded toward the complex of tents and huts.

"Yes. Katherine McNeely. I'm working with the penguins."

"How wonderful! Then we must take your advice, by all means." He turned to his wife. "Are you all right, dear?"

"Yes, dear, of course."

With a smile Joe Carter led her back toward the nearest group of penguins. While still fifteen yards away, he got down on his hands and knees in the snow. After a brief hesitation Miriam Carter joined him. As they crept closer to the penguins, a few of the regal birds retreated; others eyed the couple curiously.

Kathy joined them on the ice. "Let's make it easy for them," she said. "Down on your stomachs. Stop when I do."

Joe Carter grinned. He was a man accustomed to giving orders, Kathy guessed, not taking them. Without delay he dropped down on the snow, reaching out with one arm to help the woman beside him to follow suit.

Kathy was surprised. She had wondered if they would do it. They were within the perimeter of the rookery now, and the snow surface was discolored by the pervasive penguin guano and enveloped by its smell.

"I hope you don't mind a little guano."

Joe Carter laughed. "Young lady, I've been in more shit in my lifetime than you can ever imagine."

Even more to Kathy's surprise, Miriam Carter sniffed, sighed and flattened herself on the snow.

Kathy wriggled forward, trusting the Carters to follow her lead. They wormed toward the nearest emperor penguin, a male with a vivid orange collar. He stood his ground. With a wordless gesture Kathy stopped the Carters. They were six feet from the penguin.

The bird regarded the trio of humans for a minute, clucked and waddled back and forth in front of them. Two other birds drew closer, curious and unafraid.

Glancing at Joe Carter, Kathy saw unmasked delight on his face. Beside him, Miriam Carter wore an anxious but tolerant smile. The expression must have been as familiar for her as Joe Carter's exuberance was to him, Kathy thought.

Over the next hour they worked deeper into the center of the penguin rookery, until they were surrounded by emperors, young and old. Before long their presence was accepted by the penguins, which carried on their own squawking discourse and the normal busy activity of the rookery. They strutted around the humans on the snow, pausing to stare at them with their black obsidian eyes, cocking their heads this way and that. ("They have monocular vision," Kathy explained. "They look at you one eye at a time.")

One young chick, still molting, tottered up to them, squawking plaintively. After examining them closely, it found Miriam Carter's orange jacket and yellow sweater so natural that it poked a beak under the sleeve of her coat, searching, and, turning its back on her, tilted its head back to peer up at her. It seemed about to snuggle close, much as the young chicks pushed backward against their parents. The woman held very still, lips parted, hardly daring to breathe. Joe Carter's expression re-minded Kathy of a new father witnessing the miracle of birth.

The chick squawked again, tottered around in a circle and waddled off, peering upward at adult pairs while continuing to call out.

"It's searching for its parents," Kathy said softly. "For a moment it considered you."

"How will it ever find them?" Miriam asked. "There are so many . . . there must be many thousands."

"Each of them has a distinctive call, even though they sound so much alike to us. Apparently the adult penguins can recognize the sound of a particular chick, and the young ones learn very early to recognize their parents' calls."

There was a moment's silence. Then Joe Carter said, "They walk just like my grandson, Mike. He holds his arms out like flippers and sort of totters along."

The two women laughed.

"You should see them in the water," Kathy said. "They sail through the ocean the way an eagle soars through the air."

After a while Kathy led the couple toward the far side of the rookery, where they could observe the antics of the smaller Adélie penguins. Many of these had climbed onto the small pile of rocks or higher projections of ice to gain a better lookout, like spectators flocking toward balcony seats. Groups of other Adélies hurried toward the sea ice, and no sooner had one group set off than others scuttled after them.

At the base of the little pile of rocks a male Adélie began to bow repeatedly before a female. He threw out his flippers and tossed his head back and began a kind of ritual dance. Soon the female joined him in bowing, dancing and fencing with their bills. At the end of their performance they stood close together, the male with his head draped over his partner's neck.

Kathy explained the courtship routine of the Adélies. "Courtship is everything," she said. "That's how he wins her, a display like the one you just watched. They're nest builders, as you can see; that's what those little circles of small stones are. Early on, when she accepted him and they decided to set up house together, he probably searched for a perfect stone to give her for starters."

Miriam Carter laughed. "I told you, Joe. Just like you." Kathy was struck by the affection in her laughter.

"What do you mean?" he demanded, mock indignant.

"He likes to preen himself and bellow. When he came courting, first he danced with her, and then he gave her an absolutely perfect stone."

Joe Carter was silent a moment, as if weighing the evidence. "Well," he said finally, with an amused sidelong glance at Kathy, "there's a lot of competition out there. You do what you have to do."

When she had first seen them, Kathy had been prepared to admire the man and forgive—or at least tolerate—the woman. She was now coming to realize that she had been guilty of the worst kind of stereotyping. Her intuitive assessment of Joe Carter still stood. She would have bet her diploma that he was a chairman of the board somewhere. It was Miriam she had underestimated. But *he* hadn't, she thought. Joe Carter knew what kind of mate he had found.

For the second time Kathy felt a wistful envy.

Three hours of the tourist invasion passed very swiftly. At last a shrill whistle cut through the clamor of the penguin rookery, a sound not quite like any penguin's call. One of the tour guides, standing ashore beside a waiting Zodiac, waved urgently.

With clear reluctance the tourists began to wander back toward the boats, appearing from ice cliffs, from the camp's Jamesway, from the penguin rookery and, off to the east, from another ice formation where a group of fur seals had been found.

Joe and Miriam Carter walked slowly out of the colony of penguins with Kathy McNeely. When they reached the open ice, Joe took a deep breath of clean air and grinned. He turned to stare back for a long minute over the mass of penguins.

"How wonderful!" he said. "We'll never forget this. We're very grateful to you, Dr. McNeely."

"Not to me. To them . . . and perhaps to everyone who's trying to keep this place whole for them."

"Aren't you one of those?"

"Yes," she admitted.

"Then God bless you, my dear."

"Just be glad you came."

"Oh, we *are*," Miriam said. There was a glow in her eyes, and on her face the kind of radiance that Joe Carter must have seen forty years ago when he preened for her, Kathy thought.

They walked carefully over the snow and ice toward the Zodiacs, which quickly filled. As Kathy watched Joe Carter hold out his hand to help his wife step into the boat, she was sorry to see them leave. Usually she found tourists an unwanted distraction, and their often aggressive carelessness, their habit of trampling over everything in their eagerness, tried her patience.

But she realized that the Carters had done more for her than she had done for them. They had reminded her who and what she was. They had given her an almost forgotten glimpse of the awe and wonder Antarctica could inspire in someone who had never before seen its magical light, the splendor of its sculptured face, the astonishing variety of life along its fringes . . . life that she was convinced was seriously threatened.

A little of the bitterness she had carried within her for the past week had eased.

Sorry, Carl, she spoke in her mind to her old mentor. *You mean a lot to me, and I lost my head.*

Then do what we both want.

She had to resist looking around, so clearly did his voice answer her.

The Zodiac carrying the Carters and their fellow passengers chugged out into the water through the floating ice. Joe Carter was standing tall and straight, peering back at her in spite of the urging of the boat's pilot. Joe raised one arm in a wave. He staggered slightly as the Zodiac rode through choppy water but held his footing, erect and dignified.

Kathy returned his salute.

Volkov had said the Russian icebreaker would be in the vicinity in two days. It arrived only a day behind the *Southern Gypsy*, taking advantage of the tourist ship's open channel through the sea ice. Their first glimpse of the Soviet ship moved Volkov and Simanovich to an impromptu dance at the edge of the ice shelf, which in turn drew an audience of curious penguins.

Kathy McNeely watched the bulky ship shoulder through the thin ice. It would need all its bulk within a few weeks as the ice rapidly thickened with the approach of winter. She had been asking a lot when she approached Volkov the night before. To carry out the exploration she proposed would expose the ship and its crew to some risk if the weather should change quickly and the sea-lanes closed. The history of Antarctica was dotted with the wrecks of ships caught in the relentless grip of winter ice.

"Did you mean what you said earlier, Alex? About asking your captain to take us near last year's spill area?"

"I have ask him already."

"You did?"

"By radio. He say yes. You still wish this?"

"Now more than ever."

FIFTEEN

HANK FORBES PEERED AHEAD through the windshield of the UH-1N Huey, squinting in spite of the protection of his goggles against snow glare. The sky was clear, and without cloud cover the endless vistas of snow and ice were like white mirrors, gathering up all the light from the sky and hurling it back.

But the sun, very low to the horizon now, cast long, sharply defined shadows, every detail etched into the snow. Whenever mountains intervened, as they did when Forbes turned the chopper to follow the long slope of a glacier toward the seacoast, the day remained brilliant but without color, all black and white, shadow and snow.

Ahead of him, still far off, a tower of ice turned red, the only spot of color in all the landscape before him. It glowed like a beacon, drawing him toward it.

He glanced at his instrument panel. Sure enough, that sunlit tower was guiding him straight toward the TERCO base camp. Behind him in the cabin there was a stirring, shards of conversation piercing the muffled beat of the rotors.

Forbes grinned. Lulled perhaps by the flawless perfection of a windless day, perfect for flying, the two TERCO geologists were in a far different mood from that on the flight to McMurdo base from the Operation Second Chance camp. Under the circumstances both Merrill and Sears had tried to conceal their resentment of Forbes's blunt decision to fly Carl Jeffers back to MacTown, but they hadn't been very successful.

Merrill, in particular, had been impatient and irritable over the layover at McMurdo, necessitated by a foot-dragging NSF inquiry into Jeffers's accident. Forbes, who'd been asked to give his version of the event, had overheard Merrill raging at an NSF official over the delay. Fat lot of good that did him, Forbes thought. Officialdom never changed, even at the bottom of the earth.

Forbes glanced ahead at that orange pillar. It made him think of something he had read in a biography of Captain James Cook, the great explorer who was the first man to sail a ship south of the Antarctic Circle, seeking to discover terra incognito. Cook had had just such a glimpse of a distant ice cliff or berg set afire by the sun. He had described it as a man carrying a lantern and, in a moment of fancy, had wondered if it might be someone from an unknown race of people who dwelt near the South Pole.

Antarctica teased you that way, Forbes thought. You might think of yourself as being hardheaded and unimaginative as a garage mechanic, as Forbes did. Antarctica made you a poet and philosopher. At least it made you believe in the poetry of nature. And it put ideas into your head about what was important and what didn't really matter, what was big and what was small, ideas Forbes would have scoffed at before coming here.

Forbes had spent twenty-five years as a navy pilot, a career that had taken him from Nam to the Persian Gulf. In his last year he had been assigned to Antarctica. He was a loner, and the idea of spending a year down at the end of the earth didn't bother him; his wife had long since divorced him and remarried, taking their two children with her. They didn't even carry his name anymore.

What he hadn't been prepared for was becoming infatuated

with the place. At the end of the year, retired from the navy, he had taken advantage of an offer to stay on in Antarctica as a contract pilot. Rank and privileges gone, and some of the bullshit you had to take, but the same job with better pay.

He'd almost have paid them to let him stay.

Some pilots disliked (make that hated) the visual phenomena the Ice was famous for. These illusions distorted the landscape and confused both distance and direction. The air was so dry and clean and clear that mirages were commonplace. Icebergs might be seen floating upside down, not in the sea but topsy-turvy in the sky. Distant mountains could appear to be only an arm's reach away, while nearby objects seemed far off. Natural properties were reversed, the land taking on the transparency of clouds, the clouds the solidity of land. Odd angles of light diffused, refracted and reflected from ice crystals in the air, especially in ice clouds, produced halos, duplicate or dog suns and moons, and vertical pillars of light like rainbows stood on end.

Forbes was fascinated by all of it.

Then there were the auroras. Especially the one called the southern dawn, the aurora australis. Forbes had been told the phenomenon was produced by the interaction of solar winds with the earth's magnetic field. He didn't understand the science of it or care much. Seeing it was something else.

The auroras were indescribable blends of violet and red and green, orange and lemon yellow, each color clear but delicate, like an almost transparent watercolor. They had been called swaying curtains of colored light. To Forbes they were the veils of an invisible dancer cavorting through the sky, twisting and turning and flowing, dancing until dawn, when the diaphanous veils began to fade and fall inward, like a woman's dress pooling about her feet.

Forbes was in love with her.

Snap out of it, he growled to himself. Reality ahead.

Forbes flew down the slope of the glacier and veered off, reluctantly abandoning his sight line to the pillar of fire. He circled over a perfectly flat, featureless ice sheet whose vast, pure expanse of white was interrupted only by a tiny cluster of tents and huts off in the northeast corner.

"Nice flying, Hank!" Rupert Merrill called out from the cabin behind the pilot. "Right on target."

Maybe they would applaud when he set the helo down, he thought.

Hank Forbes liked visiting the isolated camps scattered throughout Antarctica during the summer. The men—there were only a few women among them—were always glad to see him, and not only because he brought them mail, news or needed supplies. The kind of people who could be found willing to work in this harsh environment, doing the kinds of things they did, which generally seemed to have very little to do with chasing the almighty dollar, were the kind Forbes would choose to be with. They were hardworking and hard-drinking. They weren't much concerned about appearances. They *cared* about things. They enjoyed a good laugh. Forbes didn't know if you *had* to have a good sense of humor to survive in an Antarctic camp, but the condition seemed to be prevalent. Maybe the ones who couldn't laugh didn't hang around long.

That UCLA scientist who was hurt, Carl Jeffers, was one of the good ones.

Forbes had talked to Jeffers quite a bit, mostly about what it was like to be a helo jockey in Antarctica. "I'm like a limo driver down here," Forbes had said. "Back home that doesn't amount to much, but on the Ice it makes you a celebrity of sorts. Sometimes I'm the only way you can get from here to there."

"In style," Jeffers suggested.

"Goes without saying."

He had even talked to Jeffers about his kids, fishing out of his wallet the year-old Christmas card with the snapshot of the family. That picture had hurt at first, Doris with another man standing grinning beside her, flanked by Hank's children, Greg and Gina (he would always think of them as his), but after studying the photograph for a year, Forbes had come to terms with it. They *were* a family now, a unit, and that was something he had never been able to give Doris, the thing she wanted most. Never would have been able to give it. Which also meant that he would never have been a real father, not when he was never there.

Jeffers was sympathetic. "They may not have your name now, but the other guy didn't give your son that nose."

"Not exactly a prize."

"Nonsense, it's a great nose. Fortunately your daughter— Gina, is it?—didn't get it. But she got your blue eyes and curly hair."

"Yeah, she's pretty, isn't she?"

"When you're old and gray, which can't be far off, they'll probably come down to your little retirement cottage in Fort Lauderdale to visit you."

"Hey, it'll be a cheap vacation!"

They had had a couple of drinks together, Hank Forbes hob-nobbing with a UCLA professor, how about that, Doris? Found out they both were Dodger fans and shared memories of seeing Sandy Koufax pitch, of Kirk Gibson hobbling off the bench in the ninth to hit that dramatic home run that beat the Oakland A's in the '88 World Series.

Once Jeffers asked him about the TERCO base. Had Forbes ever been there before?

As a matter of fact, he had ferried a number of TERCO's fieldmen to their camp, and he was able to describe the place to Jeffers. Not much to look at, three huts painted orange so you could spot them a long way across the ice, a group of small tents, mostly for storage, oil drums and fuel bladders, a special drill set up in one of the huts for extracting ice cores from the shelf. Like a score of similar little field bases scattered across the Ice each summer.

"Nothing else? No unusual activity?"

"Nothin' at all, Doc. Just a bunch of men doin' their jobs, tryin' to stay warm."

Jeffers had turned quiet that last day, something on his mind, and Forbes remembered he had had sharp words with Rupert Merrill. Just a disagreement, Forbes had thought. Concerned marine scientist versus oil company man, they weren't always going to see eye to eye.

But Jeffers was out of the picture now.

Having arrived late in the day, Forbes had planned on staying overnight at the TERCO base. He checked in with MacTown by radio for the weather, learned that nothing ominous was in view for the next day, though the long-range forecast was more uncertain. He chuckled when he switched off. As if the long-range forecast for Antarctica were ever anything *but* uncertain.

The air was very dry and clear and cold, one of those days when you could see the spiny ridge of mountains rising on the far side of the shelf, fifty or sixty miles away, and count the shadows, everything was so sharp-etched and close. The temp hovered around zero, and Forbes enjoyed wandering around the camp without having to wear his wool face mask. The snow surface was packed hard from all the activity. TERCO had several motor toboggans, a Caterpillar tractor, a tracked vehicle called a Trackmaster and a huge traverse tractor the size of a boxcar, all of which had left their marks in the snow. You wouldn't have thought they needed the big tractor. Forbes wondered how they'd got it up here.

Forbes ambled over to one of the men, an engineer working near one drilling hut. "How do you find out what's inside those ice cores? You don't do that here."

"Beats me," the man said. His name, stitched onto the lapel of his parka, was Hugh. "That's for the chemists back in Houston."

"You ship the cores all the way back there?"

"Uh-huh. Put 'em in that hut over there, and they're packed and shipped in special containers, in freezer holds."

Forbes grinned. "No trouble keeping them frozen while they're here."

"That's frozen history," Hugh said. "What they tell me, you lose one slice, like as thick as your fingernail, and you lose maybe a century."

Forbes shook his head. "Like they say, ain't science wonderful?"

Having relaxed by this time, Hugh chuckled. "If you ask me, and nobody does, I can think of a lot better places to freeze my ass than this here camp. We're just going through the motions here."

Forbes glanced idly around the camp. "You brought enough stuff up here for some real work, it looks like. Whatever did you haul with that big rig?"

"Oh, we used that to take the drilling equipment over to the other camp."

"The other camp?"

Len Sears, emerging from the main hut, spotted Forbes talking with the engineer. Hugh's mouth tightened. "You never heard me say that, okay?"

"Say what?" Forbes agreed amiably.

Sears wandered over. "You getting along okay, Hank?"

"Fine. Just getting acquainted."

"You're planning on staying over the night, right?"

"Yeah, a few hours' sleep seemed like a good idea. Looks like we don't have to worry about bein' blown off this shelf."

"The mountains help to shelter us from the winds, but sometimes they turn right around and we get some real howlers." Sears nodded at the engineer, who went back to his work. Sears said, "Glad to show you around, Hank, answer any of your questions."

Forbes grinned. "I can't say as there's a whole hell of a lot to see that I haven't seen before."

Sears laughed. "You can say that again."

Jeffers hadn't liked him, Forbes thought, as Sears left him. Something about Sears and Merrill had been eating at the scientist. Why should it be nagging at Forbes now?

Because of the freak nature of Jeffers's accident, he thought.

Something that never should have happened came damned close to killing him.

But that thought led nowhere. At least nowhere that Forbes was prepared to go.

One thing: Forbes spent the night in the Jamesway with Merrill, Sears and Mike Davis. He had slept soundly, in spite of the turbulent hammering of the storm. But once during the night he had been awakened. There wasn't any kind of major disturbance. Only half awake, he had recorded a sensation, thought nothing of it, drifted off again. He thought about it now. It was the cold, he thought. He had known without reflection that someone had been outside and had come back in again. In Antarctica, especially in bad weather, anyone coming from outside into a warm hut or tent wore cold like an aura around him. In a blizzard he wore it literally, for the dry snow clung to everything.

Who had been outside, and when? Why hadn't he said anything about it when Jeffers was found? Or could it have been Jeffers himself, pausing at the Clubhouse on his way to the utility tent?

Funny questions to be asking oneself.

Hank Forbes had flown a number of TERCO's people up to this site, a half dozen in addition to Sears and Merrill. Three of the faces he remembered were not in evidence that night when the crew gathered in the main hut for the evening meal. There were several men present he didn't remember, who had probably come in one of the big cargo planes with the heavy equipment. All told, eight men shared the communal supper in addition to Forbes.

How many at the other camp? he wondered. The one Merrill and Sears had never mentioned. The one Hugh got all nervous about when Sears saw him talking to Forbes.

The conversation over a meal of beans and bacon was barrackslike, both jocular and scatalogical. It quickly turned to the subject of women, its permutations chauvinistic, vulgar and wistful.

One man, a Polish pipe fitter from Hamtramck built like an oil barrel on stubby legs, launched into a description of a time when he was accidentally dumped off at a camp on the Antarctic Peninsula that housed a half dozen nurses in training for service on the Ice. They had been living there in isolation for weeks.

"It turned cold, so cold everything froze. A storm just sat down over that camp. First my ears froze, then the tip of my nose, and then my fingers and toes. And then, while I was using the john, my piss froze on the way to the hole. It backed up, and my dick froze when the water froze. I had to break the piss off when I was finished. But I couldn't do a damn thing about my frozen dick."

"What about one of them nurses?"

"I'm getting to it. I went to the head nurse. It was kind of embarrassing, but it didn't take her long to see I had a problem. Well, like I said, those nurses had all been stuck in that camp for a couple months by themselves, and they got together and decided they would do their best to help me out."

The speaker paused, leaned back and sipped his coffee.

"Well?" one of the listeners finally asked.

"Well, what?"

"Well, goddamn it, what happened?"

"Oh . . . well, it took those nurses, all six of 'em, four days to thaw me out. Let me tell you, when that storm was over and I left that camp, those were the gratefulest bunch of women you ever saw. I still get Christmas cards from every one of 'em."

Amid the scoffs and jeers and threats, Len Sears said, "You guys should see the woman at that scientists' camp where we sat out the blizzard on the way here. Every one of you would be pole vaulting from here to McMurdo."

"Not Popolano," one man said. "With that little peanut of his, he'd tip over and drown in the snow."

"What was she like?" asked another. "Come on, Sears, give."

While Sears offered a vivid and exaggerated description of

Kathy McNeely, Hank Forbes, who had liked McNeely and enjoyed her company, was silent. Finally he said, "She's not gonna be all that far away from here. Close enough to dream about."

There was a long silence.

"What do you mean?" a young technician asked softly.

"Last we heard, she was going to head along the coast this way, looking for the site of that *Kowloon* oil spill."

This time the silence was more prolonged.

Rupert Merrill said, "There's no call for getting their hopes up, Hank. No way she'll come anywhere near this camp."

"Maybe not." Forbes sensed the instant letdown in the room. "I thought I'd take a look at that spill site myself, if I can find it. Weather holds good, I figured I'd scout down along the coast and see if there's anything left of that penguin rookery that was there. It's the penguins Dr. McNeely is interested in," he explained for the benefit of those who hadn't heard about Operation Second Chance. He told about the discovery of a number of injured seals and penguins in the aftermath of the recent blizzard, offering a somber description. "No one's certain what happened to them, or where, except they fell into some oil."

"You wouldn't think oil from last year's spill would last that long in this place," one of the fieldmen said.

"They don't think it's oil from the *Kowloon.* It came from another accident."

"They don't know that for sure," said Merrill.

"Dr. McNeely was sure."

Forbes wasn't sure exactly why, but the easygoing atmosphere of the hut had subtly changed. His description of oil-saturated birds and seals had let the air out of the balloon, he decided.

The group began to break up. Several men stayed in the main hut to listen to some fresh, only slightly worn country music tapes Merrill and Sears had brought from McMurdo. Others drifted off to their own huts. Two of the scientific observers in the team went back to the drilling hut for some late-evening work.

The storyteller, whose name was Kornievski, invited Forbes to share space in his hut, which slept six men in what was, for Antarctica, relative comfort. One of the men was in the field, he said. Forbes could have his bunk.

Forbes didn't ask where the man was.

From his own observations and a little guesswork, he figured the TERCO crew at this base camp was little more than half the total number who had flown here at the beginning of summer. At least half a dozen men were unaccounted for.

When he left in the morning, Forbes decided, he was not just going to scout around for signs of an old or recent oil spill in the sea ice along the coastline. He was also going to see if he could find out where the other TERCO camp was and why nobody wanted to talk about it.

In the morning the helo wouldn't start.

Problems with machinery were chronic in Antarctica. The Bell Huey helicopter was powered by twin turbojets. Turbine engines had proved generally reliable even under extreme cold conditions, but nothing mechanical was impervious. Hank Forbes checked for frozen fuel lines and other obvious trouble spots, then borrowed a hot-air blower from the TERCO people.

After thirty minutes' labor the helo still wouldn't start.

Forbes sighed resignedly. Working on the Ice for three years had made him more of a mechanic than he cared to be, but it was not his chosen profession. Especially where working with frozen metal tools meant wearing heavy gloves in tight quarters, and the numbing cold gave gloved fingers the dexterity of baseball bats.

It looked like a long day ahead, trying to find the problem.

The delay exasperated him.

SIXTEEN

On the evening before the Soviet icebreaker was to pull anchor, Brian Hurley walked down from his camp on the glacier to the Operation Second Chance base. There was cloud cover, making the evening bleaker than any this past week. The clouds wore a rim of light, like a halo.

He found Kathy McNeely at the utility tent she had turned into a convalescent station for the wounded penguins thrown onto the ice during the violence of the blizzard. The two surviving oil-soaked seals that had been rescued had been released. They had quickly escaped into the sea. The two penguins found earlier had been set loose into the neighboring rookery, along with several others whose injuries had been less severe. A half dozen penguin patients were still being treated. Others—Hurley was not certain how many—had been dead or dying when found.

Survivor, lounging outside the tent, jumped up at Hurley's approach. Hurley crouched to accept an enthusiastic greeting, and Survivor banged him with his crutch. In answer Hurley threw both arms around the husky's neck. "That's a hell of a way to greet a friend," he growled. Survivor's wet tongue caught him on the side of his face; the moisture quickly froze in his beard.

Kathy emerged from the tent. He thought her eyes lit up a little when she saw him, but he wasn't sure. "Ready for Survivor's evening constitutional?" he asked.

"I don't know, Hurley. I'm trying to get everything done that I can. Smitty and Emil are taking over for me here, but . . ."

"You can't work all day and all night."

She glanced back at the tent, hesitating. Hurley heard one of the penguins squawk.

"I guess it may be the last walk," he said awkwardly. Damn it, why did she make him act like a fool?

Kathy smiled. "You make it sound like walking the last mile."

"Yeah."

"Well . . . all right, Hurley, I guess I *do* need a break. And Survivor needs his exercise."

The husky, turned loose, hopped on ahead of them, exploring the ice and poking his nose into drifts of snow. His agility with the free-swinging brace around his left front leg never ceased to amaze Hurley. It was as if the dog had completely accepted it as a natural appendage. In his mind it was no longer a hindrance. The bone was healing naturally, Kathy McNeely had said. Nothing seemed to be out of line. She couldn't say whether or not Survivor would have a limp when the leg was fully knitted together, but in no real sense would he be crippled.

"Will he be able to pull?" Hurley had asked her.

A shadow had crossed her face. "I can't answer that."

The drifts were deep on the lower part of the slope, and both Hurley and McNeely felt the drag on their thighs after a while. They walked in silence, trailing plumes of white as they breathed. The temperature was five above, a mild evening, mild enough to let both of them go out without their wool face masks. Hurley's beard, bristly the first time she saw him, had grown luxuriant. Droplets of ice in the beard made it appear frosted. The beard softened his features, but it had a wiry texture. She had never kissed a man with a beard before that night in MacTown . . .

"What's wrong?" Hurley asked.

"Oh . . . nothing."

"You're leaving in the morning with Volkov, I take it."

"Yes. The captain has agreed to put us as close as possible to the old emperor rookery."

"What happens from there?"

"I don't know," Kathy admitted. "There's a tractor and a motor toboggan aboard. Volkov says they'll let us go inland a ways if we can't find anything in the sea ice or along the coastline." She paused. "It all depends on what we find."

"This late in the summer, you'll be lucky if you can even get close to shore. And you won't be able to stay long."

"I know all the reasons against it, Hurley. I'm going, that's all."

They topped a fold in the ice and came in sight of Hurley's camp, still about a half mile up the slope. The red silhouette of the television crew's helicopter sat near Hurley's tent like a mutant hornet in a monster movie.

"It's pretty late in the year for you to go off on some wild junket up the glacier," Kathy observed pointedly. *And your only reason for going is personal,* she thought.

"The TV people want it. It's not my idea."

"And they're calling the shots, right?"

"They're calling the shots. It's their money. Without it I wouldn't be able to be here. It's not all that different from you scientists and the National Science Foundation," he added. "They help finance a lot of the research that goes on down here, so they have a say in where you go and what you do."

"That's different! You sure have a way of twisting things around, Hurley. The NSF isn't trying to make megabucks off our work. It's just helping to make it possible."

"The NSF doesn't finance private projects," said Hurley. "I had to go elsewhere. Scrounging up the money for another expedition is an old Antarctic tradition. Scott and Shackleton and Amundsen would all understand. Even Byrd had to hustle money."

"They weren't doing it for . . ."

"For what?"

"Publicity . . . glory . . . their faces on TV."

"Weren't they?"

They walked in silence for several minutes without seeming to come any closer to Hurley's camp and the red helo beside it. Survivor, who had hopped on ahead of them, paused to wait for them.

"Don't worry, we're coming," Kathy said. She wished she could call back some of her zingers at Hurley. What business did she have criticizing him for his motives?

The clouds lifted from the face of the sun like a curtain rising. The red sphere rested almost exactly on the horizon, like a ball on the edge of a table, as if this were the moment before setting. But the sun wouldn't drop any lower tonight. Another week or so, Kathy thought. Then there would be a widening wedge of twilight in the middle of the night, deepening quickly as the last days of summer came and the darkness lengthened over the Ice.

"Those clouds are moving in from the north," Hurley said after a while. "You'll have ocean fog in the morning when you pull anchor."

"I know."

"No one else is going? From your team, I mean."

"No, they're going to try to wrap things up. Walt Corbin has finished his project, so he's trying to tie up Dr. Jeffers's studies of the seafloor. Emil and Smitty will do what they can with the surviving penguins." She smiled as a thought struck her. "What's the matter, Hurley, do you think I need a chaperon?"

"Maybe you do. Those Commies might be planning on kidnapping you and hauling you off to Siberia. Or worse."

"They're not Commies," she said, amused. "And what could be worse than Siberia?"

"They could force you to sit there all night while Volkov sings 'Dark Eyes' and Niki plinks that fiddle."

She felt an odd sensation, indefinable and thrilling, like a small electric shock.

"You don't like my going off with my Soviet colleagues, do you? Or is it just with Volkov?"

"What's it got to do with me?"

"You think my virtue might be threatened?"

"Well, is it?"

"No, of course not." She smiled again, enjoying his discomfort. "That is . . . I don't think so. Alex is a gentleman."

"Yeah, sure. I've seen what happens down here on the Ice. You're isolated with a small number of people, and they become like your best friends in all the world, the only ones who can possibly understand what it's like here. You become a select, intimate family. You start feeling very close."

"Sounds scary. Having friends like that, I mean."

"You're not listening."

"I hear you, Hurley. I guess I'll just have to take my chances. Like you going up that glacier. This is my work. It's my life's work. Not only do I care about these people, but I care about the animals, too. Especially those penguins. That's what this sea voyage is all about. Something very nasty has happened here. I don't know what it is yet, but . . . Alex and Captain Suganov have been good enough to give me the opportunity to try to find out."

"What about Survivor? You care about him, too. I've watched you with him. What's going to happen to him?"

"Oh, didn't I tell you? I asked Volkov, and he agreed, even though he doesn't approve."

"Agreed to what?" Hurley asked, a sinking feeling in his stomach.

"To let me take Survivor along." She glanced down fondly at the husky, who thumped his tail, brushing snow from side to side. "You're right, I do care about him. This way I'll be able to continue to monitor his progress . . . and he's coming along just fine. Fit as a fiddle, you might say . . . and you know darned well that instrument Niki plays isn't a fiddle."

A shout drew their attention, allowing Hurley to ignore the comment. A hundred yards up the sloping ice sheet, a tall, thin figure standing next to the helicopter waved at them. Even at this distance Kathy recognized Hal Berkowski.

"Your master calls," she said impulsively.

Hurley winced. "Low blow, McNeely," he said. "Besides, it's you he wants. He's another conquest."

"I don't think so. Berkowski wants to take pictures of me as if I were some eager starlet."

"What's wrong with that?"

"I don't belong in your film, Hurley. Let's let it go at that."

He was silent for a moment, staring up the white slope toward Berkowski. "You don't approve of me, do you?"

"What you do is your business . . ."

"Unless I'm scuffing up the scenery. Leaving dirty footprints in the snow. Not like your friend Merrill and the TERCO outfit, prospecting for oil."

"Merrill is doing legitimate environmental studies," Kathy retorted. "If it weren't an authorized project, he'd never have got NSF permission to come here. That's below the belt, Hurley."

He grinned. "One low blow deserves another. But I really *do* wonder about Merrill and Sears. I think your friend Jeffers had some reservations about them, too."

"Damn it, Hurley, you've no right to drag Dr. Jeffers—"

"You know he did! You were there that last night. You must have heard him."

In her anger she started to deny it. Her memory tripped her up. She recalled Jeffers's somber mood that night, his desire to speak to her later in private. Why hadn't he felt free to talk to her there in the Clubhouse? It was true that Jeffers had lashed out at Merrill. He had also warned her about him. *He's waltzing you, my dear. Don't trust him.*

Hurley looked as if he wanted to say something else. She waited, annoyed to find herself anxious, wanting him to speak. She hadn't meant to quarrel with him again, much less take gratuitous shots at his Antarctic project. *We need men like him out here, too,* she thought. *Men like him found it for us.*

Another shout from Berkowski floated down the slope, its sound, in the awesome stillness of an Antarctic evening, as sharp as glass breaking.

Hurley glanced toward him, then back at Kathy. "Look out for yourself, McNeely."

"Sure. You look out for yourself, too. That's not going to be a picnic up on that glacier. Look after Survivor's buddies."

Hurley went down on his haunches before Survivor and took the husky's broad head between his hands. "Take care of her, okay? You're in good enough shape for that."

Survivor growled low in his throat, not a warning but a moan of pleasure. Hurley laughed, ruffled the dog's ears and pushed to his feet.

A gust of wind blew powder snow around them.

Hurley stared down at Kathy. For a brief moment she thought he was going to make some kind of gesture, reach for her, even . . .

"Are you coming back?"

The question took her off stride. She hadn't even thought about it. What if winter arrived prematurely, while she was still on the Soviet ship or with Volkov on the ice? There might be no practical way to return to the camp as planned.

She met his gaze, and it occurred to her that she had never seen him clean-shaven or wearing a suit or doing any of the normal things one did in a normal world. Holding a glass of wine to the light. Watching a child's face. Slumping in an easy chair.

"I'll be back," she said.

"I'll see you then."

He walked on up the slope, his boots disappearing into the

deep drifts. Behind him a stiffening breeze blew snow over the depressions he left behind, slowly filling them up.

She felt curiously empty, wishing he would look back. Survivor whined softly, as if he, too, knew he was saying good-bye.

SEVENTEEN

MIKE DAVIS FLIPPED UP THE SCREEN of his laptop computer, booted the word processing program and began to type, his gaze flicking back and forth from his notes to the five-inch-high monitor screen.

Back at McMurdo Station after nearly a week of junketing, the journalist could almost think of himself as an old hand at Antarctica. Almost.

He no longer was struck by the incongruity of pulling out his high-tech little laptop in the midst of the starkest frontier left on earth. Sharp contrasts, visual or cultural, quickly became commonplace observations in this setting.

The sparely furnished room in which he was working was in a barrackslike building near the NSF headquarters, a sort of Swiss chalet that stood out amid the ramshackle clutter of the station like a Beverly Hills cottage transported to the Appalachians. Davis's room had electricity, which saved his battery pack. Black shades covered the windows to shut out the midnight sun and the relentless snow glare. And it was warm. When he returned to it after several days in the field, it had seemed more luxurious than any real Hilton he had ever stayed at.

But that wasn't the story he was here to tell. He was zeroing in on that.

The story began on the screen in front of him. . . .

"What is happening to the atmosphere over Antarctica may shape the future of life on this planet," says Ted Kowalski, of the Ohio State University Institute of Polar Studies, relaxing with a beer in a prefab hut situated on the West Antarctic ice sheet. "That sounds like doomsday crap, but it isn't. It's real."

The evidence is becoming overwhelming, say Kowalski and Nils Nillson, a Norwegian atmospheric scientist who joined Kowalski and his U.S. colleagues this spring in a joint research program funded by the two countries. Industrial and other chemical pollutants, in particular the chlorofluorocarbons, have caused a thinning of the ozone layer that protects the earth from damaging ultraviolet (UV) rays.

"When the chlorofluorocarbons decompose in the upper atmosphere," Kowalski explains, "the chlorine atoms sink down into the ozone layer, which is extremely cold during the Antarctic winter. Then with the coming of the spring sun they become very active. They demolish and consume the ozone molecules. They've done it so well they've opened up a hole."

Kowalski and Nillson came here in September, early spring in Antarctica, when the iron grip of winter first begins to ease. Seasons are reversed on the ice, with the brief summer beginning in December and ending by the Ides of March. It is in the spring that chemical reactions in ice clouds over Antarctica, resulting in a depletion of the UV layer, can best be observed. Part of the Kowalski–Nillson study involves firing laser beams into those ice clouds to measure the chemical reactions taking place.

Higher levels of harmful UV not only threaten higher rates of cancer in humans and contribute to the potential "greenhouse effect" that may cause global warming but may also damage or destroy the microscopic phytoplankton in Antarctic waters that forms the very basis of the food chain throughout the Southern Ocean and beyond.

This joint U.S.–Norwegian study typifies the spirit of international cooperation and the open sharing of scientific information that help make Antarctica unique.

THE ICE

Another kind of hole

Bernhard Hauser, a marine biologist from Hamburg, Germany, sits patiently inside a flimsy-looking hut that is surprisingly snug on a strand of flat, wind-riffled ice, staring at a round hole cut into the twelve-feet-thick ice of McMurdo Sound. The ice within the deep hole is a gemlike blue-green.

Relaxing on a cot, William Sawyer, on a polar studies mission from UC Berkeley, is thumbing through a tattered copy of *Playboy* magazine. The centerfold, he complains, is missing.

Hauser and Sawyer are waiting for a single Weddell seal to swim from the cold depths of these Antarctic waters to this single hole in the ice, where it must come up for air. The Weddell is a large, amiable seal—this one weighs about 600 pounds and is 10 feet long—that can spend more than an hour underwater at a time. Then it must breathe. It must find or create a hole in the ice.

The two marine scientists are part of a joint U.S.-German study program. Their patient, selfless search for greater understanding of the seal's ability to sustain long periods underwater, like the work of Kowalski and Nillson, seems to epitomize the peaceful pursuit of science that has made Antarctica one of the world's great laboratories since the Antarctic Treaty was signed in 1959.

But all that is changing.

The summer of our discontent

The Antarctic Treaty ushered in three decades of harmony on the Ice —the name old hands give to this white continent one and a half times the size of the United States.

This remarkable document is deceptively simple, comprising fourteen articles that summarize the provisions of the treaty. Key among them are Article I, which states that Antarctica will be used for peaceful purposes only, forbidding any military activities; Articles II and III, which provide for freedom of scientific investigation and the sharing of the results; Article IV, by which the member nations set aside any territorial claims while the treaty is in force; and Article VII, which allows observers from any treaty state to visit and inspect all other stations at will.

But it is the seemingly innocuous Article XII that today presents a threat to the future of this remote continent.

Article XII provides that, from the date the treaty entered into force in the early 1960s after being ratified by all the signatories, any member state may call for a review after thirty years.

That time is up.

Has the long period of unprecedented, peaceful cooperation among nations also ended? There are signs it has. . . .

Davis scowled. He stared at the screen. He wondered if the subheads he had included in his copy would survive. Writing headlines wasn't part of his job; the *Times* had headline writers who did nothing else. Anonymous outside the newspaper's offices, most of them were noted within journalistic ranks for their facility with puns. Davis hoped they would let "The summer of our discontent" stay. No pun, but a nice twist on Shakespeare via Steinbeck's book title, he thought.

If the whole article wasn't trashed.

He stared gloomily at the screen.

The story was right there, close; he almost seemed to have a handle on it, but . . .

He wasn't happy.

He could hear Shafter now, that grating voice that somehow matched the wolfish grin. "It's thin, Davis. It's not just thin; it's vaporous."

"It's the story you wanted."

"I don't give a shit whose idea it was. It's your job to find the story, put it together, make sense of it. What you're giving me, Davis, is to journalism what puffed rice is to cereal. Mostly just air."

It was the catalog of horrors that fell short, Davis thought.

Oh, there were problems on the Ice, all right. That clash at Faraday between the limeys and the Argentines, for one. Davis had learned that the incident had had the potential of turning very nasty. He had also been able to verify several of the dirty tricks Sam Namura had told him about, some of which had produced lingering hard feelings. One respected scientist, whose homosexuality had been revealed by the distribution of photographs of mysterious origin, was no longer with his Antarctic mission, a fact deeply resented by several of his colleagues.

Other items of note: U.S. Navy investigators had found no explanation for some shipping snafus. The debates Davis had heard over the minerals agreement were often rancorous. And there remained widespread suspicion of the Chinese Antarctic group's eating habits at their new station on the mainland. The agreed measures adopted by SCAR, the international Scientific Committee on Antarctic Research, had stressed that the killing, wounding or capture of any mammal or bird native to Antarctica, or harmful interference with its natural habitat, was forbidden (whales were excepted, Davis noted). If the Chinese had broken that agreement by feeding off the penguin or seal population, they deserved to be ostracized by the Antarctic community.

There had been an unusual number of accidents, too, like that business with Dr. Jeffers, the UCLA scientist at the Operation Second Chance camp.

Davis shivered. He had wanted to go to the Outhouse himself early that morning, while the blizzard still howled. He had held on as long as he could, then used the emergency pail inside the hut to drop his load, drawing some muttered complaints from his companions. What if *he* had been the one to go outside? No one knew exactly when Jeffers had made his trip. What if he, an Antarctic novice, had emerged from the Outhouse to find the lifeline back to the Jamesway broken? Would he have been lucky enough to survive like Jeffers?

But accidents happened. Blizzards happened. This was a frontier after all. Conditions were often severe, almost always potentially dangerous. Nothing sinister there. The problem was—the problem with the problems—that they didn't add up to enough. There was no discernible pattern.

And for every story of discord he had heard, for every ugly incident, for every outburst of bad feeling, Davis had personally encountered something entirely different wherever he had gone on the Ice. A boisterous welcome at Vostok, the Russian station, where Soviet scientists had been eager to show him the record of their ice cores, which, plumbing the East Antarctic ice sheet, had peered deep into the earth's history to record events more than 150,000 years past. They had been even more eager to break out the vodka and almost pathetically hopeful that he had brought along a few fairly recent American magazines to ease the boredom of the coming winter. An equally warm reception at New Zealand's Scott base, Germany's Lili Marlene and the Aussie base on Commonwealth Bay. The people at any of these stations were so delighted to see new faces after weeks or months of uninterrupted isolation they had treated the American journalist like a long-lost relative. They were also eager for news of any kind about the world they had voluntarily left behind—for some of them, those who had wintered over, more than a year ago.

They made Davis think of Sir Ernest Shackleton, who had tried and failed to make the first crossing of the continent in 1914. When his ship *Endurance* was locked in impregnable ice for more than nine months and finally crushed, Shackleton and his party escaped in small boats and were marooned on the ice for more than a year. Leaving the rest of the crew on Elephant Island, in the spring of 1916 Shackleton and five of his men sailed over eight hundred miles across the stormy sea in a small boat, the *James Caird*, to reach South Georgia Island. After crossing the island on foot to reach a whaling station, the dirty, unkempt, exhausted explorer's first question of the station's manager was "Tell me, when was the war over?" The manager stared at this apparition, who had appeared out of nowhere, and said, "The war is not over. Millions are being killed. Europe is mad. The world is mad."

Like Shackleton, those whom Davis met at the Antarctic stations were full of anxious questions and frequently astonished by his answers.

Only the French had been a bit chilly. At Dumont d'Urville in Terre Adélie, Davis's reception had reminded him of the indifference—even mild hostility—he had often encountered as a tourist in Paris. Here, however, the reason soon became clear. The French were still smarting from Greenpeace demonstrations against the airstrip built across a string of several small islands near the base. The heavy construction, which displaced large numbers of penguins, also involved blasting the islands, leveling their surface and moving thousands of cubic yards of earth to connect the islands. The explosions killed an undetermined number of penguins and interfered with normal access to a large emperor penguin rookery. The widely publicized demonstrations had brought generally negative press coverage. Reporters, Davis discovered, were still viewed with suspicion at the French base.

But the story of the French airstrip was not new. Davis thought he could use it as an illustration of disintegrating relationships among the treaty nations, but how far could he take it? The airstrip was a lapse, but in other areas the French had been leaders in the drive to preserve the purity of the Ice.

Davis glanced once more at his notes. Maybe Greenpeace would save the day. If not for Antarctica, then for his series of articles.

He rummaged through the sheets of transcripts he had made from his taped interviews, found the one he wanted, pulled it out of the pile.

"Antarctica is under siege," the Greenpeace spokeswoman had declared with the fervor of a true believer. She had been an attractive young woman, Davis recalled, or else his brief sojourn on the Ice was already distorting his perspective. He usually wasn't attracted to true believers, even leggy blondes. Life had enough hard, inflexible edges without going out looking for them.

What was her name? Ah, here it was. Janet Morrison. And a few more words from Janet. "Antarctica used to be all science. That was it. But that's changing. The developers are knocking down the barricades. If we can't stop them, if we can't save this one beautiful place, how are we going to save the rest of the world?

Good question, Davis thought.

Maybe tomorrow, when he was scheduled to fly on to the new Chinese base, currently under siege itself by an encampment of Greenpeace protesters, he would find some answers.

He was still nagged by the feeling that he was missing something.

He shut down his laptop, packed it away with his notes and went through the now familiar ritual of dressing for below-zero cold: thermal underwear over his Jockey underwear, windproof trousers topped by close-weave field pants, a heavy wool plaid shirt under a Norwegian sweater, woolen mittens over gloves, boot liners inside his boots—everything layered for extra insulation. And for the final layer, his red NSF-issue parka, a hood, woolen balaclava over his face hiding the new red beard stubble, and the essential dark sunglasses.

Stepping outside, he immediately felt his skin shrivel with cold under all the protective clothing. The day was overcast. An ominous plume of smoke curling up from Mount Erebus was quickly shredded by winds. The same winds howled along the canyons of MacTown, carrying stinging snow. The muddy street outside the barracks, soft in yesterday's sunlight and higher temperatures, was frozen solid, the mud like sharp-edged waves.

Davis plodded through the relentless cold, head down, eyes narrowed to slits, toward the cafeteria. Funny how important the little things became: food, warmth, hot coffee, company.

That's the real goddamn story, Shafter, he thought. *Being in a place so hostile to life and staying alive.*

EIGHTEEN

THE FEELING OF STRANGENESS PERSISTED.

Though not appointed for tourists, the Soviet icebreaker and supply ship *Shevchenko* was comfortable enough. Kathy Mc-Neely was given a bare bones cabin about the size of a closet, but it was hardly more cramped than her polar tent. Here at least she could relax. It was warm and private, and the toilet was only a few steps along the corridor.

When she left the cabin, however, she had the sense of having stepped across a border into a strange country in which she was the only alien. She ran a gauntlet of eyes. The men aboard, Soviet sailors, hovered at a distance, staring, jumped out of her way or leaped to serve her slightest possible need. Their eyes never left her. She felt like a prized specimen exhibited in a cage.

At the captain's table for supper the first night she mentioned it to Volkov. "How long since they've seen a woman?" she asked.

Volkov laughed. "At least one year. For some is longer time. And for many, they have never been close to such a woman as yourself, *moya dorogaya*."

"I think you've been on the Ice too long yourself, Alex."

"Is not true."

The ship's captain was Anatoly Suganov, a burly, black-bearded Ukrainian who always seemed to be in the pilothouse whenever Kathy glanced up at it, no matter what the hour, as if he never left. There must have been intervals when he ducked below for a few hours' sleep, but she never caught him at it.

Suganov appeared in the officers' mess only for the evening meal. His manner with Kathy was gruff but courtly. With Volkov he was unexpectedly jovial. They spoke in Russian—Suganov knew little English, Volkov explained—and Kathy could only guess at the jokes that provoked spontaneous, table-pounding laughter.

Volkov's presence soon came to dominate the ship's company—even more than her own, Kathy thought. Her impact was an accident of sex; his was by force of personality.

Young Simanovich, in the company of familiars, was much more open and extroverted than he had been at the scientists' camp. Only when he was with Kathy and Volkov and the captain at supper did he revert to silence. She finally understood it as shyness.

"But of course, Katyusha," Volkov said when they were alone. "He is in love with you."

"That's nonsense!"

"Is no good to make it light," Volkov said.

"Make light of it, you mean."

"Just so." He smiled, making note of the idiom. "His heart is too heavy."

She glanced at him quickly, but she saw that he was not joking.

After the first day of sporadic sunshine, coastal clouds returned along with capricious winds. The air turned very cold, and the sea spray froze on the rails and decks, making footing treacherous whenever Kathy stepped outside. The sea was black under the cloud cover, the *Shevchenko* plowing its way as if through black virgin soil. On either side of the ship, thick brash ice beat time to their passage like whiskers on a drum. Kathy spent less time than she would have liked in the bow or on the open deck, driven inside by the cold winds.

Survivor, on the other hand, hated being inside. Like any dog sticking its head out of a car window into the breeze, the husky relished being out on deck, sniffing the sea air, head turned to face the winds. The cold did not bother him. When Kathy took him for a walk to exercise his leg, the ship's crew could follow their progress by listening to the clatter of the dog's metal brace against the deck.

The Soviet sailors, surprised as much by the dog's presence on board their ship as by the crutch he wore, quickly adopted him as a pet. Instead of being reserved or prickly over their rough horseplay, Survivor romped or wrestled with them as much as his cumbersome appendage would allow. Watching the sailors play with the husky or feed him scraps saved from their own meals, Kathy thought of Hurley's warning that Survivor was part of a feisty team, half wild, not a household pet.

"You've changed," she told the husky one evening—for he slept on the floor of her cabin each night. "Hurley wouldn't believe what's happened to you. I doubt he'd approve. You know what you've become?"

Survivor thumped his tail.

"A softy," she said, grinning. "You've turned into a pet."

With the dog as companion, the slow journey along the rim of the continent offered Kathy her first real opportunity to experience Antarctica through the eyes of a tourist. Until now it had been all work. Along one stretch of pack ice she watched hordes of crabeater seals scurry with startling speed over the ice as the ship passed nearby. She was intrigued and amused by a giant albatross that followed the ship for an entire day. She was enchanted by flights of small Antarctic petrels, dark wings shading back to a pencil line of white. The little birds appeared black against the pale silver of the clouds. Over the water they all but disappeared, visible only as a thin edge of white-tipped wings, like streaks of light.

Even more than the ordinary tourist, Kathy was particularly elated whenever she discovered healthy groups of penguins on the ice floes or bergs, perched on promontories of ice along the edge of the continent or, as they sometimes did, dolphining alongside the ship as if for the entertainment of the enthusiastic Soviet sailors. She spotted chinstraps and Adélies, the latter in a colony high up on a fist of black rock, and one small group of king penguins.

No emperors appeared, nor were any new victims spotted in the water or on the ice. But they were drawing closer, she knew, to the old emperor rookery. Closer, she was certain, with a mixture of hope and fear, to an answer to the latest man-made threat to the penguins and their environment.

Each morning there was thick fog or mist, making the ship's passage a mysterious journey into the unknown, its radar sweeping the black waters ahead for the presence of an invisible iceberg in their path. The mists glowed with unseen lights, the fading summer sun reflecting off ice crystals like sprinkled glitter.

On the fourth day dense pack ice forced the ship into a course farther from the coast. Later that day the *Shevchenko* pushed past a huge tabular iceberg locked in the permanent ice of a lagoon, the breeding ground for a colony of fur seals. At first Kathy thought the iceberg and its small bay were familiar, the ice of the lagoon resembling the sea ice of the oil-devastated penguin rookery she had come to a year ago. As the ship moved on and the light changed, the scene became strange once more.

The following morning the fog lifted. The ship broke out of pack ice into open water. Though the sky remained gray and overcast, an extraordinary seascape opened out before the ship. Across the floor of black water icebergs drifted in every imaginable size and shape: ice mesas and promontories, cones and obelisks, huge ghost ships dying slowly into the sea, enormous tables of ice, floating caves and arches that turned blue when the sun shot through a rift in the clouds. Kathy McNeely was reminded of western movies she had seen as a child in which striking vistas of Utah's Monument Valley provided a dramatic background for heroic adventures. Here the ocean was the black desert floor, the icebergs were her monuments.

The broken face of the continent was equally dramatic. The ship thrust past awesome sweeps of glaciers and icefalls, domes and ridges. Sometimes the ice and snow piled up like huge white children's blocks to form the shoreline. Here and there the mountains themselves descended to the sea, rough black cliffs with caps of snow.

When the fascinating icescapes and the hope of seeing more penguins kept Kathy out on deck in spite of the cold, Volkov frequently joined her. They took turns discovering signs of life along the ice edge or in the surrounding waters or identifying the flocks of birds. In such moments she felt very close to the Soviet scientist, enjoying his company, drawing warmth from his presence.

Brian Hurley would have been disappointed, though. Volkov never made a pass at her.

Not until the day they saw the whales.

They had gone out on deck together after supper. Survivor clattered on ahead to join a group of sailors. In communal silence Kathy and Volkov watched the landscape of snow and ice flow past them, as if the ship stood still and it were the land that moved. "It's like we've reached the center of the earth," Kathy murmured. "We've stopped, and the earth is rotating around us."

"Yes."

He was watching her, the full lips parted slightly, cheeks burned pink and eyes tearing from the cold air washing across the deck. But something caused her to stiffen, and Volkov's gaze followed hers.

Out on the smooth black expanse of water in front of the bow there was a great swelling, as if the ocean itself were lifting upward. There was a rustling, like a wind rushing through a forest. Then the blackness broke. A pair of humpback whales heaved up out of the deep, put up their flukes and sounded. Survivor, closer to the bow, barked excitedly.

Kathy's breath caught, and her heart raced. She realized that the ship's engine had slowed almost to a stop. Soviet sailors crowded the bow, many of them carrying cameras and snapping away furiously in spite of the poor light. Captain Suganov, too, watched the spectacle from his windowed perch in the pilot-house.

The great whales stayed in sight for several minutes, their massive bulks flowing smoothly and gracefully through the dark water. Aware of the ship behind them, they separated and slowed, allowing the *Shevchenko* to come abreast. Then they swam on either side of her, keeping pace, like tugboats escorting the ship safely through their domain. The whale nearest the ship was off the port bow, where Kathy hugged the rail. It was close enough for her to see the knobs on its huge head and the barnacles on its body. It suddenly dived beneath the surface, offering the spectators a view of its deeply notched flukes. When it resurfaced, it gave them a prolonged serenade, a crescendo of eerily moving whistles that set Survivor off again, barking as he danced along the railing, slamming his brace against the deck.

At last, slowly, the two whales dropped back, joining each other in the wake of the ship. As if withdrawing reluctantly from a stage, the giant creatures sank back out of sight. The sea closed over them, seamless.

Kathy began to breathe again.

Volkov, standing beside her, put an arm around her shoulders. The gesture seemed natural. In that emotional moment, thrilled by what she had just witnessed, the majesty of those giant creatures viewed so intimately in their elemental beauty and power, Kathy did not resist but leaned against him.

After a moment Volkov swung her toward him, tilted her face upward and kissed her. Her first thought was that his lips were cold. Frost from his beard was cool against her cheek. But there was a radiant heat from his body that was like a stove.

His arms bound her like padded steel coils. His mouth was

insistent on hers. She felt a softness within her, the desire to yield, as if she were very, very tired.

"Katya . . ."

"No, Alex . . ."

She pushed free, finding a strength she didn't know she had. Without the warmth of his body pressing against her, she felt suddenly cold, exposed to the icy blasts swirling across the deck. She hugged herself tightly.

"It was perhaps the wrong moment."

"No . . . no, it was the right moment. I'm just not—"

She realized that it was the moment she loved, the time and the place and all it meant to her, not Volkov himself. And that wasn't good enough. She might be lonely, but this was not a good trade-off. She was not, she thought ruefully, very liberated.

She remembered Brian Hurley's wry warning about the danger of the Antarctic affection syndrome. It had made her vulnerable. Aleksei Volkov would have been an attractive man under any circumstances. Here, after two months in virtual isolation with him, sharing deprivations and discoveries, after days on board ship with him in increasing intimacy, she had about as much resistance as mush.

Almost, Hurley, she thought. *Almost . . .*

"There's a Mrs. Volkov, isn't there, Alex?"

For a moment he was silent. Then he chuckled. "Yes, of course, there is Mrs. Volkov. Ludmilla. She is in Moscow. You are here."

"Are there any children? You've never talked about them," she persisted, more firmly in control—not only of herself, she realized, but of him as well.

Volkov sighed melodramatically. "There is Dmitri, he is scientist like me, and Natalia. She is very pretty like you. She is seventeen."

"Do you have pictures?"

"Yes, I have picture. Katya—"

"That was very nice, Alex. It was a beautiful moment to

remember, and that's the way I want to remember it. You're not in love with me, I'm not in love with you and that's very important to me."

There was a shading of amusement in his eyes as he studied her. "You are romantic, yes?"

"That's as good a word as any."

"Maybe you will change your mind."

"I wouldn't count on it," she said, laughing.

Volkov smiled in response. He was really a very charming man, she thought. If only charm were enough for her. Hurley had no charm at all, and—

And why was she thinking of Hurley anyway?

"I am like Soviet sailor on *Shevchenko*. Is very long time from Moscow."

"You'll survive, Alex," she said dryly. "And I'm not going to take pity on you."

He laughed outright then, the boisterous laughter that was an expression of his vitality, his robust acceptance of life, and they were friends again, Antarctic comrades, closer in that moment than they would ever be again.

NINETEEN

THE DOGS MILLED AROUND, barking and yipping and snapping at one another with excitement. They were so unruly Brian Hurley had trouble connecting the traces of two of the more intractable dogs, Muley and Crazy, to the sledge.

When the team was hooked up, Hurley found that the sledge's ten-foot plastic-sheathed runners were frozen in the snow. He freed them by rocking the sledge back and forth sideways, exciting the dogs even more.

The ice cracked, and the sledge sprang free. With a wild clamor the huskies were off.

Berkowski shouted at his cameraman. "You getting this? You getting this?"

Maneuvering for position, the cameraman lost his footing and took a pratfall in the snow. His camera flew into a drift.

Berkowski screamed after Hurley, "Come back! Goddamn it, Hurley, come back here!"

But there was no stopping now, even if Hurley had wanted to. The snow was hard and slick; the sledge fairly flew over it. Fanned out ahead of the sledge, the huskies, inactive for several days, were fresh and eager. They were doing what they had been bred and trained for. This was their element.

Hurley glanced back over his shoulder. The photographer was on his feet, brushing snow from his equipment. Berkowski was flapping his arms as if he were trying to fly.

Hurley grinned. Then the sledge dipped over a ridge, slewed through drift snow in the trough and leveled out. Hurley's abandoned camp, the television crew and its helo, the tiny Operation Second Chance camp near the ice edge and the bank of coastal fog into which the Russian icebreaker had disappeared; all slipped behind the ridge and were gone.

He was alone.

Hurley felt the same kind of release, he guessed, that the dogs felt. *This* was what he had come to the Ice for—not getting his face on the tube but accepting the challenge of one small corner of this beautiful, terrible wilderness.

To hell with Berkowski.

That first day's run was a long, steady climb up the narrow tributary of ice that branched off the main body of the Hartsook Glacier. The air was magically clear, offering sweeping vistas of endless whiteness—steep white cliffs, long smooth white flanks, broad white rivers of ice—all glittering in the sun like the bright lights of a thousand Broadways. Every rock protruding from the snow was starkly etched. The shadows were long and sharply drawn, throwing every seam or ripple of the surface into relief. And in all this vast white stillness, the rattling of the sledge and the puffing of the dogs were the only sounds.

The hard climbing of the morning gave the team a chance to settle down, find their legs and rhythm. It allowed Hurley to regain his feel for the sledge and his rapport with the huskies. By afternoon they were together, keenly attuned to one another's movements and responses, as if he were one of them.

They left the coast behind. The wind off the snow-covered mountains was clear and cold, without smell or smoke or dust, its purity absolute. It was also very dry, and Hurley's first stop was necessary to slake his thirst and that of the dogs. As always in Antarctica, water would be one of their acute needs at every stage.

At the fork where the smaller vein of ice linked with the more massive bulk of the glacier, separate plates of ice had collided with a force that caused them to buckle and break and heave upward. There was no way through. Hurley detoured almost a full mile along the broken seam before he found a ribbon of smooth ice that led him up to the surface of the glacier.

By then it was late afternoon, and he paused to take stock. The dogs had run well. There had been no serious mishaps. They had covered only about twelve miles; but it was the first day, and he was reluctant to push the team—or himself—too far.

Over the past two months Hurley had scouted his route up the glacier, planning ahead for next year's polar run. He had picked out the sites of two advance bases he would use as emergency supply depots. A flyover in the HTV helicopter had enabled him to confirm his route insofar as that could be done without being down on the ice. The trail involved two extensive but necessary detours, one around a treacherous-looking icefall and the other skirting a large field of crevasses.

The first base camp along the route, where Berkowski and crew would be waiting for him after flying ahead, was about eighteen miles up the glacier. If he got an early start in the morning, he would have no trouble—barring the unforeseen—reaching the camp by the end of the second day.

Picking out a level stretch of snow in the lee of a steep shoulder of the mountain about a mile ahead, Hurley decided to call it a day.

That night he had his first real taste of solitude.

It came after the routine of setting up camp was over. He fastened the polar tent with ice screws and storm guys. He secured a canvas tarpaulin over the sledge and its cargo of supplies. He carefully checked over each dog for soreness or limping, paying particular attention to scratches or cuts on their pads. Bones had one torn pad, not serious. Otherwise the dogs were in good shape, hardly tested by their day's work.

Then Hurley filled the Primus stove with kerosene and fired it up, both to warm his tent and to melt snow for cooking and drinking. He would keep the water pan going much of the night. In the field there was never enough water.

After a half hour's rest he fed the dogs and heated a can of hash for himself. Only then did he get ready to settle in for the night.

Preparing for his Antarctic adventure, Hurley had read everything by and about the early explorers of the continent that he could get his hands on. One book, *Alone,* was a harrowing account by Admiral Richard Byrd of his winter alone, in 1934, at the advance base he had established on the ice inland from Little America. In the book Byrd had tried to fathom what drove him and others like him toward such isolation. He explained it as the desire to be totally by himself, to experience peace and solitude long enough to find out just how good they really were.

Hurley didn't think of himself as much of a philosopher. Byrd, too, he thought, was more impressive in what he had done than in trying to make sense of it. Hurley tended to be impatient with discussion, debate, planning. It was the doing that mattered. But he felt the sense of being alone that night more than he ever had before, cut off from the world and all its trappings. For a long time he stood outside his tent. There was cloud cover, and the sun was cut off by the mountains, so he was surrounded by a kind of silvery twilight. And an awesome stillness. It was not simply an absence of sound but a force in itself, a weight of silence, absolute and concentrated. *This is what Byrd was talking about,* he thought. *This is what he felt.*

Hurley went inside the tent, hung up his goggles, mittens and face mask to dry out and slipped into his sleeping bag, shivering until it began to warm up from his body heat.

He thought the silence would crush the tent, burying him.

When the stillness broke, he jerked erect, heart hammering.

He fell back, chuckling ruefully at first, then descending into helpless laughter at himself.

Outside the tent a melancholy chorus of wails and yips filled the night with sound. The crying of the huskies was not really melancholy, Hurley knew from experience; it only sounded that way to human ears. What he listened to now was in fact an exultant song. They were glad to be in the field again. Theirs was a song of fulfillment.

When the dogs fell silent at last, burrowing into the snow to make their own warm nests, the silence was, if anything, even more complete.

In this solitude, drifting toward sleep, Hurley dreamed he saw, in the darkness of the tent, an image of Kathy McNeely's face. Hovering behind her, visible just over her shoulder, was Alex Volkov.

He saw the helo midway through the second day. It came low enough that even though he could not be certain he saw Hal Berkowski inside the bubble, he did see the eye of the camera tilted toward him and the huskies. Hurley hoped the helo wasn't going to try to sit down. The surface of the ice was rippled by sastrugi, like waves frozen in place, with hard, sharp-edged crests and troughs soupy with soft snow. The sledge had taken a pounding all day from the uneven surface, and it was no more hospitable for landing an aircraft safely.

But after a few moments circling over him, the helicopter veered off and flapped on ahead. In minutes it was gone. The stillness returned like water filling a depression.

Framed by the mountains on either side, the enormous mass of the glacier dominated Hurley's vision, pale blue in places where it was scoured clean of snow by winds, emerald green in the depths of its crevasses, but over the rest of its surface covered in whiteness, snow whiter than white.

On most of that surface, no man, no living creature of any kind, had ever left a mark.

Berkowski was waiting when Hurley and the dog sledge team plodded up the slope of ice toward the field base. The television crew had already set up a tent, securing it to the helicopter—assuring, Hurley thought, that if winds came up during the night powerful enough to pick up the helo and send it flying, it would carry the tent with it. Smothered in full Antarctic gear, for the weather had turned colder during the day, Berkowski directed his cameraman as he filmed Hurley's arrival.

Waving the HTV man off, Hurley set about pitching his own tent and looking after the dogs, a routine he never varied. This time two of the huskies had cuts in their pads serious enough to require treatment with antibiotic ointment.

Hurley accepted an invitation to join the television crew for a hot meal in their tent. The fare, frozen steaks grilled over a Primus and accompanied by pan-fried frozen potatoes and fresh bread brought from MacTown, was better than Hurley would have prepared for himself, and the crew was laughing and friendly, seemingly elated with itself.

"Great stuff, Hurley!" Berkowski assured him. "Those shots we got today are terrific. And the stuff we shot when you were kicking it off, I thought we'd lost all that, but it came out great. Even when the camera went flying, we can even use that."

"Glad to hear it."

He should have been glad of the company, the good food, the sense of satisfaction over the first two days of his climb. He found himself wishing they all would go away.

Berkowski cornered him after eating. "Hey, listen, man, you're gonna be on your own for a few days, okay? I don't want you to think we're just, like, leaving you out here to twist in the wind, you know. But we've got to head back to

McMurdo to fill up our tanks, so to speak. The boys need a break."

Hurley felt like rejoicing. He wanted to jump up and shout.

"Hey, you're going great," Berkowski said, misreading Hurley's silence. "We'll meet you up there where you marked a second base camp, beyond that falls."

"That's about three, four days from here."

"Yeah, yeah, well, it'll take us that long, you know. Listen, are you okay with this, Hurley? Because if you're not . . ."

Hurley grinned. He was tempted to test Berkowski's reaction by saying he felt abandoned but thought better of it. Getting the camera out of his face, and Berkowski out of his hair, was a consummation devoutly to be wished and under no circumstances to be jeopardized. "I'm okay," he said. "It's supposed to be a one-man run, me and the dogs against the wilderness."

"Yeah, right, right! And it's going to be a great show. Trust me on this, Hurley. It's gonna be Emmy time!"

Lying in his tent later that night, Hurley wondered why he couldn't share any of Berkowski's enthusiasm. He told himself that nothing had changed, that he was doing what he had come to the Ice to do. But it was only when he was out there on the ice, alone with the dogs, that he felt the exhilaration. The show business part of it was something else.

He thought of McNeely heading off into the sea ice on that Soviet ship. Doing something with her life. Volkov, too, he supposed. Yeah, sure, Volkov, too. *Maybe that's your problem,* he told himself. *Play time has gone on too long.*

He wasn't ready for nine to five. He might never be ready for that. But maybe he was ready to go back to doing some of the work he had been trained for.

Maybe he could think about living a more normal life.

With someone.

Hurley scowled, crawled out of his warm sleeping bag to

drop another chunk of hard snow into the water pan and struggled back into the bag.

Crazy thoughts to be having, two thousand feet up a mountain covered with ice.

TWENTY

LEN SEARS BROKE OFF HIS PACING of the long prefabricated shed that served Rupert Merrill as a combination office, radio room, medical supply center and sleeping quarters. The two bunks at one end of the shed were shared by Merrill and Sears. There were bookshelves overhead and military lockers at the foot of each bunk.

Sears shrugged into his parka, pulled on mittens and opened the door to a vestibule, a heat-lock entry with double doors that prevented cold air from penetrating directly into the shed. He quickly closed the outer door behind him.

He was back a moment later. "He's pokin' around again," Sears said as he dragged off the mittens and hung them up. "I guess he's given up on the chopper for tonight."

There was satisfaction in Sears's tone, the smugness of a man who has put something over on someone.

"I'm surprised he hasn't got it going before now. He's practically torn both of those engines down and put them back together."

Sears, who was an expert mechanic, shrugged. "Ice crystals get into your fuel line like that, you got to clean everything out. It's like those clots of blood from your cholesterol that plug up an artery and bingo!"

"You think he suspects it wasn't just accidental?"

"Why should he? You got ice forming everywhere you look. For a pilot down here, what happened isn't unusual. Forbes said it's happened to him before. I'm tellin' you, Merrill, that's not what's bugging him. He's been nosing around about *us,* asking too many damned questions."

"Is he going to be able to fly out of here soon?"

"Sure." Sears's expression became sly. "Unless you want him to have some other problem, delay him some more . . ."

"Leave him alone," said Merrill. "We've stalled him as long as we can. I don't think he's so anxious to go flying around on a wild-penguin chase anymore."

"But what if he's got some answers about our operation? Or makes some educated guesses?"

"Guesses about what? He knows we have a second camp, that's obvious. What else can he know?"

"If some of those bigmouths have been talking . . ."

"Nobody's telling him anything. They know better."

"Don't be too sure."

Merrill, whose tolerance of Sears after the fiasco at the Operation Second Chance camp had worn so thin as to be transparent, stared at his assistant. Sears was nervous—for good reason. Merrill's anger was one of them.

Over the past five years, ever since Merrill had singled him out during an oil drilling operation, Sears had been a useful man. Sears could fix anything mechanical—or rig a problem if that's what was needed. It was his skill as an oil field trouble-shooter with pumps and seals, flow line devices and drilling systems that had first caught Merrill's attention. Sears was also loyal because it was to his advantage to be loyal. Not bothered by scruples. Willing to do whatever had to be done.

A little too willing to cut corners, as it had turned out.

A useful man who was becoming a liability.

"What do you figure to do with Forbes, Lenny? Push him

out in the next blizzard and hope he gets buried? You got away with that once—so far. It won't work twice."

Sears's weather-beaten face turned gray. "You told me to take care of that scientist," he muttered.

"I told you to stay away from him! I told you to make yourself scarce. I sure as hell didn't tell you to try to kill him!" Merrill's simmering anger, contained for the past week, exploded. "You understand what you nearly did? You nearly buried *us*, Lenny! If that crazy stunt had blown up in our faces, and it's only pure dumb luck it didn't, this whole damned project would've been finished! *We'd* have been finished. Kusic would've seen to that. First order of business, Lenny: Get rid of the fuck-ups. If it had got out that someone from TERCO tried to knock off an environmental scientist who was here to save the penguins, TERCO would have been down the toilet. People are funny about murder, Lenny. They get all worked up about it."

"It was an accident," Sears protested weakly.

"Don't kid yourself you could've made that stick. It would've been murder."

Merrill thought about Ron Kusic's reaction had Sears's bungled attempt ever come out. Kusic, sitting up there in his glass-walled office in Houston passing judgment on events half a world away in miles and an entirely different dimension in reality, was not the kind of man who would show any forgiveness or mercy. Christian virtues weren't his thing.

Merrill thought he understood Kusic. He was a cold-eyed son of a bitch with a colder heart. Hard. A gambler, with the guts to risk everything if the prize was big enough. Kusic had what fight managers called a fire in the belly. Only he didn't burn just to beat someone up. He was a player in a much bigger game with much higher stakes.

Once, after Kusic had pulled off one of his early takeovers, Merrill had been with him in his penthouse apartment when that right-hand man of his, Pete Rodriguez, had brought the news that Kusic had come out on top in a bitter proxy fight. The board of directors of the small, family-owned pipeline company

Kusic was taking over had resigned in the face of defeat. Kusic was in charge.

Merrill had started to leave, thinking Kusic and Rodriguez would want to be alone to celebrate, but Kusic had waved him back into his chair.

There'd been no jumping up and down, no fist pumped in the air, none of that "We're number one!" collegiate bullshit.

Just a tight, satisfied smile.

Later, drinking champagne, Kusic had relaxed. He had talked more than Merrill had ever heard him open up, before or since.

"People are funny, Merrill. They're inconsistent. They won't take their own ideas to the limit." He interrupted himself to stare toward the new neon sign on top of TERCO Tower, clearly visible from the living room of the downtown apartment. "Nobody believes in God anymore. They don't want to admit it, but they don't. So they know that all the old morality stuff is nothing more than the sting operation of all time, something the human race dreamed up so we can all feel good about ourselves, so we can think we're better than the other animals. They know this, but they're not willing to accept what it means. They want to keep pretending."

"Rules are a useful social convention," Merrill said, emboldened by champagne and the rarity of drinking with the boss.

"You're goddamned right rules are useful. Laws are useful. Right and wrong, they're useful notions. But that's all they are. Which means . . . do you get it yet, Merrill?"

"Well, sir . . ."

"When they stop being useful to you, they don't mean diddly. Don't let them get in your way. You want to climb all the way to the top of the ladder, Merrill, I can see it in your eyes. You won't climb far with a lot of unnecessary baggage."

Merrill grinned. "I'm beginning to get it."

"Sure you are. Listen . . . my old man used to come home drunk every Saturday night and beat the shit out of me and my mom. Then Sunday morning he'd put on a clean shirt and go off to church. We had to mouth all the standard pulpit stuff, like the

Ten Commandments and the seven deadly sins. It was all make-believe, Merrill, you understand?"

"Yes, sir."

"You take those seven deadly sins. Let me tell you, they're not sins at all, except maybe one of them. I can still remember them. *Pride*—you've got to have that or there's no fuel in the engine. *Covetousness* . . . why the hell should you break your back if you can't get what you want? *Lust,* that goes without saying. You don't feel it, you're half a man. *Anger* . . . you need that so you won't ever go soft. If you're not angry with what's been done to you or what one part of society has that you don't have, then you'll be happy being someone else's gofer for the rest of your life. *Gluttony* . . ." Kusic dismissed that, too, as anything but sinful. "Listen, if you don't want to gobble up everything, all the food you can eat, all the good booze, every woman you meet, you're lying to yourself. You know that bumper sticker you see, the one that says, 'He Who Has the Most Toys Wins'? No truer words, Merrill. That says it in a nutshell."

He paused. "So what have I left out?"

"Envy," said Merrill.

"Hey, you remember 'em, too! *Envy,* that's right, more fuel in the tank, one of the things that drives you. You see what the winners have, how they live, you're green to have it. That's no sin, Merrill. You need it. What it all comes down to is this: There's only one of those deadlies left, and it's the only one that's really a sin because it's the one that will make you a loser. *Sloth.* Get off your ass, Merrill. That's what that sin is all about." Kusic chuckled, amused with his own conceit. "Listen to what I'm telling you, Merrill. You can *use* those deadlies once you know what they're all about, use 'em to your advantage. As long as you don't let them hamstring you, and most of the men you go up against believe in them, you've got one hell of an edge going in. You know what I'm saying?"

"Yeah, Mr. Kusic, I hear you."

And he had heard, Merrill thought. He'd learned more from Kusic than anyone else he'd met or was likely to meet.

He stared thoughtfully at Len Sears. Maybe he was being too hard on Lenny, but it wasn't what Sears had done that stoked his anger; it was the way he had done it. He'd been stupid, exposing the entire TERCO Antarctic operation to unacceptable risk. First there had been the penguins turning up in the ocean and on the ice near that Operation Second Chance base camp, firing up the ire of those scientists, especially the woman, who was now off on a crusade. Merrill didn't think McNeely and her colleagues would find anything, but you could never be certain. Sears should have made sure about those penguins.

Then there was Dr. Jeffers. All he had told Sears to do was to stay out of sight and let Jeffers forget about him and what he might have said. Instead Lenny had taken it upon himself to eliminate the problem.

If you're going to do something, do it. Merrill could almost hear Kusic's voice, his scornful judgment of failure. Sears had botched it. Now Forbes was a potential problem.

That was another thing Merrill had learned from Kusic: One mistake breeds another. Always. Make one stupid move, and you have to make another to cover it, and another after that. It was like a chain, everything linked.

That Sears had blundered stupidly, not once but twice, was a given. What wasn't yet clear was whether or not the damage had been sufficiently repaired. They had caulked up a hole, that was all. If the caulk didn't hold, the whole damned ship would sink.

The radio transmission from McMurdo Station that evening brought a cautionary warning about a deterioration in the weather pattern over most of Antarctica. Blizzards had been recorded over the polar plateau, and major storms were heading toward McMurdo Station and other parts of the coastline. TERCO's base was in the path of one of the storms.

"You better batten down the hatches, boys," the navy caller said.

Merrill, who was in the shed with Sears just before supper when the radio crackled into life, said, "Thanks for the warning."

"Listen, is Hank Forbes still with you people? We've got a message for him."

"A message? Yeah, he's here . . . I don't know where he is right now, but I can take a message for him."

"I guess you can pass it along. Tell Hank some reporter is trying to get hold of him, a guy named Davis from Los Angeles. He's up at the Pole, and he hasn't been able to get through to you guys by radio, there's been a lot of atmospheric noise."

"What's it about?"

"Davis wants Hank to ferry him around. Just pass it on, okay?"

"Sure," Merrill said. "We'll make sure he gets the message."

"And don't forget to tie everything down that weighs less than a ton. They say this blizzard comes with a capital *B*."

When the radio's crackle fell silent, Merrill and Sears stared at each other. Sears chewed his lower lip.

"Take it easy," said Merrill.

"But that reporter . . . him and Forbes had their heads together on the way to MacTown when we took Jeffers back. And afterward, too. They were getting real buddy-buddy. What does he want with Forbes now?"

"Don't jump to conclusions, Lenny. Maybe it's nothing to get stirred up about. Davis is just a reporter."

"That's just it! He's digging, Merrill. He's looking for something. And he's going after Forbes."

Rupert Merrill did not immediately reply. For once, he thought, Sears could be right. Why would Mike Davis suddenly be so anxious to talk to Forbes? What was he after?

"When Forbes hears about the storms brewing up, at least that'll keep him here on the ground," Sears said. "He won't be able to start snooping from the air the way he said he was going to. The storm will kill that."

"No," Merrill answered.

Decision time, he thought. Time to decide, as Ron Kusic might have said, whether or not he bought in to all the Sunday gospel morality he had heard as a child. Even if the threat to the TERCO discovery was slim, it couldn't be dismissed. The word from Houston was that Kusic was going to announce the Antarctic discovery soon. Merrill couldn't let that dramatic revelation be undermined by an ugly story about TERCO's responsibility for oil-soaked penguins or, worse, an attempted murder.

He couldn't let Forbes and Davis get together. Not now.

Win or lose, Merrill thought. Kusic was right. There really wasn't anything else.

"What do you mean?" Sears asked nervously.

"The weather's fine. Look outside."

"But—"

"No buts, Lenny. You never heard about a storm, right?"

The uncertainty remained in Sears's eyes.

"It's time we helped Forbes get out of here. Give him a hand, Lenny, okay?"

As Sears began to understand, the uneasy question in his eyes gave way to relief. "I get it. But isn't someone going to wonder why he took off? I mean, we *did* get that radio message."

"And as far as anyone will ever know, we told Forbes. But you know how these pilots are. Forbes had to do it his way. He thought he could outrun the storm."

Sears nodded vigorously, enthusiasm growing. "Yeah," he muttered. "Yeah . . ."

"Three strikes and you're out," said Merrill softly. "This time there can't be any mistake. Am I getting through to you?"

"Sure, sure, I understand . . . don't worry about it."

"Just don't screw up."

TWENTY-ONE

ANTARCTICA HAD HELD BACK for most of the past two weeks, pulling its punches, letting its weaknesses show, hiding its strengths.

On Brian Hurley's seventh day on the Hartsook Glacier, the weather changed without warning.

It had been a long day's climb. Over hard, wind-sculptured, compacted snow, on the way to becoming ice and just as slippery. Through soft snow that clung and drifted and dragged. Over two different crevasses, each no more than three feet across, but bottomless. Each spanned by a thin snowbridge.

The bridges held.

A third crevasse was wider. Twelve feet across, Hurley judged. Even where a crust of snow, which appeared to be several feet thick and as wide as a road, bridged the gap, Hurley didn't trust it. The fissure cut across the glacier, splitting it as far as he could see in either direction.

Hurley headed east on a path that ran parallel to the fault toward the steep, snow-covered wall of a mountain peak. If the crack ran into the precipice, he would be stymied. He'd have to retrace his steps and try the western side of the glacier. But

Hurley guessed that as the crevasse drew near the mountain, the glacier would be denser, packed so tightly under such enormous pressure that any split or gap would have been forced shut.

A quarter mile from the bottom of the snow cliff the crevasse narrowed to a slit and disappeared under a thick blanket of powder snow. Hurley halted the dogs. Cautiously, step by step, he walked across the snow. Under his layered clothing he was sweating. Returning, he used a pick to chop at the snow every three feet. Each blow struck more solid snow or ice beneath the powder.

Hurley took his place at the rear of the sledge. "Let's do it, guys—mush!"

In seconds they were safely across. Hurley breathed more easily.

The next few minutes had the huskies laboring again, however, hauling the sledge up a mound, floundering for traction in deep snow. Gaining the top of the rise, Hurley was rewarded with a long view over a twenty-mile sweep of the glacier to the west, where it ended at a sawtooth ridge of small, snow-covered peaks that presented a profile like filed teeth. As he stared across the way, iceblink hurt his eyes, making them water. He thought he must have been mistaken in what he saw. A field of snow rising up on the far edge of the glacier like a ghost. He opened his eyes to peer again across the way.

He hadn't been mistaken. The snow surface had lifted up like gossamer skirts in a gust of air. Now the white cloud began to break up into separate swirls, spiraling upward like dust devils on a parched prairie.

The twisters marched across the glacier toward Hurley, picking up more dry white powder as they danced over the surface of the glacier. A chill seized the back of Hurley's neck. The icy fingers slid downward as the sweat cooled on his body.

He looked around for some kind of shelter.

There was no mistaking what he saw. The blizzard was gaining speed and strength as it howled toward him. It was also gaining volume, building like the united voice of a crowd in a great stadium. Already the spinning clouds of snow were merging, losing themselves in what quickly became a solid wall of snow that blotted out the distant, saw-toothed peaks, erased the horizon, filled the sky.

The mountain slope behind Hurley offered no visible shelter from the wind. The nearest bluff was a steep, smooth face, rising five hundred feet in one sheer climb. Ahead of him the great river of ice flowed out of a distant pass that was Hurley's next goal—visible for the first time, then quickly blotted out as the blowing snow filled the pass.

There was nothing to hide behind. Nothing to blunt the full force of the blizzard.

Reacting instinctively, Hurley yelled at the dogs, "Left! That's it, left! Go, go! Come on, Dutch, show 'em the way!"

The dogs wheeled in a circle, catching the urgency in Hurley's commands. Coming about, they plunged back down the slope of the mound they had just climbed. It wasn't much protection, Hurley thought. Not much at all.

Then he saw a heel of the bluff jutting from the base of the mound of snow. Not snow but solid firn or ice. He slewed around the corner of the heel and drove the sledge deep into the snow.

"Dig in, guys!" he shouted needlessly.

The rising wind blew his words away like leaves in a gale.

He had only a few minutes before the wall of snow would reach him. He planted the aluminum poles of his tent and threw the fabric over them. A gust nearly tore the tent from his grasp. On the second try he got it in place, snugged down over the poles, the single opening facing away from the direction of the storm. He pounded ice screws into the near corners, praying they would bite into solid ice. He felt the satisfying jar through his hands as each screw sank in and held. With the other screws hammered into place, he dragged the sledge over one edge of the tent, which had extended aprons on each side that could be weighted down. There was no time to find something for the other side.

The dogs, storm wise, had already dug into the snow. Most of them were no longer visible. The roar of the storm became a scream. Hurley dived into his tent and secured the opening behind him, seconds before the storm engulfed him in mind-numbing chaos.

The wind screamed. The side walls of the tent flapped like sheets on a line. The malevolent uproar of the storm filled Hurley's mind. The murky air inside the tent, which had become dense with powder snow that clogged his nose and throat, made it hard to breathe; in much the same way the fury in his brain made it impossible to think clearly.

After a while—Hurley lost all sense of time—almost imperceptibly the assault began to diminish. The tiny, enclosed world of Hurley's tent became quieter, more stable. The shuddering din of the blizzard, muffled now, receded from Hurley's brain.

Some minutes passed before he grew uneasy over the deepening silence. The side walls of his tent, bowing inward, provided the first clear warning. When he checked the tent's entrance, he found the tunnel too narrow even to crawl through. The side had been pushed inward. He threw his shoulder against the opening, then turned around and slammed both feet toward it.

His boots smacked into snow with little effect. No amount of pushing or shoving or kicking would move the impassive weight that blocked the only exit. Hurley felt the familiar, smothering grip of claustrophobia. He began to gasp for breath. He should have been more alert. The wildness of the storm had obsessed him. He should have sensed what was happening.

The roof of the tent was sagging under the weight of the drifts piling up on top of it.

The blizzard still raged outside, as loud and violent as before. He could no longer hear it. He was being buried under the drifts, as the raging winds sculpted a new mountain of snow on top of him.

TWENTY-TWO

————————

FOR THE FIRST TIME IN A WEEK the twin turbojet engines of Hank Forbes's Bell UH-1N helicopter settled into a satisfyingly powerful whine. He opened the throttle by twisting the grip mounted on the end of the collective pitch stick, bringing the main rotor up to speed. Checking his instruments methodically, he listened anxiously for any skip in the steady flow of power.

The mystery seemed solved: ice crystals in the fuel. Hardly a mystery at all here on the Ice, where machinery commonly froze, seized up or became brittle and broke under pressure. Ice had downed more than a few aircraft over Antarctica, whether by corrupting fluids or by coating wings and fuselage until the sheer weight of it brought disaster.

Searching for the cause of the Huey's sudden engine problems, Forbes had gone over the chopper like a hobbyist stripping down a venerated classic in his garage and putting it back together. It had taken him five frustrating days to isolate the fuel problem, another two days to clean out the lines and fuel residues.

To his credit, Len Sears had pitched in at the last minute to help out. A good mechanic, Forbes had discovered, somewhat to his surprise. Working hand in hand with Forbes last night, Sears had also proved to be unexpectedly amiable. Most of the TERCO crew had been friendly all along, but Sears and Merrill only superficially. Forbes had been around the block often enough to recognize a smile that never reached a man's eyes, a heartiness that rang false. That still applied to Merrill, but Sears had been genuinely helpful, not afraid to get his hands dirty or his fingers frozen.

And Merrill, Forbes admitted grudgingly, had been generous with the emergency aircraft fuel stored here, as it was at many field bases regularly visited by helos and supply planes.

Iceblink caught his eye, causing him to gaze off to the north, where the skies were darker than normal over the Southern Ocean, mother of storms. Immediately overhead there were only patchy clouds. The temperature had dropped to twenty-two degrees below zero, and the barometer was down slightly. There had been nothing ominous in the forecast from MacTown that Sears had relayed to him.

Forbes ran through his safety checklist more quickly than normal. After all, he'd been over the entire aircraft so thoroughly these past few days he was confident nothing else was wrong. The dual turbine engines, which normally thrived in Antarctica's thin dry air and extreme cold, were running smoothly. The rotor's flapping was music to his ears. None of his instruments was frozen.

Clear for takeoff, he thought. He wanted out of here.

A cluster of TERCO's people had come out of their tents and huts to watch him, alerted by the scream of the turbojets and the rhythmic wop-wop-wop of the rotors. In the eerie stillness of an Antarctic morning their combined uproar crashed over the ice shelf and exploded in the mountain canyons like rolling thunder. Kornievski, the pipe fitter from Hamtramck, thrust a fist of encouragement into the air. Forbes waved at him and the others, not sure they could see him through the cloud of snow stirred up by the main rotor. He eased up on the collective, heard the change in pitch of the rotor and breathed a sigh of satisfaction.

An instant later he was airborne.

The sense of release and freedom was overwhelming. On land, he thought, he flopped around like a fish out of water, impatient and quickly irritable. In the air he was himself again. Maybe not an Iron Eagle anymore, but a winged creature in his natural element.

Looking down as he swung over the TERCO base, he saw Sears and Merrill standing together just outside the office shed, both men shielding their eyes with their hands as they peered upward through dark glasses. Maybe they were as glad to see him go as he was happy to be out of there.

Forbes briefly wondered if the opposite was true. It had crossed his mind, as he fumed over the usually reliable Huey, that Merrill might want him grounded. That way he couldn't go off hunting for that other TERCO camp or, for that matter, searching for evidence of any recent oil damage along the coast-line that he could pass along to the scientific rescue group. Forbes had the impression that Merrill hadn't been happy about his announced intention to fly over the coastline.

He set his course for the coast to the northwest. He hardly had need of his instruments. Below him a pair of glaciers ran out of the mountains, pointing his way toward their ultimate desti-nation, the sea.

Forbes skipped low over the nearer of the two glaciers, his skids no more than fifty feet above the snow, scanning the surface until snow glare made him look away. He was struck by the futility of trying to locate TERCO's second camp in all this wilderness. It could even be down there on the glacier, a few specks of color visible only by lucky chance. Trying to find it was like trying to spot a small boat in the middle of an ocean.

He had one clue, something one of the crew, a young engi-neer named Westcott, had said. "You really think that lady doc-tor might come looking for a fuel spill near the coast?"

"I think so," Forbes had answered. "She was making plans for it when I left her camp."

"She won't find anything now."

But when Forbes had pressed him, Westcott had become evasive. He had offered only one other comment. "If she's anything like Sears says she is, I just wish I were down at our other camp. She comes looking, she might stumble on it, you never know. I'd give a month's pay to be there. TERCO wants us to winter over, you know. It's been a long time since I saw a real live woman, and it'll be a long time again."

Down at our other camp. Which meant that the camp was at a lower altitude, first of all. And if there was a chance of Kathy McNeely's happening upon it, it must be near the coast.

She won't find anything now.

What did that mean? That there had been something to find before? Something Westcott—also meaning the TERCO crew's honchos, Merrill and Sears—knew about?

Grounded for a week, Hank Forbes had been away from MacTown longer than his itinerary had called for. In spite of his regular reports by radio, his navy bosses would be impatient to have him come home, he was so long overdue. The sensible thing would be to abandon any notions about locating TERCO's other camp or a new oil spill. It wasn't really his business. The NSF was the overseer for Americans allowed into Antarctica for research and other purposes. They weren't asking for his help.

You don't trust Merrill, he thought. By logical extension, Len Sears, for all his friendliness the last day or so, wasn't to be trusted either.

They're hiding something. He was beginning to believe it.

Given the nature of TERCO's business, the hunch suggested some kind of unauthorized energy research or drilling activity. Looking for oil? That seemed like a real possibility. There had been authorized explorations of Antarctica's oil and minerals potential by several nations, including Japan and Germany as well as the United States. But if it wasn't such a big deal, why was TERCO being so secretive?

On impulse, as he skimmed over the surface of the glacier, steadily descending from an altitude of twenty-one hundred feet toward sea level, Forbes dug around his storage panel for his detail maps. One of them highlighted areas on the Ice that were forbidden to helicopters as landing sites. SPAs, they were called, or specially protected areas, set aside because of the presence of groups of penguins or other Antarctic-based species, either on the ice or in the adjacent coastal waters, or because human activities might threaten the particular ecology of the sites. The Keep Out sign wasn't inflexible; in a few cases bases had even been permitted in or near SPAs. But the kind of exploratory drilling TERCO might be up to would certainly be prohibited.

Forbes located the TERCO base he had just left and quickly tracked to his present position over the glacier. Following its line, Forbes's finger traced a path to the coast. Just to the west of that intersection with the sea a highlighted area on the map jumped out at him.

The location of the *Kowloon* oil spill included the site of a large penguin rookery, identified by a small penguin symbol on his map. It had been designated as a specially protected area. *Off limits not only for helos,* he thought, *but for TERCO and other research groups as well.* No drilling, no subsurface blasting, no pollution allowed.

What if TERCO had ignored the designation? That would explain being closemouthed about its auxiliary camp and what it was for. It might explain a lot more. Including a new oil spill? That was reaching a bit, a long shot, but . . .

Forbes felt an excitement not quite warranted by the evidence. But he could be over the SPA in less than thirty minutes. It was a large area, the size of a county back home, and he would have to watch his fuel carefully. He couldn't afford a lengthy search.

Keep an eye on the weather, too. Those black clouds to the north, over the ocean, suggested a major depression. And now he could see something he hadn't noticed before, a pall of darkness topping the mountains to the west, billowing higher into the sky like the smoke of an enormous fire.

Forbes frowned. Time to check in with MacTown.

"Hello, Mac, this is Forbes, position, over."

Static answered him. Experiencing the same problem this morning before takeoff, he had put it down to the sheltered location of TERCO's camp.

His glance flicked toward the dark mass over the mountains to the west. It seemed to have climbed higher even in the few seconds since he had first become aware of it. Was a storm the reason McMurdo couldn't hear him? If so, he was going to have to make some quick decisions soon. He might have to sit down and wait it out.

He could turn back to the TERCO base, still a safe option. He hadn't reached the point of no return, where going back was more hazardous than continuing on his course.

No go, he thought. *Maybe it's just superstition, but you don't want to go back there.*

He had plenty of fuel, no problem there. The problem was the early arrival of a sudden, full-blown Antarctic blizzard. It didn't occur to him to question the weather report passed along to him last night by Len Sears. Storms blew up on the Ice without warning. It was a fact of life.

He calculated quickly that he was now within a few air miles of that SPA. The coastal shelf was visible in the distance, less than fifty miles away, the white ribbon of the glacier funneling toward it, white on white.

Time for a few quick passes over the area, just so he could tell himself he'd tried. He felt a little reckless. He had a natural aversion to secrecy, especially secrets that might be hiding destructive activities here on the Ice. Sears and Merrill were up to something.

Carl Jeffers had suspected them.

The thought of Jeffers, popping up unexpectedly, gave Forbes an irrational chill. He remembered the look of terror in the scientist's eyes when they carried him onto the Huey to fly back to McMurdo. Forbes had put it down to the trauma Jeffers had endured. Could there have been another reason?

Forbes shook his head angrily. Jesus, what was he thinking?

His present situation was hairy enough without trying to manu-facture sinister plots on flimsy evidence.

He concentrated on the surface below. The glacier he was following butted against a backbone of the mountain range. Beneath the skin of snow he could see the line of vertebrae that descended toward the distant rim of the continent, close enough now for him to observe icebergs out at sea, the water dark as india ink under angry clouds.

A short distance ahead, a fork appeared, a branch of the gla-cier diving off to the right between two spiny peaks. Forbes drifted over it and found himself peering down a long valley that narrowed at the far end. Must be a pass there, a place for the ice to squeeze through.

A gust of wind lifted the helo. It bounced and yawed, and he had to correct quickly with his foot pedals to keep from swing-ing around.

Hairs stirred on the back of his neck. The blackness that had appeared to the west filled half the sky now. He flew through a brief snow shower, burst into clear again, saw more snow ahead. He had to pick his holes, like a halfback running for daylight. He started to think about finding a place to land.

He had never felt really scared in an aircraft, and he had been through some hair-raising blows. He'd had to make a pancake landing once in a navy fighter whose landing gear was damaged, but he had been too busy that time to know how frightened he was. Maybe he was too dumb to be scared, he thought. Or maybe this was it—nerves jittery, sweating in spite of the cold that penetrated the cockpit and iced the windows, thoughts tumbling over each other, a sudden desire to pee.

He could ride down the valley toward the coast. The bulk of the mountains would provide some kind of buffer.

The radio screamed static at him. Above its spitting he could hear the muffled beat of the rotors and a keening sound. It reminded him of a great mass of women sobbing and crying as their men rode off to war or out to sea.

Not for you, though. No one to cry over you anymore. He won-

LOUIS CHARBONNEAU

dered if Greg and Gina ever missed him still, if they would
grieve very long if anything happened to him.

It's what you chose for yourself, he thought. *Let's not get sloppy
about it. Be glad you had them when you did.* They were the best
times, those first years, feeling a tiny fist tighten around his
finger, lifting a boy overhead while he screamed with delight.
Nobody could ever take those years away from him.

He came over the pass and funneled down through it, and all
of a sudden there was something down there on the snow and
ice that didn't belong, a yellow incandescent light, surrounded
by a halo caused by snowdrift. He reduced power and pulled
back on the cyclic. The Huey slowed, nose tilting up while
Forbes hovered, peering down into an ice canyon. A flurry of
snow enveloped him, obscuring the scene below. When it
cleared, he saw the light again, illuminating a big drilling rig,
mounds of tarpaulin-covered equipment and two sturdy-look-
ing huts.

Then the wind caught him again, a powerful draft lifting him
up, hurling him skyward. Forbes tried to regain control, heading
into the wind to maintain his hover, prepared to land no matter
what. Those huts meant shelter, survival.

The wind was too strong. It carried him along, helpless as a
leaf in the wind. He twisted the throttle grip, calling on all the
thrust the turbojets could deliver.

He didn't know how far he had been blown away from the
TERCO camp, for he had no doubt that was what it was, or
how many minutes had passed while he fought the winds. Too
far, he thought. He would never make it back.

He thought he could hear the whine of the jets over the
howling of the storm, but without warning something snapped.

The tail of the helo swung sharply. Forbes worked the foot
pedals that controlled the pitch angle of the tail rotor, that small,
easily overlooked rotor that compensated for the torque effect
of the main rotor blades, providing control for steering.

The pedals banged against the floorboards without tension.
Hank Forbes discovered fear then. It had an icy feel; it brought a

looseness in his loins; it made his heart race from the spurt of adrenaline in his blood. He didn't like the feeling or knowing that it could happen to him. The Huey, battered by high winds, began to spin, the tail swinging in one direction, out of control. Helpful Lenny Sears had seen to the tail rotor personally, checked the linkage by means of the extension shaft to the main rotors, supervised the lubrication. . . .

Forbes understood it all in those last few seconds: the meaning of fear, the sorrow of lost love, the bitterness of treachery and betrayal.

He never gave up. He cut off power, setting up autorotation of the main rotor blades. He checked his radar altimeter, his mind automatically calculating the point of dead man's curve, the calculation of height and forward speed that was necessary for the freewheeling rotors to bring the chopper down safely without power. Forty feet up, which didn't buy enough time to stop his fall, but his forward speed might be enough. He worked the cyclic stick, trying to stop the spin, brain and hands functioning in unison, adjusting, battling, calling on a lifetime of skills learned and courage won. He had the radio switch open, shouting, "Mayday! Mayday!" as he went down.

Out of control, the Huey slammed into a bluff. The main rotor dug into the deep snow and sheered off. The cabin split apart on impact. The last thing Forbes felt was a deep pain in his chest and a kind of relief that it was happening this way, sudden and sure, falling out of the sky.

TWENTY-THREE

AT THE END OF THE FIRST WEEK AT SEA the weather worsened. Anatoly Suganov, captain of the *Shevchenko,* no longer appeared at his table even for supper. Whenever Kathy McNeely braved the bitter cold and blowing snow of the open deck, she would peer up at the pilothouse. Suganov was always there, his black beard frosted by the lights behind him, staring intently into the murk through which the *Shevchenko* groped her way.

The ice floes bunched and thickened, obstructing the ship's progress. The loose sea ice merged into a solid mass up to six feet thick. When radar found a channel of open water close to shore, where ice cliffs towered more than two hundred feet straight up, the *Shevchenko* cautiously entered the passage. Out on deck, craning her neck to peer upward, Kathy saw stalactites of ice dripping from the overhanging face of the cliff directly above her, as if the ship had moved inside the ice.

The passage narrowed. The *Shevchenko* smashed at a huge ice floe until the slab finally broke. Thick plates of ice heaved up on each side of the bow and thundered against the hull of the ship as it shouldered them aside.

The channel closed. The ship ground to a stop. Everyone on deck was ordered inside.

Peering through a porthole, Kathy could no longer see the top of the cliff, a striated wall of blue-white ice, from which small pieces of ice rained down on the deck like hail.

Volkov, who had been up on the bridge talking to the captain, joined Kathy on the lower deck.

"How does it look?" she asked. "Can we get through?"

"Ship is very strong. I think it is possible, yes."

"The sea ice is freezing solid early this year. We don't have much time, Alex."

"That is why I tell Captain Suganov we cannot turn back. He agree. We must go forward."

Kathy peered out of the porthole at the ice cliff off to the starboard and ahead toward what she could see of the sea ice, now an unbroken sheet of white off the bow.

"How?" she wondered aloud.

"Is open water ahead, not far."

"But this ice is . . . it stopped us cold, Alex, if you'll excuse the expression."

Volkov smiled. "Is very good joke. I must tell Niki."

"The point is, we're not moving."

"Ship has much more power. Engine you hear is turbine—you understand?"

"Sort of."

"Has horsepower of sixty thousand. But *Shevchenko* is ice-breaker. Main engine is diesel. It is more horsepower by three."

"Three times as much?"

"That is correct."

"Does that mean the captain is going to try to smash through the ice? Straight ahead?"

"You will hear diesel engine."

Even as Volkov spoke, she heard a deeper rumble in the ship's bowels. If Volkov's translation into English was accurate, the main propulsion plant could produce 180,000 shaft horsepower, which seemed formidable.

It would have to be, she thought. The history of Antarctic exploration was a litany of ships caught and imprisoned in the ice for entire winters—many crushed like kindling. Nearly all the great men whose names were part of Antarctica, lent to its shelves and bays and ice sheets, had faced the terrible threat: the Frenchman Dumont d'Urville, whose *Astrolabe* and *Zelée* were briefly caught in the ice in 1838 before escaping . . . James Clark Ross, discoverer of the great ice barrier that now bore his name, trapped with his two ships *Erebus* and *Terror* in 1841 . . . the *Belgica,* under command of Adrien de Gerlache, icebound for the winter of 1898, with a young Roald Amundsen aboard as mate . . . Robert Falcon Scott and the *Discovery,* trapped in McMurdo Sound for the winter of 1903, the same year the Swedish ship *Antarctica* was crushed by the ice and sank . . . Wilhelm Filchner and the German ship *Deutschland,* frozen in pack ice of the Weddell Sea through the winter of 1912 . . . Ernest Shackleton and the *Endurance,* battered in the grip of the ice for nearly a year before she sank in November 1915.

Modern icebreakers were better built for the task, Kathy had been told in early briefings, and much more powerful. "Not to worry," Carl Jeffers had advised her cheerfully. "You'll be a lot safer than you are on the L.A. freeways."

The rumble within the ship rose to a shuddering roar. The whole ship trembled with pent-up force. The *Shevchenko* surged ahead, slamming into the thick plate of ice in her path. The roaring diminished, then rose again. Over and over the ship's heavily reinforced bow smashed against the ice, breaking a path as the ice grumbled and cracked and split, sometimes with a dragging scream like monstrous nails being pried out of wood.

Mists swirled over the ship's decks, freezing on the railings and rigging. Even the sea spray froze wherever it touched.

Volkov, when the ship rocked repeatedly from the impact against the ice, grabbed Kathy's arm to prevent her from falling to the deck. She made no attempt to free herself. It was comforting having Alex there, she thought, calm and reliable and reassuring. Too comforting, perhaps . . .

Over the next half hour Captain Suganov and the *Shevchenko* pounded against the sea ice, lurching forward a few feet at first, then yards at a time. When the mists thinned or parted to allow any visibility ahead, there was no change in the snow-covered surface.

The ship's radar, its electronic eyes, "saw" open water ahead, Volkov had said. Where was it?

The diesel thrust built up even louder than before. The entire ship vibrated. Survivor, who had been lying miserably on the deck near Kathy's feet, sat up and barked. A huge sheet of ice split and broke before the bow with a tremendous crack. The slabs of ice tilted upward and fell back like buildings toppled.

And suddenly the steep wall of ice beside the ship fell away. The mist lifted. Gray clouds appeared overhead. Off to starboard now appeared a sweep of thin brash ice in a bay. The *Shevchenko* broke through the last barrier of sea ice into smooth black water.

"I think you can let go of my arm now, Alex," Kathy said.

"Oh, yes . . . of course, *moya dorogaya.*"

He released his grip. She felt a warm surge of gratitude. Then Survivor whined and nuzzled her. She looked into the husky's startlingly blue eyes. Her rush of emotion checked, she patted the dog's head reassuringly. *What are you trying to tell me?* she asked him silently. *That I shouldn't mistake gratitude for something else? Is that what Hurley told you to say?*

As if in reply, Survivor lifted his left front leg and banged her leg with his brace.

"Look, Katyusha," Volkov said, an edge of excitement in his voice. "We have found it!"

The leap of recognition was unmistakable. Kathy had spent part of a bitter winter here. Some of the landmarks were just as she remembered them. To the east a tail of the mountain range trailed all the way to the sea, ending in a tumble of black rocks and gravel. The tongue of a narrow glacier curled beside the flank of the mountain. The rocks and ice rose in steep, rugged piles from the sea ice, making that shoreline virtually inaccessible. A flat expanse of sea ice between the open water and the mainland created a solid floor for the bay. Inland, the small tongue of ice merged into one of a pair of twin glaciers separated by snowy peaks. The effect was not unlike a divided highway.

Everything else was different.

The sea ice was deeper than she remembered, more clearly defining the shape of the bay. Its surface was also more broken and irregular. Where there had been a large emperor rookery before, now only a scattering of penguins could be seen on a narrow crescent of pink-stained snow and ice along the western edge of the bay.

There was no immediate visual evidence that this was the location of the *Kowloon* spill. Could Nature heal herself so quickly? Or was the damage hidden? The oil from the *Kowloon* had seeped into the sea ice, most of which had probably broken up or moved out to sea. Peering toward the pile of black rock off to the east, Kathy thought she saw the dark stain of oil sludge at its base, but that might have been an illusion. She would have to check more closely to be sure.

What puzzled her, making her doubt her own senses and memory, was the appearance of the solid ice shelf that marked the edge of the continent.

It was not the same at all.

"I don't understand it, Alex. Why is it so different?"

The Soviet scientist studied the shoreline. A year ago the ice had sloped gradually upward from the sea ice like a gentle rise from a beach. Now a sheer cliff of blue ice rose over a hundred feet straight up to a sharply defined shelf. The table formed by the cliff was nearly the full width of the bay, a good half mile across. At its western flank, above the penguin rookery, the ice crumbled into a pile of broken ice and snow.

"Iceberg," said Volkov.

"Iceberg?"

"What is your American word? The ice has calved. Broken off to make iceberg."

Kathy's gaze darted back to the blue cliff. Ice that had been invisible for centuries, she thought, buried deep within the sheet that flowed down to the sea. It seemed incredible that an entire piece of the shoreline, nearly the width of the bay, could have calved away from the mainland and drifted out to sea, but such massive breaks occurred. They were not even a rarity. In the Antarctic summer hardly a day passed without the thunder of another great chunk of mainland ice separating from its mother ice. Approaching the continent, past the Antarctic Circle, ships encountered fleets numbering hundreds of icebergs, a fantastic, ever-changing armada defending the sea-lanes.

"It is only explanation," said Volkov. "Captain Suganov showed me his charts. This is area of oil spill last winter. There is no question, coordinates are precise. It appear different but is same place. Breaking away of much ice explains why shoreline is all so steep and why bay is much larger."

"I don't see any evidence of oil."

"I am sure it will be on seafloor and in bottom ice. Niki will make dive to see."

"You've already planned this."

"Yes, of course."

"What about *our* plans?"

"We will do what you wish, my dear doctor. We will take our Cat and our tin dog—that is correct, yes?—and look for new spill."

The Cat was Volkov's strained English slang for the caterpillar-tracked vehicle aboard. Tin dog was an Antarctic term for a motor toboggan, a mechanical substitute for the dog-and-sledge transportation of earlier times. The latter term reminded Kathy of the companion relaxing now at her feet.

"What about my dog?"

"Russian sailors take care of him for you. But I think this will not be necessary."

"Why not?"

Volkov laughed. He had been amused by Kathy's careful attentions to the husky, but his amusement had given way to admiration for Survivor's adaptability and obvious devotion. "I think you will have hard time leaving him behind."

Late that evening Kathy McNeely stood on the rim of the ice cliff, staring out toward the *Shevchenko,* at anchor on the black water beyond the sea ice. The day had been nonstop activity since their arrival, Volkov supervising the unloading of supplies and equipment from the ship while Kathy explored the small penguin colony.

"Captain Suganov say he can wait only few days. Weather report we have from Vostok, Molodezhnaya and Leningradskaya, three of our stations, is very bad. Ice will soon be very bad for ship."

The Soviet tracked vehicle was large enough to provide a closed cab, and its tanklike tracks were capable of carrying it safely over broken ice and even soft snow. It had been lowered, along with the smaller motor toboggan, which was about the size of the American Polaris, from the *Shevchenko* onto a firm ice floe. From there both vehicles were driven over the sea ice to the edge of the bay just above the penguin colony, one of very few places where the steep-walled coastline could be reached from below. At first alarmed, the birds had quickly become curious about the odd vehicles, once they stopped spitting and growling. They gathered around like spectators at a construction site while Soviet sailors hauled the tractor up a rugged pile of broken ice steps to the level table at the top of the cliff, and then, more quickly and easily, the toboggan.

"Then we'll have to make the most of what time we have," Kathy said, reluctantly accepting the reality that she could spend little more time with the penguins at the edge of the bay, several of which she had already identified by her mark from the previous winter. Fortunately none of them showed signs of recent injury. Nor was there any evidence of oil in or near the rookery. Whatever had happened had not occurred here.

"You must get good rest tonight. We will finish inspecting penguin colony. If we still find nothing, we will leave tomorrow to look at ice. You are quite certain about taking dog?"

"Survivor goes with us. If there's any chance at all that we might have to be flown out, I can't leave him behind. Besides, he won't hold us back."

Volkov shrugged. "It is what you wish. I only ask because we must take food for him as well as ourselves. I will prepare all supplies."

"I hope you know how much all this means to me, Alex."

"Is nothing." He smiled. "We make good team, yes?"

"Yes," she said. "A terrific team."

From the sea ice below them, someone was waving urgently. Niki had just reached the ice in a small landing craft.

"What does Niki want?"

Simanovich shouted at them. His words, sharp in the stillness, came to them as clearly as a series of small thunderclaps. The words were in Russian, and Kathy, sensing their importance, turned to Volkov with an undefined feeling of apprehension.

"What is it? What's wrong?"

Volkov's expression was somber. "Radio message has been received. Is very bad news. There has been accident. Your friend—"

Kathy felt as if the ice were giving way beneath her feet.

"—is missing," said Volkov gravely.

TWENTY-FOUR

THE GIRL'S NAME WAS BEBI SOMETHING. The accommodating maître d' at La Ronde had provided Ron Kusic with a name and telephone number, which Bebi had thoughtfully left with him —"Just in case you might want to call," she had told Kusic. "I never thought you would, really."

"That was very clever of you."

She was a true blonde, her hair long and thick and glowing with highlights, like the hair conditioning models in television commercials. The hair had first caught Kusic's eye that night at La Ronde, where Bebi was dining with another man. ("Just a friend," she had assured Kusic. "I mean, nobody special.") But Bebi's truly stunning asset was the creamy perfection of her skin, which had apparently never been touched by the sun's rays since a reckless adventure in the nude when she was three years old. A wide-brimmed hat shielded her face whenever she was compelled to be in the sun. She applied No. 15 sunscreen liberally over every inch of skin that might be exposed. Long skirts or slacks were mandatory for outings in the open, which she avoided whenever possible. She was not a picnic girl.

Her figure was generously curved, the legs long and straight.

Every inch was pale pink-and-white. Kusic watched her fit her improbably high, full breasts into the strand of a string bikini bra, which barely covered them. Her lips were parted slightly as she frowned in concentration, the tip of her pink tongue showing between perfect white teeth.

Bebi glanced up at him shyly.

Kusic smiled. "I hear Senator Wingate stirring around on deck. We'd better hustle on up. It doesn't pay to keep a representative of the United States government waiting."

"He seems very nice," Bebi said.

"He likes women."

Not being quite sure what that meant, Bebi was silent. She wriggled a little, making sure the bikini was properly in place. "I knew it would be very special with us, Ron. I knew that first time you looked across at me at La Ronde. It was special, wasn't it, hon?"

"Special," Kusic said.

He reached out and slapped her on the bare fanny. "Better finish dressing. The government is waiting."

Bebi giggled.

He was the number two senator from the number one state, a young—though not quite as young as he appeared on television —vigorous and, Kusic had heard, ambitious man. This morning he appeared tired, as well he should, Kusic thought. He had spent the night on Kusic's yacht with Elena, a twenty-three-year-old with impressive skills.

"Have you thought anymore about what we were talkin' about, Senator?" Kusic had noticed that senators and governors and the like enjoyed being reminded of their status as frequently as possible.

"Well, ah . . ."

Bebi emerged from the cabin after a visit to the head. She wore the yellow string bikini beneath a cotton robe that fell open as she came up the short, steep flight of steps to the covered promenade deck. The almost unnatural whiteness of her skin was in sharp contrast with the tanned beauty of Elena, who lay sunning herself on the bow.

"I was talkin' about that Antarctic Treaty."

"I hope you didn't think . . . that is, you'll forgive my being blunt, Mr. Kusic, but my vote isn't for sale." Ice clinked in his glass as Wingate brandished his Bloody Mary like a weapon.

"I should hope to hell not, Senator! That isn't what this here is all about."

"Good. As long as we understand each other."

The senator had got stubborn there for a minute, got his back up, Kusic thought, but even as he spoke, his eyes slid sideways toward Bebi, who was very carefully arranging herself on a chaise in the shade of the deck awning. Lying back and closing her eyes, she let the robe fall off her shoulders.

"This isn't about bein' for sale, Senator. This is about bein' of like mind. I was told that might be the case, and I think from what I've heard I wasn't given a bum steer." When talking to out-of-staters, Kusic fell into a Texas drawl. He had been born in Omaha, leaving at the earliest possible time, when he was seventeen.

"I liked what you said about meeting America's needs first," Wingate said, "especially the needs of the very young and the very old. Our infant mortality rate is intolerable for a rich society, and all too many of our old people can't afford to care for themselves."

"That's what I mean. As far as the treaty goes, sure, Senator, I'm courtin', and I don't mind sayin' it. But that doesn't mean I'm buyin'. To set your mind at rest, that campaign contribution we spoke of, I've already faxed a letter to my office early this morning. It's in the works, and that goes no matter how you vote on the treaty or anything else. It's the man I put my money on, Senator, not the vote."

"I appreciate that, Mr. Kusic."

"It's Ron, for crissakes, you make me feel old."

The senator laughed. He seemed relieved by the direction the conversation had taken. "My guess is we're in the same age bracket, Ron."

"And the same thinkin' bracket, too. All I'm hopin' you'll do, Senator, is give this minerals agreement a hard look, and the whole Antarctic Treaty thing an even harder one. There've been signs of bad blood down there on the Ice this year, I guess you've heard. First thing you know, one of the signatories is going to decide to assert territorial claim. Then it's good-bye Susan. Uncle Sam has been playin' the good uncle, not making any claims of our own. We're gonna be left holdin' an empty sack."

"That's not going to happen, Ron."

"I sincerely hope not. Thing is, the way that treaty works, any of the involved nations can throw a monkey wrench into the works at any time, and there isn't a damned thing the major powers can do. My thinkin' is, the U.S. of A. needs a little more leeway than that, especially when it comes to developing Antarctic resources."

"What you're talking about is open exploitation of Antarctica's mineral potential." The senator sounded skeptical.

"It's gonna come, Senator. Got to. This world has only so much oil, and we've seen how some two-bit Arab can hold us up over it, same as puttin' a gun to our head. There's only so much platinum, so much gold, so much uranium—"

"You've found all those in Antarctica?"

"Sure enough, Senator. You'd be surprised what we've found under all that ice."

Wingate's glance was alert to the careful phrasing. Like any good politician, he didn't miss many nuances.

"I'd like to hear more specifics."

"We think there'll be news before very long, Senator. It'd be premature of me to say any more'n that."

"That's the kind of thing"—now it was the senator's turn to search for the careful phrase—"that might change some minds on Capitol Hill. I wouldn't sit on it too long, Ron, if there's important information not generally known."

"I tell you what, Senator Wingate. You can be damned sure, before we have anything to announce, you'll know about it. And that's about enough business for one day, wouldn't you say?" Kusic's glance took deliberate note of the two young women, Elena sunning herself, Bebi seemingly dozing on the chaise. "Trouble is, I have some of my own business I have to attend to."

"I was wondering about your plans for today, Ron."

"I've got to grab a chopper up to Houston. I was hopin' we could have a little more time to get acquainted, but this is somethin' that won't wait. I sure hate to leave the girls like this . . ."

"Maybe you could give me a ride." The senator's eyes slid once more toward Bebi, whose eyes remained closed. Her remarkable bosom rose and fell visibly as she breathed. The nipples were outlined clearly by the thin yellow fabric.

"Hell, there's no need for you to rush off, Senator!" Kusic grinned. He had an infectious, all-American grin. Someone had once told Kusic it reminded him of the young Ronald Reagan in his movie years. "Take your time, enjoy some of this good gulf sunshine. I'll have the captain take you out if you'd like to get in a little more fishin'."

"That won't be necessary."

"You're callin' the shots. You can leave whenever you're ready. I'll have my car stand by, or you can wait for the chopper. With any luck I'll be on it myself when it comes back. If I'm gonna be tied up for a while, I'll send it on down for you, how's that?"

The senator smiled. "I can hardly object, can I? Maybe I'll take you up on that fishing expedition this morning, if the captain doesn't mind."

"No problem. Let me fix it up before I go. And you girls . . ." Kusic grinned at Elena, who had wandered over to them, looking thirsty, a fine dew of perspiration visible on the brown skin of her throat and chest. "Let's not wear the senator out, okay? Man's got work to do, he just needs a little sun and air and a chance to relax."

"Don't worry, daddy," Elena said. "We'll see the senator relaxes."

Wingate was practically licking his lips, Kusic thought. Obviously he and Elena had had a good time together, but the presence of the pale-skinned Bebi was reviving him already. Kusic had an idea that once he was out of the picture, an interesting little ménage à trois just might develop.

The senator might not be for sale, but he was certainly hooked.

Because TERCO Tower had no helicopter pad, the helicopter set down at the airport, where Kusic had left his BMW 850i. Tooling in from Houston International in the sleek silver coupe, Kusic drove one-handed while he phoned ahead. His secretary ran Pete Rodriguez down.

"How'd it go with the senator?" Rodriguez asked.

"He's in the bag. Even so, I'd like you to find out which of the major oil companies in his state contributed most to his last campaign. It won't hurt to have another push in the right direction."

"Can do. I think the Senate is leaning our way on this."

"I gave the junior senator a little hint about what we might find in Antarctica if we're given a green light."

"Was that wise?"

"He's a smart guy, Pete, when he's not doing his thinking below the waist. He can see the Middle East supply of oil drying up, along with our own resources, in his own lifetime. Maybe about the time he's ready to run for president. He knows damned well we have to find new fossil fuel resources or the machinery is all going to grind to a halt. And when I dangled the idea of an important mineral discovery down on the Ice as a little teaser, kind of like a bonus for the U.S., he got real interested."

"Sounds good. You want me at your lunch meeting with Emmett Brady?"

"You'd better be there. Brady sounds worried. You can make more sense of the financial maze than I can." The statement was not entirely true, and Rodriguez knew it; but Pete did have a sharp eye for figures and the ways in which they could be manipulated.

The porterhouse steaks were big enough to lap over the sides of the large dinner plates. Emmett Brady attacked his with customary gusto. If he had bad news, Kusic thought, he wasn't going to let it affect his appetite.

The muted voices of money, power and privilege swirled around them. The sound of Gusher Luck, Kusic thought. The Steak House was in downtown Houston, but there was no hint of down-home Texas in the buff-colored booths and soft-lit elegance, except for a glimpse of Stetsons hanging on the racks behind the hatcheck girl's cubicle and the prevalence of fine-tooled leather boots under the cloth-covered tables.

Rodriguez joined them late, ordering a chef's salad while Brady and Kusic polished off their steaks. All three men ordered brandy and settled back to get down to business. Brady lit a cigar. Although Rodriguez was trying to give up cigarettes and Kusic didn't smoke, neither objected to the lawyer's indulgence.

"Heard you had Senator Wingate down for some fishing."

"You have good ears, Emmett."

"He's a comer, he doesn't make any bad mistakes."

"I think he'll go along with us on this Antarctic Treaty and the minerals agreement, once he has a little time to think about it."

Brady studied him thoughtfully. "I won't be part of any arm-twisting because Wingate likes women. That can backfire."

Kusic laughed. "I'm not talking blackmail, Emmett. I'm talking about guilt. And ambition. The senator is doing what he wants to do, but he's going to feel a little guilty about it when it's over, and maybe a little nervous, kind of looking over his shoulder. That's all it takes, especially seeing as how his constituents all want to keep driving their cars and running their central air. He'll be able to tell himself he's voting his conscience, looking out for the country. All I did was give him another good reason to see the light."

For a moment the lawyer was silent, savoring his cigar between sips of brandy. Finally he said, "If you've got any of that good news you hinted at the other day, now's the time for it."

"First let's have your bad news," said Kusic.

"I warned you, that *L.A. Times* hatchet job was devastating," Brady said bluntly. "The banks are taking a closer look at TERCO's leverage. The principal and interest on the senior subordinated reset notes aren't due until 1999; you have time. But you've still got those lump sum payments on the merger debentures due this June and again in 1994, and they must be paid in cash. If they're not paid on time, the holders of the merger debentures have the right to accelerate payment of principal on the debentures. If that happens . . ."

"It's not going to happen," Kusic said.

There was a moment of silence before Brady said, "The perception in the financial community is that it might. There are dissident stockholders, as you know, mostly those minority holders who were never happy with your takeover. You can expect a fight at the stockholders' meeting next week."

"You really think they're ready to come out into the open?" Rodriguez asked.

"I wouldn't be bringing it up if I thought it was just talk. Ron, there's a proxy fight brewing."

"I'm not afraid of a fight," said Kusic.

"How are you going to defuse it?"

"Suppose," Kusic said deliberately, "I walk into that meeting and break the news that one of our resource development teams, working in Antarctica, has made a major mineral discovery."

Brady stared at him, absorbing the impact, assessing it. "Accessible?"

"It's in a coastal area, accessible during the summer months, which is our winter here in Texas."

"You're not ready to tell me what this is?"

"Not just yet."

Brady nodded slowly, pursing his lips around the cigar. "How big is this deposit?"

"Take my word for it," said Kusic. "It's big."

"It's my understanding that anything discovered in Antarctica at this point will be shared with other nations."

"The accord hasn't been approved by all the signatories. Until it is, it's not binding. This find may influence what's still to be decided, and the discoverers will be in a strong position to influence that outcome. Besides," Kusic added with a smile, "the specific discoverer's name will be on every nightly newscast for weeks or even months."

A rare smile touched Brady's lips, though it was not reflected in his eyes. "You bastard, you've been holding out on me!"

"We wanted to be sure of what we had."

"That's why you've been pushing against this Antarctic Treaty—"

"That's right."

"—and pushing to liberalize the Antarctic minerals regime."

Kusic nodded agreement. "Time to call in some markers, Emmett. Your political friends will want to be in on this."

"It doesn't answer the immediate cash-flow problem," the lawyer said thoughtfully, "but if it's as good as you say, it should go a long way toward squashing any real proxy fight. Especially if you announce at the right time, drop the news right in the middle of the meeting. If it gets out early, the dissidents will have time to react. Don't give it to them."

"As of now, you're the only one who knows anything, outside our research people, and they're loyal."

"What about Senator Wingate?"

"I gave him a hint, that's all."

Emmett Brady mashed his cigar in an ashtray—in an odd way, an emphatic gesture of satisfaction. "All right, you must have some ideas about meeting the interest on the merger debentures."

"I'll let Pete answer that." Kusic nodded toward Rodriguez.

"We're thinking of selling off TERCO Pipeline," Rodriguez said. "There are at least two interested buyers, ARCO and Dutch Shell. I think some others will surface. It's not a distress sale, so the price should be right. A good case can be made that the pipeline company, which operates as an autonomous subsidiary, as you know, is extraneous to the future needs of TERCO."

If Brady found irony in the statement, in view of the bitter takeover battle in which the former family owners of the pipeline company were forced out by Kusic's leveraged maneuvering, he gave no sign of it.

"The cash infusion will free investment money for the Antarctic venture," Rodriguez continued, "as well as meet our immediate debt obligations."

"What about the negatives?"

"We don't see any serious problems. There's a public relations factor we'll have to address. Our discovery is located in what is called a specially protected area, or SPA, an area of special ecological sensitivity or interest. But the fact is there is no express prohibition against establishing a base within an SPA or carrying on scientific research there."

"You fudging a bit there, Pete?"

Rodriguez fidgeted, glanced at Kusic, whose shrug gave his aide the go-ahead. "Maybe a little. Naturally it was necessary to carry out some controlled drilling and subterranean blasting to get down to the mineral base. We don't believe our activity has been harmful to the environment, but . . . some of the bleeding hearts will think otherwise, of course."

"You'll get environmentalist flack," Brady agreed. "The eggheads will be in full cry."

"They're exaggerating the so-called fragility of Antarctica."

Kusic cut in crisply. "They're also exaggerating the hazards to the ecology that would be created by carefully monitored development of accessible resources. It's about time the doomsayers started thinking about the fragility of the hold this human race has on our way of life—and the fragility of the United States economically in the face of the new European market alliance and the Japanese dominance along the entire Pacific Rim, not to mention in California."

"Sounds good, Ron," Emmett Brady said. "Save it for the stockholders. I don't mind telling you, you boys have made my digestion a whole lot better tonight."

"Glad to hear it, Emmett," Kusic said. He liked a man who was what he called a player, someone who was there at crunch time. Brady was a player. "Does that mean you think a public offering will fly?"

"The prospectus is sitting at the printer right now. We can pick a date of release after the stockholders' meeting, and I'll tip off the underwriters that you're going to have an announcement. Once you drop that little bombshell, I guarantee you, TERCO's leverage is going to look a whole lot better!"

Alone with Rodriguez in the privacy of his office, an hour after dropping Emmett Brady off, Ron Kusic raged. Veins stood out on his neck and forehead. "What do you mean, you can't give me details?"

"We only have a shortwave message from Merrill, in code. You know he couldn't say much in the open."

"So what the hell did he say? What's wrong?"

"Maybe nothing. There've been some people poking around, some environmental scientists, because of that fuel bladder accident. More dead penguins have shown up. There's a chance their snooping might lead them to our coastal drilling site."

"Those goddamned penguins again!"

Rodriguez nodded unhappily.

After a moment of ominous silence Kusic said, in control

now, the molten anger cooled into hard steel, "How did Merrill let this happen?"

"He's doing his best—"

"Doing his best doesn't cut it. You know that. Merrill knows it."

"What I mean is, he's taken steps."

"So what's the problem?"

"A helicopter is missing. Merrill thinks it may have gone down in the vicinity of our lower camp—that the pilot might have been looking for it. There's going to be a search for the missing plane; that's inevitable. What Merrill is doing is organizing the search himself so he can control it on the ground. The weather is bad enough it will probably keep planes out of the search for now."

"Probably?"

"It doesn't have to be for long. The Antarctic summer is ending. From what I hear, there won't be any exhaustive search once the really bad weather sets in, not for the next six months. By then it won't matter." Rodriguez paused, wondering if he was putting too good a face on the situation, recognizing that its failure would put him at risk along with Merrill. "By then we should have the green light from the Congress on unilateral minerals exploration by U.S. companies. And TERCO stock will be solid gold."

Kusic stared at him for a long moment. Then the infectious grin came. "Not gold, Pete," he said. "But close."

Part Three

CONVERGENCE

TWENTY-FIVE

———————

BRIAN HURLEY GAVE UP TRYING to batter his way out of his tent through the lone exit. He sat back, staring at the blocked tunnel, then at the sagging walls of the tent. How long before the accumulating weight became too much and the tent collapsed?

His heart was beating like a bass drum. He tried to relax. Exertion and excitement consumed more oxygen. They also made it difficult to think clearly. Although a snow mist was now fogging the interior of the small tent, he knew he would not suffocate any time soon. The huskies slept under snow habitually. On very rare occasions, he knew, a dog had been lost to deep drifts, but normally the dogs slept undisturbed and simply dug their way out in the morning. He had to figure out a way to do the same.

Hurley considered what he might use for digging. The small field shovel was in his pack on the sledge, which weighted down one apron of the tent. He hadn't had time to unload, grabbing only a few things before escaping the storm's fury. Could he somehow reach his pack without bringing the tent and its canopy of snow down on top of him?

His thoughts drifted to Admiral Byrd again. During that harrowing winter alone on the ice, he had faced similar crises, first trapped inside his tent and later outside, unable to open the only door to get back in to safety. In spite of everything, the good admiral had kept coming back for more in later years, making a life's mission of it . . . including going around the country giving speeches to drum up financing for his next venture. *That what you have in mind, Hurley?*

It wasn't. Never had been. But he'd been at it for quite a few years now, pushing the frontiers of the world's wilderness areas and his own endurance to their limits, always with the feeling that he would one day go back to his real life's work.

Berkowski's television special is your version of the lecture circuit that kept Byrd going a half century ago, he thought.

Maybe he had pushed too far this time, but no matter how it turned out, he had no regrets. He wasn't going to second-guess coming to Antarctica or making the assault on the Hartsook Glacier. The latter had been part of the planned race to the Pole all along, and a test run had simply been a good way to end this summer of preparations.

While his thoughts wandered, he was also contemplating his predicament, one part of his brain weighing and discarding a half dozen solutions. They ranged from trying to dig his way out of the tunnel opening by hand or by using one of his cooking pans, to slicing through the right-hand side of the tent near its base to get at the supplies on the sledge. He had a knife, cooking utensils, boots, the pole frame of his cot—

He stared at the poles. The cot folded up like a stretcher, and it lay on the floor of the tent. With no time to locate and spread out his groundsheets before diving into the tent, he had grabbed the folded-up cot, which he used as a kind of brace for his packing on the sledge. He had simply thrown it into the tent as much to get it out of his way as anything else, though there had also been a stray thought about sleeping clear of the ground if he wasn't able to heat the tent.

Hurley stared from the poles to the bowed left wall of the

tent for a long time. Then he decided he'd better sit back for another minute and make sure he wasn't about to do something foolish.

His thoughts went back to his earlier ramblings. What he was questioning was not this adventure. He would never regret coming to Antarctica. It was as far out on earth's cutting edge as anyone could go, and it was breathtakingly beautiful besides. The real question was, When would he have had enough? When he finished his polar run, would that satisfy? What *was* his real life's work?

If television was going to take over all the frontiers, he thought, maybe it was time for him to bow out, to go back to something whose excitements came too slowly and painstakingly and almost invisibly to attract the nightly news cameras. Something like archaeology. Not that he had found its challenges dull; he had simply been lured away by another kind of challenge, more immediately exhilarating.

Strange thoughts to be pursuing at a time like this. Did it mean he was finally growing up? Maturing? Or was he reassessing his goals because he could no longer go to sleep at night without thinking about Kathy McNeely, imagining what it would be like to be with her, fantasizing the most unlikely scenarios . . . ?

Where was she now, she and good old Alex? It was kind of too bad, he thought, that the Commies were now the good guys.

He felt some pressure against his temples, and the clouded air in the tent was thick in his lungs. Maybe he had been a little too optimistic about how long the oxygen would last or how much air penetrated deep powder snow.

A creaking sound caused his scalp to crawl.

The noise came from the vertical center pole of the pyramid tent. The polar tent had changed little in its design for most of this century, in large part because it had proved to be spectacularly successful in resisting even the fiercest katabatic winds. But in seeking a protected place to raise the tent, Hurley had inadvertently exposed it to a different kind of hazard, a massive buildup of drift.

He thought the center pole had shifted slightly, tilting.

Hurley located his skinning knife and drew the long, serrated blade from its sheath. As he did so, a small piece of nylon rope fell out of the sheath.

Hurley stared at it. He had cut several pieces from the rope that had been used as a lifeline at the Operation Second Chance camp. Each one, like this, had sharp, unfrayed edges where it was cut—exactly like the end of the rope that had supposedly been snapped by high winds. It wasn't exactly proof of anything, Hurley knew—he was no forensic scientist—but it was enough to keep his uneasy suspicion alive.

He turned his attention back to the poles of his folded cot. After picking them up, he set both poles at the center of the sagging wall of the tent. He had to force them into position at an angle of approximately ninety degrees. Once in place, they stayed there, fixed by the pressure against the fabric from outside.

Hurley wondered whether his desperate plan would work, what the odds might be, whether anyone had ever done it before. (Was that the ultimate test for him, he wondered, the lure he couldn't resist?)

He couldn't think of anything else that had a ghost of a chance, and he couldn't wait much longer. Waiting, letting things happen without taking action of his own, just wasn't in his nature. He donned all his snow gear, except for his dark glasses, which dangled from a strap around his neck. Then he picked up his knife again, hefting it.

In that moment, looking down the long tunnel of his life as it had brought him to this moment, Hurley experienced without warning the keenest, most excruciating regret he had ever felt. *McNeely,* he thought, *if I get out of this . . .*

He brushed the doubt aside. Planting his feet wide to brace himself, he looped one arm around the six-foot poles of his cot. With his free hand, in one savage swipe of the knife, he slashed through the double-layered wall of the tent just below the spot where the poles were wedged against the fabric.

Snow engulfed him. It filled the tent like water bursting through a hole in a dam. Like water, it erupted first through the rent he had made toward the bottom of the tent, spilling around Hurley's feet. With a soft thunder the torn side wall of the tent collapsed. Snow clogged his eyes and mouth and nose and ears; he was drowning in it. Blindly he thrust the poles he was holding upward through the snow. They shot through the soft powder, and for an instant he saw a flash of light before the avalanche of snow poured over him once more. The poles were torn from his grasp. He was thrown off his feet, pounded, slammed onto his side.

Hurley clawed frantically upward.

His right hand struck one of the poles. He hung on to it. Quickly he found the other pole. He began to push the ends back and forth, widening a channel they made through the settling drift.

He pushed the poles upward. Following the direction of their thrust, he managed to get his feet under him. That gained him more leverage. He jerked the poles back and forth again, feeling snow cascade around him. Then he tried to follow them up through the drift.

It was like swimming in quicksand. The soft snow yielded easily, but more of it filled the spaces he created, giving him nothing to drive against. With each clawing stroke toward the surface he seemed to slide back just as far. His movements became frantic, wild, the crazed lashing about of a drowning man.

The poles shot through the top of the drift into the open, and light flowed around Hurley—light and air, pure, sweet, dry, cold air that filled his lungs with pain and bliss.

Seconds later he flopped out of the disintegrating channel he had made and rolled slowly down the gentle slope of the drift.

The howling winds had diminished. There was still blowing snow, but not as violent. The white darkness was easing.

The drift wasn't as deep as he had feared. The tip of the

center pole of his ruined tent, tilted at an angle, projected a foot above the snow.

As if Hurley's scrabbling had alerted him, one of the huskies burrowed out of his snow cave and stood up, shaking off a white overcoat of powder, and stared at Hurley. It was Muley, the dog he had named for his brother. Behind Muley, to the left and right, there were other minor cave-ins and shiftings of the snow as, one by one, the dogs rose grumbling to the surface.

Much to Hurley's surprise, Hal Berkowski was waiting for him at the advance base. Hurley saw the camp, and the red helicopter with its HTV logo on the side of the cabin, from a distance of about two miles, at the top of a long cascade of ice that resembled a falls, as if the tumbling water had been arrested in midair. It was, in fact, an icefall, an almost perpendicular wall of blue-green ice that was impossible to climb. Hurley had observed it from the air at the same time he had spotted the level ice shelf above it that offered an ideal place for him to set up his second advance base. The shelf had the bonus of solid snowpack nearby where the helicopter could land safely. He just hadn't expected Berkowski and his crew to be there so soon in the aftermath of a blizzard.

It took Hurley over an hour to cover the two miles by a circuitous route around the falls. When he finally reached the shelf and came in view of the camp, he saw two cameras trained on him from different angles. Hurley was tired and hurting, thirsty and hungry, and the bile of anger that rose in him against the cameras' invasion was almost uncontrollable.

Berkowski clapped mittened hands in nearly silent applause. "Fan-tastic, Hurley! Terrific stuff! We got the whole scene there —one man pitting his raw courage and will against nature, a tiny little speck of humanity crawling up the face of that wasteland of snow and ice—beautiful, man!"

"Great," Hurley muttered.

"How about some good stuff with the dogs, huh? You know, hugs and kisses, we made it together, guys—okay?"

"I do that anyway," Hurley snapped.

He checked over the huskies for cuts or tears in their pads or any other sign of injury. They all had come through without visible harm. They were tougher now than when they had started this climb, stronger rather than weaker, though Hurley knew full well that that could change over weeks of hard pulling. Not this year, he thought, clapping Dutch on his broad head, going to the others one by one, Muley and Crazy, Oscar and Kipling, reliable Sam and good-natured Bones (pulling his share of the weight now) and the quietest, steadiest, most affectionate of them all, Vixen. He could see the red light on top of one of the TV cameras. *They make it all seem like an act,* he thought, *like a product commercial.*

In the tent where coffee, hot and strong, was waiting for him, with a savory stew simmering in a pot over the Primus stove, Berkowski pestered him with questions. "Hey, you got through that storm okay? I guess you did, you're here, right? That shit was blowing through the streets of MacTown, let me tell you, I thought it was never gonna stop. I didn't know if we'd get up here in time to catch you."

"I'm surprised to see you."

"Hey, you didn't think we'd let you down? No way, man! This is for real, the real thing. I got to admit, though, it didn't look good for a while there. They say it's been blowing snow over half the continent. Everything's been grounded until this morning when we took of. I was afraid we'd never get off the ground." He broke off, suddenly remembering something. "Hey, this pilot, I think you knew him, he was at that camp down on the coast for a while . . . he didn't make it back."

"What do you mean?" Hurley asked, chilled by the offhand revelation. "Who are you talking about?"

"Guy named Forbes. His helo went down. They say he got caught in one of those blizzards."

"They found him?"

"No, there's a search party, I understand. Some guy named Merrill—his group have an ice core drilling operation going not far from where the chopper disappeared—he's organized a search. With the weather like it's been, nobody's been able to get to Merrill's camp. And hey, that scientist you're sweet on, the one they call the Bird Woman, she and the Russians are trying to find the missing chopper, too."

"Jesus," Hurley whispered.

"Yeah," Berkowski agreed. "Hey, it happens down here, you know? Lot of stuff happens. That's one of the things we have to get on film, that crazy, dangerous feeling, like anything can happen, one minute you're alive, the next minute you're at the bottom of a crevasse or you're drowning in snow or freezing to death."

"Maybe I can help," Hurley said. He was thinking again of the piece of cut rope he had saved after Dr. Jeffers's accident. Now Hank Forbes seemed to have met with an accident of his own.

"Huh?" Berkowski laughed. "Yeah, sure, Hurley, your dogs can sniff out the frozen corpse."

"One more crack like that and I'll give Dutch one of your legs for breakfast."

"Hey, let's be cool here, man, what did I say?"

"Nothing, you were just being a jerk."

"Fuck off, Hurley. You're just a hired hand here."

"Not anymore. I want those topographical maps of yours, the ones you showed me before I set off. I want to know exactly where that helicopter went down and how I can get there from here."

"Are you crazy? It's got nothing to do with you!"

"It's got everything to do with me. There's something wrong there. I don't know what it is, but I can go places with the dogs you can't get to any other way, especially if the winds are bad and you can't get in with helos."

"Hurley, you're not listening!"

"I'll need another tent," said Hurley. "I trashed one of mine,

252

and I'm using my spare. I don't want to go without a spare if I can help it."

"You're not going anywhere!" Berkowski's voice rose a notch.

"If I can get there, I will."

"You're making a fucking film. You hear me, Hurley?"

"Of course, I can hear you. You're shouting. The film will have to wait, okay? This was just a trial run anyway."

"I'm telling you, Hurley, there's no way you can do this. Besides, you couldn't get there. They say there's more bad weather coming, maybe lots of it. Summer's almost over down here. We've only got a few more days to shoot if we're lucky. You can make it up to that plateau where the glacier pops through the mountains. I've already got some good shots of it, panoramic stuff. All we need is you trudging up the last mile, you and the dogs."

"Sorry," Hurley said.

"Sorry doesn't cut it!" Berkowski was yelling now. "Sorry's no good, Hurley."

Hurley set down his coffee mug, glanced regretfully at the stew simmering on the stove and said, "My dogs need food and rest. I'll be leaving in the morning."

"You can't do that!" Berkowski screamed at him.

"Just watch me."

"But you made a deal!"

TWENTY-SIX

"WHEN WE FIRST STARTED STUDYING IT CLOSELY—mind you, that was only about five years ago, and we've learned a lot since —the hole was only a small one." The speaker, a small, bright-eyed, energetic man with boyish features and youthful enthusiasm, was an environmental scientist. He reminded Mike Davis of TV's Doogie Howser playing scientist rather than doctor. "I came down early this time, in August, because the hole really opens up in the Antarctic spring. There's a catalytic action triggered by the sun's first rays. By mid-September there was no ozone layer over this entire continent—just a hole! Do you understand what that means, Mr. Davis? Antarctica is half again the size of the United States, and this ozone hole covered Antarctica!"

Mike Davis, plodding alongside the scientist as they made their way toward the aluminum dome of Amundsen-Scott Station, the United States South Pole facility, had given up trying to make notes. His ballpoint pens kept freezing, and his notepaper, made brittle by temperatures approaching fifty degrees below zero, cracked and tore. "You're saying it's getting bigger," he said.

"Of course, it's getting bigger! That's because we keep dumping more and more of our man-made chemicals into the atmosphere."

"The question is," Davis suggested, rousing himself from his almost total concentration on how cold he was, "is the condition irreversible?"

"Ah!" The scientist, Donald Martin, who was from Ohio State University's Institute of Polar Studies and had spent the past spring and summer months conducting sophisticated studies of chlorine compounds in the stratospheric clouds over Antarctica, slapped his bear-paw mittens together emphatically. "*That* is the question. Perhaps more to the point, is the human race's suicidal campaign to destroy this planet reversible? I hope you'll be asking those questions in this story of yours."

"I'll try," Davis mumbled through cracked lips.

Venturing reluctantly out of the 165-foot-wide geodesic dome that covered the base, Davis had accompanied Martin on a walk to the old polar base that had preceded the modern domed facility. Known as the Old Pole, it was a ghost base now, visited surreptitiously by those brave or foolhardy enough to try to descend into the sunken shafts. Davis had been warned against going down because of recent cave-ins, and he hadn't needed much persuading. The old base was being crushed by the enormous weight of the surrounding ice, as easily as he might crush an aluminum beer can in the can crusher gadget he had recently installed on the wall of his kitchen back home.

The South Pole was not anything like Davis's expectations. He knew his somewhat mystical conception had nothing to do with the reality. There was no "pole" as such. A striped pole like a barber pole with a mirrored globe on top represented the center point of the earth's axis (a smaller version nearby was said to mark the exact geographic location). National flags were planted in the snow surrounding the barber pole, incessantly flapping in the wind, their colors vivid against the endless expanse of snow.

That was another thing Davis hadn't been prepared for: the

absolute desolation of the place. It appeared to be completely flat as far as you could see in any direction, an endless white sea of sharp-edged sastrugi. There was nothing to arrest the wandering eye—no growing thing, no living creature, nothing but the frozen waves of snow and ice. Robert Falcon Scott had got it right when he finally reached the Pole—too late to achieve his dream of being the first. "Great God!" he had written in his anguish, "this is an awful place. . . ."

Davis shivered. Forty-eight below when they had set out this morning. His head ached, and so did one tooth; he had lost a filling, which had simply crumbled from the cold, and there was nothing he could do about it. Even though he walked slowly, he was huffing and puffing, his breathing affected not only by the cold but by the thin atmosphere at this altitude, some ninety-three hundred feet above sea level. He'd got high the night before on one beer.

Okay, so he had done it. He could write about the South Pole honestly, say he'd been there, touched the Pole itself, or the barber pole that stood for it, even visited the Old Pole. Now get back inside.

The sun, resting on the horizon, was a white ball seen through an intervening haze. It reflected in a mirror image off the silvery skin of the aluminum dome, and another version of it burned high in the sky, a false sun, brilliantly white against the blue. The dome, which covered the living and working buildings of the American polar station, was about a fifth of a mile from the Pole but was moving toward it, Davis had been told, at the rate of about thirty-three feet per year.

It boggled the reporter's mind, the idea that this enormous ice sheet, more than two miles thick and a thousand miles across, wasn't just sitting there; it was *moving*. Which meant that everything constructed on it was also moving. The geographic pole remained a fixed point, but everything set down on the ice moved, the U.S. base being no exception.

The two men paused at the top of a long, inclined ramp,

broad enough to accommodate a large truck, that led down between walls of snow to the U.S. station under the dome.

"Will you be leaving here soon?" Davis asked.

Martin peered up at the sky. "That hole is closing now. Yes, I'll be going home; only a handful of people winter over here at the Pole. But I'll be back next spring. We have to stay on top of this. We have to know, Mr. Davis . . . is that hole still spreading through our atmosphere?"

Inside the dome it was nearly as cold as outside, but here the cold was without wind, a penetrating chill, a motionless presence. Stretching across the snow floor of the dome were the heated buildings, single and stacked, their few windows pouring light into the dimness, as inviting as lighted windows in a house at the end of a long, dark winter road.

The two men fled inside.

"You've got to go there," another journalist had assured Davis a few days earlier, over cards and beers at a MacTown bar. "If you haven't been to the Pole, you haven't really done Antarctica."

"Why? From what I hear, there's not much there."

"It's a symbol; it's the Pole, for God's sake! Besides, for the people who work down here, the Pole's the essence of it all. I mean, it's the coldest, driest, windiest, emptiest place on earth. Also one of the horniest. You don't have any women in your party, do you?"

"No."

"Just as well. But you've got to go there, Davis. Otherwise this Antarctic exposé, or whatever you call it, is a fraud."

Having just returned to McMurdo Station from the new Chinese base in East Antarctica, Davis was temporarily floundering, not sure of his next move. The Pole was there. A venerable LC-130 Hercules cargo plane was ready to take him along with a few other "distinguished visitors." Davis had argued with himself, which meant arguing in his mind with Shafter; in the end Shafter won, as usual.

He had spent two days at the Chinese base of Ling Po, which was located on the coast of Enderby Land not far from the Soviet base of Molodezhnaya. Davis had learned that, in the hasty construction of its first Antarctic station on King George Island in 1984 and 1985, China had brought in hundreds of construction workers and masses of equipment, bludgeoning the environment as the base was built and disregarding the agreed measures of the treaty, specifically a provision against killing seals and penguins to feed the large numbers of workers. The reputation earned at that time had followed the Chinese during the intervening years, resurfacing over the establishment of the new base.

Davis found no heaps of seal carcasses or other evidence to verify the rumors. In fact, the Chinese had been at pains to open their doors, if not their hearts. They had provided the visiting American journalist with shelter, information about their scientific research, free access to every part of the base and endless quantities of vegetables, noodles, chicken and rice. They were reserved but unfailingly polite. Their scientific spokesman, a man named Cheng, explained his team's interest in marine living resources as being focused on krill. They now understood the agreed measures, he told Davis; they would not violate them. The Greenpeace protesters who thought otherwise were children misled.

The Greenpeace delegation numbered some twenty or so ardent young people, women and men. They had set up their own camp facing the Chinese base at a distance of about a quarter mile. They created human barriers to block the paths the Chinese took to their boats. Defying frostbitten noses and fingers, they chanted slogans and unfurled protest banners demanding that the Chinese "Stop the Killing!" and "Save the Seals!" Beleaguered Chinese scientists and their silent support workers seemed more bewildered than angry over the harassment.

The demonstrators were openly hostile toward Davis. Why was he staying with the seal killers? They thrust still photographs in his face of dead or bleeding penguins and seals. When he tried to learn where and when the pictures had been taken, they became angry, shouting him down. When he suggested that the new Chinese base seemed to have been constructed with considerable care for its minimal intrusion upon the environment, a young woman cried, "You're justifying minimal rape!"

They made him feel old and cynical and used, partly because he saw himself in their passionate faces, the young rebel he had been in the sixties.

Davis took photos of Greenpeace members in their small boat trying to block passage of one of the Chinese landing craft out of the inlet toward their support ship, anchored offshore. He dictated notes into his tape recorder for a story of the confrontation.

Shafter would like it, he thought. The story had punch and drama, and it was readily linked to significant environmental issues. But it left Davis dissatisfied. It wasn't the story he had come to the Ice to find.

He was having dinner with Don Martin and one of the DVs who had flown in with him from McMurdo when Jack Benteen, their pilot, joined them. Davis had been exposed to people shaken by bad news or real tragedy too often to miss the signs.

"What's wrong, Jack?" he asked.

"One of our people is missing—a helo pilot, Hank Forbes."

"Missing! How long?"

"Oh, shit!"

"What happened?"

"Did he crash?"

The exclamations and questions spilled around the long table in the mess hall, a table famous for the collection of photos of naked women it preserved under its glass top, captured in all manner of improbable poses. No one was looking at them now.

Benteen suddenly remembered that Davis had been trying to

contact Forbes shortly after they arrived at the Pole. "You flew with Hank, right?"

"Yeah . . . a good guy."

"The best. You never got hold of him?"

"No, the communications chief here at the Pole tried, but there was too much interference."

"Yeah, that's what happened when he went down," Benteen said slowly. "He flew into a blizzard. He sent a distress signal just before his radio went silent. It was logged up here and at McMurdo, but apparently he wasn't receiving. . . ."

"You're sure he went down?"

"There's not much doubt." Benteen was silent for a moment. "What did you want to talk to him about?"

"It wasn't important. I just wanted to hitch a ride." Silent for a moment, Davis added thoughtfully, "He told me he couldn't fly a helo safely in high winds."

The pilot stared at him. His eyes were red-rimmed. "Hank knew better. He shouldn't have been up."

"How could it happen?"

"Transmission has been bad all over the Ice this past week because of the storms. He must not have heard . . . and it must have been clear where he was when he took off."

Another accident, Mike Davis thought. Like the others he had looked into, it seemed almost predictable in this hostile environment.

"Where was he? When he vanished, I mean."

"He'd been at some USARP camp." Benteen used the acronym with the derisive meaning commonly employed by some Antarctic hands who were nonscientists, spelled out as Useless Scientists Attempting Ridiculous Projects. "They're organizing a search party now."

"Who's organizing a search party?" *Where, when, how, who,* Davis thought. *Get the basics.*

"These TERCO people . . . the guy in charge."

"Merrill," Davis said. What was wrong with that picture? he

thought. Merrill and Forbes hadn't got along. What did Merrill care about what happened to Forbes?

"Huh? I guess so . . . yeah, Merrill."

"When did all this happen?"

"Hank's been missing since yesterday morning. Over twenty-four hours." Benteen shook his head. "Too long to be out there if he went down."

Mike Davis put down his mug of coffee, excitement building. "Could you get us there?"

Benteen stared at him as if he hadn't heard right. "You serious?"

"Dead serious. Can you take me there?"

It was the story, Davis thought. He had a hunch, and for the first time it felt right.

Benteen, who was a navy lieutenant commander and accustomed to obeying orders, said slowly, "It'd be my ass. There's too much shit out there."

"Bad weather?"

"Especially near the coast. And there's more to come."

For a moment the reporter was silent, letting his question hang between them, watching Benteen squirm. *You're using him,* Davis thought. Then he added to himself, *Make it good.*

"You were a friend of Hank's?"

"Hell, yes."

"Do you know where this TERCO camp is?"

"Yeah, I've got a pretty good idea."

"Do you ever take your Herc into areas like that?"

"Sometimes, if conditions are right."

"Or if it's important enough?"

Benteen stared at him.

"Can you take us there?"

TWENTY-SEVEN

THE TRACKED RUSSIAN VEHICLE rumbled noisily but efficiently over the level ice sheet, its harsh growl the only sound in an infinite wilderness of silence.

Fog had crept over the ocean, obscuring the Soviet ship. By midmorning the sea itself had withdrawn from the stage, leaving only a rugged landscape of snow and ice under a gray sky. The temperature, Aleksei Volkov noted on setting off, was thirty-two degrees below zero. The gray day and gusting winds added to the chill factor.

The cab of the tractor vehicle, which to Kathy McNeely resembled something put together in someone's backyard out of an old van and some tank parts, was overheated, but there was room for only Volkov and McNeely. Survivor rode in the back on a platform, his face lifted happily into the cold breeze. Behind the tractor came a small train consisting of two cargo sleds, one carrying supplies, the other a motor toboggan. The toboggan was there to provide access to areas the larger, clumsier tractor might not be able to reach—or, Volkov observed, emergency transportation back to the ship should the tractor break down.

THE ICE

The tractor plowed across an ice stream, rattling and bouncing over the rough surface. Ice streams were offshoots from larger glaciers and tended to move much faster, sliding toward the coast at four hundred meters or more annually rather than the stately ten meters or so of a typical glacier.

An hour after they set out their way was blocked by the steep face of a glacier. After casting about for most of another half hour, Volkov found a seam the tractor was able to navigate, struggling upward at a steep angle. It brought them to the top of the glacier. Staring inland over the formidable sweep of this river of ice, Kathy thought of Hurley, climbing the even more demanding Hartsook Glacier, not in a heated tractor cab but on foot with his dogs.

At least Hurley was alive. She knew that much.

She had waited, painfully breathless, the blood pounding in her ears, when the first word came of an accident. "Your friend . . ." Volkov had said, and a bearded face had leaped instantly into her mind, blue eyes slightly mocking (or so it seemed to her), an arrogance in his grin (or was it only a determination as strong as her own?). She had tasted a bitter sense of loss that made her tremble. Then Volkov had said, "The helicopter pilot. There has been no word from him. He flew into a storm and vanished."

She grieved for Hank Forbes, but she couldn't hide even from herself the relief she felt that it was Forbes, not Hurley, who was missing. Was that guilt the reason she had been so ready to join the search for the missing pilot? It was a question she couldn't answer for herself. No shrinks available on the Ice, she thought. Maybe there should be. They would be kept as busy as construction ants.

The face of the glacier was laced with sastrugi, making the trip across it slow, laborious and punishing. The tractor's rasp rose higher, and she felt the edge of every spine of ice vibrating through the vehicle. Slammed around inside the cab, she had to hold on to a brace in the door panel that served as a panic bar. Her jaw tightened to keep her teeth from rattling.

"It is not far," Volkov shouted above the tractor's din. She didn't know if he meant the far side of the glacier or the canyon they had selected as their goal.

Radio signals Forbes had been sending just before he disappeared had been heard at the TERCO base camp in the mountains and at the listening posts at the South Pole and McMurdo Station. Triangulated from these coordinates, Forbes's approximate location at the moment of his last message had been pinpointed. Kathy McNeely had been surprised to discover that the pilot had been flying toward the coastline where the *Shevchenko* now anchored, the vicinity of last year's *Kowloon* oil spill. He had also been close to the continent's edge when his last, desperate call was heard.

From the Soviet vessel, Volkov had communicated by radio with the TERCO base, where a rescue attempt was being organized and mounted. He had talked with Rupert Merrill. Afterward, in the *Shevchenko*'s small lounge, he told Kathy what he had learned. "Rescue party has long way to go. We are much closer. This company, TERCO, had smaller field camp closer to place where Forbes was flying, but it is shut down." Volkov frowned, his heavy black brows knitting, as if this revelation were in some way significant.

"What do they say Hank was doing? Why was he flying in our direction?"

"Merrill say, Forbes was wishing to help our search. He was looking for oil spill or damage to penguins and other animals."

The words pierced, painful as a splinter driven under a fingernail. "He was so decent," she said, remembering the pilot's amiable grin, a kind of casual grace in his economy of words and matter-of-fact courage.

"Is not certain he is dead."

"But they think he is?"

"Is very possible," the Soviet scientist admitted. "But he is resourceful man, I think. For such a man there is always the hope."

"Are you suggesting what I think you are, Alex? That we go look for him ourselves?"

"It was your wish, my dear Katya, to search for oil spill. Our tractor is ready for this. It can take us along the coastal shelf as far as possible." His finger drew a line across a map he had rolled out, indicating the edge of the ice shelf and moving along the coastline to the east. Where the finger paused, east of the two landmark glaciers visible from the ship, he said, "Here is canyon. It climb into mountains. And here"—his finger tapped a spot not far inland along the path of the canyon, a blank space on the map between two ridges—"here is where last signal was sent."

Kathy stared at the blank spot with rising excitement. "If we can reach that canyon, if there's a way into the mountains . . ."

"We will be looking for oil spill, look for penguins, but it is also possible for us to go as fast as possible to this canyon. Then we will see."

"I would be very grateful, Alex."

Volkov shrugged, grinned, began to roll up the map. "It is, what you Americans say, we catch two birds with one stone. I would say kill, but there have been too many birds killed."

"Far too many."

"Do you believe there is some link? The oil . . . the birds . . . TERCO?"

"I can't tell you exactly why, Alex, but . . . probably. And I think we can find it. If we keep searching."

They slept that first night on the ice in one tent, Kathy and Volkov, with Survivor lying between them as chaperon. Hurley wouldn't have approved, Kathy knew, but the arrangement was about as far from a love nest as she could imagine. Just two cold, weary people, crawling into their sleeping bags as soon as they could, still wearing protective layers of clothing.

Anyway, it was her business. Thoughts of Hurley were becoming a bit of a nuisance, as persistent as a bad conscience.

Up early, they broke camp, packed up their gear and fired up the tractor. Its unmuffled snarl broke like a thunderclap across the field of snow. An awful sound in this land of such pure silences, Kathy thought, like running a dune buggy around inside a cathedral . . . but in the early morning, on this barren ice shelf, it was comforting to hear. It was the sound of survival.

Volkov communicated with his ship by shortwave radio before they started off. "Weather forecast is not good," he informed Kathy. "There is depression building over ocean. We may have to turn back sooner than we wish."

"Not yet, Alex."

He nodded slowly, not surprised by her answer.

Shortly before noon, plodding eastward past the second of the two glaciers in their path, they came to a wide ice shelf near the bottom of a canyon. The shelf was serrated by crevasses, and Volkov drove the tractor very slowly, picking his way. After a while he stopped, leaving the engine running. Like Kathy, he had been relieved to have the engine start so readily this morning, and he wasn't about to risk restarting it.

Kathy and Volkov walked over the hard snow to the edge of the shelf. Survivor hobbled along behind them. The table dropped off in a sheer plunge to the sea ice a hundred feet below, a break so clean and sharp it could have resulted only from a monumental split in the ice.

"Ice break off here, I think," Volkov said. "Make very large iceberg."

They were standing at a corner of the bay. The cliff on which they stood had suffered at least two massive recent breaks. The first of these had exposed a wall of blue ice that stretched more than a thousand feet across the inner curve of the bay. She would never have forgotten such a dramatic feature, Kathy thought.

"This cliff wasn't here a year ago," she said. "It wasn't like this then."

"Much has happen here. But is no oil. Few birds are left now; it is too late in summer. I think we will not find what happen now."

"Any chance it could have happened farther inland?"

"Penguins would not go so far from water, I think."

"Unless something attracted them. They're curious creatures, Alex."

Volkov turned his gaze toward the mountains. A little earlier, while they were traversing the second glacier, a gate had seemed to open in the mountains, revealing a glimpse of a long, snow-bound valley rising between snowbound ridges. It was not visible from their present position, but it was somewhere in that valley, if Volkov's mark on his map was accurate, that Hank Forbes had disappeared.

"Let us go back," he said abruptly.

"But why?"

"Back to tractor, I mean. I wish to look at map."

Back in the smothering warmth of the cab, Volkov donned and then removed a pair of reading glasses, which quickly steamed up; it was the first time Kathy had seen him wear them. He handed her the map on which he had marked the location of Hank Forbes's last radio transmission.

"Is quite close, I think, is it not so?"

"It could be."

"It will not be easy to find small helicopter in all this. . . ." He gestured toward the mountains. They both were aware of the challenge, not only to find a way to climb to that snow valley but also to avoid the many hazards along the way. "We also do not know how far Forbes might have flown after radio signal. Even if he went one, two kilometers . . ." Volkov's shrug was eloquent. If they were even that far off in their calculations, and if the snow had drawn even a thin veil over the downed chopper, they would never find it.

"We have to try, Alex."

"Yes, *moya dorogaya* . . . we will try."

TWENTY-EIGHT

"THE SON OF A BITCH is flying here," Len Sears said.

"With a weather front warning out?"

"Yeah. I guess you know what that means."

"What do you think it means, Lenny?"

"The snoop knows something."

"If he *knew* anything, Lenny, we'd have heard about it. And if Forbes knew, he wouldn't have been able to hide it for a week."

"I told you Forbes was always sniffing around, asking questions."

"Which means he was trying to *learn* something, not that he already had the answers."

Rupert Merrill studied Sears thoughtfully. Outside the long shed that served as TERCO's field headquarters, a big Trackmaster was waiting, its engine rumbling, steam rising into the cold air from its exhaust stack. The news that Michael Davis was en route from the Amundsen-Scott Station had been unwelcome, but it was nothing that couldn't be handled if they kept their heads.

And Sears kept his nerve.

Lenny had changed since that business with Dr. Jeffers. *A guilty creature,* Merrill thought, *looking over his shoulder all the time.* Some men were hardened by the kind of act Sears had committed. Others came unraveled. Sears was acting more and more like a member of the second group.

Merrill wondered if he could safely leave Sears behind at the camp, with Mike Davis and, presumably, others coming to help search for Forbes. But it was either that or send Lenny down to the other camp—with a fifty-fifty chance that he might encounter other would-be rescuers coming from below. The latest radio signal from the Russian ship had spoken of a search party setting out, including the American woman. Jeffers's close friend, Merrill remembered. Dr. McNeely.

"I'm counting on you, Lenny."

"Sure, I know that. Nothing to worry about."

"But I *am* worried."

Sears's flush darkened his already weathered face and neck. He was feeling very unlucky again, even though Merrill had assured him it was highly unlikely Hank Forbes and his helo would be found at all, impossible that Forbes would be found alive.

"I told you, I can handle it."

"Be cooperative as hell, especially with Davis. Tell him anything he wants to know, within reason. Let him talk to the crew; they don't know anything about Forbes except that he was here and he flew off on his own and everyone thought he was a great guy. Nobody has anything to say against him. And I've already spoken to every man in the crew about our lower camp. If Davis or anyone else asks about it, it's no secret. It's just a field camp for some core sample drilling at a different site, a small operation, no big deal, and it's already been shut down for this season."

"But if anyone gets there—"

"I'll be there first, and I'm shutting it down. By the time I'm through, it'll look like just what I'm saying it is, a small field research camp. So we're taking out a few rock samples; nobody has to know what they are, nobody will care. Right now it's

Forbes they're interested in. Give them all the help they ask for, Lenny . . . but stall."

"How am I supposed to do that without making them suspicious? Especially this reporter."

"They're not going anywhere on foot, Lenny."

"What if they try to fly down? They'll be ahead of you."

"Nobody's crazy enough to try to fly one of those big cargo planes through these narrow canyons with the snow blowing."

"A helo could——"

"Did Davis or anyone else say anything about a helo?"

"No, but Forbes was one of their guys, they might——"

"The helos are grounded all over this damned continent," Merrill said. "You heard the order out of McMurdo yourself earlier today. Davis is coming in a Hercules. I'm surprised McMurdo is letting it come here."

"What if they want to use some of our equipment? We've got another tractor."

"Lenny, use your head. I think it's not at all unusual if we're short of fuel—after all, this is the end of the year for us here— or if some of our equipment isn't running. You can handle that, right?"

Sears nodded, his expression sullen, taking the last question as an implied rebuke.

Lenny was fast becoming a liability, Merrill thought. Maybe it was time to think about a replacement.

"When are you leaving?" Sears asked after a long silence.

"Like right now."

"You heard the weather report; you could get caught if the storm moves in fast."

"I won't get caught. And that Trackmaster can go through just about anything. It's not like it's my first trip down to the lower camp."

"You shouldn't be trying to handle the rig alone. I could drive and keep it running if anything breaks down."

"I need you here, Lenny. I'm taking Ben Carmichael with

me, nobody else. He knows how to handle the tractor, and he also knows how to keep his mouth shut."

Sears appeared, if anything, more sullen.

Maybe, Merrill thought, giving Carmichael more responsibility wasn't such a bad idea. Maybe it was an idea whose time had come.

Brian Hurley's run down the mountain had begun more than twenty-four hours before Rupert Merrill left TERCO's base in a powerful Caterpillar tractor. The Trackmaster would rumble its way across open ice and bulldoze through deep snow without slowing, maintaining a relatively swift fifteen-mile-per-hour pace, most of the time with little regard for the terrain. It would be slowed frequently, however, by the need to detour around pressure ridges where two deep plates of ice had collided in an upheaval or where the drifts were too new and soft to carry the heavy weight of the tractor.

Hurley was traveling almost as fast, the downhill run nothing like his labored journey up the Hartsook Glacier. He had set out at midnight, having taken only a few hours' sleep at his second camp. Hal Berkowski, expecting further heated argument in the morning, was taken by surprise. By the time he was roused from his hut, Hurley had the dog team hitched up and running.

It was twilight at that hour, the first time the sun had been invisible since early spring. Though the silvery half-light lasted less than an hour past midnight before the sun rose again, it was a reminder to Hurley that time was running out on this Antarctic season. He was astonished to discover how little he cared about his own plans or Berkowski's tantrums.

He followed the finger of a small glacier, one of a pair visible on Berkowski's map that cascaded down the mountain slopes toward the ocean, reaching the coast in the vicinity of the infamous *Kowloon* oil spill. There were hundreds of such river roads across Antarctica, reaching like the legs of an octopus from the mother plateau toward the sea. Perhaps because this one was a relatively young, fast-moving glacier, it proved to offer surprisingly few serious obstacles for a single sledge and a team of dogs. Its rapid flow had prevented the formation of dangerous crevasses, and its surface registered few of the dips and spines of the underlying rock strata. Even the infernal, ever-present sastrugi were smaller and less punishing than usual.

Though the going was easy, the sledge lightly laden—Hurley had taken on only the minimum supplies at the last camp, principally food for the dogs—he stopped every few hours to rest the team. Each delay increased his anxiety. He couldn't shake the feeling that Hank Forbes's accident was part of a pattern, related in some way to Carl Jeffers and that cut lifeline. If he was right, if one or both of these incidents had not been an accident at all but deliberately caused, what he was looking at was murder. And it meant that everyone closely associated with the two men and their activities might also be at risk. Especially if—like McNeely—they wouldn't leave it alone.

He didn't stop to give himself a few hours' sleep until the sun set, not long before midnight, and the eerie twilight returned, painting the icy landscape in luminescent shades of pink and lavender. By then he had been traveling around the clock with only brief rest stops for the huskies. Dutch, though he wouldn't give up, had picked up a cut on one front pad, and all the dogs were showing signs of fatigue.

Hurley raised his tent, treated, fed and watered the dogs and fell into his sleeping bag. He hadn't realized until that moment how close to exhaustion he was. He estimated that in the twenty-four-hour run, downhill, he and the dogs had covered close to one hundred and fifty miles.

He woke shortly after six o'clock that second morning.

The sledge team settled in quickly and found its rhythm, pushed by downslope katabatic winds stronger than they had been the day before. The winds stirred up light drifts, reducing visibility, increasing Hurley's sense of lonely isolation, along with the anxiety he could not shake.

While Hurley was scraping the last of some frozen eggs and

sausage off his plate that morning and preparing to break camp, Rupert Merrill was at TERCO's base camp, ordering the Track-master to be fueled up and made ready. When Hurley stopped to give the dogs their first rest, shortly after ten o'clock in the morning, Merrill was preparing to leave his base and weighing Len Sears's shortcomings in this crisis.

By that time a pressure system over the Southern Ocean was making itself visible in a dramatically dark and gloomy sky. The depression surged south and east toward Antarctica. As the winds grew stronger, the clouds thicker and blacker, and snow began to fall, the great depression spiraled in toward the coast-line east of the Antarctic Peninsula.

From the United States stations at McMurdo and Anvers Island, and from a dozen international bases scattered around the edge of the white continent, storm warnings went out to all ships and aircraft.

When the warnings came, Merrill had left camp. Though Hurley carried shortwave radio equipment, he had made no attempt to communicate with his last camp or with one of the NSF listening posts within range. With Merrill also temporarily out of touch with his base, neither he nor Hurley knew clearly what was coming.

TWENTY-NINE

————————

THE SEEMINGLY SOLID SURFACE OF SNOW collapsed under the weight of the Soviet tractor. It hung halfway across a chasm. One set of tracks lost all traction, clawing at the air.

As the split in the ice opened up, Kathy McNeely cried out in alarm. The vehicle tilted downward. Reacting swiftly, Alex Volkov braked and reversed. The rear tracks dug into the ice, stopping their forward tilt. The tractor shuddered to a stop, nose and forward tracks dropping over the edge of a crevasse.

"*Yob tvoyumat!*" Volkov cursed the tractor. "Katya, quickly! Get out now!"

Kathy didn't argue. She popped open the door of the cab, clambered onto the rear platform behind it and released Survivor from the short length of chain attached to his collar. The back end of the tractor was sticking up in the air, its nose down; it resembled a big duck drinking. The snow beneath it was hard.

Kathy started to help the husky down from his perch, but he was ahead of her, hopping down with the three-legged agility that never ceased to surprise her.

Volkov appeared beside them. "I will release the two sleds. If tractor goes down, at least we will not lose everything."

"Maybe you shouldn't get back in that cab yourself, Alex."

"I will try to back out."

Her instinctive protest died in her throat. She was uncertain of the tractor's capabilities on snow and ice in a situation like this. Surely Volkov was more knowledgeable.

The growl of the tractor's engine rose louder as Volkov increased power. The tracks began to move, grinding into the skin of snow and the underlying ice. The tractor lurched, slipping sideways. It heaved backward about a foot before it lost the distance gained.

The tracks cut deeper into the ice, but the vehicle could not back away from the edge of the crevasse. The loud rasp of the engine died away to a muttering idle.

Through the windshield, which was fogged on the inside, Kathy could make out the indistinct shape of Volkov's head in his fur cap bobbing up and down vigorously as he swore at himself and the tractor.

He opened the cab door and threw out a length of wire antenna. At Volkov's direction Kathy quickly stretched the antenna out to its full length. After a few minutes of fiddling with the shortwave radio, Volkov spoke urgently in Russian. Guessing that he was calling for help, Kathy stepped back to survey their situation. Her glance fell on the motor toboggan before swinging toward the pass into the mountains they had been heading for.

Clambering cautiously from the tractor's cab, Volkov jumped to the surface. Though the vehicle didn't move, its position, half in and half out of the crevasse, remained precarious.

"I have call for help," the Soviet scientist explained. "Tractor must be pulled back. *Bozke*! Is too dangerous to try to do any more alone."

His glance flicked toward the ominously darkening sky. The clouds were moving very fast, driven by strong winds at higher altitudes.

"How long before they can get here?"

"They bring second tractor for pulling. They must bring it

275

from ship. It will be five, six hours, maybe longer. I think it is safe to wait inside cab, where it is warm."

"You're not going to get me to sit in there for six hours, teetering on the edge of a crevasse!"

"Then we will make shelter," Volkov replied. "We have our tent, and there is time. It is quite certain storm is coming. Only question is, how bad it will be."

"I don't want just to sit here and wait, Alex."

"We must wait for men from ship. I must use radio signal as guide to make certain they find us."

"One of us has to stay here, I agree. But we still have your toboggan. I could go on up through the pass and see what I can find."

"Is not such a good idea, I think."

"It's a great idea, and you know it."

"I don't think you should go alone, Doctor. Clouds are moving very fast, you see? If blizzard comes . . ."

"I'll turn around and head right back as fast as I can go. But that's all the more reason for me to make a quick run up there now. We may not get another chance."

"Is too dangerous."

"I promise I won't take any foolish risks, Alex. And if there's nothing there, I promise that's it. You get your tractor out of trouble and we'll turn around and go back to the ship. We're blocked off from continuing along the coast here by those ice formations to the east anyway, and we can't go very far inland with the weather as threatening as it is."

"I do not like this, Katya."

"Just show me how to start this toboggan. I've driven one just like it at our camp, so it's not like I'm an absolute novice. What can go wrong?"

"Many things can go wrong. It can turn over; you see here what can happen." He scowled in the direction of the beached tractor. "Or motor can fail and not start. You will be alone—"

"I'll take Survivor with me."

"Is not the same."

"Stop arguing, Dr. Volkov. You know darned well this is the best option we have. I'll go on ahead, just far enough to convince myself there's no sign of Hank's helo or an oil spill or anything else along this route we should know about. I'll be back before your men get here from the *Shevchenko*."

"If storm come . . ." he argued lamely, accepting defeat.

"I'll come barreling down the mountain. Believe me, I'm not about to let myself be caught up there in a blizzard!"

They were brave, confident words, and she would soon recall them with a far different feeling.

There was a splendor in being alone in the snow valley. Fantastic walls of snow and ice rose on either side of her, sculpted into blocks and towers, hiding the underlying shapes of the mountain rock. The awesome silence was shattered only by the rasp of her small motor toboggan, which ran on rubber tracks with metal claws, chugging at a steady five miles per hour.

A layer of soft snow covered the hard-packed surface beneath, but the powder was not deep enough to impede the progress of the toboggan. A large windscreen shielded her from the strong winds blowing down the long valley toward her, and there was room for Survivor to ride on a second seat directly behind hers.

She saw no evidence of human presence, though she was certain that the small TERCO camp could not be far away.

Darkness came before she had been an hour in the valley. She had been so intent on her scrutiny of the snow terrain ahead and the challenge of picking out a safe pathway for herself that she had paid little attention to the ominous blackening of the sky behind her. Then, quite suddenly, the sky disappeared. The endless day turned into surprising night. She had to turn on the toboggan's single headlight, which sent a spear of light outward over the white surface and reflected off the first whirling flakes of snow.

The blizzard struck with stunning force. The snow valley,

clear just a few moments earlier, was obscured by falling and blowing snow, grainlike, hard and stinging. The silence was filled with a rising rush of sound.

Kathy tried to turn back. The wind howled down upon her from behind. Clouds of snow whirled around her, so thick the headlight was able to penetrate them for only a few feet. Her vision was reduced to no more than an arm's length in any direction.

She felt the gusts like physical blows on her back. Her lone headlight seemed to vanish, remaining only as a dancing brightness of snow crystals against the toboggan's windscreen. She could no longer be certain in what direction she was moving, where the toboggan was taking her. Helpless as a blind person, she drove slowly through chaos.

The toboggan tipped over the crest of a snowbank and slid downward, out of control. Near the bottom of the bank it tipped over, throwing Kathy and Survivor out into the snow.

Panic thudded in her breast. Though the motor kept on racing, at first she couldn't see the vehicle. Then a smudge of light —the headlight—drew her. She was aware of Survivor beside her, struggling out of the snowbank, giving a single excited bark.

She tried to right the toboggan. It weighed more than she had thought, or the grip of the snow was tighter. Her boots slipped on hard ice, and she fell against the machine. Out of caution, then, after a moment's hesitation, she shut off the motor, praying that it would restart later.

With that alien voice silenced, she was left to confront the roaring wind. It assaulted her senses, numbed her.

After a brief struggle she tilted the toboggan upright. It balanced precariously on edge for a moment, then flopped erect.

But a wall of snow, steep and soft, the bank down which she had tumbled, now rose ten feet before her. There was no way the toboggan could climb it.

She had left the headlight on, and a glow to her left caused her to turn toward it. She gasped. The light, though dimmed by drift in the air, penetrated an ice formation, blue-green in color, with sharply faceted faces to its many shapes, which formed a cluster like blocks of crystal. And the light revealed a hollow space at the base of the formation, an ice cave.

She didn't wait to analyze the fierce new hope that gave her the strength to drag the toboggan over to the cave's entrance, then haul it halfway inside. Working feverishly, she unloaded the emergency supplies packed on the back of the machine, grateful once more for Alex Volkov's foresight. Within a few minutes, guided by the toboggan's headlight, she had ground-sheets spread on the icy floor of the cave, her sleeping bag rolled out, a small Primus stove beginning to shed a faint wave of warmth through the cave. When she turned off the toboggan's headlight, the flickering light from the stove danced within the walls of ice, painting a mysterious and incredibly beautiful grotto.

She hung her parka on the front of the toboggan to dry out. Then, shivering uncontrollably, she crawled into the icy folds of her sleeping bag, where she continued to shake for long minutes, until her body warmth began to dispel the chill.

Survivor crept onto the groundsheet beside her and placed his head between his paws, watching her by the pale green light.

"Hurley will be mad as hell when he hears about you sleeping here with me instead of outside. Can't you hear him yelling?"

—*Where am I supposed to get another dog?*

—*There are plenty of dogs. The Kiwis have them, so do the British, the Aussies, the Argentineans. You won't have any trouble replacing him.*

—*You've ruined him.*

—*He's not ruined, Hurley, he's just more civilized. He's learned to enjoy a few of the comforts of his new station.*

—*Women!*

That was something Antarctica had done to her, she mused— one of the things. She now spent an inordinate amount of time either talking aloud to a dog or carrying on these fantasy conversations with Brian Hurley.

Of course, the latter weren't conversations, really. They almost always descended into conflict. Heated, stubborn arguments. But not always . . .

—*Don't you like women, Hurley?*

—*Sure, I like women.*

—*You have a funny way of showing it.*

—*Sometimes . . . it's not easy. Hell, it's never easy.*

—*My God, I think you're embarrassed. The great Hurley, blushing. Does that mean you don't have a girl?*

—*Yes . . . no. That is, I do have a girl. She doesn't know it yet.*

How absurd, she thought, to lie here inside an ice grotto, a light like a candle flickering nearby making her think of a house of worship, the surface ice behind the Primus stove melting from the warmth she had brought inside, turning the wall smooth and sleek, then freezing again as soon as it slipped out of reach of that small radius of heat, the wind howling outside, snow so deep she might never dig herself out, and all the while she filled her mind with schoolgirl fantasies.

She wondered where he was now, whether he was safely out of the storm's way, whether he had reached his goal, climbed to the top of the glacier, tasted the joy of achievement.

—*I never meant to put you down, Hurley. What you've done . . . it's something.*

—*I know you didn't.*

—*How could you know?*

—*I saw it in your eyes.*

Absurd, she thought.

THIRTY

JACK BENTEEN HAD KNOWN THE RISK he was taking, but he was committed. Even his commanding officer at McMurdo had been reluctant to give him a direct order against his flight plan. After all, one of their own was missing.

With a single passenger rattling around in the big cargo plane, Benteen was past the midpoint of his flight when the first radio message alerted him to the existence of a major depression forming over the ocean. The blackened skies ahead of him, heavy dark clouds climbing like the Montana thunderheads he remembered from childhood, had already conveyed their own warning. The urgent signal from the South Pole listening post only confirmed what Benteen was already feeling in his gut.

By then it was too late to turn back. That's what he told himself.

He was going to race the storm to the TERCO base, and if he didn't win . . . well, ol' Hank Forbes was gonna have some company.

*   *   *

A side wind rocked the plane. Benteen felt the Hercules shudder from the force of the blow. "Shake, rattle and roll, you bitch," he growled. "Just give me five minutes more."

"Do you always talk in song titles?" Mike Davis joked.

The reporter had taken the copilot's seat next to Benteen, having come forward from the empty cargo area when turbulence caused the whole aircraft to rock and shimmy. Benteen glanced at him. Davis looked pale and queasy.

"You're not gonna be sick, are you? This airline doesn't supply urp bags."

Davis's expression mirrored acute misery. "Just get us down."

Benteen grinned. "Hey, this trip was your idea, remember?"

"Don't remind me."

The pilot's grin lingered as he turned his attention back to the controls, but by then the expression was a kind of tic that no longer related to what he was thinking or feeling.

The depression, always fiercest where it struck the Antarctic coast, had hurled winds in the upper stratosphere over the mountains, bringing ice clouds and a rare snowfall to the polar plateau. Benteen had raced toward the coast at lower altitudes, not exactly puddle jumping like a helo pilot but giving a good imitation. In the illusory atmosphere created by the rising storm he seemed to be brushing the mountain peaks and ridges with the tips of his wings as he followed a chain of the Transantarctic Mountains on a twisting course toward the sea.

For a while he remained above the snow flurries, but as he descended, he passed through ice clouds and curtains of drifting snow. His cocoon of visibility began to shrink.

"You strapped in, Davis?"

"Yeah."

"Do you believe in God?"

There was a moment's silence. In the circumstances Mike Davis found himself taking the question seriously. "I guess so. I'm not sure who He is, though. Do you?"

"You fly down here on the Ice long enough, you become a believer. Anyway, it won't hurt to pray a little."

"You think He's on our side, Jack?"

This time Benteen was silent for a time, so long that Davis thought he wasn't going to answer. Then he said, "I don't think He takes sides. I mean, if you're gonna do something stupid, He's gonna let you be stupid, you know?"

"Jack, I—"

"That's not a complaint. You try to do something that's right, He's gonna let you do that, too."

"What you're saying is, we're on our own."

"Looks that way."

They had descended between two flanks of the mountains, flying over the cascade of a minor glacier perhaps thirty miles wide. The pattern of glaciers was familiar to anyone who had flown regularly over Antarctica, who had seen how these walls of ice pushed down from the polar plateau through mountain passes, filled depressions and valleys, smashed everything in their path, ground smaller peaks into gravel, moving inexorably on, year after year. A veteran of five years on the Ice, Benteen was sometimes startled to fly over a familiar glacier and see how far it had advanced since the last time he noticed it, as if it had happened overnight.

After checking his gyroscope, he made a small correction in his flight path, turning a couple of degrees east. "There ought to be another canyon over this way," he said, talking more to himself than Davis.

"How are you going to see it in this stuff?"

Benteen grinned. "Hell, we're not into the real snow yet. If it's blowing hard when we come down . . ."

A head wind rose up and smacked the Hercules as if it had run into a wall. To Benteen if felt as if the big plane had stopped in midair. A heavy vibration built up quickly, until the whole aircraft seemed ready to shake apart. It was during that moment that Benteen, peering out at wings that flapped like a bird's, saw how much ice had already built up on them.

They swooped down over a long, enclosed valley, which was exactly where it was supposed to be, and what did you know about that? Maybe God was on their side after all. But you could never let yourself get too sure about that, because in the next instant they were flying through heavy snow, flying blind, instruments only, descending faster than Benteen liked because of the excess weight building up on wings and fuselage, coming in over an ice shelf that was supposed to be wide enough and level enough for a safe landing on skis, but that supposition was based on your being able to see where you were, watch the ground come up to meet you. All Benteen had were pencil lines of light on the screen before him, lining them up the way a kid played an arcade game, and if you won, if he won, the prize was getting to stay alive, able to play the next game.

Suddenly they flew out of the stratus of snow, which lay like a lid over an ice shelf with about a hundred feet of relative clear sandwiched between them. Benteen whooped with elation. He experienced an infusion of awe, as if he were witnessing a miracle. Then he was too busy to think, adjusting his flaps, feeling the side winds buffet the aircraft brutally, cursing the winds under his breath, all the while bringing the Herc down in a sort of dance because of those side winds, until there was no longer room to dance. He could see the buildings of the field camp then, or rather some lights strung over the huts, visible through powder drift.

He set the skis down gently, a lover's caress, praying that the snowpack was level and hard enough and that it didn't hide rocks or troughs that would flip him over if one of the skis struck them. He bounced into the air once, twice, touched down and felt the runners skate over the surface and knew that he had pulled it off. He experienced a quiet, fierce inner pride, something he could never describe or fully explain, very fleeting, but the kind of moment he lived for.

Slowing, flaps down, beginning a wide circular turn and taxiing toward the lights that glowed mysteriously through blowing snow, "Hey," he said, "not so bad, huh?"

Mike Davis was speechless.

THE ICE

*　　*　　*

The cataract of ice that Brian Hurley followed toward the sea plunged down the mountain in a steep, sometimes precipitous slide. As he picked his way through seams and folds, across washboard snow plains and down smooth slopes, Hurley came to understand that the conditions making this downhill run so swift would make the same glacier appallingly difficult, if not impossible, to climb. At times the sledge careened down steeply angled faces almost out of control, the dogs running effortlessly, Hurley jumping on the back of the sledge for a free ride.

He was never aware of the pass Hank Forbes had followed to a snow valley east of the nearest chain of ridges, which formed one containing edge of the glacier. Hurley's road remained open and clear before him. The map he was using, taken from Hal Berkowski, showed the approximate location from which Forbes had sent his last signal, somewhere in these mountains but closer to the ocean. The rough calculation provided by the map did not indicate that, in fact, the signal had come from the other side of the peaks.

Hurley would later be astonished by the distances he and the dogs covered in that headlong ride down the glacier.

Then the blizzard swept in from the sea to meet him.

It came with screaming winds and biting, icy snow. For the first half hour he kept going, driven by the uneasy foreboding over Kathy McNeely's situation that had accompanied him on the whole journey. As the sky blackened and visibility closed down, making it impossible for him to see beyond Dutch, the lead dog, and soon not even him, Hurley knew that he had to stop, hunker down and wait out the storm.

He found a flat spot on the snow that gained a little protection from the bulk of an ice ridge but did not threaten his tent with heavy drifts. The tent blew down twice while he was trying to erect it. On the third try he managed to pull his storm guys taut and sink his ice screws before another gust of wind tore the tent loose. He used some of his supplies in crates to weight down the tent's apron. This time he brought more of his essentials inside. The huskies dug shallow caves for themselves in the snow, and at last, exhausted, Hurley crawled into the tent.

His hands shook and his teeth clashed audibly while he filled his Primus stove from a fuel can, located his Primus prickers and lit the stove. The flickering flame was almost as welcome as the immediate waves of warm air. Outside the tent there was no longer any light, only the massive blackness. There was no glacier, no sky, no mountain, only the dark fury of the storm.

The blizzard found Aleksei Volkov alone where he had taken refuge in the cab of the Soviet tractor. The rescue party from the *Shevchenko* had never reached him. The tractor remained balanced on the brink of a deep crevasse. Snowdrifts quickly built up around the vehicle, and he had the vague hope that they might help keep it more stable.

For the first two hours he kept the tractor's motor idling, even though it meant consuming precious fuel, in order to keep the heater blowing inside the cab. Then the engine coughed and died. Repeated attempts to restart it failed.

Like many vehicles designed for use in Antarctica, the tractor had an auxiliary, battery-powered hot-air blower, used principally for warming up a cold engine before starting. It could also provide heat for the cab. Volkov decided to use it only periodically rather than run down the battery pack.

The swift turn of events had been devastating. He had little fear for himself—he could wait out the blizzard in relative comfort even if his comrades were unable to get through to him —but Katherine McNeely had been caught up in the snow valley by the suddenness of the storm's arrival. Volkov had started after her but was soon driven back when he briefly became lost. To continue on foot during the heart of the blizzard would have been suicidal.

He could only wait, engulfed in the maelstrom of wind and

snow that blew so hard the stinging crystals etched patterns in the windows of the cab like corrosive sand.

Wait, and hope that Katya had found shelter in time.

The sailors from the Soviet ship at anchor outside the bay had succeeded in raising a second Caterpillar tractor to the top of the ice cliff just before the blizzard swept over them. Niki Sima-novich had planned to lead a contingent of five men from the *Shevchenko* to join Volkov and retrieve the other tractor from its hazardous situation.

The storm stopped them before they could get started. Ice clogged the air intake. After lengthy preheating and coaxing, the tractor's motor came fitfully to life. It stumbled for a minute or two. Then a crankshaft pin, weakened by the cold, snapped like a toothpick.

As the savage winds tore at the men outside and rocked the heavy tractor, it became clear that repairs were impossible.

The would-be rescuers retreated to the bottom of the cliff. There, on the edge of the sea ice, they were marooned. The wind-whipped waves raging between the ice and the *Shevchenko* made the sea impassable for the small boat and even for the military-type amphibious landing craft they had used to ferry the tractors from the ship.

Through the heart of the storm, Niki and the Soviet crew waited on the ice, partially sheltered from the fiercest winds by the bluff behind them but increasingly vulnerable to severe frostbite. Niki, with yellow blisters forming on his hands and his fingernails turning black, was even more afflicted by self-recriminations over his failed rescue attempt, and his fears for Volkov—and the American woman. He thought that if they were not found alive, his own life would be unbearable.

Within sight of the small group of men, the remnants of the emperor penguin colony crowded together on the sea ice, huddling for warmth. Nature had endowed them with remarkable protection against extreme cold conditions, but the younger chicks, born at the beginning of this summer season, had feathered coats not yet as thick and dense as those of mature adults. They were more vulnerable to severe snowfall. These youngsters bunched together in scrums for mutual warmth.

Many of the adults, safer at sea during such a storm, remained on the ice, plaintively calling for the chick that was now so nearly ready to leave them on its own journey. Finding it, they offered their own bodies for warmth and shelter.

The snow built up on the ice. After a time the mass of birds became almost invisible, their shrill calls fading, no longer audible in the wild keening of the storm.

THIRTY-ONE

MIKE DAVIS HAD HOPED to be in time to join the search party; he was too late. Rupert Merrill had left that morning for a small field camp closer to the coast from which the search for Hank Forbes was being carried out. It was the first Davis had heard of a second TERCO camp.

He said as much to Sears in TERCO's office, where he sought refuge from the gale winds sweeping across the ice shelf. "I didn't know you had another camp."

"Yeah, well, it's a smaller operation than this, just some core sampling in a different location to compare with what we've found at this level."

"That makes sense," the reporter said, wondering why Merrill hadn't seen fit to mention it before.

"From what they figure, our lower camp is close to where Forbes went down."

"How do you suppose it happened? You wouldn't think an experienced pilot would make a mistake like that."

"How do I know? How does anyone know why these things happen?"

"I thought maybe, you being here when he left . . ."

"Listen, Forbes left on his own. He flew into some shit. It was his choice, going where he had no business."

"Oh?" Davis's journalistic antennae rose, quivering. "What do you think he was looking for?"

"Whatever it was, I guess he didn't find it."

Evasive, Davis thought. And touchy. What had made Sears so hostile toward Hank Forbes—and so nervous about answering questions about him?

After a moment he asked, "How many men do you have down there? At your other camp, I mean."

"Four of our guys are still there."

"Have they been out searching for Forbes?"

"Yeah, no luck. Merrill went down there to direct things personally."

"Alone?"

"Him and Carmichael."

"Who's Carmichael?"

"One of our engineers," Sears answered curtly.

Not one of Sears's buddies, Davis guessed. Or was Sears put out because he had been left behind? Something didn't fit. If Sears hadn't got along with the helo pilot, why would he be angry about being left out of the search party?

The drift snow whirling about on strong winds had reduced visibility at the camp to a few feet in any direction. A lifeline had been strung between the various huts. Cautiously following one of them, Davis found Jack Benteen in one of the long huts that served as sleeping quarters for a half dozen of the crew. He shook hands all around, jotted down names, exchanged routine comments about the blizzard and accepted congratulations that he and Benteen had got down in one piece.

He didn't need Benteen's gloomy assessment about getting into the air again soon. "Not until this blows over," the pilot said. "We pushed our luck, Mike. Now we're stuck here. I just hope it isn't this bad down below. If it is, they'll never find Hank."

"Is it usually this bad closer to the coast?"

"It's usually worse."

Davis, who was feeling dry and parched, gratefully gulped a tall glass of water. He became even more grateful when one of the men fished a beer out of a bucket of snow and tossed it to him. He had an image of a television commercial with him as one of the guys having a great time guzzling beer down on the Ice. He took a chair and popped open the can. Maybe some of TERCO's crew would be more forthcoming than their boss.

"Any of you guys know what Hank Forbes was up to when he left here?"

He looked around inquiringly. The hut had gone very quiet all of a sudden. Several of the men exchanged glances before one spoke up. "He said he was trying to help out some scientists he'd met, something to do with injured penguins."

"The Operation Second Chance group?"

"He didn't say what they were called."

"Must be them," Davis said easily.

"He didn't say much of anything." Len Sears's harsh voice came from behind Davis. The reporter jumped nervously; he hadn't heard Sears come in. "I told you, we don't know what he was after. Dead birds, maybe."

"Looking for another oil spill?"

"We don't know, okay? He was just here for a few days. He had a wild hair itching him, he took off and that's it. Give it a rest, Davis."

The reporter smiled his best smile. "Just doing my job, Sears. A helo pilot disappearing is news, even in these jaded times."

Something *was* wrong here, he thought. And if his reporter's intuition was working at all, Len Sears was very close to coming unhinged. Jittery, eyes darting back and forth from Davis to the men in the hut, all of whom were uneasy or tense in a way they hadn't been before Sears arrived. A man ready to explode.

After an awkward silence Davis said, "I guess you haven't heard anything new from your people at the other site."

"In this storm we're not hearing anything at all. I was just on the radio. All I'm getting is interference."

Sears glared at the other men.

No one said anything.

It was that way through the rest of the afternoon and into the evening, with Sears hovering around or appearing without warning whenever Mike Davis was alone with one of the crew or looked as if he might be.

Dinner in the mess hall was unusual in Davis's Antarctic experience, for there was none of the expected casual joking and caustic banter. A pall had fallen over this base, Davis thought, that had nothing to do with the blizzard. Undoubtedly the storm was making matters worse, but there was a worm eating away inside this apple, hidden, turning it rotten.

His first breakthrough came when he had to use the toilet. Hugging the lifeline carefully, mindful of what had happened to Carl Jeffers, Davis made his way through blinding drifts. Could a freak thing like Jeffers's accident happen twice, a safety rope snapping in high winds?

The toilet facility was a small hut placed over a hole dug into the ice. Davis had used it shortly after landing, and at the time he had wondered how long it would be before this portion of ice and everything deposited in it would work its way down to the sea, carrying its own pollution.

The shed was dark, and he groped his way inside, feeling the walls. His hand touched something that moved, and his heart froze.

"Take it easy," a husky voice whispered in the darkness.

"Jesus Christ, who are you? You scared the piss out of me."

"That's what you came here for, isn't it?" The stranger chuckled. "Keep your voice down."

Davis's heart had gone into a high-speed gallop after the

initial frozen moment. He waited for it to slow down. "Why?" he whispered back.

"Sears."

The laconic answer seemed to say everything. Davis studied it for a moment. The bad vibrations he had sensed in the crew's hut and later at dinner had not been his imagination.

"Who are you, anyway?"

"Kornievski."

Recognizing the name, Davis immediately attached a square, blocky figure to it, a face with a big jaw, reddish brown hair, a nose that had been broken more than once and seemed to have been shaped the last time without any bone.

"What's going on?"

"A lot of us don't like some of the things that have been happening around here. Mind you, I don't think one of us is losin' any sleep over what TERCO's doing."

"What *is* TERCO doing?"

Kornievski did not answer the question directly. "Half of us have been oil field roughnecks, everywhere from Texas to Saudi Arabia and places in between. We're not World Park types, if you know what I mean."

"I think I do. Is TERCO looking for oil?"

"We were last year; at least we did some exploratory drilling. Then we started to track some mineral deposits. That's what Houston is after now. But that's not what's bothering us."

"Okay, what is?"

"Forbes." Kornievski was silent for a moment. "He shouldn't have gone up that day."

"Was the weather bad?"

"Not when he took off, no. But he had no warning."

"Benteen says TERCO would have been informed of a storm moving in. MacTown knew Forbes was here, had been for a week."

"Forbes didn't know about a storm. I talked to him before he fired up. He said it was clear, no problem."

"If a blizzard warning was sent, how could Forbes not have known?"

"You figure it, Davis. Maybe he didn't get the message."

The reporter tried to absorb this suggestion, shocked by the implications. "Listen, where can we talk besides here? Sears is going to be wondering what's keeping me."

There was a moment's silence. Then Kornievski said, "I think I said enough."

He brushed past Davis. The door opened briefly, letting in a blast of cold and snow. The figure disappeared immediately.

The reporter closed the door swiftly. He was shivering, not only from the cold.

THIRTY-TWO

BRIAN HURLEY DID NOT WAIT for the blizzard to exhaust itself completely. There was always the risk that like a fighter who had thrown too many punches, it would revive in the brief interval between rounds. He had endured similar Antarctic storms that lasted off and on for a week. As soon as he sensed a diminishing of the high winds, and visibility lengthened out to a dozen paces, he struck camp, hitched up the dog team and set off. The huskies, rested and eager once more, rent the cold air with sharp, excited barks.

The sledging was much slower and more difficult than before the storm. Most of the time the huskies were elbow-deep in fresh, soft snow. Every yard was gained by punishing effort. Luckily, after about a half hour, they broke out of heavy drifts onto a steep, open slope where the high winds had swept the surface clear of new powder, and the sledge's pace quickened.

As the wind continued to slacken, the dense curtain of blowing snow gradually lifted. The snow-covered peaks appeared to the right, their flanks achingly white with new snow. Soon the whole Antarctic panorama opened up before Hurley: endless fields of snow sculpted into free-form shapes by the wind, heavings of black rock, layered hills and crags of ice creating fantastic, multicolored formations. And far ahead, beyond the blunt prow of the glacier, a glimpse of water, gray as the clouds overhead.

An hour later, charging downslope from the lip of the glacier, Hurley rounded a dogleg turn and glimpsed a ship at sea. It lay at anchor in open water some distance to the west and about a half mile off shore—the Russian icebreaker. Some kind of vehicle, a pinprick of bright red, stood at the edge of the bluff that overlooked the wide apron of sea ice, too distant for Hurley to be certain what it was, although the presumption was that it was some kind of tracked vehicle.

Relief choked him up, made it hard to breathe. Volkov and McNeely must not have started their land search before the blizzard interrupted them. She was safe.

His gaze swept the bay, continued eastward and riveted as shock coursed through him.

Still far off, hardly recognizable as human, a single tiny figure struggled across a vast plain of snow. It must be a man, he thought; it couldn't be *her*. Hurley's mind refused to accept that possibility.

The man hardly seemed to be moving at all—certainly he made no progress—but as Hurley started toward him, he saw that the figure, hip-deep in snow, was actually moving in a circle.

Blindly.

The snow had crusted across this shelf just enough to support the weight of the running dogs and the light sledge. They raced toward the floundering man. When they drew closer, he stopped moving. He raised his head to peer wildly about him. He had heard something, Hurley realized: a yip from one of the dogs, a rattle from the sledge—small, sharp sounds carrying far in that immense stillness.

The figure remained motionless, staring blindly as Hurley drew closer and closer. *Snow-blind,* Hurley thought.

A man bulky in his heavy clothing, which included a red

NSF parka. A man wearing a fur hat, bear-paw mittens, heavy boots.

"Volkov!"

It was a moment before Hurley realized he had shouted the Russian's name aloud. Volkov turned toward the sound.

"Yes! Yes, who—"

"Hurley! My God, what happened? How did you get here?"

"Our tractor—it was on edge of abyss, a crevasse. It fell. I jump clear. . . ."

The scientist was exhausted, swaying on his feet. His lips were cracked and bleeding. He was without glasses, and the signs of conjunctivitis—severely inflamed eyelids and eyeballs—were obvious. Even without strong sunlight, the snow glare could cause extreme pain and diminished vision to unprotected eyes.

"I fall when I escape from tractor," Volkov said, as if he were interpreting Hurley's silence, "lose sunglasses."

Hurley asked the question he dreaded. "Dr. McNeely wasn't with you? She's back at the ship?"

"No, no!" Volkov burst out, plainly in distress. "That is why I am here. I thought to find her. We separate before storm."

"Where is she? Damn it, man, how could you let her go off alone? What was she trying to do?"

Volkov's blind, raw gaze stared past Hurley into his own anguish. "She take toboggan and go to search for missing helicopter pilot."

Furious, Hurley grabbed him by the shoulders and shook him. Volkov staggered back, too weak to resist. "Are you crazy? How could you let her do that?"

"She was insistent; I could not stop her."

"The hell you couldn't. It was your toboggan!"

"You must understand, I did not approve. Katya—Dr. Mc-Neely—is not a child, Mr. Hurley. She is strong-willed woman. She has what you say, very much mind of her own. She would do this no matter what I say."

"Why didn't you go with her?"

"I must stay with tractor after I call for rescue party to bring another vehicle. Katya's concerns—mine as well—were quite legitimate, for the missing pilot, Forbes, and for penguins who have been hurt, to find how this could happen. It is not for nothing she is called Bird Woman."

Hurley's anger began to drain away, leaving a residue of fear. "Where did she go?"

Volkov shielded his eyes, trying to peer in the general direction of the mountain ridges immediately inland, east of the glacier Hurley had followed. He could see a little, Hurley thought, already calculating Volkov's chances of survival if he were left alone. His comrades would be here before long in that red tractor.

"There is a valley in those mountains," said Volkov. "It was there Forbes disappeared. Katya take toboggan to go there. She tell me she know how to drive it. You understand, there was no storm yet. She promise to turn back if weather become bad. But it happen too quickly. She is there . . . somewhere."

His wave encompassed two chains of peaks, a snow valley that was not visible.

"I'm going to have to leave you here," Hurley said bluntly. "I have to find her."

"No! I go with you."

"That's not possible. You're in no shape to go anywhere. For one thing, you're blind."

"I can see little. Is getting better. You have extra glasses, perhaps?"

"I can give you those, but you'd only slow me down."

"I know where Katya was going. She has map, but I have study it. You will need me to find her, Mr. Hurley."

The Russian's stubborn insistence renewed Hurley's anger. But if there was any chance that he was right, that Hurley would need his knowledge of Kathy's goal, the possibility of taking him along had to be considered. He could ride in the sledge if he couldn't keep up.

Besides, Hurley knew, in the final analysis it would be very difficult to abandon him without knowing for certain that he would soon be found.

"You were going to try to walk into those mountains to find her?"

"Yes."

"You must care a great deal for her."

Volkov's ravaged eyes sought Hurley's. "Of course, my friend. But it is you she care for."

The simple statement, so assured, so heavy with apparent knowledge, stunned Hurley. Had she talked to Volkov? Opened her heart? He was both envious and elated—and instantly plunged into despair. Poorly equipped and unprepared, she had been trapped by the blizzard somewhere in that white wilderness. How could she have survived?

"There is camp somewhere in valley, an American company of geologists. She may have found refuge there."

"TERCO? But their research base is higher up. I talked to some of their people. They're doing core drilling at an altitude over twenty-five hundred feet."

"This is smaller field camp. It is close, Mr. Hurley. There is also rescue group trying to find missing pilot. So there is hope for Katya. We must not give up hope."

"No," Hurley whispered. "We'll find her."

"Then you will take me with you?"

Hurley nodded. He didn't really have a choice.

THIRTY-THREE

WITHIN HER GROTTO, carved like a chapel out of crystal ice, Kathy McNeely listened to the howling tumult outside her shelter and thought of Dante's Inferno, as if the many voices of the wind were the screams of countless lost souls. After a while she dozed off in spite of herself, more fatigued by her struggle up from the coastal plain to the snow valley than she had realized.

When she woke with a start, the voices were silent. She tried to sit up and was restrained by her sleeping bag. Her heart pounded with a nameless fear of the dead silence. Beside her, Survivor sat up, watching her, curiously alert.

Crawling out of her bag, she was immediately chilled. Hastily she pulled on her heavy sweater and wind pants over the clothes she had worn to bed and draped her parka over her shoulders. The Primus stove still burned low, and she turned up the flame. She was both hungry and thirsty. Water first, she thought, for herself and Survivor. Then food. What had Volkov put into the bag? Tinned fish, she found. Brown bread. A can of Del Monte fruit cocktail—where had he got that? she wondered, amused.

Pleased that she was able to smile.

When she had relieved herself in a corner of the grotto, feeling oddly guilty, as if the act were somehow sacrilegious, she warmed the fish in a pan and spooned out some of the fruit. Her thirst and hunger slaked, she gave Survivor the rest of the fish and turned her attention to her predicament.

She had decided the silence was not threatening but the opposite. It meant the blizzard had moved on, or at least the worst of it.

She edged past the motor toboggan, which was half buried in snow, and peered out of her ice cave. The wall of snow rose a dozen feet above her, almost meeting a brow of blue ice projecting from her crystal cave. Through an opening at the top like a narrow transom she could see a wedge of gray, cloudy sky, a pattern in motion changing quickly as the clouds scurried on.

She glanced at the toboggan. How could she ever drag it up through that soft, sifting snow?

Could she even climb out herself?

And what of Survivor? She was past underestimating his intelligence and adaptability, but could she really expect a three-legged dog with his fourth leg in a cast to climb straight up through twelve feet of powder snow?

There has to be a way out.

Her training was in science—in studying facts, evaluating their implications, reaching empirical conclusions, searching for alternative explanations. She had, lately, found her heart occasionally ruling her head, but this was no time for emotion, either false hope or irrational fear.

—*Use your head, my girl.*

—*Shut up, Hurley, I'm thinking.*

She could stand on the toboggan. Where would that get her? Three feet up at most. Step off into that white powder and she would be right back where she started.

Climb, she thought.

The grotto was her salvation.

It was a broken formation, like a work of architecture built over time by a mad, untrained artist, a thing of unpredictable beauty and no logic. But the ice was hard. Its many facets offered potential steps, ledges, handholds, unyielding surfaces.

She dug a length of nylon rope out of Volkov's supplies and tied one end of it to Survivor's collar. "No way you can climb with me," she said. "You'll have to wait till I can haul you up, okay?"

When she clambered onto the first block large enough to provide a step, the husky tried to follow.

"No!" Kathy said firmly. "Stay! That's Hurley's word, right? Stay."

She was back down herself in a moment. Her mittens slipped off the smooth ice surfaces, providing little purchase. She had seen something else in Volkov's kit while rummaging, an all-purpose tool that had a blunt end for use as a hammer, a hatchet's edge and extension spikes at the top. It would have to do.

She began to climb the outside of her cave, picking and gouging at the ice to create rough niches for gripping, even using the tool as a hook to pull herself up. It was slow, tiresome work, and her legs were soon quivering from the strain. Once her left calf cramped, an agonizing seizure, stalling her in place on the wall of the grotto until the muscle unclenched. She was sweating under her layered clothing. Her breath froze on her face mask.

And she inched upward.

Ten feet above the floor of her cave she crawled out onto a small ledge. Pushing erect, she looked out over the surface of the snow valley, pure white drifts extending across the valley to the wall of mountains on the far side. To her left the ledge offered access to what appeared to be older, hardpack snow.

It took her another five minutes to pull Survivor up onto the ledge with her. She peered down regretfully at the back end of the motor toboggan. There was no way she could raise it to the surface on her own.

"We're gonna have to walk out of this place, Survivor," she said aloud.

With the storm's passage, she assured herself that Volkov and his comrades would be looking for her, but she didn't want to stay where she was. They might miss her. She would go to meet them.

"You hear a tractor," she told the husky, "bark like hell."

She edged onto the snow, hugging the promontory of ice at her back, testing the surface gingerly with each step before transferring her weight. After a few moments she gained more confidence. The snow was firm, crusted, easily supporting her.

A peculiarly shaped mound blocked her way. She wondered if ice or rock lay underneath the snow. Followed by Survivor, she circled the mound. A view of the bottom end of the valley opened up. The blizzard had covered all trace of her passage across the snow, as surely as it had hidden any evidence of Hank Forbes and his helo. The knowledge was a painful admission. Alone with her dog, on foot, she had to abandon her search.

The snow collapsed beneath her feet. She gave a startled yell. In the same instant there was a rumbling above her. Suddenly the whole face of the bluff was moving, sliding, pouring down upon her. She was caught up in a small avalanche and hurled off her feet. She heard Survivor's bark before he disappeared under the snow. Like a swimmer bowled over in heavy surf, she was rolled and tumbled head over heels down a short slope before coming to rest. She swam frantically upward, trying to reach the surface.

She burst out of the snow, gasping for breath, her heart slamming against her ribs. She sucked in great gulps of air while the adrenal rush slowly eased. A final trickle of snow whispered past her down a shallow slope.

A whimper of pain triggered both relief and fresh anxiety. *Survivor!*

The dog lay on his side in the open, thrown clear of the slide onto a wide, flat ledge of blue ice. Just beyond was a shoulder of exposed rock.

Beside that, uncovered by the avalanche, was a portion of the shattered tail section of a helicopter. The small rear rotor was missing.

* * *

Survivor seemed unable to get to his feet. His hind legs scrabbled at the slippery surface feebly. Kathy McNeely feared that he had reinjured his fractured shoulder when thrown onto the ledge. She paused beside him, murmuring meaningless, soothing sounds, her hand reassuring as it rested briefly on his flank. Then she crept past him, edging slowly around the hump of brown rock.

The nose of the helo had split apart, exposing the cockpit and cabin as if they had been opened up for a cross-section view of the interior.

Hank Forbes was still strapped into the pilot's seat, leaning forward as if he were peering at something in his lap. Frozen in death, his skin was blue, a darker color than the translucent blue of the ice.

She was not sure how many minutes passed before she was able to approach the broken shell of the aircraft. She became aware of being cold, of shivering, of a pervasive sadness that settled over her like a physical weight.

Kathy approached cautiously, testing the surface. Here the snow had solid underpinnings, whether of ice or rock. Here, when the helo had plunged out of the sky, it had encountered nothing soft. It had broken apart on impact. A piece of the main rotor protruded out of the snow twenty yards away. A portion of the windshield was stuck against the ice above the crippled plane like a mounted trophy.

She did not need to touch the body, sheathed in ice, to know that Forbes had been dead for some time. What startled and dismayed her was the discovery that he had not been killed instantly in the crash. He had died slowly, alone, trapped in his seat. Her impression that, in death, he was staring at something in his lap was not mere chance.

His left hand held a page torn from a notebook.

The paper, made brittle by the cold, ripped easily when she tried to free it from Forbes's hand. A small corner remained in the viselike grip of his fingers. She made no attempt to pry it loose. She held the remaining fragments cautiously, piecing them together.

She was almost afraid to read the words scrawled on the tattered pieces of paper. They were confused snatches of phrases and words written in agony, with the full knowledge of death hovering near. They composed the testament of a dying man—admissible in a court of law, she seemed to remember—and they were a searing accusation: "Broken back—broken ankle—tail rotor tampered with—no accident—Jeffers—Sears—Merrill—check rotor—ask TERCO re drill site."

The horror of it was too immense to grasp immediately. Her thoughts whirling, she tried to reject the implications. Forbes had been in enormous pain, perhaps delirious, imagining things. But she didn't believe it. The price he had paid to record his last thoughts had been too great.

Someone had tampered with the helo.

Please God, no, she whispered to herself, *not Carl, too!*

A sound from Survivor, not quite a growl, alerted her. She scrambled back from the open cockpit, turning, fear trickling from the back of her neck down her spine.

Rupert Merrill stood at the top of a snowbank, staring down at her, silhouetted against the gray sky. "What did you find, Doctor? Notes?"

Kathy couldn't speak.

"What did he write? Gibberish, I suppose."

She did not answer.

Merrill stared in silence for a moment. "I'm sorry you found him. I really am."

His regret seemed genuine, but when he started down the bank toward her, half sliding in the snow, she felt immobilized with fear, like a bird hypnotized by a snake.

THIRTY-FOUR

By EARLY MORNING the banshee howl of the blizzard had diminished to a steady gale on the ice sheet where TERCO's base camp was situated. Visibility remained limited to a few feet because of blowing snow.

Unable to sleep, Mike Davis had filled some of the time interviewing a few of TERCO's crew, including two geologists who were involved in extracting ice cores from the shelf for study. They spoke enthusiastically about their work, causing Davis more confusion about TERCO's activities. Were his doubts misplaced, or was it possible that Merrill was playing some kind of double game, having some of his people carry on legitimate research while others were involved in secret, even forbidden exploration?

He had to talk some more with Kornievski. Get him alone without Sears in the background. That wasn't going to be easy, it seemed. Didn't the guy ever sleep?

On impulse he decided to brace Sears directly once more. Maybe what he needed was a little push. He found Sears in the shed that served as the camp's HQ as well as sleeping quarters for Merrill and his foreman. Sears offered coffee. Davis took note of the corner of the office crammed with radio gear and asked if there had been any late news.

Sears grinned. "MacTown says there's a storm out there."

"No kidding?" Davis found a folding chair and hooked it toward him. If Sears had decided it was time to be friendly, he would take whatever he could get while the mood lasted.

"Did Merrill get through okay to your other camp? Have you heard from him?"

"The signal was all chopped up; I could only hear bits and pieces. But he got there."

"That's some kind of stunt in a blizzard, isn't it?"

"He was driving a Trackmaster. Those things can keep going through just about anything. We'd established a safe route, no crevasses or anything like that. Merrill's only problem was getting lost when the blizzard hit before he and Carmichael reached our camp. I guess it was touch and go at the end, but they got through."

Sears was being positively loquacious, Davis thought.

"You mind telling me what research TERCO is doing at that other site?"

"It's no secret. We're doing some core drilling, same as we do here."

"That's all?"

"Who've you been talking to, Davis?"

"Anyone who'll talk to me. Nobody says much. I guess they're not supposed to. You're looking for minerals down there? Is that it?"

"Some of our guys are geologists. Sure, we want to know what's in the ground under this ice. But that's not the primary reason we're here."

"I heard it differently."

"Well, you heard it wrong."

The two men stared at each other in silence. Sears had papered over his earlier edginess, but it was still there under the surface. Like any experienced reporter, Mike Davis knew that people could often be goaded into saying or revealing more than they had intended if you kept after them and asked the right questions. Sears, he thought, was vulnerable.

He adopted a confidential tone. "What have you found down there, Lenny?"

The question came out of nowhere; he hadn't even known it was there until the words were out of his mouth. For an instant something naked and frightening flickered in Sears's eyes. Then it was gone, so quickly Davis wasn't sure what he had seen.

"You *have* been asking questions."

"That's why I came to you. I figure you can give me the answers everyone else is afraid to give."

"Nobody's afraid of anything. I told you what we were doing."

"Come on, Lenny, what's the harm? I'm going to find out anyway. You might as well give me your side of it so I've got it straight. Isn't that in TERCO's best interest?"

"You've got TERCO's best interests at heart, eh, Davis?"

"All I want is the truth." When Sears didn't answer but continued to stare at him in silence, Davis had a reckless impulse. Sears was near the edge. Push him over and see what happens.

He glanced toward the shortwave radio. "Were you here the other day before Hank Forbes took off?"

"Yeah, I was here."

"Didn't you get a weather report that morning or the night before?"

He watched Sears's eyes closely, but he couldn't be certain of the reaction. Something was there, but it might only have been anger over the persistence of the questions.

"How come Forbes went up in that helo when there was a storm warning out? Didn't he know?"

"You've got it all wrong, Davis. Forbes was here when that weather report came in. Hell, he was the one talked to MacTown. Going up that morning was his own decision."

Sears had to be lying. Why would an experienced pilot like Forbes ignore such an obvious danger signal? What was Sears covering up? Had he and Merrill withheld the information from Forbes? My God, that was— Davis felt cold. Sears saw him shiver and, unaccountably, grinned at him. "You think you have all the answers, don't you?"

"No. But I've got a few of them. I'll get the others."

"Yeah, I guess you will." Abruptly Sears stood up. Mike Davis flinched, then shook his head ruefully at himself when Sears reached for his parka and fished his outer boots from under a bench. "You want to know what TERCO is doing in Antarctica? I'll show you."

"What do you mean? Go out in this blizzard?"

"The worst is over; it's not so bad now. Anyway, we're only going across to the storage shed, and there's a safety line. Come on, you wanted some answers; I'm offering them to you."

"What's in the storage shed?"

"Ice core samples waiting to be shipped out. Mineral and rock samples, too."

"They wouldn't mean anything to me. I wouldn't know what they are."

"I think you will. Hey, you're supposed to be a science reporter, right? Come on."

Davis hesitated. Sears's mood swings bothered him, but how could he reasonably refuse? Maybe he was about to learn all there was to know about TERCO's activities on the Ice. It was a chance he couldn't pass up.

The cold struck him like something alive, tearing at his clothes. Snow and ice built up quickly on his face mask even in the short distance between the two huts—no more than twenty yards. Thank God for the lifeline! He could barely make out Sears's thickly padded shape a few feet in front of him, plodding through deep snowdrifts. The scene had a strange, luminous glow from the spotlights mounted between the buildings of the complex. Although they shed little useful light, they made the snowflakes and ice crystals dance and glitter like sprinkled gold.

No one else was about. Some were playing cards; others asleep. No one saw the two men trudging through the snow.

Davis followed Sears into the narrow shed. Sears closed the door behind them, and for a moment they were in total darkness. Davis could hear Sears's ragged breathing. Even the brief struggle to walk between the two buildings had winded both men.

Vaguely uneasy, Davis wondered if he had made a very bad mistake.

A light flared on. A trouble light, Davis saw, plugged into a cord that must be connected to the camp's generator. Sears hung the light from a hook overhead. Glancing around the single room, Davis saw elongated boxes, most of them closed and ready for shipping, stacked along one wall. Each was about five feet long and six inches square, large enough to hold one of the ice cores extracted by a specially designed drill from deep within the ice. Two of the cores rested on a long table in open boxes.

Davis shivered. "It's cold in here."

"Yeah, it has to be to store the samples. This is our freezer chest." Sears seemed to find this amusing.

"That's it?"

"You wanted to see some other samples? What do you think of this?"

Sears picked up a small rock, about the size of a grapefruit, from a pile against one wall. Similar brown rocks, mottled with yellow streaks, filled several boxes. Sears handed the rock sample to Davis. "What do you think of that?"

Davis almost dropped it. "Jesus—what? It's so heavy!"

"Yeah."

"What is it?" the germ of an idea formed. "Uranium?"

"Bingo!"

Davis stared at the marbled rock. Was that what TERCO's secret activity was all about? Was it a major find?

"I don't know all that much about uranium, Sears. Enlighten me."

"You remember when people were digging for it? Joe Treasure Hunter going out on weekends, thinking he would strike it rich? That was back in the seventies."

"Yes, I remember."

"Back then, uranium went for over seventy dollars a pound —that was for enriched U-235, not raw ore. A lot of it was found in the U.S., mostly small veins, in Utah, New Mexico, up in the Black Hills of South Dakota. Then the environmental freaks got off against nuclear power. There was a big backlash. That Chernobyl disaster in Russia didn't help. By 1990 nuclear power plants were being shelved all over the U.S., and the price of uranium ore was down the tubes."

"How far down?"

"Maybe eighteen dollars a pound if you were lucky."

"So what makes this so special, Sears?"

Sears' grin was mocking. He was enjoying himself. "What you gotta understand, Davis, is, this stuff is going to get more valuable no matter what. We've looked into it."

"I bet you have," the reporter said dryly.

"The Department of Energy's projections even in 1990 had the price per pound going up to forty dollars by the year 2000. And climbing. That was before the Iraqi crisis and the disruption in Middle East oil production. After that the DOE's upper reference case projections more than doubled."

Davis whistled softly. "Eighty dollars a pound?"

"That's just the beginning. As oil becomes scarcer and more expensive, nuclear power is gonna look better and better. There's no telling where the price will go in the next thirty years. But that isn't the half of it, Davis."

"I'm all ears."

"Yeah. All the ore in the U.S. and Canada comes in at yields of maybe one percent or less of high quality uranium oxide. Not high grade stuff, but workable. That rock you're holding in your hand—our lab has analyzed other samples just like it we found here. It assays at about sixty-five percent pure uranium." There was a glitter in Sears' eyes now, a kind of manic glee. "Only one other place on earth was there ever anything like it. That was in Katanga in the Belgian Congo, where we got all our wartime uranium we used to build the first bombs, the ones we dropped on Hiroshima and Nagasaki. The Katanga mine, some of that ore was just lying there in the open, waiting for somebody to pick it up, it averaged sixty-eight percent pure ore, the richest ever. You know what that makes ours?"

"Number two," Davis said slowly. "The second richest uranium deposit in the world."

"Number one now," said Sears. "That African mine is dead. Played out. A hole in the ground. And it never was very big . . . maybe forty thousand tons of ore at the outside."

"What have you found here?"

"Our preliminary surveys indicate at least a half million tons of ore. And it's not even very deep, Davis. That's the funny thing about uranium ore. It's forced toward the surface in reefs or spurs. That's the way it is here."

Davis stared at the rock in his hand. "God help Antarctica," he murmured. "Why are you telling me this now? Is TERCO going public with it?"

"Not yet," Sears said. "And you already know too much."

Davis was still looking down at the yellow-streaked piece of ore when, out of the corner of his eye, he saw Sears' arm swinging. He ducked from the blur of motion. The blow grazed his skull. Davis's sudden movement prevented the rock in Sears' hand from smashing into his temple.

Even the glancing blow he took knocked him off-balance. Pain exploded in his head. Dizzy, he staggered. He felt his legs wobble. He had once fought in Golden Gloves matches, and he remembered the sensation of being tagged by a blow solid enough to rattle your brain and turn your legs to the consistency of oatmeal.

He stumbled against the long table, grabbed it to keep from falling.

Sears stalked him, grinning, holding the rock like a weapon. Davis was defenseless. He had dropped the piece of rock he was holding when he was struck.

"You must be crazy! You can't get away with something like this; there are too many people. They'll find me."

"Maybe they will, and maybe they won't."

"It's not worth it, Sears. It's—"

Murder, he thought. As Forbes had been sent to his death? Pushing Sears to the brink and over, had he unearthed something so deadly it meant that he also had to die?

"Like I said, you know too much," Sears said calmly.

Davis had retreated as far as he could. He tried to keep the table between them as Sears advanced. He thought of children playing games, dancing around a table, taunting each other.

Sears pushed the table over. It crashed to the snow floor. One of the open boxes smashed, spilling a long core of ice onto the floor, bits and pieces of history disintegrating on impact.

Davis looked for a weapon, anything to defend himself with. There was nothing.

Sears lunged at him. Davis ducked under his arm. He almost made it past Sears to the door, but Sears reached it ahead of him. Another blow with the heavy rock glanced off Davis's shoulder, numbing his arm.

"Goddamn it, you really are crazy!"

Sears might not have heard him. Nothing would sway him now; he was out of control. Something must have happened— perhaps something Davis did not yet know about—to sever his connection with humanity.

Sears rushed him again, swinging the chunk of rock.

Behind him the door crashed open.

There was a moment when three men were frozen in a tableau: Sears facing Davis with his arm lifted, the lethal piece of rock in his hand; Davis retreating and Kornievski, halting just inside the open door while snow sifted across the floor around his feet.

Len Sears swore. He turned to face the intruder. Kornievski moved his bulky figure with surprising speed. He held a long piece of one-inch pipe in his hand. With a single blow he struck Sears's arm. The heavy rock flew out of Sears's hand and broke into pieces where it hit the floor.

Sears screamed in pain. Kornievski, ruthless, an oil field

roughneck who had been in more brutal fights than he could remember, didn't wait for Sears to recover. He struck again with the length of pipe, smashing it against the side of Sears's head.

Sears dropped like a sack.

Mike Davis, his brain whirling, head and shoulder aching, stared at the man who had saved his life. "How—how did you know?"

"I was watching. I should've got here quicker."

"You got here—" Davis stared down at Sears, whose head was bleeding. He was having trouble finding words for the simplest thought. Nobody had ever tried to kill him before. "—at a very good time."

"You okay? You're bleeding a little."

"I'm okay, I think. It's cold in here." In fact, he had never felt so cold before. "Let's get him back to the other building. Then I think . . . it's time you told me everything you know."

Back in the warmth of the headquarters shed, with Sears securely tied up and laid on his bunk, Mike Davis was euphoric. Even with the swelling lump on his head and the bruise that made his shoulder ache, even before Kornievski began to talk, Davis knew that he had the story of his life.

THIRTY-FIVE

"WHAT DO YOU HAVE THERE, DOCTOR? Let me see what Forbes wrote."

Kathy McNeely recoiled, but Merrill quickly circled the prone Survivor, giving him a wide berth, and snatched the note from her.

"I see," he said, digesting Forbes's last words.

"You're one of those who want to sabotage the Antarctic Treaty, aren't you?" said McNeely.

"I'm not sure what you mean."

"I've heard stories about too many accidents—disruptive things here on the Ice. Were some of those staged? Is TERCO involved?"

"That's very astute. The answer is yes, we've sown a few seeds of discord when the opportunity presented itself. The treaty is obsolete. You have to understand, Doctor, it isn't a national thing. It has nothing to do with that at all."

"What happened here that you had to cover up?"

"That's a harsh phrase. We've made a very important discovery. It was necessary that word of it didn't get out prematurely. Unfortunately there was an accident. Just one of those things. A fuel bladder ruptured, spilled a few thousand gallons of diesel oil. If those penguins hadn't been in the vicinity, no one would ever have known."

"But the damage would have been done."

Merrill seemed not to have heard. "One of my men tried to bury the birds. Obviously he didn't do a very good job. It's not easy to bury anything permanently here."

"What kind of company, what kind of men, would authorize such things?"

"The people I work for are simply good businessmen, Doctor. They're not evil. They don't wish to harm animals or the environment capriciously. You'd call them ruthless, I suppose; I would say realistic and practical. There are untold riches beneath the ice of this continent, more than we guessed. They can't be left untouched, unused."

"So your bosses countenance anything you do, no matter what."

"My superiors are not interested in how I accomplish what I'm supposed to do. They are *very* interested in whether I get the job done."

"And you're perfectly willing to destroy what has been part of this continent for millions of years. You'd say the annihilation of a penguin colony, for instance, is simply an acceptable cost of doing business."

"Don't give me that sentimental hogwash, Dr. McNeely. You know better. The ecosphere won't be harmed in the long run if a few penguins are dislocated or killed. Nature is tough— damned tough. Particular animals don't matter to Nature. We're all replaceable. Nature doesn't give a damn about emperor penguins or spotted warblers or any other species—including humans. You're trained in biology. You know perfectly well that ninety percent of all the species that have ever been on this earth are extinct. The ecosphere isn't untouchable. It's always changing, always adapting. Twenty thousand years from now Antarctica might not even be here, and it won't make any difference what we do to it."

"We're caretakers of what we have—of what we've been given!"

"We're caretakers of *ourselves*! You think we don't need what's buried under all this ice?"

"You've done all this—decimating a penguin colony, destroying the environment, sabotaging the treaty—for a ten-year supply of *oil*?"

For a moment Merrill was silent. Then he said, "Not oil . . . at least not this time."

"What then?"

"Uranium. A mountain of it, sixty times richer metal than any supply we have in the Western Hemisphere. We goddamned well need both oil and uranium if we're going to produce enough energy to last through the next century. Us, Doctor— *this* species!"

Kathy glanced down at the fragments of Hank Forbes's notes. "Individuals don't matter," she said quietly.

Merrill was within a few steps now. She looked at him directly, unafraid.

"Are you going to kill me, too?"

Merrill gave a kind of sigh. It made a small cloud of moisture in front of his face for an instant. There was ice clogging his face mask. She wondered how long he had been out looking for her.

"I saw your light, just briefly," he said, as if answering a question other than the one she'd asked. "I had to wait until the storm passed to find you. I thought it was someone in distress. I'd hoped to rescue you, Doctor."

"You tampered with Hank Forbes's helo. I think you must have tried to kill Carl Jeffers, too. Is there no limit?"

"I didn't want any of this," Merrill said harshly. "Do you think I'm some kind of monster? Jeffers was an act of stupidity, never authorized. Forbes . . . that was desperation. Desperate men do desperate things."

"Not all men—only a certain kind."

Merrill shook his head. "We're all the same, Doctor. You

317

should know that. Some of us are more fortunate than others. We're never forced to find out what we would do if we had to."

He was trying to put a reasonable face on evil, Kathy thought. It was the practical thing. It was necessary. It made possible a higher good. Perhaps men driven to embrace evil had always found a way to forgive themselves.

Without warning he rushed toward her. Scrambling away from him, Kathy found herself forced out onto the snow. The drifts impeded her, but they slowed Merrill's headlong rush as well. She circled him, trying to get back to the ledge. Angling to head her off, Merrill caused her to move farther to her left than she had intended.

He wanted another accident, she thought. He meant for her to disappear, as Forbes and his accusation would disappear once she was out of the way.

She sensed a change in his pursuit. He was following her cautiously now, slowly, cutting off available escape routes while crowding her backward. She glanced over her shoulder fearfully, half expecting to see an accomplice, someone closing off retreat.

What she saw was a glimpse of blue ice almost at her feet. She understood instantly that Merrill already knew it was there.

Trembling, she edged along the rim of the crevasse. Glanced in the direction of the grotto where she had sheltered from the storm. On the nearby ledge where he had been thrown by the avalanche, Survivor was on his feet. The long piece of rope she had used to haul him up from the grotto still trailed from his collar. If she could get that far, she thought, she might . . .

What? Merrill was bigger, stronger than she. He might even have a weapon. What could she fight him with?

Despair shook her, gave way to rage. Damn him! She wasn't going to give up! She wouldn't make it easy.

She turned, defiant, as Merrill closed in on her.

"I'm really sorry," he said. He actually sounded sincere.

"You'll be sorrier!"

THE ICE

She tried to run along the rim of the abyss, slipping and stumbling in the soft snow. When he was almost upon her, she swung to face him, knowing surprise was her only chance. She threw herself at him, trying to knock him off-balance.

They wrestled briefly. Merrill caught her arms, held them. Behind the frost and ice clinging to his face mask were eyes that held none of the regret in his words, eyes cold and determined.

"If you'd only let it alone . . ." he said.

"Then you'd have got away with it!"

She glimpsed movement in the snow behind him, but she dared not let herself feel hope or show it in her eyes, which were locked on his.

He was strong enough to lift her up, swing her off her feet toward the crevasse. Struggling, she tore one arm free, swung her gloved fist at his face. Instinctively he twisted to evade the blow, and for a few seconds she was reprieved. He slammed his hand viciously across her face. The impact was cushioned slightly by her own woolen balaclava, but the blow was still hard enough to stagger her.

With a snarl that took Merrill completely by surprise, Survivor attacked.

Crippled though he was, he was 150 pounds of angry dog hurling himself at his enemy. The first slash of his teeth tore the quilted padding of Merrill's jacket. Merrill panicked, trying to get away. The dog's weight crashed into him, knocking him backward.

Instinctively Kathy McNeely reached out to save him when Merrill teetered on the rim, his arms windmilling wildly. She grabbed for his arm, a piece of his clothing. Instead she caught the rope Survivor was dragging behind him.

Merrill felt the emptiness opening up beneath his feet. He screamed.

In the instant of toppling backward, he caught hold of Kathy's leg. His hands clawed, raked, held on. She felt herself being dragged off her feet, pulled after Merrill as he dropped into the crevasse.

319

She cried out and, still holding on to the rope, slipped over the edge. She plummeted ten feet into the chasm before crashing against a lip of ice. The impact knocked the breath out of her— and broke Merrill's grip. He gave a bleat, like a frightened animal.

Her boots skidded off a tiny foothold, and she started to slide again.

She stopped, dangling at the end of the rope, fifteen feet into a pit so deep there was no longer any sound of Rupert Merrill falling.

She swung slowly, brushing against the wall of blue ice. The rope had somehow got twisted around her arm. In her confused state it was a moment before she remembered that the other end of the rope remained attached to Survivor's collar.

THIRTY-SIX

"I DON'T HEAR ANYTHING," Alex Volkov said.

"The dogs did—look at them."

The huskies were unmistakably excited, some of them yipping and whining, others dancing and milling about, Dutch snapping at anyone within reach.

"What was it?"

"I'm not sure. It might have been . . . a howl."

Volkov did not say that the wind sometimes spoke in voices that ranged from a whisper to a howl. Hurley's disappointment was too obvious, too terrible a burden.

After waiting for a long moment, hearing only the stunning silence, Hurley pulled the team together. "Go!" he called. "Go, let's go!"

Five minutes later, laboring through deep snow up the center of the snow valley, scanning the horizon for any sign of life, knowing that Volkov's vision, however eager he was to help, was still limited, Hurley felt another leap of hope. He stopped the sledge.

"There—listen!"

This time Volkov heard it, too, and Vixen suddenly lifted her head and let out a mournful howl, answering the cry that came from somewhere ahead of them.

"That's a dog," Hurley said. "And there's only one dog that could be here in this valley: Survivor!"

"Yes, I hear it. It came from off there—to right."

"Are you sure?"

"Yes, yes, my sight is not good, but my hearing is better. I am sure."

Hurley had no need to urge the huskies into a lunging, straining effort. They broke out of soft powder onto crusted snow and increased speed, climbing a long rise. Along the way the silence was punctuated by repeated yips and howls from the unseen dog, each cry closer, each one increasing the team's eager excitement.

Topping the rise, Hurley felt almost unbearable frustration. Nothing! There was only the unbroken sweep of snow, contained by walls of rock and ice. Where was the dog? Where was Kathy?

Survivor's howl rose once more, trembling in the still, cold air. Hurley's gaze darted toward the sound. "Go!" he yelled at the husky team. "Find him!"

The dogs took him unerringly toward the sounds. Within moments Hurley glimpsed something that told him he was about to learn more than Kathy's and Survivor's fate, the answer to another mystery: pieces of Hank Forbes's missing helicopter.

Then he saw Survivor, standing, legs braced, at the edge of a crevasse.

There was no sign of Kathy McNeely.

He stopped the team with difficulty, jumped past the uproar the dogs were making and ran stumbling through the snow toward Survivor. En route he observed the rope attached to the husky's neck, looped through his collar.

And saw the tautness of that rope.

"Katya!" Volkov shouted.

"Alex! Alex, is that you?"

Hurley knelt beside Survivor at the edge of the fissure. For a

moment he couldn't speak. He was almost afraid to touch the
dog, whose legs and muscles were quivering with strain.

He peered down into the blue-green depths. "Kathy . . ."

"Hurley—oh, my God, Hurley, help me!"

"Hang on—don't talk, don't try to do anything else, just
hang on!"

"We must pull her up," Volkov said. "Quickly!"

"No!" Hurley took charge. "I have another rope. We can't
take the chance. She might not be able to hold on if we try to
pull her up. I'll go down after her. You'll have to help Survivor.
Take hold of this line. He looks as if he's just about finished."

Hurley turned the sledge around, tied a long nylon rope to it
with the other end secured around his waist and aligned the dog
team to pull away from the crevasse.

He let himself down over the edge of the precipice and
played the line out slowly, foot by foot.

"Hurry up, Hurley." Kathy's whisper was magnified within
the crevasse, which was no more than three feet wide.

She was only about fifteen feet down, and he was soon beside
her. She was suffering from cold and fear and almost certainly
some frostbite. Her face mask was almost completely covered
with frost and ice. He looped an extra length of his own line
around her chest and under her arms, fumbling awkwardly with
his heavy mittens until he jerked one off and let it drop into the
void.

It went more quickly then, even if his right hand was soon
cold. When he was sure the rope was tight enough, he put his
left arm around her. With his right hand he tugged on the line.

"Go!" he yelled up at the waiting dog team. "Go, you beautiful sons of bitches—pull!"

Kathy McNeely sagged against him as they started to creep
upward, sliding against the perpendicular wall of ice. He turned
to place his own body between her and the wall.

Holding her with one arm, feeling tears freeze into icy drops
on his eyelids, Hurley knew that he would never want to let go
of her.

THIRTY-SEVEN

THE PRESS CONFERENCE PETE RODRIGUEZ had set up in TERCO's Houston headquarters began at ten o'clock in the morning. The conference room was jammed. Standing near the paneled double doors at the back of the room, Rodriguez recognized the financial writer from the *Los Angeles Times,* others from the *Wall Street Journal,* the *Washington Post* and *Forbes* magazine. They weren't the primary concern, he thought; they understood the game. More problematical were the skeptics from *Time* and *Newsweek,* the sensation-mongers from television news stations looking for tonight's news-at-eleven hook and the stringers for the supermarket rags. And most dangerous of all was a staff writer from the *L.A. Times* following up on the big story that newspaper had broken under Michael Davis's Antarctica by-line. Davis himself was still down there, trying to dig up additional information.

What a mess! Rodriguez thought.

Ron Kusic entered the room briskly, causing first an interruption in the buzz of conversation that filled the room, then a babble of excited questions that rose to shouts as each reporter clamored for attention. Kusic, smiling, held up both hands, palms out, gesturing for silence. He looked tanned and fit and confident, Rodriguez thought. Suit and tie this morning instead of the yachtsman's outfit; good. The latter wouldn't have played well in brief TV bites, too much the rich man's image. Funny how people loved that stuff; it filled the pages of *People* magazine—the rich, after all, were America's royalty—until something went wrong and they smelled blood.

"I have a brief statement," Kusic said when the room had finally quieted down enough for him to be heard. "Then I'll be happy to answer your questions." He waited for a full minute, letting the silence deepen until the shuffle of a shoe was audible, the clearing of someone's throat at the back of the room. "This is a very sad day for TERCO," he began.

"What about Antarctica?" the *Newsweek* staffer blurted out.

"I'll get to that," Kusic answered coolly. "As you know, there has been a tragic accident near one of our research camps in Antarctica. A helicopter crashed in the vicinity. One of our key people, Rupert Merrill, a fine geologist who headed up our research program in Antarctica, was directing the rescue effort to find the missing pilot. Unfortunately that effort was too late to save the pilot . . . and Merrill himself is missing and presumed dead."

More shouting erupted. With a thin smile Kusic waited it out. *Good,* Rodriguez thought; *he's controlling it, making them hear him out.*

"As you know by now, TERCO, like a good many other companies from several nations, has been engaged in exploratory research in Antarctica. Legitimate research, I might add, under the auspices of the National Science Foundation. One result has been the discovery of a remarkably rich uranium deposit, which will be of immeasurable value to the world's energy needs and particularly those of the United States. Efforts have already been made, sensationalist efforts in the face of a genuine human tragedy, to find something sinister in that discovery and in our work in Antarctica. There is nothing sinister about it. TERCO's findings do not even directly benefit TERCO since any mineral exploration and mining in Antarctica will be controlled by the community of nations involved with that continent."

"Then why was TERCO withholding information about the discovery?"

"What about the man who attacked a journalist?"

"Are you saying Merrill didn't know what was going on?"

"Doesn't TERCO think sabotage or attempted murder is sinister?"

"Who gave Len Sears his orders?"

The rain of hostile questions made Pete Rodriguez squirm, but Kusic seemed unfazed. He held up his hands again. "If you'll just give me another moment . . ."

It was several minutes before the uproar quieted enough for Kusic to continue. "Let me finish, gentlemen—and ladies." He smiled at a woman in the front row from the *Houston Chronicle*. "First of all, there was no cover-up. Let me emphasize that. We did not see fit to announce our findings in the matter of the uranium field until our laboratory had been able to analyze the deposit samples. That is not a cover-up; that's normal procedure. This is Texas, and most of you know the oil and energy business. You don't start shouting, 'Oil!' until you know what you've got. I might add that responsible journalists do not use words like *sabotage* or *attempted murder* without any evidence to substantiate such an accusation."

"Hank Forbes left a note; it was found," the *Post* reporter said sharply.

"I've read a copy of that note. Forbes was a dying man, in extreme pain, obviously delirious. He made an error of judgment, attempting to fly his helo in bad weather, and unfortunately he went down. Those are the facts. The rest is simply wild speculation."

"What about his tail rotor being tampered with?"

"The tail rotor has not been found. I repeat, there is no evidence of anything sinister about that helicopter crash. There was a terrible human tragedy; it's irresponsible to try to make it something else. I would expect such questions from our friends with the *Star* or the *Enquirer,* not from a responsible newspaper."

"Your man Sears attacked Mike Davis, tried to kill him." The *Los Angeles Times* writer was on his feet, his face flushed with anger.

Kusic stared at the writer. "Let me address that. I wonder if any of you know the degree of stress involved in working for long periods under the extreme conditions of isolation and climate present in Antarctica. Most of the people who are allowed to go there under NSF guidelines are subject to psychological inquiry before being cleared, to make certain that they can cope with and perform under those conditions. From what we know at the present time—and the facts are still somewhat sketchy—an engineer in our research team, Len Sears, who had been in Antarctica for a year and a half, wintering over this past year, apparently went berserk and attacked this reporter, Michael Davis, who had been questioning him extensively. Davis, we know now, had been in Antarctica for the express purpose of trying to find support for a story about attempts to sabotage the Antarctic Treaty. I leave it to others to question or justify his motives; I'm not in the news business. We do know that he found no evidence to substantiate such a story. What appears to have happened is that he was in the wrong place at the wrong time, when a man who had been under too much stress for too long a period snapped. What went on between the two men, I have no idea. Maybe Davis antagonized Sears in some way he's not telling us about. I don't have to tell any of you that reporters can sometimes be aggressive and"—Kusic smiled—"irritating."

It was his first real blunder in the press conference. Most of the journalists were on their feet, shouting angrily.

"Davis isn't on trial here. TERCO is!"

"Don't you think the destruction of a continent is a little irritating?"

"What about that penguin colony that was wiped out?"

"There *is* evidence," the Los Angeles writer shouted. "Davis has the testimony of a scientist, a Dr. McNeely, whom your

man Merrill tried to kill. What did you have down there, Kusic
—TERCO's branch of Murder Incorporated?"

"That's irresponsible!" Kusic snapped. "A hysterical woman,
someone lost in a storm—"

"She says Merrill admitted trying to sabotage the treaty!"

"Merrill's dead!" Kusic retorted. "He can't defend himself.
The fact of the matter is, he had courageously organized and
was attempting to carry out a rescue search under nearly intolerable conditions, and in the course of that attempt he lost his life.
Merrill is the victim in this case, not Dr. McNeely. She is, I
understand, something of a crusader for penguin rights, not human rights. She was angry over a regrettable rupture in a small
fuel bladder that caused injury to a few of her precious birds.
Under the circumstances, perhaps her perspective is suspect."

"Jesus Christ!" one of the reporters swore under his breath.
"Will you listen to him? Next thing, he's going to blame the
penguins for Forbes's accident!"

As the questioning continued, Pete Rodriguez found himself
practically rejoicing. By God, he was going to pull it off! Some
of the reporters, particularly the local TV people, were beginning to back off, giving Kusic the opportunity to smile into the
cameras. Others were shaking their heads, talking to themselves.

Then the reporter from the *New York Times* raised his voice
above the general hubbub and caught Kusic's attention. "Are
you denying any responsibility for what's happened in Antarctica, Mr. Kusic? The oil spill and the attempt to cover it up—
are you washing your hands of the whole thing?"

Rodriguez saw Kusic focusing on the questions. He had a
keen, concentrated expression that Rodriguez knew, like a cat
ready to pounce.

"I'm glad you asked that, Tom," Kusic said, addressing the
reporter familiarly. Kusic's expression became sober, his voice
lower. "I'm not denying that TERCO must share responsibility
for these events. Our people were there, carrying out legitimate
exploration, but mistakes were made. It seems evident that an
overzealous man in the field took it upon himself to undertake

measures that would never have been authorized by me or anyone here in Houston. Len Sears was not responsible for that fuel oil spill, but he attempted to bury a few deceased penguins in an apparent effort to hide what happened. That cover-up, if you wish to call it that, was one field manager's poor judgment; it was never sanctioned by TERCO's management. The fuel tank rupture was not reported to our Houston office. Sears also attacked a reporter with intent to commit bodily harm. That, too, was an individual act. Because Sears was a TERCO employee and we placed him in that situation, we must bear some of the burden of responsibility for his actions. I believe most of you will recall that in the recent past a president of the United States was tarnished by the actions of a subordinate who took it upon himself to authorize or carry out unsanctioned activities in the field, in the sincere belief that he was fulfilling his commander's wishes. I believe this situation is analogous, and I accept responsibility."

"Len Sears," one reporter exclaimed. "The new Ollie North!"

"Mr. Sears is presently being held at McMurdo Station," Kusic went on. "We've requested permission from the NSF to fly a team of medical specialists to that site for a psychiatric examination. I suspect they will find that he is a man driven over the edge. He deserves our pity, not our condemnation. . . ."

Pete Rodriguez opened the door behind him and slipped out of the conference room. His heart was pounding. Like Rupert Merrill down there in Antarctica, he had looked into the pit of oblivion. Unlike Merrill, he had drawn back from the abyss.

Kusic was winning, he thought. He was turning the whole thing around!

Pete Rodriguez's euphoria and Ron Kusic's satisfaction in the aftermath of the news conference were short-lived.

The call from Emmett Brady came shortly after noon. Kusic

listened, asked a few questions while Rodriguez watched him and slowly put down the phone.

For a long moment he was silent.

"What is it?" Rodriguez asked finally, becoming more anxious the longer he waited.

"Brady wanted to know if we were watching TV."

"Why? What's happened?"

"Senator Wingate was holding a press conference the same time I was. He's come out in favor of the Antarctic Treaty and the minerals regime. He's denounced TERCO."

"That son of a bitch! We can nail him—"

"We can't touch him. And that's not the worst of it."

Rodriguez waited.

"It didn't play, Pete. The dissident stockholders are calling for an emergency meeting of the board of directors. Brady says their support is increasing by the minute. Our bankers say the cash payment on the debentures will have to be made in full in June; no leeway. And our underwriters"—Kusic's mouth twisted in a bitter smile—"have let Brady know there's no chance for the stock offering at the present time. Enough of the small buyers have been turned off."

Rodriguez felt sick. The bottomless pit was opening up at his feet again.

Kusic swiveled his chair to stare out the tall windows behind his desk. For the first time Rodriguez became aware of how dark and gloomy the day had become. A gray curtain of rain was falling over the northern half of the city, moving slowly toward TERCO Tower.

"Penguins!" Kusic spit out the word. "Like little men in tuxedos. Can you believe it?" Kusic swung his chair around. His face was as gray as the sky behind him. "Who really gives a shit about a bunch of goddamn birds!"

Late that evening the TERCO offices were quiet. Lighted windows still defined the shape of the tall building with the blue neon logo at the top. Some cleaning personnel—two women and a man—emptied wastebaskets and ran a vacuum cleaner in the executive suites on the top floor.

Alone in his corner office with its panoramic windows, Ron Kusic drummed his fingers on the huge rosewood desk, which was immaculately clear of papers or other debris except for a clock-calendar and a telephone.

He stared out the north window at the sleeping city. The window remained streaked from the afternoon rain. Drops of water glistened on the glass like dew.

Kusic's eyes narrowed, the eyes of a hunter. Relentlessly opportunistic, his restless brain was already casting about, searching for new prey.

One opportunity—the Antarctic option—would have to be shelved for now. But there were plenty of others out there, Kusic thought, just waiting for someone sharp enough to spot them, bold enough to accept the risks. TERCO still had assets; they could be gutted to make way for expansion in other directions.

He glanced at his Rolex, which read 9:55 P.M., shrugged and reached for the phone.

THIRTY-EIGHT

A WEEK AFTER ESCAPING FROM AN ICY GRAVE, and more than two thousand miles to the northwest, Kathy McNeely opened the window of the rented Toyota minivan and drank in the cool, moist air. Behind her in the back seat, Survivor leaned forward, pushing his nose to the window. Brian Hurley, at the wheel, glanced toward her but said nothing. They had both been silent during the drive, Kathy subdued, Hurley picking up on her mood.

It was cool and drizzly, as it had been since the transport plane from Antarctica—one of the last flights to leave the Ice before winter weather made air travel too dangerous—set down on the wet macadam at the international airport outside of Christchurch. The view from the van was of gray clouds sitting on green mountains, mists of rain drifting across green fields. Temperature in the fifties. After summer in Antarctica, New Zealand's version of early winter seemed practically balmy.

"There it is," said Hurley.

"I don't know why I'm so nervous."

The hospital was white frame, a huge three-story building with wide porches spanning the front, surrounded by acres of tree-shaded lawns. It reminded Kathy of a grand hotel built in the United States in the first part of the century.

They found Carl Jeffers in a large private room on the second floor, sitting in a white wicker chair by an oversized window overlooking the lawn and rain-shrouded hills. Portions of the Sunday paper were scattered over the bed and on the table beside him.

Jeffers glanced up at the sound of their footsteps, and Kathy felt her heart squeezed at first glimpse of his ravaged face. Then she saw his grin, and the biologist popped to his feet with familiar energy. "Well, it's about time!" Jeffers exclaimed. "Didn't anyone tell you it gets cold down on the Ice in winter?"

"I've heard the rumor." Kathy's joy threatened to spill over, either in tears or foolish gushing. Word about Jeffers' condition back at McMurdo Station had been sketchy at best; no one was even certain he was still in New Zealand until Kathy confirmed it with a telephone call from the Kiwis' Scott base.

Jeffers embraced her, peered into her eyes, reached up to brush away a tear from her cheek. "What's that? Don't tell me you were worrying about me?"

"Maybe a little."

"Nonsense! I've been getting better by leaps and bounds since I heard what those bastards tried to do to me. Blind, malevolent Nature I had trouble dealing with. The human version of evil is too familiar to be so frightening."

"I'll have to think about that," Kathy said.

The scientist turned toward Hurley and gripped his hand. "I heard what you did, you and Alex. God bless you both."

Looking uncomfortable, Hurley said, "You're looking good, Dr. Jeffers, considering."

"Ah, yes, considering . . . ."

There was a brief moment of awkward silence. Jeffers found a chair for her. Hurley sat gingerly on the edge of the bed while the scientist returned to his chair by the window. Jeffers was putting on a good show, Kathy thought, but he hadn't quite worked his way past the trauma of his experience on the Ice.

"Don't look so miserable, my dear, you remind me of Ruth. I really don't need any more nursing. I'm being released this week."

"Your wife is here? In Christchurch?"

Jeffers nodded. "She couldn't wait for me to come home, I can't understand why. She's been hounding the nurses—they call themselves sisters—for two days, she thinks I'm neglected. The sisters have really been wonderful, by the way." He paused. "I'll admit I had some rough going for a while. It was finding out what really happened, and what TERCO was trying to do, that got me going again. I've something to concentrate on besides thinking about freezing to death."

"That sounds more like you."

"That reporter's story in the *Los Angeles Times* has made quite a splash here in New Zealand. It's even made me a bit of a celebrity. The Kiwis take their ecology very seriously. I'm supposed to be on a talk show panel on TV when I get out of here, if Ruth will let me." Jeffers smiled indulgently.

"Don't rush things, Carl."

His expression sobered. He stared from Kathy to Hurley. "I'm not sure we have all that much time, Kathy. The Kusics of this world aren't going to be sitting on their hands. They've had one temporary setback, that's all. They'll be back for more, wearing garments of respectability and concern to generate better PR."

"There are a great many people of good will who've been shaken out of their complacency," Hurley said. "If there's any way you can look at what's happened and see good coming out of it, that's a plus."

"People forget," Jeffers said.

"Then it's up to us to remind them," said Kathy. "Alex Volkov wants to set up some kind of international conference of scientists concerned about Antarctica's future. You'll be hearing from him. He wants you to be part of it."

"I don't know . . . ."

"People will listen to you, Carl . . . now more than ever.

You've seen what can happen, the lengths to which a few will go to serve the profitability of corporations, regardless of the cost to others or to this planet."

"I can be a point-man, you mean," Jeffers said wryly. "Take advantage of the publicity, get my two cents worth on TV."

"Like Cousteau," Kathy McNeely said. "You're a public figure now, a survivor, a kind of ecological hero." She glanced at Hurley. "Sometimes publicity isn't all bad."

Jeffers's glance flicked between them, questioning. "Speaking of survivors, what about that dog of yours? He's with you?"

"He's in the car. Hurley didn't think the nurses would appreciate bringing him in the hospital."

"Too bad. I was looking forward to the good sisters' reaction when he came banging along the hall with that crutch of his."

For a moment Jeffers was silent, turning to stare out the window at the misty rain. New Zealand had its own kind of beauty, Kathy thought, saturated in green. In her mind's eye she looked past the hills toward another landscape, so much harsher, colder, vaster . . . endless expanses of white, a world without color or softness or pity.

The scientist was watching her. "You're going back, aren't you? Next summer?"

"Yes, Carl."

He turned to Hurley. "You too?"

"I still have a glacier to climb."

Jeffers shook his head. "You're not still fighting like cats and dogs, I hope." There was amusement in his eyes as he asked Kathy, "Or has he seen the light?"

Kathy grinned at Hurley. "You want to answer that?"

"I've seen it," Hurley said. "and I'm suitably dazzled."

Carl Jeffers chuckled. "And so you should be." He was silent another moment. "I think it was Thoreau who said, 'In wilderness is the preservation of the world.' You wouldn't think it would be so difficult for the human race to achieve that level of rationality. It won't happen by chance, or wishful thinking. We have to make it happen."

Kathy McNeely smiled. "I think you're going to be terrific on TV, Carl." Her smile broadened into a grin. "And if you need any pointers, you can always ask Hurley."